Journal from Ellipsia

Books by Hortense Calisher

IN THE ABSENCE OF ANGELS

FALSE ENTRY

TALE FOR THE MIRROR

TEXTURES OF LIFE

EXTREME MAGIC

JOURNAL FROM ELLIPSIA

HORTENSE CALISHER

Journal from Ellipsia

Little, Brown and Company · Boston · Toronto

LIBRARY OF CONGRESS CATALOG CARD NO. 65-21355

FIRST EDITION

Published simultaneously in Canada
by Little, Brown & Company (Canada) Limited

PRINTED IN THE UNITED STATES OF AMERICA

To C. H.

Contents

Part I

1. Hobbies

ALTHOUGH the amphitheater lent to Linhouse for the occasion was a small one, it had all the usual properties of a rotunda, plus one. From his chair in the wings, looking past the large object — as yet he knew no other name for it — which he had managed to set mid-stage last evening, he had a full view of the place. After a while, he took from his pocket a couple of buns he hadn't had time for in the coffee shop earlier and munched them, regarding the hall. Intended for use by the Center's "medical" faculty at those surgical moments when abstract principia had to be humanly applied, its sealed, delicately thermostated air could also be steriled, though such weren't his instructions today. Such must rarely be the case at an institute whose researches were so advanced that any practical application of them almost surely had to be performed elsewhere, preferably off the grounds. Indeed, among Fellows whose professional prefixes were almost always either bio, geo, phys or astro — with here and there an "anthro" or, like himself, "philo" — the term "medical" was altogether a misnomer — there was no such faculty. The term was a leftover from the will of a richly misguided donor, to get the bulk of whose bequest the institute had had to build this minor, neglected wing furnished with eccentricities among which a lecture hall capable of being temperature-controlled to all the half-degrees Fahrenheit between freezing and near-boiling was by far the most understandable.

Meanwhile, the men and women Fellows, who with their assistants, wives or secretaries, were now beginning to straggle in, were having to do so through doors regularly spaced on the hall's perimeter, opening from that encircling corridor whose light could have been violet, but today, like the general demeanor of the staff, was quite ordinary. No reason why there should be anything unusual in an event bound to occur now and then at any institution, other than that the deceased herself had asked that it take place here. Or – as was known only to Linhouse – that she had asked for it at all.

From his own new-member's tour of the entire Center three years ago, he recalled some of what he had seen through the many doors in the opposite wall of the corridor above, each of which led into or toward a maze of more complicated facilities. He had been told that none of the latter, taken alone, was in any way unscientific. On the contrary, each had been the latest of its kind, and might still be, if the Center hadn't succeeded in misinterpreting the funds left for their care. Now and then, a Navy or Air Force team made use of one or other of the available setups, and there was always some newcomer to the staff who was sure to seize with delight on the very study cell for him, only to be defeated before the year was out by the very incoherence of his surroundings. The oddity lay in their haphazardness. Soundless exits of the tiny cells for parapsychological experiment lay cheek-by-jowl with the ironclad demispheres of various "ray" sciences whose prefixes were now intermingling, or with the foolproof glass-and-filter labs of those whose very names were not yet stabilized – all these in turn abutting on a series of model test rooms and tunnels for either projectiles or personae, bright little offices where the buboes of plague could be isolated or a computer had *Lebensraum* to brood, tight little fun-rooms where a man could survive without sleep or stimuli, recover from air-bubbles in his blood, learn to freeze or to fly.

The donor of all this, a simple banker chap who, as he himself said, knew no more of science than the next man, had merely wished to hedge his bets. Just as humorously, he had demurred at the trustees naming anything after him; unlike those sad prey of the jokesters, the breed of Titsworth and Klingenstein who from birth must have been dying to see themselves monumented up there in stone, a plain Jacob Hobbs had no such need – not that the undergraduates could do much with that name. The trustees, reminding him that institutes like theirs had no undergraduates, left him unaware that kittenplay with the language often rose with higher learning. And knowing more than he about the modesty of donors, they let themselves be persuaded to reduce the height of the name carved on the facade to seven feet, and to replace a statue first projected for the entry with instead a simple fellow's profile medallioned in bronze, scale one foot to the inch, embedded unobtrusively in the marble floor. So it was that, of the audience now steadily arriving by twos and threes or one and one, a probable half had said over the shoulder to a secretary, "Off to that memorial service for the vanished Mrs. Jamison. In Hobby Hall, if you need me. Can't think why they're holding it there." And the rest, murmuring in the susurrus of telephone gossip, "I gather that Linhouse is the one who . . . mmm-hmmm," had added, "Why on earth there, though? . . . Okay, I'll meet you there. *In*side. On Jake."

Earlier, in the coffee shop, Linhouse had overheard from the booth behind him enough to know the general trend.

"Somebody always dies over the summer," said the man of the couple. "Never fails."

"Officially *lost*, she's supposed to be. Somebody at the

bank was holding a letter saying if she hadn't come back by a certain time the house was to be disposed of. And they got a letter later, from some district officer – would that be Africa? Anyway, that's what *I* heard."

"– like Amelia Earhart, hmm. Over the Galapagos."

"– New Guinea, maybe. After Jamison died here, she went back once herself, you know. Brought back a lot of stuff the museum had to turn down – except for him, she wouldn't ever have been on the staff. This time they say she went without telling anyone where."

"– and thirty years later, a race of Western blonds. Not *blond* exactly . . . what was she."

"– *I* never thought she was so attractive."

"Women didn't, honey."

"She was like some of those convent-bred liars I went to school with, butter wouldn't melt in their mouth. And of course you never knew for sure if they *were* liars. But they sure knew how to rile the boys."

"– cold cat, though. Doubt if she'd start a race."

"Maybe not with *you,* dear. . . . I gather Jack Linhouse is, er . . . making the speech."

"Oh that's right, they were at one time, weren't they. Why him, I always wondered."

"Men do. *Honey.*"

She, she, she. Where *she* was concerned, this had always been the general trend. He'd managed to leave without finding out who the couple were, just as all the past week, after assimilating the shock of the news – the house was to be sold, and the bank was assuming – and of having to think of her at all after these long, self-curing months, he'd gone about fulfilling the terms of her request without letting himself consider them too closely. In the same way last night, while he was lugging that bequest of hers over here on the platform – and "lugging" was scarcely the word – he'd managed both not to be seen, which, considering the thing's peculiarities might well have made a stir, nor to think about the matter too cautiously afterward. Almost complacently, he'd managed not to learn a great deal. As to why the least vain of women should have wanted this elaborate vanity of a service—though no one knew he hadn't instigated it. As to where she'd gone last February and why, and how her bequest had come back, from wherever it had come—to be found waiting for him, in her house. Or whether it had been there ever since she'd left. He hadn't seen it there a year back, not in his day. Altogether, the question was whether his own not inactive mind could stay off the whole business until that thing there, presumably bearing some record of a journey, might enlighten them all. As yet he knew nothing, and preferred it so. It wasn't that he believed in her so firmly. But it was such a nice anodyne, after all she'd put him through, to have her believe in him.

To Linhouse, still so shaken by the circumstance that had fallen on his calm, summer's end return to the Center—and still sweating from last night's getting to the hall what now rested on the low platform before him—it was at first incredible that few among the audience coming in had cast a passing glance at it, and none of those who'd done so had stopped before it, rapt—as he'd half expected. Nobody had paused, either to kneel down before the great thing under its bell-glass, or to touch that inches-thick but perfectly clear substance, or finally, to raise that cover and lift the thing beneath—with a cry. Having lifted it himself, he was sure of the cry.

On second thought, he understood why not. Hobbs Hall was a Madame Tussaud's of odd objects and apparatus, among which only the most ordinary thingumabob would be unusual, a can opener say, or a milk bottle. Or perhaps nobody finding even these would credit their simple use in this place, the opener surely made of magnesium, the milk bottle power-driven. In the quietest corners of this building one was likely to come upon, say a color organ, posing its still more silent sunsets. In this rotunda itself, a button he was shortly to press, as per her letter of instruction, would produce music, electronic music no doubt pushed to those ultimates which, as a concert buff, he was curious to hear. Around this place, the most unusual object would be what? A baby, probably. He looked out at the audience. Perhaps some hard-pressed wife-of-staff had brought one. No, no babies so far. The audience itself, then. In the increasingly exaggerate halls of science, people did have a tendency to look at least as funny as milk bottles. For unique objects then, he and his colleagues, as instant photoplasm first class, would have to do.

He looked out at them with some irritation. Except for a few mavericks of the word, like himself, almost all were members of what he chose to think of as the *really* physical sciences, the rest belonging to those which were nearly or partly so. It was perfectly possible that to quite a number of them the object in front of him — and them — *was,* in a sense, ordinary. "Oh, mnya-as," one might drawl, "Hed one down in the department. Hed naow luck with it," or, "Marfelous! Neffer before het I upper toonity to upserve —!" or even, "Golly! This must be the one the aborigines brought down from Popocatepetl, just last year!" Then why hadn't the writer of said letter chosen somebody from this talented array to execute her ceremony? He could answer that at least. She'd known him to be willing. He could be trusted not to refuse to make a fool of himself over her in public — having once done so in private.

And a fool he would again be made. He stiffened suddenly, at the entrance of the Center's publicity officer, a plump type with a smile on her like a soft cut in apple pie. In front of his colleagues, who had after all known of his connection, he had been prepared for ridicule. In turn they would have come prepared at best to submit to the ritual fifty minutes of eulogy and music anywhere allotted to a bygone member of a community, at worst to amuse themselves over his devotion to a woman whose disappearance from these parts had been rather more notable in his life than in theirs.

"A memorial service, you say," the provost had said on the telephone. "Dear me, I'm so sorry to hear . . . I did hear she'd left here . . . last year. Dear me . . . so young, I hope there was nothing out of the . . . of course she had no real connection here, except as Jamison's widow . . . hmmm . . . Do you know . . . has she by any chance left a bequest?. . . . on her own . . . mmm, yes. Of course the museum is very grateful, has always been, for what *he* left them . . . nothing like it in toto anywhere . . . I tell you what, Linhouse, you handle it, on your own, see? . . . No, I trust you perfectly . . . to get it official would take half a year of red – *mmm* . . . you know how these things are. Aah, and no need to have it under the aegis of the museum." Terminally, the provost had sounded as grateful as if he'd been pleading with Linhouse for hours. "Thank *you,* Linhouse. And see my secretary if you want anything. Perhaps some of those little engraved cards."

And so Linhouse, still in the shock of having to do anything at all, had seen to the secretary, to the posted notices, the arrangements for the hall – to in fact everything, including last night's experience. Or rather, *she* had, through her serenely imperative letter, awaiting him after so long. His judgment, admittedly already impaired, had been further taken in, he supposed, by the fact that her letter to him had arrived conventionally enough, through her bankers. And it had been after all what anyone strains to honor – a last request.

What he hadn't been prepared for, was the press. Had he need to be? The publicity officer – whose name always escaped people, though they never managed to do the same with her — was always reassuring everyone that her function was as much to *sup*press; it was certainly the case that even the *Times* had a special reportage for such scholarly failings as might be called human. And what the tabloids could do with a vanished anthropologist, much less the picture of this one, was inexhaustible. He looked down in the audience at Miss What'shername, at that face flattened to a smirk by constant snubbing, and couldn't trust it. Perhaps it shouldn't trust him.

He reached up behind him and pushed number eight of the row marked "Lights" on the concert-size switch panel. The surgical glare muted to what seemed at first an ugly, nightclub rose. Number four produced a cinema dark of no use to him, but just right, he supposed, for the sound screen above the panel. He touched number eight again, as per the letter in which everything had been so femininely specified — the sheer silly gaiety of it even now reaching out for the works of him better than any pinch of perfume.

Number eight's glow was opera intermission rose-velvet really, a Covent Garden glow. Clear enough, nothing furtive. In it, the large bell-glass covering the "object" looked, except for its size, harmlessly like two cherished ones on his own mother's mantel, even to its base of some black stuff close enough to their polished teak. Did bell-glasses normally come, however, to a height of something under five feet, by a width of over two? Could they be blown as thick as this and still remain more pellucid even than his mother's? And granted all this, could they then be —?

In the new light, he could still see the provost seat himself, other friends arriving. What might Linhouse be the agent of having brought here, to this storehouse where so much that was sinister to his eyes went unnoticed? Or, to the men out there, who hadn't spent their lives nosing Greek as he had, was the object housed there in front of him (and even the one property which had made it so alarmingly easy to get here) so run-of-the-mill that any half-dozen of them could at once laughingly name it? From his world now so shaped by their alembic, he looked at them with humility, as men of his sort must nowadays. Jolly lucky he hadn't at this point to name it to *them*, since the stigmata of his misspent life were apparently graven in him, even to his eyes. For ever since last evening, his eyes had kept telling him what the great shaggy oval under the glass was, and yet couldn't be. In a certain shame he bent his glance away from all those sanhedrin out there in the front row, and stole another look. Yes, and for all its oddness. What it still seemed to him most to be, was – a book.

He'd never seen one like it of course, a cylinder book, or one shaped like a dirigible flattened at either end and resting upright on one of them. Between these, the concentric leaves or pages, thick as discs, came naturally to their broadest circumference in the central pages, declining at either end to the smallest, which were of about the size of a child's phonograph record, or a modest lily pad. The gradual, elliptic curve of the page ends, or cross sections, was counterparted by that of the spine and covers, these shagged to a thickness too vaguely patterned to be called tooled, yet not coarse, as if the broad hand of its maker had sometimes dreamed of Florentine. It was a book made by a Brancusi, or else a very gifted aborigine. And he thought he knew what the leather was, of which its entirety seemed to be made. In his childhood's home library in Wiltshire, there had been books and even other articles made of what had then been called Hungarian leather, alum leather, or plain "white leather," this made, according to his grandfather, by a process called "tawing" that kept the natural color of the skin. In that library's shelves of anything from early parish registers to proceedings of ecumenical councils, there'd been books which to a five-year-old child had seemed almost as large as this one and some of shape almost as queer. And as that child, he'd been bred early to the presence of a certain beingness that persisted through all their thicks and thins, from the quartos that could lame a toe, to the silk missal that lay on the table like a handkerchief. For all he knew, this one, when uncovered, might talk on tape, or hum in braille, or even shoot out some gamma or gas which would require a memorial service for everyone here – nevertheless, he still recognized that presence in it. It had the *being*ness of a book.

And now to face the music, in more than one way. An hour's introit, to allow people to gather, was standard at these nondenominational performances. His watch now said two-thirty-five. The invitations had said three. He would give them an extra fifteen minutes for latecomers. Turning to the panel, he flicked a switch, to quick disappointment. The place was wired, like any other, for Muzak, which now began its mindless brain massage. He sighed. He'd been asked to sit with that thing over there from the time it was moved here. It had been almost dawn when he had settled it in place here.

Keep it company, she'd written, *it's quite a prize. Once the mechanism is moved, it must be allowed to regain equilibrium overnight, or for at least five hours, at a temperature of 71°.*

He'd kept it company; by God he'd slept here, on a couple of turned-down seats, going out like a truant for his coffee and a washroom shave.

An hour beforehand, raise the temperature in the hall to 74.6°. Please be exact about that. Afterwards, you have only to lift the glass and it will function perfectly. Just give the crowd some music meanwhile. And there really ought to be a crowd, you know. I'd like about fifty. So invite perhaps a hundred. Any music will do. With the sharpest ear for the spoken word, she'd had no ear otherwise.

Clearest of all, in the arrangements she'd foisted on him, was the evidence that she'd had absolutely no regard for what his feelings might be throughout them. Never had had much of course, at any time. As had been clear enough a year ago when they'd parted. Still, she might have remembered his severer musical tastes, and that it would have assuaged his feelings to – that he would have been happy to choose – Or had she known better how he, listening, was likely to memorialize her? Perhaps, with that sense of style which in women must be never wholly separable from intelligence, she'd known herself as not one best recalled in passacaglias. Listening – it was the "Vilia Song" beloved of Muzaks – he began to smile.

2. Soft Muzak

AT FIRST glance an olive type but not really, she had what Linhouse's grandmother would have called a georgette skin – pale, without oil, not thin – and her brows had a penciled, brushed look which, though natural, gave her face a made-up emphasis even when fresh from the wash-basin. With men, she had that charged yet careless manner they recognized at once and returned to endlessly, to be addressed either as men or as "boys" of her own age, but never, with the usual stance of her countrywomen, as sons – since the age of six she had been a jampot for boys. Almost at once a man sensed that the usual ploys invited by her elusively median appearance – "Were or were not her eyes hazel? Was she really more of a redhead than a brown?" – had all been tried and returned many times before, yet she always answered as if these were new, causing her to be spoken of as "a French type" by those mistaking for flirtatious the warm-cool smiles which Linhouse had reason to know were not manner, but a personal thing no Frenchwoman of his acquaintance had ever been guilty of – somewhere, she didn't care. Had she been a beauty, hers would have been of the kind that is either outside fashion or makes it; since she wasn't sugarlump pretty, her attraction couldn't be pinned down.

This had been its fatality for him, God knows; she could not be pinned down.

"Oh —" she'd been saying at a party where, unintroduced, he had stood at her elbow, "if I weren't of the white race there'd be more names for my indefinite mixture — *mahine, grayling* —" and she had gone on to list several more abstruse but apparently similar terms he'd never heard of before. He already knew her to be an anthropologist, one of no special distinction — he'd been told that also. This was the way it went with the few women on the staff here; the Center, instead of choosing fearfully brilliant survivors of competition with the most distinguished male colleagues, discriminated rather more thoughtfully, tending to settle for a few mediocre women scholars who might then be taken as evidence that the others didn't exist to be found.

He recalled now that he had been smiling at this private thought when, finishing her sentence, she had seemed to address her smile particularly to him: "Guess I'm what might be called a white octoroon." Even as their eyes met — she must really have been replying to some speech of the Austrian heavy at her other elbow — he had sensed that it was merely habit on her part, to make any man seem particularly addressed. Later, he thought of it as a power she couldn't discard. At the time, he'd nodded, but not answered. In his own way, he was knowledgeable enough about women. And later on, as the campus had let him know, she had indeed singled him out.

He had slept with her. According to gossip, since her widowhood no one else had. Still later, they'd become one of those couples who were invited together; in the easy droppings-in of the life here she'd been discovered at his flat, he at her cottage; since this was a civilized community the worst was known of them without comment, and the best — i.e. marriage — hoped for. And what had endlessly preoccupied him all that year together and beyond it, down to the very moment when her letter had led him back to her house to find the object now on the dais, was — what it could be, what in God's name could it be, about which she didn't care?

In their sexual moments, though no grunting peasant girl for whom the exchange was nearest to the intake of food, she was normal enough, fully as much so, he suspected, as many of the nice matrons hereabouts and most of the fast ones, both of whom would have been disillusioned to the bone if told either that sexual exchange was quite Europeanly their own purchase money in the buy-marts of life, or that on this basis it might still be enjoyed. She too wanted her exchange, but whatever it was it wasn't any of the usual, not marriage. He'd never had an affair in which there was less sense of the marriage topic coming up — and this was unnerving. She was always unnerving him.

Once, when in his arms — was it their last day? — she had revealed herself so far as to say, of the sexual act itself, "Oh well, it's the nearest, isn't it, the nearest we can come in this world, to *nothing*" — and when she saw his face, full of attempted Freudian concern for her and real concern for his own vanity, had at once hopefully amended it. "Oh, I mean — to talk *your* language —" by which she meant philosophy, though he was technically a classicist — "the Something that is nothingness." She often tried to talk what she thought of as his language, just like any respectable doctor's wife or professor's moll, and with about the same success. This effort had been one of the most womanly things about her. And the only proprietary one, if it was that, which he now doubted.

For it was earlier on this same occasion when they were as a matter of fact still lying together on the extraordinary couch she had brought back from New Guinea only to find out later it was fake — she *was* a poor anthropologist — that he'd discovered why she had singled him out.

"But *why!*" he'd said, outraged. She'd mistaken him, she said, for a physicist. No, not any special one — just a physicist. "Unless you were planning to go through the departments one by one!"

"Now, you know that isn't so," she had countered, calmly enough. "I've never wanted to be one of those academic how do you say it, *het — hetaira.*"

He'd had to laugh. And he supposed it was true enough; since the death of her husband, the Jamison who had been a good anthropologist, she hadn't slept around. As an older man with whom she'd gone off so young, her husband had been willing enough to train her for the travel she was so eager for, and they had lived happily enough.

"He first got interested in me because I belonged to a tribe," she had informed Linhouse on a still prior occasion.

"Uh-huh, of course," Linhouse had answered — she was on his knee at the time — fully aware of what she must have been at eighteen. What the boys around the jampot must have thought of her going off with a fifty-four-year-old man, he could well imagine. And he knew that her name had been Wertham or Wertheim, that she had grown up in Pennsylvania.

"No, really. I'm from a religious sect, the Amish. That is, my grandparents were. The 'plain people.'" She'd had to explain this to him, adding rather seriously, "*We* were lapsed ones. My parents, that is. There aren't many of those who are lapsed, you know. But we were." This was the one glimpse he had had of her earlier life, beyond a remembrance that once, when he'd suggested driving down to what he by then knew was referred to here as the "Dutch" country, meanwhile thinking of the trip British style as a picnic tour of, say Lancashire, with some good old churches on the way, and some inns of course — she had replied, "No, I never go back anywhere. The farm's there, but *I'm* not. So why try?"

All his memories of her, of this woman who never went back anywhere, were like that, leading circularly into one another, heading him only to that nowhere in which he still refused to believe she was. On the couch, that later and last day, he'd been as furiously bereft and confused by her as any of those earlier, presumably non-Amish, wretched boys.

"Why a physicist!" he had bleated again, taking the insult for a professional one, where it hurt him less. "If you were fancying he'd train you up to be one, isn't twenty-eight a bit late to start? They get their major insights earlier than the rest of us, you know. Like poets."

As he said it, light broke, or seemed to. There were women who had, it was said, not so much a natural bent as a natural *bending*, who performed very well, or perhaps only, in the hypnotic wake of another being. These women were not the helpmeets of great men — the wives of Rembrandts and Disraelis, carriers of the cup, the helmet and the nose drops; these were the disciple types who galloped the desert a length or two behind their sheikhs, reached the crest of the Jungfrau in time to see *him*, their guide, planting a flag there, or flamed down the Ganges of the intellectual life alongside beloved mahatmas who were still very much alive. After all, he thought expansively, she had tried to learn his language.

In the tender ray of this, he'd been about to apologize for his nastiness. Before he could do so she had replied calmly, "Much too late, at *thirty-four*." Until then he hadn't known her exact age, and he found this directness as annoyingly unfeminine as her refusal to see his nastiness. She never either took or gave the bitchy backchat which at once refreshed a male's sense of superior rationale. To be a bitch, a woman *had* to care.

"So you settled for a philosopher," he said. "Who turned

out to be a classicist." He was too low to ask again – why. If indeed she knew. No, no, that was the worst of it. Medium as her coloring, her mind might be, but one always got a firm impression that she knew her mind.

"Oh, but there're things you've taught me –" From whatever distance it might have wandered, that personal look of hers always returned just in time. "What you told me Descartes said, for instance – or was it Comte? *Me imperturbe.*" She pronounced the Latin impeccably, may eempairtoorbeh, whether or not she was familiar with it, with a delicately parroty ability she did have, to mimic the sound even of inflected dialect – Chinese, Navaho – tickling the labials with the lightest tongue, sliding oboesque through diphthongs that were utterly orient; it was here, in their recordings, that she had best helped Jamison. Watching her pout the Latin, he mused that the inner arch of her mouth must be shaped by all this *bel canto,* like a Bali woman's perhaps – if the Balinese sang.

"But I've been thinking –" she said. Her American was ordinary enough. "I – me imperturbable in the world, the universe. But how could he, anybody be, as long as he still admits the I – me part?"

He planted a kiss on the mouth, and sought its arch. They were lying together even closer when he heard it whisper, not teasing, from that pool of annihilation he'd thought satisfied. "But they're the ones who *know,* these days, aren't they. The science people. After all, that's what it means, doesn't it – *scientia?*"

It had taken her a long moment to answer his gruff "Know about what."

They were still close, yet all sad leagues apart when she said softly, "About – about Elsewhere."

Yes, he had heard that hungering, *traveling* voice, and not heeded it. Travel had always been for him her one snobbishness; he'd even heard her say that the much-traveled were like celebrities, at ease only with their own kind. If, she said, one wished merely to speak of Paris with love, or Africa with wonder, or a Flanders winter with warming, reminiscent hate – or perhaps, like two ski addicts, only of that burning up of space which was a mutual need – the others always stood about, sour and envious at what they took to be boastfulness, or worse yet, pulled a kind of moral rank of their own, armchair people listening to the rackety talk of fools who risked the front row at Le Mans.

"Why – you've been almost as many places as I have!" she'd said at their first meeting, with what he'd taken to be the American mixture of cheek and dotty charm. He hadn't been to her Africa, but he knew his Europe of course, and even (unlike her) his Russia. His having been to Australia also had fixed him as once upon a time having been at least in the archipelago of some of her weird island diggings – and he had been to "their" Asia. Though not what was here called "an Oxford man," he had been more than once in the small close of Merton, Jamison's college.

"Worn stone," she had said dreaming, while the Austrian man beside her – who had never been farther from here than Vienna – now looked on at them. "Worn stone and live green." And then, with full face again – that cool lamp – "And all the sparrow-sex voices."

He'd thought he understood that right enough, a woman's signal to him whom she recognized as man. "Now, now," he said with the proper coyness, "just what do you mean by that!" and they were off, to all the exchanges which obviously were waiting to kindle between them, and had – in spite of her slight mistaking of him, and his great one.

His mistake had been awesome. To think of it that way lent his scrabbling actions, then and since, the only sort of dignity these could have. He'd fallen into an error of emotion about another human being, at the deepest level on which such could be made. It was only an error of reversal—a plaint whose echo could no doubt be heard above many a circle of the damned. He'd merely forgot, or not until now learned, under what actual light every human being was to be seen, approached, and if possible honored. What she hadn't seemed to care about—he knew it now because he knew it for himself—had been merely the bramble and shadow behind which she had cached whatever it was she *had* cared for so ungovernably, enough to leave her world for it. In that light, every man he saw now seemed to carry his own meaning before him, plain as the nose on Cyrano; every woman, if one troubled to receive it, shook it out like the perfume of nakedness, no matter what concealing garments of gesture she wore. A hundred times or more she must have told him what it was, silently handing him it the way children pass one another an icicle, holding at last only its shape. And when she said it aloud he hadn't heeded, much less listened with every cell as he would now, for the clue of it, for the way she'd named it as if it were an actual country—Elsewhere.

If he'd known that this was to be the last time he saw her intimately, would he have listened more carefully for the key to it and her? He doubted so. In the nine-month interval since, the affair had died in what had at first seemed to him no more than one of the several more or less familiar ways such affairs did die, no differently for him, he'd always supposed, than for other people—i.e. other men. Women had their own versions of these things, blueprints somewhat intensified, of what they had long accustomed the world to think of as their side of it. Accordingly, they never *imposed* agony. Since the collapse of his own early, brief and only marriage—to a young woman too high-minded to leave him quickly and honestly for the kind of maintenance she really wanted and ultimately left for – he'd understood this, and had managed never again to be agony's recipient. Normally, per the blueprints, women *under*went it. As a friend on the sidelines, he'd sometimes watched this process, powerless to convince the sufferer that if the man in question gave signs of stopping an affair, it needn't be because he was thinking of another woman, or had never thought much of *her*, or had gone away in order not to think of her; it might well be merely – that he had stopped. On occasion, he himself had been of use in supplying that consolation which was the crudest and the best. Either way, for women an affair never died – and was never consciously begun – without a "because." But to him it had always seemed, contrarily, that between these poles of exchangeable agony there were innumerably more connections between men and women which, flickering to a stop just short of love or law – just went out. He'd become tolerant of this in his own life, though never without a sense of loss – for his choice of women, as of ideas, was never made or relinquished without feeling. In both realms, though he knew the ideal to be a pursuit, not an end – it was always with a spinal sadness. A philosopher can know better than to hunt the philosopher's stone, and yet suspect that the very act of knowing this is as sad as it is wise.

Nor is there anybody more humbly expectant of change than a man who despairs of the absolute. Yet she'd surprised him all the way, this Janice Jamison of the name so like the fake trademarks of the Sunday clothing ads, or even when halved, so cloying – Janice – that he'd long since taken to thinking of her as "she." Now and then he'd even addressed her so: "Come here, *she,*" in a teasing which she'd accepted quite without comment, as if Jamison had already inured her to the faintly ethnic cast of his own image of her as perhaps a charming bit out of his ballad collection, or his personal totem for her sex generally — a pidgin English "she." And all the time, with Jamison, where it may have, must have begun, and with Linhouse later, she'd been thinking on, dreaming on: Elsewhere.

When, in the next ten days or so, another meeting had somehow not been arranged, he hadn't yet been alerted; she'd always been vague on this score — though lively enough when finally met and reminded. And under her careless power for the personal, a man could take even this for flattery, as if only his presence was aphrodisiac.

He winced now, brought out of his Muzak wanderings by the thought of it, and glanced at the uppermost tier of seats in which a threesome was just settling. Was there any significance in the fact that Meyer Spilker and young Anders, the very-young-but-a-physicist Anders, had come in together? No, he knew better now. If Linhouse hadn't been enough to keep her from her dreams of an elsewhere either metaphysical or sexual, neither of those chaps would have been his successor.

Meyer was here because, as senior member of her own department, he was bound to, and because, given the old-fashioned "good works" ritualist he really was, he'd have put in an appearance anyway — it was proper. In the Polish or Russian village, painted by Chagall, from which Meyer's grandparents would have come, a certain iron kindliness, scarcely separable from duty, had been part of the moral code; in Meyer, generalized sponge of all isms related to the liberal, that same code, though by now boringly sociological, was still active; if only because of the good Old Testament death wish, Meyer was sure to turn up at any ceremony for which the bid was marked "in memoriam." And Lila, one of those malleable Midwesterners, by now grown to be his exact other half, was of course here also, between the two men.

"Tippy" Anders was here with them because last year, as new staff like the Spilkers, he'd taken on rooms in their overlarge house and the alignment had continued, for reasons that nobody looking at him — or at them — would ever impugn. For, though Lila, genial haystack in beads, had good legs and skin, and Meyer was even handsome, together they had that air, so common to couples here in the States, of having left the romantic arena forever; it was possible to imagine them procreating, but only with each other; they had become all parent. To this unity of flesh they had added an even less disseverable one — that of shared views. The Spilkers' was one of those happily educated households — once peculiar to campuses here perhaps, but now endemic almost everywhere even in a better financed America — whose ideal number of children, pets, cars and sailboats was forever overflowing missionarywards; at dinner at their house one was forever stumbling over a darkish somebody in native dress or just out of it.

Though their preference ran to persons of color, and Anders was one of those extremely white Americans who so often seemed to come from the minor towns of upstate New York, perhaps this very aura — as of the last stage of whitedom — had qualified him. At twenty-three, wearing lenses thick as chips of Steuben crystal, his hair already moulting, he seemed to be ageing backwards, to the nineteen of a very old chick. Something about him, not as simple as sexlessness, certainly not rooster, nevertheless linked him elusively in the mind to genus bird or fowl, and if the observer-eye concentrated, became clearer. Looking at the back of Anders's head, recalling what discoveries had already cracked from within that membraned oval, had circled and belted this universe and were now brooding toward others, any member of the warmer-blooded species found himself filled with awe, as once the ancients perhaps, before the mystic properties of Egg. Frontface, he had the turned-up features of a merry-andrew gone solemn, and again that high oval, the apostolic forehead. One ended up equally uneasy. This could hatch.

As Linhouse watched, the three of them walked down to the front row of what in a theater might have been called the loges, and seated themselves centrally. Though they couldn't see him, Lila had already turned on the worried stare she allotted those who, under suspicion of breakdown or home troubles or racial ones, might possibly be candidates for care. At her right, Meyer's face, less at-the-ready, kept the benign gloom of a person whose sympathies lie with the mass. On her left, Anders's face wore — though less noticeably than the back of it — its resemblance. All three, directly in line with the object on the platform, seemed not to notice it or perhaps had already classified it according to their lights, as an artifact known or unknown, a machine with or without a name. What these three and the rest of the audience had said of Linhouse beforehand and now were thinking — a lover about to open his liaison's legacy thus publicly — was best not imagined, and already had been. But at his wildest he should never have imagined either of the men out there as his successor. Last year at this time, however, he'd done precisely that.

When, after a month, her vagueness could no longer be so classified and yet couldn't be pushed to anything more definite — either way, pure curiosity had moved him to look about him. Women didn't stop, without reason. Someone else was the likeliest. Pure curiosity, he told himself then, had almost entirely motivated his side of the whole affair. What had motivated hers seemed to him, a man of normal vanity and conquests, so entirely natural he hadn't questioned it — in spite of her "mistake." Still, no one could blame him for wanting a look at her next. For one thing, the scope here was so peculiarly limited. For a second, in this all but closed community, it was almost impossible, honor aside, not to find out.

Fifty miles from New York, rimmed by the Ramapo Mountains on the one side and the Hudson River on the other, the enormous gift mansions of the Center's rambling estate, where not enfiefed by geography – or perhaps intellect – were so by regulation. Some of the most valuable scientific facilities in the world were here, plus the kind of government research which, though the Center wasn't state-owned, inevitably went with such. Visitors of note came often, guests of the staff also. Some were heralded; others came quietly; all were met with aplomb. Nobody felt himself followed. Yet in such a few square miles, no matter how irregularly and munificently landscaped, there were only so many private houses to go to, each cot rather clear in its vale – and so many faces to see at them. Against the marble of the greater buildings, moonlight was sharp, shadows black, and even in rain or snow, nothing clandestine. And the bushes were so often barbwired.

It would be one of the new men, since he knew so intimately her opinion of the present staff – the one uxoriousness of their affair had been the sharing, suddenly open to two single strangers in a community largely paired, of those infinitely cozy malices of the newly married. Not long before, he himself had been new. At the Center, aside from the women and a few men in outmoded corners of the humanities like his own, the procurement of its very special scholars was exaltedly international and the turnover small – of last year's six new male staff members, two had promptly been hijacked to California and two had been of that advanced age which sometimes still did accompany distinction. A few members, of whom he knew nothing, had been on leave. Of the two who were left, Meyer, one of those tall, rawboned Jews of Lincolnian feature, Meyer Spilker – anthropologist, had seemed more likely, until Linhouse, invited to dine, had seen both that organizational household – where in that schedule would there be time for adultery? – and better, had seen Meyer with Lila. There remained: Anders, who in himself seemed a remainder of the race itself, of those of its more questionable qualities which since the days of *Pithecanthropus erectus* had been debasing its limbs to the glory of its head – unless Anders were something unconscionably new. Anders was preferable. As one's successor, a freak always is. And there still would have remained Anders, after all, theoretical physicist, latest hero of post quantum mechanics theory, and possibly of women – who by nature and history were always updating the Hero – if not for the last evening on which Linhouse, or anyone else, had seen Janice Jamison.

That had been in the February of what now, in early December, scarcely seemed the same year. Looking back, the last two years of his life fell as neatly from him its core as the segments of a fruit artificially forced. The two terms of his first year here and their affair, broken only by his annual summer visit to England, mother, and Sloane Street. His early return in August to the Center, where Janice had stayed on in her cottage. Their easy resumption, during an Indian summer slowly bronzing to fall, of that fixed rhythm of time, ergo of love and a good many other things, which was more often than scholarship the real secret of a scholar's devotion to the academic life – faint monastic reflection as it was, for some only a religious one, of seasons and duties pre-ordained. Her avoidance of him had begun that November; then came that period when he glimpsed her now and then in the way of things here, but no longer by arrangement. His way home from office to flat lay straight down the lane on which she lived; it was only after he realized that they no longer met there even accidentally that her "vagueness" ceased being vague. The scheduled life could of course also be marvelously useful in nurturing the first tucked-in smiles of amorous interest — in the beginning he'd seemed to encounter her everywhere. How the same could be managed in reverse was now brought home to him in those walks, increasingly wintry, on which each day detached its brittle leaf, delivered its more umber dark.

He could have phoned, but didn't. The walks kept up both his dignity and the thread of what he refused to name. No one who saw him embark down the untrafficked lane need know that he now passed her door without entering it. From remarks passed idly, "Where have you two —?" she seemed to be staying as socially quiet as he, and gossip still had them together. Others here were also being retiring; though there were no students here, hearts were still sensitive to the academic systole and it was now between terms, that lull of the year when people left and returned on plans accomplished before these were public, and Argus gossip even slept. She hadn't gone away. He was still here. On his lone walks, these facts — though later at home he saw himself as the lone undergraduate in a forest of senior sense — served to make him feel that they were still together.

Mountain climate is for teatime, and tea had been their time for love, replacing the siestas that would have been Tuscany. Her house, originally a gate cottage, later on in its modest history remodeled by the estate owner for a lady retired from La Scala, had the characteristics of both eras. All its downstairs sitting-room life, like that of most saltboxes not overshrubbed, was accessible to the passerby. On the three sides of its second story, the little bedroom windows with their priscilla curtains flared against the dark like an open picture book. But at the rear, a story-and-a-half addition looked out through harlequin-leaded windows on a high close of pine, its one room blind to the road unless the passerby knew the pattern cast by the panes when there was a light behind them, a motley shine scarcely connected with them, more like a watermark of a perilous coastline beyond the trees. Each evening, though he wanted neither to see her nor be seen, the lights, bright on three sides, dark at the rear, gave him all the silhouette of what he wanted to know.

On the first night he saw that pale watermark, he walked on faster than usual. There was, he told himself as quickly, no agony. Though he'd never known her to use that room when alone, imagining her to be doing so was no easier, since he'd never seen her there in clothes. In that atticless house, this room had served for one, holding whatever of Jamison's collection hadn't gone to museums, plus all of hers which would never be asked for, including that couch. A great many objects, grinning, sawing the air and pendulous, were in that room, large ones — made of wood, fur, teeth, hair, shell, stone, bone, and all full of the ferocity of our beginnings, also numbers of those sadder exquisites of domestic use, or the whittlings of a primal afternoon — the buttons, pipes and shards now offered up from merged hands and now all ideographed to the same communication. It was a superb place to make love, not out of any lechery of the exotic, but because, tossed there on all that wrack, the survivor felt himself that supreme exotic, the man who was still alive. Against the La Scala lady's mantel, at either end of which a carved Italian cherub, affixed rather clumsily, flew and hung, she always leaned for a minute, standing between them like a third carving budded there — one no good at flying but resolute of foot, smaller than angel, larger than cherub — and of more definite pudenda than either.

For a few nights after, he drove home, through town. When he resumed his walks, each evening that faint flotsam of rear light still shone, like the phosphor of a wreckage seen only by him. Whoever was visiting her must walk there also; there was never a car standing. Her Renault had been disposed of some weeks ago, this overheard by chance at the town garage, where he hadn't dare ask further. Yet he'd never encountered anyone on the path. Twice he had seen her at a distance, once only the back of her lime-colored suit far ahead of him on the supermarket line, then gone, the second time from across the library reading room, where he had raised his head from study of a catalog to see her staring at him gravely — before he could smile, she had moved one hand from the wrist *comme-ci comme-ça,* and disappeared into a carrel. Then and there he'd disposed of her; only his own celibacy had continued her charm. He'd arranged to be away over the coming weekend and had alerted some rackety friends in New York. Selection here, he now saw, could be so highly unnatural. Let Anders continue the marathon.

But before the weekend, on the snowy Thursday dusk before, as he sat under the flaring chandeliers of the much more ordinary hall where the entire Center was gathered for a speech by a visiting eighty-year-old astronomer, of the customary distinctions, who was to be Linhouse's guest for the night — there, in that public light, with all faces tipped toward that rather delightful old whale-spout on the platform, sense was at last granted him. It came like a grace, smarting but welcome, fallen on him from those advanced universes of which old Sir Harry was now speaking. Before Linhouse stole away, ostensibly to go on ahead in preparation for his guest and the drinks to honor him, he looked over the hall once more, row by row. No, she wasn't here. Everyone else was.

Sir Harry's expressed mission in this country was to woo home those British scientists who had been bled away from their country's service by gross American offers; the Center's privately expressed hope was to bleed away him. Both sides were delicately showing their medals. All the Center's luminaries, attended by every scrap of staff, were here. Over there was Meyer, marshaled at the head of a departmental claque from which only one was missing. And there— He had no trouble finding him. Anders was on the platform. She was the only one not here.

As Linhouse tiptoed out, the speaker, stretching his cosmorama so that even the secretaries might see its limits, had just dubbed the sun a third-generation, run-of-the-mill star. From Sir Harry's tone, it seemed doubtful, in that case, that he would consider spending his declining years up the Hudson. But the old man could be thanked in another quarter. *Houseguest.* Absurd that it hadn't occurred to Linhouse before. Whomever she'd had there all these weeks, perhaps months, was being harbored in the house.

Outside, snow was falling steadily, helping him obscure his real reason for driving instead of walking. On that quiet lane a car motor could be heard, and he would see to it that a car door was slammed. In the far corner of himself that had still been critic, he wished more than anything not to see Jack Linhouse sink to an even lower level of Paul Pry. To those who, like his former self, had never had such an obsession, he could now report that its sensation — as of helium in the head and lead in the shoes — was desperately tiring. Especially so if, with the same schizoid keenness, its owner disapproved of it as highly as if it had belonged to somebody else. On her doorstep, the car motor left chugging, he waited in what he did recognize — an onslaught of the tenderness, false as hope, which could vine any doorway in one's mental life, no matter how dubious a one, let one only know for sure that one was leaving it.

Later on, from the short vantage of the next night (in his plane seat as emergency duenna to the suddenly taken ill Sir Harry) he'd seen how lucky his own awkwardly hiccuped greeting might have been for her, allowing her to cover, with his confusion, some very much more grave lack of it in her. There'd been no scene – for one thing, she'd been fully and calmly clothed. If, instead, she had come to the door in any one of the snatched-up mandarin-coats or cleverly managed serapes in which, during his own tenure, she'd used to answer an inconvenient bell, he might have learned more than what he had – that in this house there was something important to be learned. But not many embarrassments were harder to bridge than the formal meeting, after some estrangement, of two parties who'd last seen each other in the nude.

"All that wiggery!" Sir Harry, opening his eyes after takeoff and refusing a pill, resettled himself. "No – I don't mean all this –" The takeoff had been extra deluxe, in fact floated on music. "– and I'll keep my seatbelt, theng kew. I meant last night." Under the eye of last night's doctor, he had told the provost that if popping off was the question, it had come to him that now *or* later, he would rather wait for that event at home. The provost, much disappointed, had declined to bear the responsibility of Sir Harry's making it there alone.

"Good of you to volunteer, though," said Sir Harry now, "to accompany me."

"Glad to," said Linhouse, smiling truthfully. Toward such sound old persons as well-seasoned with the oils-and-vinegar of life as this one, those who above all still carried their hardness of mind like altar boys the holy vessel, Linhouse had the veneration of a man who dared to hope for an old age of the same. "Also, free ride home to mother. She won't visit me here." He looked outside. "Here" was already well over the Atlantic.

"Ah?" Sir Henry stretched one long, tentative leg into the aisle, his fists still grasping the armrests. He'd waived the windowseat to Linhouse. Despite his elaboration, last evening at the party, on the undoubted existence, as admitted by most astronomers of his school, of life on those hidden stars behind the cosmic dust, beyond the Milky Way, the immediate heavens, dark blue and drifting, seemed to interest him not at all. It came to Linhouse, sharply watching his charge — could it be that the old boy was afraid of flying?

"Ah —?" He turned, just enough to scrutinize Linhouse. "Good to know that some of, er — us — still want to stay at home." Head forward on his neck, he made that most English and useful of sounds, a hairy, noncommittal snuffle — "Mmmph?" — as far toward interrogation as he could decently go.

Linhouse smiled. His quarter-cousins, the English, wore their politeness as they wore their braces, and for the same reason, to hold in and up a part of the natural man — in this case a curiosity not as innuendo as the French, nor as loose as the American, but as savage as either — and in their own gaming way quite as well rewarded. The old man wouldn't dream of asking what any young native chit at the Center would have chirped out of habit, and been given the answer to with her handshake — as to exactly what Linhouse, clearly a hybrid, *was*. Indeed the old boy would be more content to dart at it from corners, puzzling it out. This game of origins and professions could last the trip — which for Linhouse, mentally still back on that snowy doorstep, might have been preferable. But his job was to sustain the old man, not exhaust him. He'd therefore given his dossier as ingenuously as the States had accustomed him to doing, as freely as once, holding a hand, he had been made to give it to *her*.

"Father was three parts Irish. I was brought up mostly by the fourth part, in Wiltshire. Mother's an American, from Maine, if you know what that is, sir — but brought up partly in London. They married there, came —" he glanced at the window and away again, "here. My father fell in love with the States at once, from then on refused to leave it. Dead now. Mother always fancied London, wouldn't live anywhere else. We children were shared out between, divided, not always evenly. I didn't get to stay very long in the States until I was grown. Harvard. She's got a brother at the Fogg, you see. Mother. But you might say my share was rather more" – Linhouse had given a slight bow – "on *our* side." He had leaned back. Done rather neatly. He could do chit-chat well enough, except on doorsteps.

"Gahn!" The old man shook his head, not at the information, Linhouse felt, but at the pace. The personal having been dealt with so much too summarily, he took the next step of politeness, that of general ideas, not too profound. "Solomon's decision, eh. I happen to think that a man divided against himself isn't such a bad idea. Liked a spot of difference in a person, my generation did. Really did, not just say. Expect we're the last to feel comfortable with it." He chuckled. "Hundred years from now, to get any differentiation, may have to *take* to sawing the babies in half."

"Because of genetic changes? Or psychological ones?"

The old man made a face – a grown man asked by Johnnie to taste his alphabet soup. "They're not so separate, you know. In the long run, psychology's only what attaches to the other things. In the long run." He looked down at his fists, carefully unclenched them and put his hands on his thighs. "No, it'll be a matter of safety, don't you see. Perfectly natural. For the young especially – ever watch a litter? When the physical world seems to be breaking up, everybody tries to be one and the same animal, mmmph? Or person." He made a horse-jaw and smoothed it, telegraphing a joke he could still disown, if badly received. "Natural legacy too, of all this monotheism of the last few thousand years. Now that the people are to take the place of God, seems proper there should be only *One* of them, don't you know."

Linhouse laughed, for the joke, and for the old gent's mannerly try at switching the talk to Linhouse's realm – that soup. He made a try at a return. "And the world's to be one and the same place too, hmm? Or dozens of the same."

"Ah, that is American of you, that worry. Or rather, their side of you. All so afraid they'll seem gauche for liking places that way." He smiled. "Your provost or what d'ye call 'm, apologized to me for the sameness of his house. Had to tell him I didn't bother much about the difference of places."

"Not even – out there?" They were above the clouds now, on a clear, fleece night.

Sir Harry looked sideways, delicately, and away. "I know the principle of heavier-than-air machines as well as anybody," he said grumpily. "A nursemaid took me up in one of the fun-machines at Brighton, unfortunately early." Then he winked. "I can be as psychological as anybody, too." He leaned back, and once more relaxed his arms. "What's out there is *space*. Not *place*, either nostalgic or political."

"Not just something for the Foreign Office, hmm." Linhouse's comment fell worse than flat in his own ears – it was the kind of chummy remark the untraveled made to him. She had been right. This was the way even a philosopher felt with these interstellar men nowadays. Even with one who wouldn't look out of a window at twenty thousand feet up. "Still," he said kindly – the old boy was only human – "you do hold with Lovell and Shapley? I gathered so, last night. That there *is* life out there?"

The human old boy sat right up. Humanity in fact purpled him, not stinting that extra cragginess of forehead, eyeball and temple which so often gave skinny old men of distinction a look of having twice the number of features they'd been born with. "They –" He choked, and recovered. "– they . . . hold with *me!*"

A moment later, seeing Linhouse's alarm, he touched a

hand to Linhouse's shoulder. "Sorry. That's the real nastiness of getting old — these absolutely uncontrollable rushes of ego. I'll be snuffling my food next. Same last-minute greediness." He coughed and looked away, to allow a mutual recovery of reticence. Then he forced himself to look steadily out and into that moving blue-black — at this height unstarred or coddled with cloud — which was being consumed by the plane but not diminished. He continued to look there, as if age had given him the courage.

"We all hold," he said. "There isn't a chance that there isn't life out there. Or perhaps a proportion of one against it to — ten to the twentieth power number of chances — it does exist." He turned away from the window, then back. "I don't know if you know anything about this sort of —"

"Nothing," Linhouse said at once. It occurred to him that his own stance, voice, in fact whole mental field, was that of a man facing a firing squad. "Absolutely nothing."

His seatmate made the humble, sideways nod that a mandarin must get tired of making. "Well, let's see — half the stars in the Milky Way have planetary systems, you know. . . . For life forms resembling ours, what you'd ask first would be —" He shrugged. "Does it have water in a liquid state? . . . And so on. And so on." He gave up, confronted by how to choose for this child at his knee. "Yes, there'll be life." He sighed. "Yes. Life."

Linhouse stared out there with him, looking at a lesser distance however, say from wherever they were now — well past Gander — and back. It shouldn't take much more than that — say the time jump from London, between some streets less genteel than Sloane, and those of a town fifty miles up the Hudson — to cure him of the jolt that a woman had given him, in preferring some man from out of town. One of the first things he'd do when he got to London would be to take the boat that went down the Thames to the Greenwich Observatory, where time was monitored for the world over. Take a girl there for the day, that's what he would. He turned back to Sir Harry.

"Even beings like us, hmm? Or not too much different." He was surprised to find himself hoping so; never would have thought he held that much brief for the race. But now he could feel for his fellow beings with the possibly kindred passion of a man left behind.

"Bllmmph – ha!" The ejaculation was enough to startle some heads up front. Sorted from the old man's repertoire, it appeared to be a major sneeze of amusement.

"Anders!" he said out of his handkerchief, when able. "That's what *he* thinks. Told me so at your party. 'Universal biochemistry, first off!' he says. 'Check!' says I. 'Or that's what they say.' 'Convergence,' he says then. 'Beings with the same needs, molded by the same natural forces, come to resemble. I assume you grant that!' 'Granted,' says I. 'Or that's what they tell me. I'm only an astronomer.' 'Well, Sir Harry,' he says in the most benevolent way, nodding that conic section he uses for a head, 'don't you worry now, they're going to be very like you and me.'" The old man exploded into laughter again, where Linhouse joined him. He continued. "'Oh, good-oh, *very* nice,' says I, 'but you know I do worry a bit. Hope they won't be too like us, you know. Don't know about you, Anders, but I've got to have a woman once in a while.' . . . May Rachel – that's my wife – forgive me . . . And do you know what he said then? Trying to chaff, of course. 'I've allowed for that,' he said.

"At heart he meant it though, don't you see," said Sir Harry. "Poor dreary little snipe, they're always the ones, aren't they. Fancies his own image just like God did, poor little bugger."

Linhouse was silent for a while. With an effort, he wrenched himself away from that doorstep. "Bright, though." Since

Anders first shone in his cradle, it must have been the thing to say.

"Oh, very. Left your government, you know — Project Ozma — to do radio-telescopic work on his own. Broadcasting directional signals, electrical impulses. Hoping to receive. That sort of thing."

"Ozmo," said Linhouse dreamily. "The way they name them. As if they themselves can't quite believe. As if they still have to personify, in order to keep sane. The way primitives do. To keep their place in nature." Too late, he remembered that his seatmate belonged to those he called "they."

"Like your hurricanes here," the old man said slyly. "What was that last one in the newspapers — *Edna?*"

"They do it alphabetically." Linhouse grinned, and suddenly stretched as high as the plane's confines would let him. Edna, Frances, Grace, Inez — no — Helen, Inez — Janice. He felt healthier, suddenly. The thing always to keep in mind, when a woman got one down, was that there were such a lot of them. "I'm misplaced at the Center, you know. I'm only a phil — classicist. The Carthaginian heresies are about the last I've heard of. Or is it Carthusian?" He felt lightheaded, if not gay. "Tell me. What Anders is doing — is it tenable?"

"Oh, quite. What a government pays money for usually is, you know. Your place just gives him more leeway. To go off on his own track. Yes, quite tenable." He looked at his seatmate with that benevolence Linhouse had grown used to receiving at the Center — the distant pity with which Linhouse himself two hundred years ago might have gazed at men who professed no Latin. "There's a cosmic evolution going on all the time, you know — new stars, new galaxies. Someday an Anders will hit the right one. We're just — out of touch."

"Oh God," said Linhouse. Frivolity was the only answer.

"More messages. What hath God wrought, and so on. The music of the spheres, on Princess telephones?"

"Simple arithmetic, more likely. Plus and minus. Then a primer will be sent. We'll learn how to decipher. We already can receive." His voice faded as he looked minimally at Linhouse, and the window.

"And will Anders find his mate out there?" Linhouse's voice, if the old man had been attending, had been nasty, sick once again with its obsession. Back there, the light in the rear room of the house had been on, cast on the pines. Anders had still been on the platform, of course. But the light could have been waiting for him. She had done that for Linhouse sometimes.

And now he himself was a pinpoint in space, receding, in a space neither nostalgic nor political – nor even cerebral. Up to now he would have said that space, if it existed anywhere supremely did so where the hope of the world also rested – in the human head. Men on doorsteps knew better. Space was only what was between people. Even better, space was its own inhabitants, was its people. It came to him now, almost happily, that he was one of those who would never be able to see his universe except through his own quotient. Even if – under something newer and more tenable yet to come – he were to be the last man to do so. He saw himself as the last classicist, raising that banner. I accept that universe, he said to himself, to her. Mine. *Me perturbe.*

Alongside him, the old man had smiled at the black stuff in the window, saying something under his breath which sounded like "eld" or "of eld." The smile was the one with which old men stared at their future from easy chairs. "We're babes there," he added. "And you may take that as tenable also."

The plane, not a jet, was now bumping a headwind, its

engines noisier each time it lifted from a pocket. What he said next was drowned, but from the shape of his lips, that same first syllable. Despite the droning, he continued to shape it, like an S.O.S. to a Land-ho too far off to be of use, but still sighted. When it came clearly, in the moment when the engines cut out, it sounded to Linhouse as if he were calling. "– *elled.* Almost all of us think it likely. We'll have been excelled."

In the sudden deadness, passengers up ahead were looking at each other uneasily; this circling, suspended silence was connected in their minds with landings at airports, and the plane must be still mid-Atlantic. To Linhouse, no pilot, but once a parachutist, this free-floating sensation always brought back the spinal release of that mystic moment in the jump when one attained terminal velocity – when gravitation itself could do no more. It had been his one relationship to that world of the upper air which the man next to him was used to probing on such outer terms as made his own a nothing – and it too had been in the realm of the personal.

He glanced at Sir Harry, at that old face now whitening in the bridgeless gap between its first nurse and what it knew. Against politeness, Linhouse put his hand on the other's clenched one, and held it there. Space was personal. Then the engines took hold after the drop, and once again they were riding.

"I'll have that pill after all." An eighty-year-old pink returned to his cheeks, with the water Linhouse brought him.

"Anders," he said then. His voice was colorless. "Shan't ask what you have against him. Shouldn't underestimate him at his job though, I shouldn't." He leaned back then, closing his eyes, clicking together teeth still his own, as if to nip between them this moment of nonreticence. His eyes reopened.

"I mind me –" he said, and now he was only a charming old

man with a wandering voice and a leftover manner, "of what a very nice American general once said to me. 'Mrs. Partridge,' said he — that was his wife — 'Mrs. Partridge is like you, sir. Never really lets her weight down in a plane.'" He slept.

And Linhouse was left free to return to his doorstep — hers. This moment before obsession always took over again was like those nights of his boyhood when, tucked down and ready, he waited before the red room of his sexual daydreams, half hating the curtain to rise. Then, once again her door opened to him waiting there, the motor chuffing away behind him, in the snow-still air. And once again he quavered out his sparkling first-and-only line, bubbled up out of him like the lackluster air in an all-night glass of carbonated water.

She'd been clothed, of course; he'd had time to see that. It may have been for a moment they hung their heads over this. He'd had no time to sense whether or not the house behind her was swollen with man. The aura of sex, recent or to be, had always before seemed to him as apparent in that otherwise empty house as the echoes of a beautiful quarrel, but he'd had no time to stand there this day, listening. All his senses had been receiving the sense of what was no longer in her — vanished, he was somehow sure, not merely for him alone, but for all. For — he no longer felt himself particularly addressed. Nor would any other man feel so now — this was the surprise. For he could feel that it was not merely the case that she was lost to him only. She had managed to lose that gift which he had thought her powerless to discard.

Sex had still been in the structure of that face well enough, in the willfully squared lip, the cabinet glow of the eye, the brow arched like a tiny lion whip over it. But could there be — for a woman or man — a willed menopause of the spirit, visible only in whatever it was the eye was now fixed on? As long as he stood still, that focus seemed to be through him and beyond him. But when he pressed forward to enter, her barring movement gave her away. Whatever she was vestal to — for that was the air of it — was in the house. It must be a person of course — whether or not this little island-craver understood it herself, her discipleship was surely, like his own, to the space that clotted about and in people. He had stood there transfixed however, in the full knowledge of all that this woman could push him to: first, obsession, and now such perversion as he'd never dreamed himself nearing, any closer to than in the worn grooves of his Greek translations. For if she were to ask him in, saying, "Stay!" with who-knows-what possibility in that subtly anthropological smile which the backroom had sometimes induced in her — he could see himself conniving. He could understand the emotions of a man willing — not eager, but willing — to undertake a ménage of three.

In his airplane seat, Linhouse groaned. To occupy himself, he fiddled from his passport case a plastic wheel, souvenir from some other airline, which when properly spun and read provided the relative times of day between "representative cities" — i.e. airstops — everywhere. Only pick a station — Karachi, say — for in the midst of all this whirl of the wheel one must oneself be *some*place — and the status of the entire rest of the world would then be clear, spooning its cereal, or deeply sleeping on the dugs of love. He spun the wheel. In San Francisco they were —, while in Bangkok —, while in Seattle —, but meanwhile, where was he? To use the wheel, one had to posit oneself somewhere.

He glanced at the old man beside him, now perhaps roving those vast Alhambras which his inner vision was used to; what were the dreams of astronomers when not of nursegirls? In the Moorish tundra-dark at the back of, say Alpha Centauri — the only one of those sky-names Linhouse had heard of, as chief star of the nearest constellation, or perhaps it was galaxy – what were they doing there now on the peaks of their excellence, in relationship to, say –? Pick somewhere. He picked a doorstep under snow, on a Ramapo evening. Once more he waited there, dreadfully willing. Once more, from heights unscalable by him, she bent on him the traveler's stare for the untraveled, before the door closed. . . . And after a while, in the way of these clockwork episodes where no one ever forgot his lines whether answered or not, the door reopened and his one line came round again.

"It's I," he said, or babbled, once more. "I saw the light."

3. Wives, Fathers, and Converts

At LONDON Airport, the old man was taken in charge by his Rachel, no disciple, but a wife of certain sharp, foreign strengths that were at once evident in the muted, soft-coal air. A woman with a nose, she stood tall and long-necked within full dark draperies, awaiting them at the gateway like a black flamingo, and when the two of them left, the effect was of Sir Harry being carried off – and vastly pleased at it – under one superb black wing. Linhouse, invited to dine with them the following week at their flat in Holland Park, found him much improved, looking jauntily younger, and thinking of returning to the States after all, spurred on by his wife, who had never been there.

Rachel – pronounced the French way, and otherwise called Madame (she refused to be a ladyship) – had actually been born Sinsheimer, a German refugee-from-Hitler, who by her service in the Resistance had long since been translated into French. A woman of somewhere between fifty and sixty, she had the self-contained beauty of one able to live up to such a magnificently hooked nose; all of her – sleek-knobbed hair, daubed brows and a strong skin now and then pink-wattled with energy – gave an impression of having been pomaded backwards from it. As Sir Harry's third wife she was still his "young" one, no indication being given of where his place was in her succession of husbands — he was clearly so delighted to be the incumbent. If she wasn't a disciple, then what was she?

To Linhouse she appeared first off as one of those foreign women who were translated very quickly but never lost the hard core of themselves; whether what they kept was a kind of femininity, he couldn't say. It appeared to him that she too might be a traveler, and for this reason he studied her carefully. In her crow-satins and midnight crepes, always some Gallic manipulation of the many colors of black, she had as many pockets as a concierge (she must have had them made that way), these currently inhabited by one or more of the *Cahiers* of Péguy. She might be a Catholic convert then, at least some of the time — why Linhouse thought of it that way he couldn't say either, at least not at their first dinner. When it came about that, because of a worrying illness of his mother's, he wasn't going to leave the country immediately, the three of them had several dinners.

On the second, it appeared that she was a Socialist, though not of the British variety, her husband's, which she despised.

"They have no *clarté*," she said, setting the word down on the cloth like a solid, where it sat like a small candle burning. "Look at him, he takes a title."

"Before I knew you. And only for service in the War Department," said Sir Harry. At other times he was driven to protest his lack of aristocracy by citing his background — father a brewer, and not a rich one — and his university — Leeds.

"I accept the aristocracy," she said with a grin — and Linhouse for the first time was faintly *reminded*. "And the money, if we go to America, but it's the lack of style. Politics, yes — *la politique d'abord*. But 'ere it 'ave no mystique."

She drew out one of the notebooks, entitled *De la Grippe,* then another, *Encore de la Grippe,* and yet another, *Toujours de la Grippe,* while Linhouse, pocket-dazzled, wondered where she would light – nearer hypochondria or Christian Science? – until he was made to understand that Péguy had written these particular issues during a bout of influenza. They were dated 1900. When it came out that she was now, almost three quarters of a century later, a passionate Dreyfusard, he thought he understood her better. He'd met women, men too, who yearned impossibly backwards toward eras temperamentally theirs, couples knocking about Greenwich Village in raccoon coats, talking of what "Scott" said (and they didn't mean Sir Walter), women who after the third bourbon of being some man's "good sort," spoke tearfully of bustles and *la belle époque,* and ordered a chartreuse. It was just luck even now for instance, if half the bright schoolboys in Britain got safely past the *Yellow Book* and out the other side. He himself, for all he knew, had come to his profession by some such pass, an early Greek or Roman one. There was only one trouble about Rachel – he couldn't quite pin down her era. And the next time, what dropped from her, from reticule or marsupial pouch (how could he tell which?), was a mixed bag indeed: a pamphlet, *Tea Ceremony in Role of Japanese Women;* a reprint, this much-thumbed, of a lecture by her own husband, if Linhouse's eye was accurate – Ἔλλειψις ; also W. H. Hudson's *Green Mansions,* and a volume by Chateaubriand. She tucked them all back.

Was she a feminist? Did she travel, or yearn to? He asked her.

To the first query, Sir Harry answered for her, making his wife the little bow of a husband so much at one that he could speak. "In a bisexual world such as ours, women physically own the civilization already. Both sexes spend their lives concealing that from each other."

"Ah, we don' want it, this world," said Rachel. "We amuse ourselves – *s'amuser?* – watching you work for it. For what you could have by default." She spread her hands. "*Non! Ce n'est pas ce que je veux – féminisme.* It is an invention of man, that."

"What is it you want, nowadays?" Linhouse spread his own hands. It was catching. "Women, I mean."

She inspected her nails, but tossed him a keen, kind look, as if aware that someone in particular had entered here. "For it *not* to be nowadays, mebbee? 'Arry is right. We are very civilize'."

He looked up, to find 'Arry regarding him not nearly so kindly.

They were momentarily alone, she and Linhouse, when he asked her the second question, on the eve of the couple's departure for Bucks, where Harry had a house, half observatory and almost all glass, built for him by Mary, the second wife and the rich one.

"Marie, I love 'er," said Rachel. "A big damp *pavillon*, we cawn' go there except summer. A mad, impossible 'ouse, not at all *convenable*. But we can watch the stars there. And if 'e get lumbago, it is Marie who get the blame."

Though so critical of the country, she never expressed any wish to leave it. Indeed, after the manner of the country itself, which had a way of tricking foreigners into its own prides, she could be distressfully local, ranging over the whole flower field of English accent, for instance, like a lady-in-waiting hunting patterns for a lambrequin to be embroidered for the Queen. She was likely to inform them mysteriously that Wykehamists spoke through cotton wool, Harrow and Marlborough men through linen, or to hush the man on the telly with a cry of "Kent!" or "Bethnal Green!" Though her mischief was better than her ear, once more Linhouse was reminded; wasn't anthropology after all only localism to the *nth?* One couldn't of course imagine Rachel on any man's knee. In bed, an odalisque a la Jacques David, was where his mind (if it was his mind) placed her. But a teasing kinship trembled in the room. Perhaps it was the mockery of those who belonged to a tribe.

A lurid thought struck him. "Marie?" he said, low. "Is she – does she *live* down there?"

"Oui."

"Oh."

She let him simmer in his own cleverness.

"In the spirit," she said then.

"Oh, *dead!*" In his relief, he spoke rather loud. The aberrations of one's friends could make one queasy, if they came too near.

"Non." Suddenly she burst into an uncontrolled laughter he'd never heard from her. All considered, it seemed to him a little late for it.

"Oh, it was very *comme il faut,"* she said, when she had finished. "While she was down there. In Bucks. And 'Arry, *grâce à Dieu,* was at a congress in Cairo. Before Suez. An' before 'e meet me." Her proud head equated the two.

"Oh." No need to be that *spirituelle,* was his tone.

"Non," she said "– not divorce." She crossed her fingers over her mouth, and its belated smile. *"Disparue,"* she said. "She disappear."

Had he held an icicle in his hand again, there for a moment? Even now, looking back, he couldn't say that he consciously had. These days, even the most ordinary man walked under the weight of so many crowns he changed with every step and never even saw, the crowns psychologica, parapsychologica and perhaps even astrologica – clouds of wire-and-fireflies gathering in on him once again from all the phantasms at which men, since Erasmus, had been daring to laugh.

But he did ask his question. He must have thought he was changing the subject. "Do you never want to travel?" he'd said. "Elsewhere?"

She'd looked past him, out of the window, over her glass of valedictory champagne. From her expression, she might have been seeing luminous Barbizons above the gray-prickle London street. But what she said was, rather anxiously, "In America, they will take good care of Harry?" She even pronounced the "h."

Just then, Harry himself reentered, carrying his farewell gift, a scholar's compliment, that same pamphlet of which Linhouse would probably understand only the title. He presented it, then put an arm about his wife's shoulder. "She wants me to go ahead of her to America, imagine! She thinks I'm strong enough!" His cheeks were slightly oranged by drink. He looked down at Linhouse, who was much the shorter man, with mettle. "And I may do. There's an international congress at Berkeley in the autumn; they're willing to pay my way." He squeezed her shoulder, bare through its nun's veiling. "But I'll come back to bring you over, eh. Didn't know I was training her up to be my assistant down at Bucks, did you, Linhouse? She had some math at Göttingen, before the war. I've some hobbies of my own down there; we may show that chap Anders a thing or two yet. Women are remarkable, you know, at some of these very painstaking operations. Getting so, once she gets down there, I can scarcely tear her away.'

They stood there, arms unexpectedly laced about each other's waist in more than friendship, like the *mère* and *père* of a family inexplicably not present in photographs, valiant couple in their separate primes, who were now about to ascend to a bed where they might still find comfort in some massive reticulation of limb. It came to Linhouse — such hot flashes of insight came to the deserted — what the resemblance was. The smile under that nose of hers could still pearl so freshly, and with the same perverse calm – of creatures who might have been promised the end of the world on Tuesday. They none of them knew what they did or didn't care for. They merely had the pockets made, and kept them at-the-ready. They were all of them natural converts.

Lids lowered, she was accepting both the praise and the squeeze. "I so look forward to the time down there," she said.

Linhouse thanked them once more for dinner and pamphlet, promising to send on a small publication of his own. "Wish yours were all in Greek. Might have more chance of understanding it." The dedication caught his eye. *To my Wife,* followed by: $ay^{M} + n = bx^{M}(a - x^{N})$.

"You understand that, I suppose," he said to Rachel. She nodded on her long neck, her eyes very wide. He waited. She didn't tell him. He said good-bye rather brusquely. When he turned again at the door, she hadn't moved and seemed still to be staring at him, as in some primitive or else very sophisticated drawing, from one long Etruscan eye.

The following week he saw his mother safely through her successful operation and contentedly ensconced in a nursing home where she could settle down to being "the pretty American who is really more like us" – a role she'd been playing most of her life, and was now, except for the prettiness that had lasted best, getting harder and harder to define on both sides. She'd spent her life getting away from that same State of Maine which had provided her with enough stamina to do so, this energy of hers in turn having been mistaken by his father for that sexual one of which later performance had shown him to be so in need.

"The Americans have an orgiastic climate, a Puritan heritage, and whole infusions of mixed bloods," his father had written happily – and finally. "They want most to be a political nation but their own climate and distances have outwitted them. The subsequent melee is wonderful. No, I won't come back."

Privately, Linhouse knew his parents had gotten away with blaming temperamental differences on national ones. His father, correspondent for a London newspaper and circuit lecturer, had always been careful to send very good maintenance, to keep a respectable housekeeper for visiting progeny, and never to be seen with young women who had too much fringe. Meanwhile he had sent volumes of Chesterfieldian advice to all, those letters to his wife usually ending on a sharply human note: "Send for Betty, I've had enough of her," or "Time for Patrick, isn't it? Good God, he'll scarcely remember me!" His wife in her own meanwhile had kept her calendar full, her causes and acquaintances visited, a circle of admirers of the opera-escort type dancing round the Maypole of a lively establishment, and almost certainly no lover. So, with the help of Atlantic crossings almost as common as mailings, the personal facade of the family had been preserved.

It followed that of the four children conceived before it had become a facade – while his mother no doubt was thinking of dynasty and his father wasn't thinking – all had emerged like Linhouse, with a strong sense of the personal quotient. None had been too shaken about psychically to make good enough use of a dowry so suspiciously regarded by the century; all, within the aberrations of that century, were leading exactly the dull to vivid lives of people brought up exactly otherwise. Perhaps they hadn't yet made full use of it.

Linhouse, who by his and his grandparents' preference had been reared by them, was the quiet one; no one had ever said dangerously so. As one of the sawed-in-half who more normally came of divorce, he found himself no more reserved in the face of experience than was wise, still open to it with enough of the élan that most probably was meted out in the egg. Maybe he *was* a divided man. He accepted differences between nations, between people, between the sexes – and on this last score, was rather certain of his own. This seemed to him comfortable. As a human being, exclusive of his larger social obligations, he expected to itch, to weep, hopefully to love, and regretfully to die.

Particularly re the itch, of course, the words of Linhouse senior, deceased, now reverberated. "If the children are to spend that much time in England with you, they must be made to understand what a marvelously topical people they are among. Politics is *not* the full explanation of my countrymen. Early in life we are taught to sympathize rather than to feel, and we have absolutely no short-term talent for domestic drama, i.e. 'scenes.' That's all right, the children will get enough of that over here." After some digression, to the effect that Americans rarely had sympathies but always thought they had feelings, he continued. "As to summer plans. Our personal system, like any, was simpler when the children were young. But advantages still accrue. Summer romance, for instance, is particularly pretty in England, or used to be. The English are by no means sexless, indeed are well able to produce downy-rose girls and Anglo-Greek boy babies in moments of absentmindedness, especially if there is a touch of Irish in the family. But their deepest emotional shock is after all sunlight, and it is no wonder that in the long, greenish instances between they are forced to develop the pools, the literature and the society, and an addiction to warm drink. One must never forget also that 'chaff' is merely their natural defense; such a range of sympathy demands a constant cutting down of the candidates for it. The result of all this being that it is absolutely the ideal place to get rid of an emotional encumbrance!" As usual, the letter had a postscript. "N.B. Though Patrick is acquitting you admirably at Harvard — June marks splendid! — he's a little under the weather otherwise and is joining you shortly. Send Jack."

So Jack had been sent. In actual presence, his father hadn't seemed nearly as wise — or perhaps had known quite well that his wisdom was of the epistolary kind. Certainly he'd done better with whichever children and countries happened to be at a distance. And now, from the severest distance, he was doing best of all.

For it was true, Linhouse thought, lounging on a summer's day, at his mother's flat, near one of her bell-glasses — the spirit of ridicule ran through this land like rheumatism; it was impossible to die of love here. Shelley, who hadn't, slept Victorianly, his marble limbs sprawled in a crypt at the Oxford which had thrown him out in the body and readmitted him in the statue, surely the most naked thing in England. After that visit and other weekends, sailing-club or walking-tour, alone or accompanied and all as friendly as field, stream, and pub could make them, Linhouse sat for some days in the park with his mother, who was now convalescing.

Watching the pigeons, he understood even less why birds were the favorite fauna of the English, but more about the local attitude toward what might be phrased monosyllabically: Hop. The girl he'd chosen for his trip down the Thames danced at the Windmill Theatre but had turned out to be a bishop's illegitimate daughter; her mother, it appeared, had remained in the vestry of life. The girl and he spent the night together, not without some political conversation.

He began to seek the company of other children of misalliance like himself. Almost everybody these days seemed to think himself or herself one of them — it was too simple. The days passed with a rubble and a twink, from furnace-groan — they had central heating in a way — to cufflinks and all the other knickknack medley of domestic sounds and routines that so easily became the permanent nostalgias of life. If he were to choose the coziest, it began to be the crowd of teacups waiting in the pre-dark of the kitchen cabinet in Wiltshire, in the house he would never again see. His vocabulary changed again with a natter and a patter and the echo of dozens of words a man could never decently use but kept hearing, the wireless keeping up the class war anxiously, Cockney on the Underground like two whelks talking, and the toy talk of two homos in Soho, two somos in Oho saying, "Oh all that sort of thing and tiddly-pom." England redivivus. He was no longer in agony. Travel had cured him, or repatriated him. Like a good native son, he began to think of France for a change, but since money was ever more pressing – returned to the States.

On his return, by boat, the skyline smashed his teacups. Ah, stunning life, he thought, as the cab sped him from the docks, and he waited with respect for this land to assault him. The torn selvage of all coastal cities fluttered by him, all estuaries of the same debris, of what rust could and did corrupt, shot through with a nostalgia of oceans deserted for the single dull thud of land. He passed under the very mammoth that had brought him. Brave flashed the luxury bric-a-brac shops – stores. He thought with dread of his long-sealed flat – apartment. All along, he knew quite well what was happening.

In the naphtha gloom of the garage where he waited for his storaged car to be brought down to him, he was assailed by a sudden vision of the real, the right and the primeval – some copper beeches he'd once seen, kneeling with them in their own root mast, their tops several golden heavens away, in the profound air of Sussex. The grass there, so green. He forced himself quickly to think of sequoias, trees on this side of the water, and only as far as next summer's adventure.

He promised himself; as an experienced traveler, he knew what he was dealing with. The movable fantasy—already on the move. In the melancholic of other returns, he applied honesty. To all the vanitie of space, he now replied. That no country really waits for one personally, on any side of the water, that the home one is the most topical of all. That all travel—no matter how palmy, or how upflung the finny sail—is only an outer bruise on an innerness that speeds with light. He wasn't thinking of, preaching to, anyone in particular, elsewhere.

Looking round the garage, he reconvinced himself of the ultimate fantasticality of right-where-one-is. Carefully, for himself, he rehearsed the small fantasies of the route home: first the guilty twilight of Harlem—a dream of which had sometimes stopped him in his tracks in Paddington, then the all-purpose plaid handkerchief of suburbia, and finally the dark, polite verdure—nowhere near so savage as Scotland, of his adopted hills. When the attendant came with the car, he tipped him. Sinking but resigned, he refitted himself into the car. The man leaned on the window to give him a friendly warning. Be sure to avoid midtown traffic; the latest astronaut was being welcomed home there, with confetti.

She was in the back room. When he entered her house, several nights later, letter in hand, he was almost convinced of it. To be haunted it is necessary only to feel oneself the ghost. He had come in from that doorstep at last. Inside the little downstairs with its steps going straight up, the two sitting rooms, bowing at each other from opposing mirrors, were as neat as a "restoration" from some Williamsburg of memory. The curtains were impossibly clean—he heard her word for them, "priscilla," rustle again in her mouth, and saw how she looked at them with a touch of the farmgirl's satisfaction in having what one is supposed to have. Once (the day he'd suggested a drive to Pennsylvania) she'd told him about the severe house-habits of the "Dutch" – what kind of housewifery had been going on here, in this sealed house? And once, going on into the back room, he'd at first thought himself alone with all that welter of stuff, then caught sight of her, asleep he thought, on that long New Guinea couch, but when he bent over her there'd been a sudden gleam in the lashes and she'd murmured a bit of Dutch talk at him. "*Wann dich ime busch ferlore hoscht, guk ame bam nuf.*" He'd made her write it down for him afterwards, meaning to have it engraved on a Christmas bangle. "When lost in the woods, look up a tree."

It was all he had of her, except for the letter he was holding. Carrying this, he tiptoed toward the back with stilted step, unable to keep out of his gait a dream that princes were still needed here. And with his hand on the light switch, he'd made his discovery – rather early for a philosopher, circumstantially sad for a man. He knew what it was for which he did care.

Still in the dark, he pondered it, as if he hadn't a world of time to do it in, or, since he was surely going to find her asleep there, he had to get it straight before he turned on the light. Was it in her difference from other women – that in the dark all cats weren't gray? Perhaps, a little. But he'd known women who were far more different – novelties against whose planes, mental or physical, a man was hard put to it to recline. Was it only sexual choice then, merely sex, that ess-shaped giggle of the cosmos, which held him here to hope against hope that when the lamp glowed she would be standing between the cherubs, a median, white-budded plant just enough different, at the small fork of her, for him? Perhaps – a little. Or more than either, that man even in his psyche was only a part-time Narcissus? Was it that he loved – as men had learned to call it – because in one final way, and a number of frivolous ones, she was different from him?

The answer he got was the worst: that he was still speaking of her to himself in the present. At the flip of a switch he would see straight ahead through a window, out where a light made a coastline of trees. If, by a similar projection, he could be his last winter's self walking by, it could know who was inside here. In a way he could. For he understood what he cared for. And he knew who was here. The pain of being thus double was ugly. There, in the dark, his own memorial service was long.

When he snapped on the light, it was no longer needed; dawn was growing, entering the room with its gray usurper's stride. The room seemed unchanged, holding the same host of immoderate objects still covered by the same moderate dust – as if in this most miniature time lapse, each had been awarded its exact pinch of the dust of time. Nearest him, a poggamoggan – *War Club of the Plains Indians, Authentic* – lay crossed with a small archeological steal, *Gold Armband, Sutton Hoo* – fake. Carefully his glance edged toward the corner where lay all New Guinea. Alone there, the long couch still sailed. He turned his head slightly to the right, toward the mantel wall. The cherubs still flew. She wasn't standing between them. Even if he hadn't had the directions in her letter, or had been a newcomer to all the wild wrack that floated this room like a Sargasso, he couldn't have missed what was.

It stood there under the glassy shape which was so clearly only its covering, and it had only the one quality. Everything else here strained or pleaded under a confusion of so many, the smallest shard in some way beating upon the world, on with it. If the total medley here could have been heard, it would have been an irregular one of all kinds of human loops and eddies stretching to be heard above and outside the concentric itself of sound.

This object stood imperturbable, above and outside them. The quality it seemed to have most was a self-containment, of a creation not necessarily – though he'd never seen anything like it – unique. If, for instance, all the snowflakes in the world, instead of being so crazily versatile, had been shaped to a compassionately single design, then any one of them would have what this had – the poise of the One. In the far corner of himself that loved one-ness – or perhaps machinery – he restrained an impulse to kneel.

Instead, he got a move on – his normal response to that impulse. Else he might have been mooning there yet in his solitary longing, instead of being so healthfully exposed here to act it out before what now appeared to be an audience close to the hundred he'd invited. One might almost think that he indeed had been observed on the way here – what right had she to expect that he'd be some sort of Godiva for whom the town would draw its blinds? A thrill nevertheless went through him at all she'd expected of him, for which, in the range of conceivability, he might yet be rewarded. It was the thrill of which heroes were made, as he well knew. He couldn't help it. Getting that thing here, as her letter had predicted, hadn't been all that strenuous. She'd merely failed to warn him that it might be ludicrous. For, anyone chancing to see the complementary rhythms between him and his charge as they made their way here together, might well be excused for assuming that *it* had been getting the move on him.

Suddenly the Muzak went off, leaving him on, to manage as best he could by himself the stealthy current of time. Had he been asleep? What in God's name was he doing here? Out front, the audience held up to him that massed sunflower face which all lecturers know – but his was not the simple platform fear. He had been born to this one, he thought as suddenly. He'd been born to *this,* to the right-here and the now, sent forth with eyes, ears, balls and ever-valiant tongue to function along his voyage of discovery, all to suffer pains or joys still unknown, including the adventure of the death that would be the end of him and them – and in all of this he was an amateur. To the end of this mélange that both frightened and beguiled, he would be one.

He covered his eyes with his hands, wishing that all his organs had complementary sets of hands to cover them, or at least some more generally anonymous skin. If, at best, there were only some repository – of professionalism – to which he might apply. He understood quite well that this was merely the Fascist fear, possibly the God-making one also – and that only his flesh was feeling it. Hard lines that only his flesh was also understanding it. For meanwhile, he knew quite as well that in eighteen or so minutes by his watch he would be getting to his feet on performance of business which might be less daily than most, but had at its heart the same fear that was dormant in any, and might attack a man when he was merely staring at his own cuticle – the ordinary citizen's stage fright and inner self-amaze. He wasn't having any revelations, by God. Any clam-digger might have this sudden sense of fear, or any Linhouse – or any Anders – and probably not when Anders was belting the universe either, maybe when he was in the middle of a shave. It might come upon one on top of a mountain or a woman, on errand or in urinal, in the movie houses of crowd, or at the weekend sandbeaches of alone. No doubt everybody knew this particular sensation as well as Jack Linhouse. It might be called the oracle of the cuticle. It was the moment when the Muzak stopped, and more clearly than in any foreign land, one stood knee-deep in the utter fantasticality of right-where-one-was. The cure for it was obscure as any of his mother's for heartburn or hiccups. Since he hadn't a lump of sugar or a glass of water, he held his breath, then breathed deeply. And had his revelation. This was why one traveled. To get rid of just that.

Just then, a knocking came, apparently at one of the upper doors. But, these doors, like those in any supermarket, were opened in the modern way, by crossing a beam of light with one's body — the kind of door at which, when set up for entry, it was almost physically impossible to knock. Maybe it was the younger generation knocking, as in that line of Ibsen he'd always despised for its patness. Go away, he said to it silently — *I* am the younger generation. Or was, up to last week. Sure enough, this not being the theater, it went away. Besides, he said after it, we have enough people, all she wanted. Every seat he could see was filled.

He checked his watch again — twelve minutes now — took from his wallet the engraved program with its carefully worded note of explanation, slipped under it the part of her letter she'd asked to have read, put the letter's other sheet in his hip pocket, and stood up, remembering that at the near end of the basement passage which debouched backstage, there was a toilet. Just as he stood up — bless action for being the cure one always forgot about — a hand was placed on his shoulder. A bear or a ghost, which will you have it, he thought as he whirled. You know which.

The old man seemed taller than he remembered him, unlike most old men. Since last seen, his skin had become the swart color that aged men come to by way of sun or liver. From his dress — the white tennis flannels and dark jacket of any number of first acts marked *Summer: 1914* — it was hopefully the former. Which must mean that Sir Harry had been to Berkeley for his conference.

"Why —!" Linhouse kept his greeting hushed, but held out his hand. It took him a long moment to realize that his hand was being refused.

The old man lowered down at him, using his height so that Linhouse's head was forced back on his neck, his eyes at close range to that handsomely troughed upper lip, to the cleft, like the finish of an interrupted penstroke, in the chin.

"What have you done with her?" said Sir Harry.

"What . . . have . . . *I*?" With each word, a different hazard came to Linhouse's mind. Were they thinking — they couldn't think — that he himself had somehow effected her disappearance, disposed of her like a Landru, cut her up and washed her down a drain? Or they *had* thought — and Sir Harry, here en route home and known to be his friend, had been sent — how else would he have found the back way to the podium? — to forestall the scandal of a ceremony. Or — No, it couldn't be. Old as Jamison had been for her (fifty-four to eighteen) — *eighty* to thirty-four? Could it be? A magnificent man to look at, tellingly lively with his own wife. And an astronomer. Why couldn't it be? Coming back and forth here, always for the most internationally apposite reasons. And all along, he could have been the new one.

"You were the last one she showed any interest in." Sir Harry's voice was hoarse but polite, like a judge who had been up all night over the transgression of a junior. "When I came back, she was gone. Leaving me a letter. All but saying she was here with you."

She. She. She.

"You too!" said Linhouse. "And I didn't even know you knew her!" In the eyes above his, he saw at last how it looked to others, that small pigtail flame of obsession. "But as for my —"

"You must be out of your mind!"

"— you must be out of your mind."

They said it simultaneously. But mid-chorus, Linhouse had already seen it — what the resemblance was. "Sir Harry —" He spoke gently. "May I see your letter?"

It was handed him, the fingers shaking now. He read little more than the few lines above the signature. *When you know the circumstances you will not blame, even though it is the second time for you. My last words are loving. There is a long chance . . .* (here some indecipherable figures) *that we shall meet again. Go to America.* And below the signature, a small postscript. He didn't really need to read either. The letter was in French.

When he handed Sir Harry his own letter, it seemed almost, if not quite, an even exchange.

Finally each raised his head, but each averted sideways, like two cuckolds.

Sir Harry spoke first. "Ah, I see. Your ceremony, then."

"Mmm." There was a pause. "Perhaps – might we meet afterwards?" And perhaps, like two cuckolds, they would enjoy it.

He looked down at Sir Harry's letter before returning it. *You may guess,* the postscript said. From the signatures, one wouldn't have thought the two women had much in common. The signature on his own letter had been round and not very characterful – the farmgirl, the jampot. This scrawl was black and taut, the footprint of an eaglet. *Rachel.*

"I'll go the way I came," said Sir Harry after a bit. It was his apology.

"Mind the stairs. A bit tricky."

"Ah yes, thanks – doors up above on the blink, it seems. Stuck tight."

"Ah, that was you then. Knocking. Sure you can find the way now?" It was a toss-up as to which voice was the more perfunctory. Neither one of them had moved.

"Oh yes indeed, I was taken round the whole show here very thoroughly last time . . . One setup rather like mine in Bucks, several million pounds worth more powerful of course . . . Nothing like it even at Berkeley; Anders gets pretty much what he wants." At last he moved. "No, don't trouble, always find my way, old Army habit. Sorry if I've delayed – and . . . well . . . carry on, eh?"

Then, at last, they let themselves look at one another. No, they were not out of their minds. But how extraordinary that they weren't.

"But –" Linhouse faltered. For there must be some connection. Anders? He tested it. "Anders!"

Sir Harry caught his meaning at once, as neatly as any sibling. But shook his head. "No, no. Oh no, my dear fellow. Not him. At least – not *Rachel* . . . That is to say – nothing against your young woman." He flushed – the clean neo-Socialist pink of those who still find the need to apply standards to people. "What I mean to say – ah what a tangle! – not where anyone could think it was you." He said it with a bow.

Pure Pinero, thought Linhouse. Those flannel pants. Somehow, balk as we may at the ordinary fantastic of our century, there are always these honest little diversions into real unbelievability, to keep us going. Those pants. Father had some just like. And if I'm to last, I ought to have had more to eat than that bun. And I ought to take a leak.

"Sorry not to have been more of a connection!" he said, with a gulp. "But there must be one, you know. Really now. Unless it's your experience that women just take off like this regularly!"

In immediate horror, he recalled that this had been Sir Harry's experience – twice. It was unconscious malice on his own part, at having been kept from that leak. As always after these slips, he yearned to say to his opposite: For the sake of humanity, let us love one another – I love you. And how I hate Freud.

But Sir Harry seemed not to have heard. For one thing, the Muzak had begun again, as if insisting that it was now a quarter past three. Also, with the ease of six-feet-four over five-feet-nine, he was looking straight past Linhouse. He had seen the object.

Linhouse waited for the old man to speak — "*Hul*-lo!" perhaps, then — "Hul-*lo!*" But the old man said nothing.

Linhouse waited to be asked what it was, so that he might reassure himself with his own answer: "It's the record of a journey — you saw her letter." Then, with a shrug, "I'm to let it play, for the crowd." Or perhaps, owing to their linked circumstance, he need merely give a flick to the letter, remaining dumb. And Sir Harry, mum-dumb also — so related were the co-deserted! — might pass over it with merely a nod.

In which case, what would *he* himself feel then? He had that terrible premonitory sense of being on the edge of identifying in himself a feeling he would be unable to bear — that sense of half of him plodding away from himself with steps nightmare slow and these fated only to find themselves returning, indrawn again to the monster at his own center — the cephalopod that floated on its own arms and wasn't going anywhere. He waited for his good kind friend, the astronomer — *scientia, scientia* — to recognize it — the object? the feeling? — and tell him what it was, in a voice not too far from the one in which nursemaids dealt with natural miracles: "Thunder is the clouds knockin' together. Days is longer in summer, because. Coo, love, hands away from the fire. It burns."

But the old man, head lifted, did none of these things. He did what all the others out there hadn't done. Stood rapt.

Finally, his hand fell on Linhouse's shoulder, and gripped there.

By its transference, Linhouse recognized his own feeling. He didn't want to know — what he wanted to know about her. Or to get to know, by any extension of hers, her Elsewhere. On the small unknowns larger ones always rested, eagles taking off from the linnet's wing. If there was a Great Pyramid shape to knowledge, then it must balance on point, upside down.

His shoulder was free. He heard steps tiptoeing away behind him. On a sigh of readiness from the audience, he walked center stage.

Here, he was as brief as she'd asked him to be, outlining what was known of her disappearance, topped by some remarks in stock encomium style, most of them in the program already. This was in order. There wasn't a wet eye in the house — never was, at these things — but no one snickered. And when forewarned of the probable length of the "reading," nobody got up to leave.

In conclusion, he gave them their part of her letter, an equally stock *ave atque vale* effusion of the sort which only the dead and the living dare exchange. Doing so, he saw how cleverly she'd managed to sink, in all this redundancy, almost no fact. Any auditor must take as official what was all so bloody conventional; even the provost must be relievedly thinking that, as so often happens at universities, everything had already been authenticated — somewhere else. For, cleverest of all, she'd managed, without precisely saying so, to attach the object to Jamison himself. It now had the beautiful, secret authenticity of the one trove which that generous man hadn't been able to relinquish, its origin as open to their surmise as that of a bottle picked up at sea — or from the ziggurat of Babylon, or the pithoi of Knossos — by a hand much more securely dead than hers, and one in life a member of the National Academy.

And now, as per instruction, a stenographer, previously alerted, tripped up to the platform on signal and seated herself with pad and pencil in a chair set at a discreet distance. *Tape won't do,* the letter had said. *Nothing electrical. And make it a girl.* One of the younger departmental staff, the secretary had a head as pretty as a painted bead. Inclined forward within that wimple of her trade, the round collar, it lent the object a final halo, as in those charades the onlookers were already so well trained to — she might have been leaning toward a dreadnought, or a tube of shaving cream. Her expression was just right for either. There was just enough room between her and it for Linhouse to get by.

And so at last he bent down to it, his hams up in that unfortunate position which says to the world, Dromio to master, "I invite your foot." Was that a snicker? Arms encircling the bell-glass, he lifted. Its weight this time surprised him newly, as much as he could handle, no more than that — no less. As he placed it well back in the wings, relief flooded him. *I know how you feel about machines — that intense way you drive,* she'd written. *No need to be afraid here.* As usual, she'd misunderstood him. Like many a bumbler with mechanism, it wasn't the machine he feared, but his own veneration of them.

He reseated himself, dragging his own chair very modestly nearer. Last night, this morning, all nerves he supposed — but he'd managed. Or *it* had. For as he sat back, another twinge came from the half of the letter in his hip pocket. *Relax. It will cooperate.*

Shed of its covering, the object itself looked less formidable; perhaps refraction had enlarged it. Had it ever been quite as tall as it had seemed? Though still svelte, it had lost some of its shagginess, even of its beingness, enough for him to conceive of it as after all merely some new model, either still in the design stage or elegantly foreign, of any one of the sound-squeezers, life-compressors, which a modern yawner must keep in his living room. He was surprised to find again how extraordinarily this circumstance always depressed him: that, of all the objects the necromancers kept offering him for the tickle, the cure, or the kill, none had ever really transcended his own senses — that first strict magic of himself as he was; none had been able to be that different.

He waited, watching this object so much the locus of itself — yes, it still had that quality. Was it moving, had it already an imperceptible quickening? Across from him, that audient face of knowns and unknowns waited also — always, no doubt even in the anchorite's questing cell, that sunflower of brothers. He saw how the tableau must look to them — like a nineteenth-century soiree-séance on animal magnetism perhaps — allowing for the maestro's stubble and little Trilby's pert knees? Or a demonstration of what everybody had come here to laugh at — the new talking machine, the new wireless, the new . . . — in which nobody sensible quite believed.

Above Linhouse, the Muzak plainted and fell away altogether, a drawer shutting on cheap knives. In the quiet, he heard from that antechoir implanted in him at the beginning, the thin oboe and countertenor of his own hope. Oh believe, believe in the polar of the unknown; it will ennoble us. Well, he would listen, he was always listening really, either in that achingly sexual undertow in which one listened to one's own undercurrents half one's life, or with that intellectual cupping-of-the-ear which had been the persistent other half of his. It was impossible of course that the two currents be facets of the same.

There was a stir in the loge. Sir Harry entered, drawing the attention of all, and walked slowly through, down to the vacant front row where he seated himself, dead center, with the same stiff articulation. Apparently, he'd had no trouble getting in; he was undisheveled. But he was unmistakably in that high state which is hard to decipher — joy at journey's end, or the elevation of sorrow? He had lost one thing perhaps, and come within sight of another.

Less than a few feet apart, Linhouse, staring at him, dared not look away. If the object was opening, it was expanding as slowly as a flower; if it spun, the Tibetan whirl of its atoms was so wild that it seemed still. He didn't need to look; he was seeing it, refracted through the eyes of a man who believed.

The world is still forest, he thought. What is coming? I smell difference. I am afraid.

Sir Harry's eyes answered him, as if the old man's hand were again on the younger man's shoulder, pressing it as once Linhouse's own had held that old wrist. They gave him back his own message. Space is personal. Let us be afraid together. We must fly this air.

Out of the corner of his own eye. Yes. It had moved.

4. Send Jack

THE top "page" or "cross section" – that lily-pad circlet, was now at a rakish angle to the rest of the great cylinder, sitting atop it like a fatigue cap or a sailor's beret. Yes, it had opened, and already was speaking or trying to, and the familiar sound which was emerging, though not yet coherent, was utterly consoling. It was the cyclic whirr of static, that mewl and screech which, from the days of the first stylus on wax, has reassured the anxious that somewhere at the helm are not spiritual hands but practical ones, under whose reasonable dialing only an encompassable nonsense will shortly emerge. God himself would be easier believed, thought Linhouse, if he would only learn to clear his throat perhaps, in some such preliminary voice.

Meanwhile, breath bated, his blind hope waited for quite another voice. Algiers, Dar es Salaam. She'd once spoken of going there. Tbilisi, the Kara-Kum Desert, El-Gumruk. Gheit el Inab, to Zoo, Nouzha and Antoniadis Gardens. The cackle and glurr of the static began to seem to him a language, not cognate, barely Middle Eastern. And over and above it, through it, didn't he hear, or hallucinate, a small Christian voice in that Islam, fresh and willful as the new teacher in some one-room schoolhouse of space? "Not *oy*. Not *ay*. *I!*" His tongue sought that arched palate. But then, in that Kubla

Khan of calling voices, did or didn't he hear another, a second pilot-one, harshly *lycée*, but speaking as if immeasurably farther than lunar and droning on to no one but the Om, the Omphalos. "*Une* et *une*. *Une* moins *une* . . ." and even more fading, barely streaked across the ear, an algebraic babble, ending: "*Axiome. Hypothèse.*" To that first voice, he thought he heard an answer. To that second, indomitable one — none. Fantasies, both of them. Then, opening his eyes, he saw, first row dead center, a pair of old eyes opposite, dreaming closed.

At that moment, the bedlam of catcalls on the recording rose to that decibel which sometimes preceded a breakthrough into sense — or silence — to headshakes and the snap of a dial, no use trying, must be a storm somewhere round. Then came a silence. Into which a voice suddenly said: "— I." Then, more strongly, followed by a pause: "I am —"

An accepting rustle of confidence went over the members of the audience — they knew their voices. Machines had special, overserious ones, drier and clearer than their own, and of a certain invigorating silliness — this was a good machine.

"Yes, *I!*" it suddenly said, very much louder. "Imagine." It was the firm, story-telling voice of the kiddie programs. There was another pause. A cuckoo-clock strangulation. Then it said with triumph, in that same ingenuous super-tone, pseudo-tone: "This is a book!"

The audience gave one dreadful blat-blurt of laughter, immediately stilled. Into that perfect acoustic of its own shock, one of them said, just too late for privacy, "Oh, God's balls." It was the laugh that was the more shocking, to hear any such genus of men as were here utter, like a society of rooks, their savage distaste for themselves. One sometimes heard that same cawing at the theater — at bitterly intelligent plays which never had good enough endings. It was the sound clowns made, or naturals, when the deformity they had been carrying about with them was at last properly recognized. No Jesus himself, Linhouse had a glimmer nevertheless of the martyr's wish to depower that ridicule by taking it upon himself. For, once a group of men could mock past a certain humor any of the better intentions by which they lived, then every man in it was cast adrift. From their hung-down faces, all here had already recalled who and where they were. If he got up – to what other point of order could *he* rise?

But, oh relief! The machine, with the most charming composure – as if it had heard but not minded – was going on, taking over the task of composing *them*, like the prize guest after a gaffe at a dinner party. What it did was simple. Once again it became clearly and grossly a machine. All its attributes were simple, insofar as he knew them, including an air of spontaneity which would have been unnerving if he hadn't surmised this to be subjectively in him. For, it began giving out that high-grade echolalia, once the property of mystics and vaudevillians, which now could be piped anywhere from bank to parish house – the noise that sounded like language or like music according to the needs of the listener, but so comfortingly never really was.

Under its smoothing cover, Linhouse could reflect that any machine was awesome until you knew the limits of its authority – a mechanical milker, until you recalled that it could get it but not give it; an airplane, until you saw it floundered in the sea. Even those computers about whose ability to run amuck the world was now so anxious must be the less impressive according to your own ability to conceive the limits of their variables, and if you could remember that they could run amuck only in terms of what they were. Just plunk down beside one any bit of what Linhouse still liked to think of as "instant protoplasm" – a hoptoad, say, or a baby — and unless the bloody contrivance had been devised to do everything these could (which of course was always possible), let it rattle all its Valhallas, chances were it still couldn't like them wet its pants, or hop away. He understood quite well that this was a philistine notion to harbor in the company of all these savants, but he suspected that it was by just such notions that, in their company, he might after all survive.

Glancing up, he saw by the secretary's artificially stretched dimple that all hands were calmed to boredom again. He himself would feel safer once he knew the limits of this thing's spontaneity, which to him gave it almost the aura of personality, a mild one, rather like that of a gentle, scholarly visitor, or tourist with ethnological interests perhaps, ready to bumble out among the conventions of a place that was new.

Just then, the object riffled itself tall, again in a motion so quick that one scarcely saw it, except for its breeze received in the blond tendrils of the head of the nearby girl bent over her pencil and pad. Was the thing "tall" or "short," "great" or "small" — until one knew its function, how could one tell? Again he wished he knew what it was "set" for. Had he the right to assume, for instance, that it was not a secretary-eating machine? Just then, this time in reassuringly single voice, it spoke.

"Every journal," it said, "has a secret desire to be found." A pause allowed each spine in the audience to squirm pleasedly under the warm suggestion that it alone was to be the finder. "This one is dedicated . . . to the Jamison who found it." The voice, though nasally purer now, was not yet sexually identifiable, or rather, elegantly asexual, perhaps that of an Elizabethan actor who in his earlier days had played Rosalind, or, in these times, that of a cultivated Lesbian not quite recovered from a bad cough. "And — *in memoriam*" — the falter in it was indeed a winning one—"in memory of those sessions in the little back room . . . where it learned . . . yes, where it learned what it is, to be a man." In the pause, the secretary's pencil flew, then blond head and the pencil were raised again, competently waiting, so that the next words, also faltering, seemed apologetically addressed to her. "What it is, to be woman and man."

Linhouse got up, overturning his chair. Hoax, hoax, a bitch and a hoax, his pulses said to him, their final wavelength arriving in a red clutter in his brain. The result was that he simply had to go. As he righted the chair, and left the stage, the recorded journal was embarked on a list of what it termed "credits and acknowledgments."

When he returned—a toilet bowl being sometimes better for self-lecture than the pool of Narcissus—the listing was still going on, and had even attained a comforting academic drone, easing reminder of how many eccentricities the mother church, Universitas, must forever pay host to, as well as of the fact that, among her many mansions, there were dozens of little back rooms which had nothing to do with him. He stood in the wings.

"—to Professor Schlovsky, of the Sternberg Astronomical Institute, Moscow.

"—from the *Third Cambridge Catalogue of Radio Sources.*

"—the two-hundred-and-ten-foot dish antenna at Parkes, Australia.

"—reconsiderations of the Heisenberg uncertainty principle.

"—studies on the C-field compatible with a steady-state universe."

Again he felt like a man facing a firing squad, all a blankness there, behind the guns. Were there such institutes, catalogs, universes? Or was this eccentricity? Whatever, surely it was not *Janice* Jamison?

He crept forward, Audience normal. Rows of tipped, soup-plate faces, twelve-inch dish antennae, astigmatic white. Sitting down again, he surreptitiously munched at a bar of chocolate found in a pocket while in the washroom. If all this still seemed kosher to that crowd, as long as it made sense to their sense, or to somebody's, it was all right with him. This was a compromise he'd come to early on, for a fact in his senior year, when he had bumped into the quantum theory in an old book of Russell's and had decided: Call a halt; this is as far in these matters as a word man can go. Take him all and all, on an average and for a' that, for that ordinary creature of blood and vesicles this had still been *very far*. From that time on, he'd decided to accept the benefits of all this magic (the burdens had not yet bubbled up) — just let somebody else watch the pot.

And since then, he thought, he'd come even farther on, about as far as some old peasant woman from New York's Italian quarter, who had never heard the word "biopsy," but would let her breast be lopped off at a sign from some invisible in lab white, who said what he saw. In the same way, if somebody pushed a button now, and the news was brought to Linhouse by certain magnetisms he had always trusted without understanding them, he would, like any Aztec to the sacrifice, in five minutes prepare to die. Meanwhile, classicist though he was, he wouldn't even admit to fearing the gift-bearing Greeks. He'd use all the jack-in-the-boxes they brought him, trot down all their movable carpets, breathe their peculiarly tonic air as fast as they mixed his formula — like a little king who, by jumping in and out of all the π-diamonded crowns which were brought him, kept himself from knowing that he had been deposed. Okay, let them keep the magic going if they wanted — just let them *keep* it magic — to him. Only when the world of mathematical science came and stood in his middle distance did he get nervous — and resentful that he could spit back at it words only. It wanted him to understand it. It wanted to cozy up to him and be ordinary together, did it? *He* was ordinary, dammit. By God, this was *his* equation. And it was all he had.

"— of Mount Wilson-Palomar Observatories.

"— of the Institute for Advanced Study at Princeton.

"— of the Southwest Institute for Advanced Study.

"— of the University of California at La Jolla.

"— for changed concepts on Hubble's Law; on the Schwarzchild Radius."

And here and a hubble-bubble it came, creeping toward him on the legstalks of what he did know to be real, of places he had been; he had even looked into that two-hundred-inch telescope — he had been, alas, on Palomar. Actually, what worried him was that at best, half-knowledge was all that was expected of him — and that the half was expected only from his side. *Nox est una perpetua dormienda,* he had murmured into the telescope, coming out ever so coyly, timidly, toward the middle distance common to them both. Though his astronomer-guide hadn't happened to know Catullus — *or* Latin, not that this worried *him* — he had asked politely enough for translation, and hadn't been at all surprised to hear that night, our night, is (shall be?) a perpetual sleeping — merely that anybody should bother to say it, and that, once said, the sentiment had been lasting. Snobs, both of us, Linhouse thought, munching the last of his chocolate. Chap would never know that the eternal dark of the distances in that big lens of his had already been projected, past-present-future, by the miraculous placement of a three-letter third-person singular common form of the commonest verb. *Est.* And I will never see into his lens. And yet, for all the panjandrums in the press, I'm yet to be persuaded that this is wholly a pity.

"— Soviet Astronomical Circular. Schlovsky on Schmidt on Wheeler-Oppenheimer, on General Theory: $E = MC^2$."

And here it was. For here was something he did know, or at least in a half-baked way could identify, in somewhat the way his own father, who had known about as much poetry as you could put in a pipe, had used sometimes to sigh to him, " 'Drink not too deep of the Pierian spring,' Jack — that's Pope. Can't think of the rest of it." A little knowledge is a dangerous thing. Even parlor "relativity" these days, to a man who knew no calculus. It took him a shaken minute to recall exactly where he'd picked up this choice bit of lore. Parlor. Hers.

On that day which — if he'd known it to be the last one — what could have been his loverly research? . . . Lovers are walked to the door with, in saltbox houses whose sitting room windows give directly upon the February dusk, at this time of year no thistledown blowing through them, but light, gloaming remarks float the room; time is mentioned, not Time but "time" only, and no glint of farewells, but suddenly she says it, bending down to a letter seen to have been slipped under the door, perhaps with the bell they had let ring unanswered earlier: "Jeepers!" — and how take seriously the elsewheres of a woman whose only oath was "Jeepers"? — "Jeepers, another letter from $E = MC^2$, it's about time she answered"; and he asks, laughing, perhaps blowing out a bit of thistledown he isn't aware of: "Secret agent?" and she replies, on a laughing breath back to him: "That was his private nickname for her — Jamie's first wife. We started a correspondence over the estate, and once in a while we still write." Jamie had kept his vow never to marry another beaky intellectual; after that, as Linhouse must recall, there had been the Maori girl who died — "and then, me." And he replies, "Nonsense!" puffing it into the ear he then kisses: "— that man never exactly built you *up*, did he!" and she shrug-smiles, with the look that can't help being jampot, and he almost takes her in the back room again — oh witness, that he was no better about her than Jamie — but she, head downcast, the blue airmail letter still in her fist, says no. And "What's the name mean — EC et cetera," he asks, in the random of a man so refused, and she identifies it, not that she knows what it *means* — as Jamie had, to her.

And this is how he is now able to identify — not that he knows what it means either — the most famous equation in Einstein's General Theory of Relativity.

On that note, as good as any other, he had left her. The next time they spoke, it was on that doorstep. But — no . . . But *no.* Just before he leaves, happening to glance at the familiar red-blue border of the same form his mother always writes on, he says, negligent of his own last words: "British, is she?" Last words, last words. And, indifferent to her own, she says them. Hers. "No, her husband is, they live there, sometimes. No. French."

And now intuition creeps up from behind, up and onto the shoulder blades of a man who personally has never even been able to stand the modern way of referring to it, the way they like to beg the question by saying a person "intuits"; it hops up, and there, leg around his neck, it *sits.* The women. The women, the women, the women — lost and/or disappeared, the women. Somewhere he had missed the connection and somewhere he has got it, the Trojan women, the Trojan — It is four o'clock of a darkish afternoon in Hobbs Hall, not Hades, and we have been gathered here, tympani, tympani, and the doors are closed — tympani-*tum.* And the voice on the stage is still going on, elegantly furnishing credits and summaries; is boredom the potion we're being given? *Mille basia, Lesbia,* oh, give me a thousand kisses and all that — or phrase it more simply — *hop!* Two thousand years of it since ever they can remember, and all very nice too — they accept the universe. And issuing from them meanwhile, all the little Galileos, sons husbands brothers fathers and uncles – all the only ones getting to look into the lens. *Est.* But what if a too sudden century or so unbinds not only the feet of the mothers, the girdles, but their pencils – their brains?

Oh, Catullus. Is this blue-airform informed, bluestocking voice, from wherever she now is, or was – Janice? Who wanted a physicist. Oh Catullus, is this Lesbia now?

"– and in conclusion," said the voice . . .

And what does she want of us?

"– If it shall appear that I have said anything worthy –"

Trust the women not to take over the world without a great deal of preliminary conversation.

"– do not attribute any such wisdoms to me, please –"

Or was that still a male idea – taking over? . . . *Say please, Johnnie dear.*

"– but credit my teacher."

Who was in all probability Jamison. And this archaic, Indo-European utterance, with its overlay of Philadelphia or perhaps a touch of Merton, was merely some Uncas he had picked up and educated, his final chef d'oeuvre, excavated from the customary Gold Bug spot on the usual archipelago between the two significant rocks.

Then why does intuition . . . *sit?*

"– and should we not credit all of them from our earliest days, those mistresses of the infinite detail –"

And what does the witch-bitch want of me, leg-necking me here?

He glared out at the hall, singling out, along the rows, various harmless wives, lab assistants, amanuenses, Lila, Miss Apple Pie. When one wanted to get the mind off Woman, it was often useful to take a look at women. Those down there were as solidly glazed forward toward the talking book as if it were a Four-Speed Wash-Dri one of them was shortly to be winning; these were not the wailing Trojan elite he had in mind.

"— to all those unknown but constant signalers, devotees of knowledge, here and elsewhere —"

He summoned his acquired knowledge of women: Anna Karenina, Madame Bovary, Tess, Lysistrata, Madame de Maupin, Fanny Hill, Moll Flanders — Fool! — all created by men. His mother, then: who had done as she chose, and let his father interpret her from the other side of the water. Other recalcitrant, but finally passive ladies. Old Margaret-I-accept-the-universe-Fuller, put down with a "Gad, she better!", the final male answer, by old Carlyle, rumored impotent, but a man. Acceptance implies a choice however — what had been lurking, still lurked, in the tundra-dark of all the Margarets? He summoned all his own knowledge of the stubborner ones, his former wife, his last lover: what do the women do, these days, when they want, when they don't want — ? At the base of his spine, something plucked a guitar string and then was silent. They leave.

"— your language. I shall never have full control of it, of complications which, forgive me, I once regarded as unnecessary. But now it seems to me that if here long enough, one may grow the tongue for it —"

Yes, only some Ishi, hairy Ainu, last aborigine whom somebody has taught to prate square root; the complications are mine. Nothing that jukebox can say will ever approach the complex humanism of an empty stomach.

"— other apology. I had thought to find you — And instead, I find you —" A choke. A pause. "Now consider me that savage — the civilize' being who think himself to be among savages."

And Linhouse stood up again, ready to — shout? Smash? Run? Who could say. But he had the connection. "*Yes,*" said a voice in Holland Park. *We are veree civilize'.*"

"— with thanks to this Center for providing opportunity. And for the marvelous facilities of Professor Van Wert Anders, without — as they say — whom — And now, as you like to say here, I will cut the cackle." The top leaf of the book, all this time infinitesimally moving in an arc leftward, gave a last tweedle and lay over, giving way to the next one, which infinitesimally rose in its turn. "Herewith, my journal. Herewith . . . oh I am so proud . . . *I.*"

In the loge, a voice said something inaudible; then Anders's head wobbled up on its long stalk. "Cut the . . . cut the . . . !" it said scratchily. "Cackle indeed!" It was a voice common enough to the professions here, a growing boy's voice, testy as an old man's. Ordinarily its timbre, that of a good square heel steadily treading eggshells, would have gone unnoticed. Now all heads in the auditorium turned to it, perhaps not for the reason its owner thought. "Nothing to do with this," he said, ". . . miles out of my field . . . primitive peoples . . . not my beckyar-r-d." From behind him there was somewhere a girl's giggle, quickly quenched. It was true though: except for the har-r-d uptstate "r's," his voice was exactly — like the box.

"Anders —" Naughton the provost's thick white shock of hair was trimmed to fall forward like that of certain bluff American business types, over a big face of healthy indoor red. And like them, he was very used to dealing with a republic of children, on whom the power, the money, the credit might nevertheless so often depend. "A while back, didn't Security report some funny stuff down at your lab?"

"Oh, I'd forgotten that, sir. Why yes, looked as if somebody'd tried to run the works, and my notes were disturbed. No damage though. And I've no such apparatus as — as *that.*"

Another giggle, locus indiscernible. For some reason, he didn't know why, Linhouse turned to look sharply at the secretary-doll, if only because this was what she looked like, a ventriloquist's vis-à-vis, this one warm and breathing, but with the same little tucked-in, stationary smile which could be talked up into half a dozen different comic imbroglios. In any caste society, women notoriously were the first to step over the stile. But this little cipher, in her starched wimple, didn't look the kind to; she certainly didn't fit his image of those women who might after all exist only in his head – the elite. As he heard his own name pronounced, a little ear of caution unfolded, within it a gray, grayling echo. Neither had Janice.

"Yes, sir?" he said.

"I'm afraid perhaps this goes beyond the bounds, normal bounds of a memorial service." Naughton looked about him, for seconding. Not a head turned. "Wouldn't you say?"

"Yes, sir." I'll take ten lashes, sir. Norms are norms.

"Could you perhaps enlighten us, beyond that letter you read us –"

"As to what, sir?"

"As to what that gizmo – as to, ah, er – where it came from."

" 'Fraid I can't, sir." It was never so hard to appear ingenuous as when one was. Try American. He turned up his palms. "Search me." And then found himself patting pockets with real concern – had he dropped her letter at the loo? He found it. "All I have is the rest of the directions. They call for –" He checked it. "One interval, halfway through, where the large television screen is to be switched on."

"These unsolicited – bequests." The provost sighed. That he could clap his hands together now with prebendary firmness was one of the reasons he had his job. "Well, then – *De mortuis,* of course. But I think I should say, without any disrespect, that our time has been sufficiently preempted, wouldn't you say, eh. Let us disband."

Someone spoke, from next to Anders. "But what if — what if it's meant to tell us what happened to her? What if she's still somewhere, and there's a message?"

This voice, almost a wail, was Lila's. Linhouse stood absently, paper in his hand. Lila's as he had always known it, silly-motherly, borne along on the ever-ready gush of her "views." And there she was; he could see her. But it was also quite definitely the voice — if one felined it a bit, rubbed its fur the wrong way, for a few sexual sparks — of the woman he had overheard this morning in the coffee shop. And Meyer, her husband, had a sociologist's organ tone, real ruby-throated Wurlitzer. "*Honey, honey,*" she had said. But the man with her hadn't been Meyer.

There was an interested murmur of assent, dissent.

"Well, then — let's say that those who wish to leave are at liberty to — Or perhaps Mr. Linhouse would prefer a show of hands. All who feel that we ought to hear this out —"

All the women. Several of the men had not voted, but now two or three were getting up to leave, when Anders, still standing, spoke up again. "Naughton —"

"Yes, Tippy? Oh, if you've recalled some reason your name might have been injected here, or on that lab incident, perhaps you'd better come priv —"

"As to that lab thing — at the time, I had an idea that it coincided with certain arrivals here — but never mind that —"

As Anders stopped short, Sir Harry opened his eyes as if from an alert sleep, and very quietly, quite without show or reference to anybody speaking, got up, walked down the aisle past the few rows intervening between him and the stage, his profile toward the object, his body negligently toward them all.

Anders's great white booby head, flushed pale yellow by

a light in the ceiling just above him, moved totally, as it always did, to observe him; none of his features ever seemed to make use of themselves separately; perhaps this helped give power to the brain. "It's not my beckyar-r-d. But just where are the controls – on that hurdy-gurdy?"

"What do you mean, Anders?" The provost. "You don't think –"

"Don't think." The head moved left, right, slowly. One wouldn't have been surprised to see its fontanelle winking. "Notice."

"Ah, *yes*, Tippy, I get you. Stop me if I'm wrong." As always, Meyer's richly psychological voice sounded as if it were demonstrating – or ratifying, from a constant pool of agreement – the omnipresence of social goodwill. "It's ve-ry responsive, isn't it. It waits."

"For wha-at?" But Lila's faintly gushed scream, now that Linhouse had heard that coffee shop change, seemed to him a pretended one – even if she herself didn't know it. It encouraged him to step forward on the rostrum.

"Perhaps the literal directions given me might be of use," he said. "I don't know a rap about electronics of course, or even if that's how – or even where this thing – but it's occurred to me that it must work at least partly on temperature. This hall – perhaps I neglected to say that this hall was specified. As you know, it's very delicately thermostated, among other things. And the room where I was asked to, er . . . pick up this thing, happens to be an air-conditioned one, very specially done for a private house. It's the room where Jamison kept his artifacts." Sad shards of a primal afternoon, afternoons. And a long couch, that still soars.

"Let me read you the directions," he said. He read them. *Keep it company . . . Once the mechanism is moved, it must be allowed to regain equilibrium overnight, or for at least five hours, at a temperature of 71°. An hour beforehand, raise the temperature in the hall to 74.6°. Please be exact about that. Afterwards, you have only to* — et cetera. He even read to them with excerpts here — the part that specified a live secretary. *Tape won't do. Nothing electrical.* "And it just occurred to me, I know I'm sticking my neck out, among all of you — but that it just might be keyed to — body temperature." Fool that he was, he even glanced inadvertently at the secretary.

And in the very moment of performing his function, knew almost for certain, with the surest misery he'd had yet — what his function might be. To keep it light. Keep it light. Keep it light, and Jack's the one to do it. For in the surf of snickers which were at once politely stifled, the hall's acoustic, equally delicate, brought up to him a "*Warm* bodies?' and a "The *back* room?"

She'd required a physicist, and maybe she'd got one, but for this end of it, a classicist was doing fine. Keep it light, that's the way she would do it, the way they all would, with God knows what embroidery on the side. Keep it a frivol. Send Jack.

From the pit, no problem to a man of his height, Sir Harry stretched out an arm, not to anyone's rescue, though Linhouse at first thought so. In the stage light, his long fingers, parched but strong, and heavily graced with a marriage ring, tested the aura of the — hurdy-gurdy — but did not touch its tawed leatherskin, or lift its sections. What a specimen he was, with his guardsman's length of limb topped by that craggy Epstein head — a man to the *nth* of his powers and his age. He lowered toward the assembly, clearly seeking out Anders, and finding him — by Anders's heavy, crystal "noticers." "Yes," he said. "Ye-es, it's —" He stretched his jaw, as if for a joke. "Set for — people."

"— kah!" With this gasp of disgust, Anders sat down.

The assembly sat heavy with embarrassment, remembering

both who these two were, what heraldic listings followed their separate names in all the peerages of science — and perhaps who they themselves were. Looking out on the spelled hall, on faces sucked by its fluorescence, Linhouse, though he knew most of them, found them hard to distinguish one by one in any live, idiosyncratic character; they seemed momentarily more and more like rows of dummy claque, a house of cardboard personages ready to be skittered by some wind.

The gizmo suddenly gave a whirr, a small, comforting, anciently mechanical one — exactly the pre-chime snuffling made by the clock Linhouse's mother perversely kept at odds with the Chelsea statuary and *japonerie* in her drawing room — a cheap Hartford pendulum, farmhouse mantel clock, from home. What it said next was said so softly that only Sir Harry, head cocked both to it and the hall, like the impresario of a trained-animal act, might hear. He blinked, but said nothing.

"What did it say?" Linhouse whispered.

"A dedication."

He was determined to count for *something*, here. "What?"

"You already know it. The simple formula for Ἔλλειψις — the infinite ellipse, or elliptois."

Linhouse shook his head. They were all like that, these men, even this one who still seemed — and took care to proclaim himself? — a nineteenth-century one. They were no longer expected to know Greek beyond a tag or two that might have slipped into their concerns sideways. But when it came to *their* formulae, they expected *him* — Ah. He suddenly did what he could do — put two and two together.

Behind them both, the machine now spoke softly but distinctly. "$-ay^M + n = bx^M(a - x^N)$." As far as Linhouse, with his mathematical lacks, could tell, it spoke excellent — French.

And now, on the crest of the great book, a second disc lay back, a new one arose. "Journal from Ellipsia," it said, in English again. "*On!*"

The lights dimmed, theatrically. Old ruses, old stratagems, returned to him, from Xenophon? Farther, much farther. Who would know that he had not dimmed the lights? What separate authorities could not be gathered here?

Beside him now, Sir Harry called clearly into that lulling pink-dark. "What say, Anders?" The call stretched as if across an abyss. "What sa-ay? Are they going to be exactly like us?"

As Linhouse's eyes accustomed themselves, the old man's face emerged again beside him. It was, he thought, a finished face, in the triumphant sense of the word. Death could merely abstract from it, and nothing be added, not even a tear.

"Yes," it said, to itself now. "On."

Part II

1. Say *Au Revoir*

ON, ON, on and on, *on;* and on, and on, on. The paradox about distance is that quite as much philosophy adheres to a short piece of it as to a long. A being capable of setting theoretical limits to its universe has already been caught in the act of extending it. The merest cherub in the streets here, provided he has a thumbnail – and he usually has ten – does this every day. He may grow up to be one of their fuzzicists, able to conceive that space is curved, but essentially – that is, *elliptically* – he does nothing about it. He lives on, in his rare, rectilinear world of north-south gardens, east-west religions, up-and-down monuments and explosions, plus a blindly variable sort of shifting about which he claims to have perfected through his centuries, thinks very highly of, and, is rather pretty in its way and even its name: *free wall* – a kind of generalized travel-bureaudom of "across." It follows that most of his troubles are those of a partially yet imperfectly curved being who is still trying to keep to the straight-and-narrow – and most of his fantasies also. His highest aspiration is, quite naturally, "to get a-Round"; his newest, to get Out.

And he will too, though in his current researches he may have reached only so far as the Omega particle. In the phenomenology of all peoples, the mind slowly becomes curved.

At least that is what Ours are matriculated to, and I had seen nothing to contradict this, during my all-to-brief sojourn in Bucks. Ah, what a mentor was there, was mine, though except for once, I never saw — as she taught me to say — Her!

As I taxied once again along the upper solitudes, trying not to arrive instantaneously at destination — which is of course Our main problem here — I thought of Her with considerable leaning. Leaning is to Us what yearning is to You — but that story will emerge later. The hardest thing to learn here — and still not mastered — is how to get about pornographically.

Meanwhile — and what a concept that is to a being accustomed to Ever — like standing *à point* as the meteors of thought surge by! This place is simply teeming with time. Excuse me. It is scarcely my fault if everything you do here is so attractive. *Meanwhile,* I was having my own practical problems, as I elided in and out, intent on not overshooting the mountains of the Ramapo. Omega particles indeed, to say nothing of such heavinesses as the baryons, neutrons and protons into which they here have finally divided that grossity of theirs, the atom. Let them try iris-ing in, as I had done the first trip, from slightly more than thirteen billion light-years away, while receding therefore at more than the speed of light and hence invisible, on radio-telephonic sources purporting to emanate from a nubbin of matter still acting flatly against its own spherical. On the darker side of which, for this my second trip, moonwise at their eleven o'clock (what a statement!), amid a smear of foothills, these directional signals would just probably be sending again, if She was able to arrange it, from apparatus just like that in Bucks — in an environ likewise named monosyllabically. (They yearn for our One-ness constantly. They are indeed a touching people.) *Hobbs.*

At the point where I reentered their ionosphere, the dear curves of Our being — which they term "body," and I must not forget to call "my" — nearly reversed themselves, but thanks to the extreme elasticity of our mental curvature, these held. Shortly after, I entered that condition, common enough among us, which however sounds so regrettably silly in their language — and is indeed almost impossible to gauge in one where the *amount* of things so consistently takes precedence over their *unanimity*. There's no help for it. I became more Here than There. From then on it was easier; they tell me that things done for the second time here usually are. A "second time" is one facet of their concept of two-ness that I had no trouble with, a kindly sign that the curves of our not quite cognate worlds do somewhere intersect. As I crossed, the far, reddish spectrum of Out There faded, gradually receded, whelmed by the increasing blue ozone of Right Here. From twenty thousand up, the daily height of their own traffic, once again their planet looked as extraordinary as any planet of a universe must look to the resident of another, up that close. Yes, I had done this before, experiencing no difficulty with their numerical progressions, and almost none with their time-sequences. It is only the two-ness of people that still gives me unutterable pause. In Bucks, I was told that monotheists here suffer almost the same tension over the many-goddedness which with us is so restful, all Our people being One.

I was told this by Marie, the mentor I found the less interesting, certainly not dear. Under less compelling circumstances, I should almost have dis-esteemed her, which with us is almost the end of negative emotion, opposite to the "leaning" which is all but forbidden, and at about the same distance from the norm, which is "to alike." But here, it was their very difference — that word, that word — which excited me:

two of them, two She's, and already so unalike. And as I was soon to know, this was nothing to another difference still to come. Which difference, they assure me, is to blame for all the others. Be that as it may, as I came in closer, almost to cloud, sure enough, I smelled it for the second time. Miles out to star, you can smell it, the sharp tang of the variability here.

I hope I am allotting the sense data correctly, that is, each to its proper organ. One of the purposes of the preliminary teaching session at Bucks was to instruct me in the art of doing this. To visit here, to sightsee as it were, would be impossible under any continuous fusion of the senses such as we have; luckily we do have, unified but not inextricably, all your five. Sight and hearing are with us of an acuity and extension which to you would be! – and smell also. How indicate this, the way we function, to the uncurved! Suffice to say that, by means of an unbroken concatenation, we hear space, see time, and smell thought, the whole process being a warning one, directed not outward toward enjoyment, but inward against *change* – any tendency toward this being immediately corrected centerwards. As for the sense of taste, due to the nature of our sustenance (do I not do your technical language rather well?) this is necessarily de-emphasized. But as we airfeed, which is as close as I can get to what we *do* do, we are often suffused with a generalized but delicate carbonation. There remains – the sense of touch.

And here, since both Ours and the beings here are creatures of flesh, not only of the same plasms but almost of the same cellular structure, the natures of both do, in one respect, very affectingly resemble one another. Our flesh, within its integument, is said to be of the tenuosity of veils, capable of supporting the insupportable; an ichor – to your pork. But let there be humility on both sides. Because of Our lack of protuberance without, and Our imponderability within – in fact because of that very serenity of curve which suits us to distances of a continuum which to your asymmetry would not be habitable—we are under repulsion to surround Ourselves, each of Us, at least for domestic purposes, with an electrical field which bars us from any intimacy with objects, and—in theory—between Ourselves. Whereas you, by reason of the extraordinary conglomeration of extruded shapes, organs, compounds and ligatures, and above all weights common to every one of you—are deliriously bashable! According to my mentor, by almost anything or anyone, anywhere.

And is it not then remarkable, that under such separate states of affairs, across all the galaxies of consciousness, You and We should both suffer from an almost identical . . . spiritual shame? In the final sense, then, do we not beautifully, *elliptically*—touch?

Which is what so excited both me and my dear mentor, and from the moment of my arrival in Bucks was the constant roundelay of all our conversation, this, because of the still fragile state of my sensibility, conducted entirely by intercom. (Until that fairly frightening adieu.)

"Whereas—" said She, in the language agreed upon for Monday, Tuesday and Friday. Wednesdays and Saturdays she taught me to converse in her native one—too volatile by far. As beings of negative gravity or mass-gravity relation, we understandably ground better in the heavier languages. Sunday, her day off, she practiced her own Elsewhere. So it was, by such routines, they taught me a number of things at once—from Days of the Week to all the primary facts of Differential Experience: National, Linguistic *and Individual*—just as you teach your young to color-count-read. I was even learning to daydream qualitatively, in tints and adjectives, and even with what I fancied might be heroines, though as yet I had never seen one. Sunday is white, gloomy, rich, British, and Protestant. Sunday is Marie.

"Whereas—" said my dear mentor. Though as yet I had not seen any of them of either kind, I imagined Her. Longitudinally oval, like myself—and pinkish too. But. But with a spot of difference somewhere. Where should it be—where? This was as far as I could go. I could never decide.

"Whereas—" She said, "the Ones in Ellipsia can only *lean* together, in sad-sweet contemplation of their Sameness—"

Ah, their She's, what teachers they are! Tongueless as I am, I found a vibration to answer her. "Where-ere-as!"

"And we," She said. It was still strange to hear her say "we" in the sense of a two-ness or more-than-one, in contrast to the elliptic We—our only equivalent to her "I." In the very first lessons, when we could communicate in little more than signals, she had told me that I would graduate into comprehension here only when I fully understood the pronouns. As, in all their magnificent hierarchy, I now do.

"And we—" I answered. "No, no," I corrected myself—at the time, I could give the responses only by rote. "One begs pardon. And *You*—"

It *was* hard. At home of course, collectively we referred to ourselves as Ours, not too far afield from the practice here. But if One of us encounters One of us, the form of mutual address remains One. There is no transmogrification into "You-ness." The rule to remember for Us—She commented later that the very sound of it soothed the irritations of this world—is that One and One are One. We have Our plural, but singly we are the same. Never, never, does One and One make Two.

"Oh, la, la!" She said. "*One* begs pardon?" Over the intercom there came a mutter: *Comme c'est chic, ça,* perhaps not intended to be heard.

"We beg pardon," was my limp answer. Oh, it's all very laughable, once one has the language of any Elsewhere as completely as you will have noted yours is now mine; how I can skip flealy from uppercase to lower, in the pronoundest sense of any occasion. But memory still pains. Those first tingles of the singular!

"Come, come," said the intercom, but softly. She was ever kindly. *"N'ayez peur, mon vieux . . . mon fils . . . ma soeur . . . ?"* There was even a giggle. After all, there were certain perplexities on her side – what, after all, was my *gender?* And I could not help her. If we in Ellipsia have gender, or once had – there is a myth to the effect that we once had, and that it still may be recovered – it lies deep to-down the inconscious. I know that there is hope – that just as the crustaceans regenerate limbs lost to the sharks of time, so we – But I could not help her then. I did not know.

"Come now."

To say what was next expected of me took more than a moment, in which the very veils of my finer flesh rent themselves . . . or congealed? Then, our rote habits and disciplines being very useful here, as they knew, I was able to say it: "I."

This was the crux of it. Even now I sometimes lose the ego-ness that is needed to make that feeling – that moment when the One rouses from the everslump of curve – and stands up *straight.* When the One becomes: a one. Even now, I am prone to give the old, collective answer.

"I beg pardon," I said dutifully.

"Bon," She said. "So far, so good. But it would be even more perfect if you say, 'I beg *your* –' Eh?"

As I had soon learned, She is never quite satisfied – this is why they make good teachers. Though this may give them trouble when they visit us, much as they may think from here that they will want to move forevermore only in the Circles of Satisfaction. Once, when I had questioned her very seriously, She had answered: No, to be fair, not to be satisfied was a characteristic of *both* halves of Them. Though it would not have been polite to tell her so, I was glad to have some slight fears allayed. For consider: even at home I had after all been One not content with Our circle – and if that should by any chance be an indication of gender, then – No, I did not wish it, somehow. And somehow, I did not think – No. I couldn't be. Good God – Marie had taught me that phrase. Good God – suppose I should be a Marie!

"Oh, sorry!" I said now, absently. "That's what I should have said of course. 'I beg *your* –' But I'm afraid I rather lost the train of thought. Please remind I. What was I begging pardon *for*?"

I never knew where in that great glass house their side of the intercom was located, being more than content to keep to the room specially prepared in advance for me. This was more on my part than a natural contentedness of disposition. For, until I had undergone the full program, including – besides dispensing entirely with the electrical barrier we switched off only secretly at home – Weightfulness, Visibility, and above all how to reduce Instantaneity – it was dangerous for me not to; language was only the first stop. So I was quite reposed to be where I was, learning their seasonal changes, snow to sprout, as I could view them in the great woodpile that pressed against the glass, accustoming myself to this uneasily irregular countryside, after Our calmly monolisting Ovaloid – I had no idea how half-cognate you and we are, until I saw your Sea. But at the time, I couldn't get over how stock-still, relatively speaking, everything seemed to be here. In the one non-glass wall, there were shelves holding books of instruction in an electro-braille not unlike records we have preserved, plus some enormous blown-up photostats of the greater carnivores and herbivores, all this to serve until my inner gyrations reduced themselves to the needs of print. Now and then, animals and insects of the minor domestic sort were patrolled across the glass, in a reverse of zoo – or perhaps, in order to show me the causality here, they were let fly to dog me of themselves. For, after Two-ness, there comes the other great thing to learn about a variable world in a state of semi-decontrol — that they here cannot wholly distinguish between the tides of causality and accident. Even when dealing with objects, one has to distinguish between these two hallmarks very carefully, since matter here comes in such an onslaught of forms. So, as yet they have not learned how to so classify events here. That is why, at home, every effort is made to have Events take a circular continuity. For, neither have we.

At this moment, for instance, there was such absolute silence over the intercom that I even wondered whether, in the daily sessions where my pair of mentors, working together from the office, had me practice how to plod time-space as they do, slowly, courting every possible friction instead of avoiding it — whether, by intent or not, they hadn't drained so much instantaneity from me that they were already gone.

"Mentor!" I said. I had never had this feeling before; of course, most that they have here, I had never had. Loss? A kind of fleshly desolation. "Mentor!" I said again, and then, pleading, the word that she had now and then let me use on a Saturday. *"Mère!"*

Silence. It hurts — the vacuum's first, puckering awareness of what it is. I began to understand more of what it would mean for a One to try to become a "one," or even to live in that world. To grow all the feelings I would need, could I do it; could I bear it? All these to be coursing undictated, tiger after lamb, lamb after tiger, through the beautiful, flickering glades that the beings here must have inside them? — It had not yet been thrust upon me that, according to my needs, these pains would be thrust upon me. According to my needs.

Then the intercom vibrated, stuttering under the timbre

of the message it carried. The walls of the room, being non-conductive glass, held me fast, bordering my instantaneity, else what a vast, electrical spreading might not have occurred? As it was, Her words went right through me.

"*Chéri!*" She said. "*Chéri.*"

Yes, the words went through me, and dispersed themselves. And somewhere within, a little of their irradiation clung. Little by little, by such exercises, is weightfulness learned.

"*Chéri,* I suppose you know what you've done?"

"What?" I could not have phrased it, but I already knew. That too is a feeling!

"You've learned it. You've done it. You 'ave said it as we do, without thinking. The 'I.' "

Yes, I knew I had learned it, plus something else with it, as yet undefined. For this was the paradox between our worlds, that whereas in *my* world, where all the Ones of Ours undulate so steadily together, it might be thought that the energy so collected would allow us to learn many things at once, such is not the case. We are too quick for horizons. At home, we can learn only one thing at a time – that being, generation after generation, what we are. But with you, who can both move and stand still just slowly enough to be variable, nothing is ever learned without a little physic of something else clinging to it, perhaps to adjudicate, perhaps to beguile. Oh adaptability! Oh, impossible not to praise each of us, but you, who have been Two and now are "one," perhaps a little more. For it is my opinion that your complications exist to comfort you in your solitude.

"Yes, I know," I answered then, "but please, let's not think about it just yet. Let's go back to giving the responses shall we?"

But sadly, both of us knew that the lesson was over; that almost all of them were, between us. At home, in the curved stream which almost counterfeits Ever, any direction is amiable, but here, in this bigotedly back-and-forth place—*got it!* This was the extra bit of medicament. In this place, it's damnably hard, if not impossible, to go back.

Yet, sadly-angry, I tried. "And whereas," I said, in the catechism, "whereas the Ones in Ellipsia can only lean together in contemplation of their Sameness. And whereas the Twos here on Hearth have so outbeasted tranquillity in their couple-ations—"

Yes, I was already growing *unalike,* like them. Moreover, like them, willy-nilly, I tried. And sadly-angry too. *See it?* These bittersweet antitheses are the bases of all feeling.

"Remember what I told you," She said. "Repeat it, perhaps. Repetition is *still* your comfort."

I repeated it. That once I reach "I-ness," our dialogue is over. That I will shortly become visible, more and more so, this being the progress of all fleshly studies. At which point I must leave here, *sans*—"

"*Sans delai.*" How soft the intercom's voice was now.

"For I will now start a new dialogue. Or rather, a *second* one. Which will teach me how One and One make Two-ness."

"Bravo," She said.

"And that—" I hesitated, half hoping. "And that this dialogue is to be—with another person. Not with you."

"*Vraiment.*" Confusing her days—that is, her languages—was often with her a sign of emotion.

"Madame—" I thought it best to be formal. At home, with every spawning from the great crater of Matrix where lie the lava pools that continuously and perfectly, in direct relationship of gravity and material, bubble Us upward, thousands of Us, One and One, there are always a few of the newborn who arrive colder in temperature than the rest. Often, these are to be seen gathered around the crater, shivering. The rule was to ignore these orphans, and until now, I had. "Madame . . . would it not be possible to . . . stay . . . and have this dialogue with . . . with *you?*" I concentrated a minute. "*Avec . . . toi?*"

Her answer came crisply, in the other language. "I have my own development to consider. Have you forgotten my remarks on that?"

That our dialogue was not as One-sided as it had come to seem to me. That, according to our joint great idea, she had her own Elsewhere to consider.

"To tell the truth," I said humbly, "I had. It must come with I-ness."

I heard her laugh. Is it possible that only a small string-box inside them makes such a sound as that, and not a whole choir of the cells? So she says.

"But this new *one* will be of which kind?" I asked. Remember that as yet all the more recent knowledge I had of them was abstractly radio signal, though by an ever more intimate connection. From a galaxy at the farther red shift of the spectrum . . . to Here, was already so immense an accomplishment—or so microscopic, to use an antique word—that the measurements of what we have done must occupy both ends of the project for eons. For there too, our worlds a little resemble. Act first, then consider. There too, we are a little cognate.

"Will it be another She?" I said.

"All our members are She's." She had never before said this. "Sympathizers of the . . . other sort . . . may exist, but for safety's sake are not encouraged." And then she said what in Ours is supposed to be merely unthinkable, but here is almost certainly cruel. "Since you have no gender—what difference does it make to you?"

Yes, they are a little untrustworthy. Even She.

"Difference is what One is here to learn," I answered, not

so humbly, indeed feeling more I-ness than ever before. "It has even crossed the mind that One might acquire it."

And here I was definitely concealing. For We too, unanimous as we are, have Our myths, our legends, our hopes. And Our legend is that we are *not* of One neutral indivisibility. Mark you, this has nothing to do with individuals as governed — we aren't political. Our myth, our angelic myth that consoles us when we too, even in all our lovely Oblong, shrink a little, a little droop, from normal convexity, is that a One of us, therefore all Ones, have within them a heavenly bit of gender, of which, under the Oligarchy of One, we are not supposed to know. And which, perhaps, *may be vestigial.* Yes, you and we are cognate, cognate beings all. For as you dream of one day rising to be like Us, we dream of once having been like You.

Our hope being, of course, that — perhaps under the aegis of One of us — each may discover his own gender.

"Indeed, you are getting on." Her tone was almost Marie's. "Don't think we 'aven't thought of it. We can only 'ope and trust that if anything can be done, proximity will do it. Reared by She's, each of whom will do 'er best, there is a good chance that you might be one."

"Ah." Ah.

We both paused.

"You really think so," I ventured.

"Mmm." She seemed to be reflecting. "Well, it would be one way of preserving the balance 'ere."

Balance, mind you. We of course are in a state of perfect equilipsium. What they call balance here is only a sort of jiggling. "But I thought you didn't approve of Here. Then why maintain it?"

"We-ell —" Her tone was less Marie, but . . . I didn't know what it was. *That's* what it was. It was exactly a tone to induce such a feeling.

"Well," She went on. "After life as a She here, then in turn, you people may wish to return There."

"But then —" I almost cried it out. "But *then* —" Then where was all the even exchange which belonged to our idea? Our mutual idea. I was learning more about she-ness. No wonder they were the pioneers here. Their thinking is curved to begin with.

And further, on a rectilinear planet, or at least one organized to be so, wasn't Her thinking a bit —? I couldn't find a compound word to fit it, either in any of the languages I carried instant knowledge of as a One, or in either of the two I had slowed down enough to share with Her. And yet, as I brooded this, I felt the most peculiar . . . tenderosity. Was it even . . . a poke of gender? But *which!*

"You're right, Mentor," I said. "It's time for me to leave."

And then a thought struck me. Dreadful ones so easily do here. "Not — it isn't going to be Marie!"

She made that round sound again, though her next words were rather thin and stretched. "No, Marie's development 'as been very *rapide* of late, in fact better than me. No-o — not Marie." And then she made the cluck-tick which characteristically ended the lesson.

"Wait!" I said. "Not so fa —! *Pas si vite!*"

"Oh, la, *la!*" she said. " 'Ow quick you learn to slow down, eh. You 'ave been a remarkable pupil."

"Oh, I dunno," I said. I hope always to cherish a certain loyalty. "Any One of Us might have done the same."

In farewell, I hovered between the two languages. Having a choice was so — tiring. *Adieu?* "Good-bye," I finally said. "And — we'll always be friends, eh?"

Can an intercom *smile?* From the depths of the depths — or perhaps around the corner — it answered me.

"*Au revoir!*"

2. But Not Good-bye!

WHEN she had gone, *I* was left behind. It was the first thing that struck me. And that it was not a mere matter of subtraction. These are the observations which must be immediately recorded by the traveler into an affective world, before his own flesh takes on the qualitative tinge of his surroundings. We, who are still incompletely numerical, shall be unable wholly to tell you the What of Us, just as You, frozen median between words and numbers, will never quite be able to give us all your Why. Between beings each so mixed as You and We, this is bound to happen. But primers are beautiful, even though they must always imperfectly soar. They are like the poetry which occurs here when thought thickens toward the curve, and with us, as the arc strains to remember the time when it was perpendicular.

In Ellipsia, when some of us leave, there are always some left behind, so it is less noticeable; we are people of concerted action, in an action-at-a-distance world. But this time, on being left, I found myself immediately extended in I-ness. I was immediately and suddenly provided with images of myself which were both outside me and beside me, hopping along in a sort of trio with "I," and always referring back to it. I was of course experiencing my first concentrated dose of your Right Hereness.

Conceive of it, the first time a being of such instantaneity as mine does this, as if a butterfly whose waverings are measured in light-years might arrest itself on the wee presto of one minute, and affix itself there. Less strange to you perhaps, who are trained to bear it from birth, but for me this sudden attack of "one-ness" — and before I had heard there might be a partial cure for it — was terrible in the extreme.

This is how it was. Before it becomes forgettable — this is how it is. I saw myself, a great, amorphous being, veiled within its own veils, lying in its glass cage. I could see the trees, and myself looking at them. This stage lasted for some time, peculiar, but only a tickle of suffering. Strangely enough, the cage was a help to me, dictating to me such boundaries as I must begin to have here. Finally, a squirrel approached the glass, one rounded corner of it, where the walls joined. From outside, he was at the lower left-hand corner, from within, at the lower right-hand. He stood there, like a signature — it was thus I learned those simple locations, to me so profound. After a while, he was joined by other small animals, not all of his kind, but some, so bringing it about that I did not make note of when he himself was gone — and so I acquired the idea of genus among them. Genera that were separate from me of course, who was still lying there. And this — was almost pleasant. As they continued to course before the glass, coming and going, I understood that this had been happening all the while, and that this rhythm was in its way also a helpful enclosure. Until now, I had not been seeing them, that was all. And then it happened. I sensed all their paired eyes at the glass, an army of them, seeing me: and looking out, seeing them — Mine. They were here in all their eyes to bring home to me how and what was human. The rending came then, such a flesh-clap to a plasm untrained to it. Here I am.

All considering, I came out of it pretty well, and quickly too, especially since the room was so lacking in any array of objects — your classic method by which to forget yourselves. I suppose curved objects would have been of less use to me, and my mentors were afraid, with reason, to subject me too bruisably to the square. Or perhaps it was by design that I was left thus alone, to complicate. For, exactly as with you, it was my confusions which went into action at once, to get me down off that dread apex of solitude. The trouble with me is that I had so many of them. And unlike you, all so primal.

The sense of variability, when it invades a One, is like a rape. Or so I conceive it. It makes one sick of philosophy, for one thing. For another, an exchange of shames takes place. Or rather, your shame becomes our pleasure. As, I assume, happens in reverse, when Unanimity attacks visitors to us. In any case, things with me became more concretized — though nothing to what they would be in the second dialogue.

Once I had calmed down, the glass once again nothing but a prospect of a view, its avenue however extended now toward a distant pergola hitherto unobserved — always something sneakily added! — I found myself able to do, be, *and* think a number of things at once, in a manner which was indescribably — well, you know. I was able to move about, daintily slow, just as you do, and in spite of having no feet, more or less as you do, and also in much the same *balance*, if you like, that you maintain with your surroundings — which you are able to maintain despite the fact that in a closed laboratory such as this room must have been, there would be no known experiment which could determine whether the force that is pressing the observer's feet to the floor is gravity, or an upward acceleration of the laboratory. Ah you dears, imagine that!

To add to my pleasure, suddenly become aware of the shadows cached even in unmirrored glass, I was able, by a kind of grossly wide peekaboo-ing, to conceive of myself as of a certain height and axis, these later determined as of approximately seventy-eight inches end-to-end, circumference at waistline elliptically appropriate. At home, though we do not lack characteristic of a sort, we are an uncolorful, unselfconscious people. Looking upon myself now, I described a pinkness up to now seen only on the brink of imagination. I turned once or twice before the glass, seeing poised on its end, at an angle of not quite ninety degrees from the floor, a long, roseate form, full of senses which were by infinitesimals beginning to separate themselves, its surface smooth and continuous as the skin of a stone of perfected shape – clean, unmarred and closed, not an arc out of curve, and no orifice anywhere. It did not occur to me to quarrel with this. Altogether, my person seemed to me a not undistinguished one to represent its place of Origin.

The next complication then asserted itself – I began to brood over the conversation just past. When, across all the coaxials of unimaginability, your pulsings began to be received by us (and who shall say which one of us is the future of whose past?), it had been taken as a matter of little interest and not much honor; we had long been angling for recognition from a quarter rather more advanced. For, as some of Ours had long since calculated – if there was a uniform expansion of the universe, and if the motion of expansion were reversed into contraction, like a moving picture run backward, why then, the entire known universe would converge to a single point, indicating the hour of its birth. Ours have long since found themselves capable of peering past this theoretical birth of the universe, into the beyond. Yours, as you no doubt know, have long proclaimed that Nature forbids you ever to peer as far even as *that*. Indeed, Ours and Yours in that field lamentably resemble one another in blaming the limits of their own nature on Nature; We even have a school which miserably contends we shall never see beyond the beyond, to the Beyond.

But consider – in order that our attitude may be forgivable. Although it had taken you, according to my studies since arriving, from your Newton's day down to this, to learn to send signals at all, and these suggestively childlike – it was borne upon us almost at once that you thought yourselves unique. A form of life that deems itself not merely the Highest but located on the Only deserves a rebuff or two – and there We were but half as culpable as You. Knowing in fact, according to such apperceptibilities as we were in command of, how crowded things already were – we forgot all about you. Even the total amount of radio noise emitted by your planet is so weak, so cosmi-comically unimportant, it is no wonder that when your persistent nagging was once again reported to the Orifice, the tenor of Opinion should be, in Our idiom: "Silence in the Quorum house; the monkey wants to Quote."

But then . . . ah, then!

Just as I was dwelling on that next eventuality, I caught a furtive movement outside the glass, in the far distance (sic!) near the pergola, a movement of figures which my astigmatism, still not reduced to scale here, and never by reason of my shape to disappear entirely, could not quite make out. Then they vanished, a reminder that I too must soon make my debut outside.

My thoughts returned to that next episode in our mutual history, romantic episode it must surely be called according to my education in your libraries, though this may have been rather too specifically confined to say for sure.

But fancy on it! Suddenly, out of the blue (you are sending primers by now) our lackadaisical receptors are aware that a new set of beings has taken over your sending stations. We of course think of these beings as a *set*, not being disposed to conceive of individual Ones, much less of differences in temperament among them. In contrast with the old set, this new set appeared to be — oh these compound words! — let us say *brightly-stupid,* where the former set had been *stupidly-bright*. The new climate of transmittance had therefore an aura of humility about it, which inclined at least One listener to listen further, longer, and somewhat apart from the incestuant stream of his follow beings.

And now comes the romance, or is it legend, or is it folklore? For is it not axiomic with you, in one or the other of these areas, that in time of Newtonal need, an 'ero (as She pronounced it) shall always appear? And 'e will be One, more than likely, from the first bubble of birth somewhat apart from the Others. Though, strangely enough, 'e will be in the end more touchable than any of them. And finally — 'e will more than likely be a runt. This helps to develop temperament. On a genderless planet, said the primer, to develop a bit of temperament would be enough. And that was the story. For, across all the bent light-rays of contingency, One of us was able to do that.

I couldn't help another peek in the glass, at my new limits. As yet, I had no idea as to what size a being of my new height would be considered here. To say nothing of that other definition of me which I wanted so badly to — *prove*. But I knew one thing. 'E 'ad done it. And 'e or she, 'e was Me.

So, via that lonely-lovely band of enthusiasts, my arrival here had been effected, with all arrangements neatly made. Because of the disparity between Our state of advancement and yours, details of the trip were most easily taken care of from Our end. The accommodation devised here, however, has been utterly ingenious — that is indeed your talent. From Here on in, the path to the climacteric of our adventure seemed immortally clear, even a path which, across the billarions between, might become well worn. And up to now — up to the moment when I turned modestly away from further self-ing, and toward the curved book-wall which held the great folios of electro-braille, and the blown-up photostats of all the dragons that have stalked their little globe — up to now, I had never:

Doubt. It comes with I-ness also, and it is not a great stalker, but an army of squirrels. Almost fainting or sinking — what a feeling it is when the *I* wobbles like that! — I steadied myself against those helpful shelves, repeating the conclusion of the catechism:

"Resolved: That for those who wish to emigrate from either side, there shall be set up a means for an Exchange of Persons." Yes, that was our great adventure.

And having concluded, I started over again: "Whereas —" and went through it completely. For purposes of holding oneself where one is, there is nothing more tonic than a catechism firmly repeated. For, with each circle of it, I found I could toss a doubt overboard: It is not the means for the project that bothers me, nor the risks to those at home, who must be prepared to undergo what I had, nor that I may lack recruits, even though I cannot as yet assure any One what gender would be theirs. Ah, that's better. Ah, *here*. I am still Here.

If anything, it was Her confusion, at the end of our talk, which was most worrying me now. Not mine. Why, I was even clearheaded enough now to be able to find that compound word — to describe her state of mind — which had earlier eluded me. Since, at home, what we use for language *begins* with monosyllable, and thereafter concentricates inward, while Your Babel proliferates every which way, it is no easy task for a One to choose words here, much less combine them. Yet I did it! I found the exact word to describe her temperament: *silly-unsafe*. Curiously enough, she hadn't seemed so in the beginning. Silly-unsafe. And why this should provoke in me, even as I said it again, that same tender feeling — was still a mystery to me. Suddenly it was clear to me, what was happening. The process was taking over. Even as her intellect swelled gently into curve, mine of course — and hurrah for it — was straightening out. Did this mean I was giving evidence of gender, or acquiring it? One thing at least I now suspected. It was unsafe to assume that they would let me choose.

Idly now, and much less nervously, I rested in my niche, carefully avoiding either end of the wall where, though still rounded, there was a kind of corner, no doubt placed there to get me used to the idea. Quick as I am, it seemed to me impossible that I should learn anything more this morning. But in addition to the discovery that I have just recounted, and to my having found that it takes approximately thirty-five rounds of the catechism for my temperament to settle itself, surely a useful prescription to have — another residue remained. Revolving slowly at my usual angle of inclination — somewhat less acute than the angle at which the gyroscope forever aims at the same point in the heavens — I contemplated this fact, as newly embodied in Me. An army of doubts can be terrifying, perhaps even return one, in total consummation, to the vacuum. But apparently one generalized little itching of it is just the friction to hold us down to the variable. I couldn't get over how self-contained a certain measure of doubt had helped me to feel. I couldn't get over looking. For what did I see but that I was now — though still rather too delicately for plebeian purposes — rather more visible than before.

And what should happen then, but that, no sooner than emerged from the pinkness of that joy, I should be assaulted by, provided with — oh, sneaky-sneaky, your diversions are *endless!* — another. I saw on the shelf, just parallel with my top curve, or perhaps an inch or two below it, a small open book I hadn't noticed before. And looking into it – how . . . can . . . I . . . say . . . this . . . slowly enough? I had become slowed down enough to – In fact, as I now know, except for a nucleole here and there or possibly a particle, I was standing stock-still, still enough to . . . I could read.

Not without design, the book was one containing many soliloquies. Though as yet I could only read *instantly*, the whole book being plain to me at one gulp-glance, I found that by repeating this process, I could manage to linger here and there, to savor. I rank this, among all the experiences I have had here, as perhaps the – well, I suppose I should reserve judgment. But – a fact you may be ignorant of – since at home Our life, or Life, is in its serene totality considered a work of what you would call art, we have none of your lesser muses. So, you may understand what I was up against as I first read – such contortions and coagulations, such strenuosities as who would conceive language or anything else here would curve toward? – I was adaze. And *au contraire* to all my practical training here so far, the business of which had been to separate the data of those senses which in me already acted totally – to indoctrinate that an eye alone is the see-er, that one tastes with the tongue only – this book of verse seemed almost suicidally intent on going back to the mélange. And from this plunge, what a rainbow of the variable, as if the lenses of many telescopes large and small had been melted down in a pot where all the other sensations besides vision were already waiting – what flapping banners of color, what marble pictures, eaten by music! Good God! – I was glad I had been given that phrase, by whatever duenna. And beneath all of this, a contra-dicting, of such an imperative as I had never met before, as if all the muscles of mind were at work *against* shape of any kind, against it and number and quality also, dragging up, ever up, out of the potpourri, in a neap tide toward its own pure moon. Good God.

What saved me from going back, for good, where I came from? Yes, I confess it, there was a moment there when I thought of it, when balance rocked on balance, and I hung between our two worlds like a jack-in-the-box in the pit of the gondola of a balloon going around infinity. I ask you, very humbly. What saves *you*?

All I now remember is that, dizzying myself against the shelves, at what must have been an acute caricature of my customary angle, I asked Me, to be sure in the manner of the soliloquy, yet with something of Myself added: Can I bear it? Can these veils support – the insupportable? Can this integument – withstand it? Can a One who was clearly not intended to – be a "one"? Can I bear all this *here*-splitting?

And cautiously-furtively, from somewhere withonward, I was answered. Not vocally, not even with any of the facilities of language – whose little games and pastimes I began from that moment to despise. It was . . . as if many images fluttered toward me to console me as I myself would wish to be consoled, to prove me the center of their circle, as mathematically as an old-style geometric proposition: Yes, you can if you stand up *straight*. Once you learn the quantity of your own *strength*. If you'll just stand up straight, and be a –

Where these intimations might be engendered, I had no idea, as, firmly now, they goose-stepped toward me impeccably from all directions, until finally, by the most brilliant of maneuvers – *hup*, one, two, *hup* – they co-imaged in me, henceforth their center. *Halt!* And slowly, slowly, I felt myself – from without but from within too – pressured up toward the perpendicular. One by one, each image came forward, gave me an invigorating punch, and retired smartly, fist still ready-clenched. You are straight. You are strong. You are hard. You are hardstrong. You are straight. Each of these blows was accompanied by a distant background music as of yo-heave-ho's and encouragements. "*Steady me boyo and up you go!"* In a final rain of blows, I was hoisted. And above all, gasp, punch: You are never. You are never, punch. Silly. You are never silly, punch. Punch, punch, punch. Never. You are never silly-weak, punch. Never silly-soft, punch. You are never, punch, in any way *curved.*

And suddenly – *"wuddya know, boys"* – there I was, perched on top of Myself, a good bit higher than any of the gargoyles I had seen looking out over Paris. After the first surfeit – miles and miles of it and what a view – the world was mine if I could only stay up there – a few doubts came by, but nothing to worry about, a few ravens. You wouldn't have thought them enough to make me almost afraid to look down at myself, to wake up.

At last, I was emboldened to dare to look at myself once again in the glass – and wuddya know, indeed. I was a dream. To be sure, I wasn't any more visible than I had been, and no further changed in outline, no bumps, no holes. But there wasn't a sign of the horizontal or the acute about me. I was a perfect dream of the vertical. This is it, I thought; this is really it. This is How I Am. And a last punch hit me. *You are safe.*

3. Out

WHEN a "one" of the beings here first begins to suspect that he is acquiring a character, or as you like to say, firming one, the first thing he asks himself to do is to test it, in order to find out what it is. And in my progress toward becoming one of you, I was no exception. Since, at home, character is unmixed with gender, I was perhaps under even direr need to do so, being totally unable to distinguish between them. Perhaps both were acquired at one strike here, which would certainly be by far the most economical, I found myself thinking, then scalded myself for hanging on to an idea which was far too much like Us – such was not the style in which they would handle things in this marvelously spendrift world. They would certainly be more haphazard about something so important here. And there must be some prescribed one of their hazards which would be the proper test for what I now had.

How I was to find out by myself what this test was for a few paltry minutes perplexed me, until it occurred to me that I need only put my trust in *what* I now had, and perhaps it would already be influential enough to instruct me how to test it. It was time for a little self-exhortation. "I am straight –" I said to myself, "*very* straight." And I am strong, perhaps not *very,* but . . . quite? I feel certain that I am about to be — whatever it is that I am about to be.

After a few round-rubbings of this, I looked down at myself and found I had indeed worked up a glow. Why, I had no idea, I thought self-admiringly, that I was so hot-threaded! I must be getting pinker-blooded all the time. And though by now somewhat winded, and though it was well past the hour for my midday inflation, without pausing to so refresh myself, I went on, conjuring my image. "I am — whatever it is that carries its own weight, stands fast, and talks short. I intend to fight for my rites. I am a being of few words. Or as soon as I get over my initiation, I intend to be. I intend to act. And there isn't a curve in my body!"

This last wasn't true, of course; indeed, quite a large part of my statement was couched in words which were unfamiliar to me, but certainly must have swum up out of my own innerstink. But, if I were ever really to get over being an ellipse — that carefulest of beings bogged in the middle-mean — this was all part of it. "This is all part of it!" I almost shouted. Yes, I almost shouted. Up to then, you must understand, I had spoken only by means of an all-over surface vibration, but now this appeared to have localized itself somewhere above my diameter, narrowing its timbre but widening its volume. That I not only had a voice, but that its first real utterance was almost a shout, was not this enormously encouraging to what I had in mind?

And just then — I fell back, exhausted. Indeed, miserable to report, I fell back so thoroughly that I found myself far beyond my former angle, far gone past even an acute case of it — in fact, I was pure horizontal.

Now, ellipses, like the horses I had seen in some of the photostats, never lie down in this position; unlike you, they are never even caught dead in it. Pride goeth, I thought, lying there. How it would have alleviated my misery to know all the positions you are really capable of — that this was all part of it too. But at the time, all I could find was a whisper in which to excuse myself to my image. "It's because I don't know my own strength as yet," I said. Don't say *as yet,* came the caution. I spoke up, still with a sigh. "Rather, I am simply a being who doesn't know its own strength." When there was no reply, I took that to mean that I might continue in this vein. "Probably, I am a creature of such strength that it would be dangerous for me not to know the limits of it." Silence. "Maybe I ought to test my strength-hood, not for itself, but for the sake of the weaklings I will surely encounter." Quite a pause after this one, too. So at last I dared to say it. "Try me. What *is* the test for what I believe to be my —" But since I wasn't really sure whether it was character or gender I was applying for, I simply shouted again, this time, "Try me. *You just try!*" And found myself miraculously on my feet — that is, vertical — once more.

And not only that — even braver. I went round the room, and anywhere I met myself in the glass, which was everywhere, I said to it, "Come on now, think you know the test, huh; come on now, brother!" Brother. Where does one get those ideas? But when the answer came it was right from my authority in the glass there. It was only a whisper, quietly-firmly, as such answers should come, but I heard it. "Want to *step outside?* I dare you. Why don't you step outside, and *just see?*

And since my intended being was not one to refuse a dare, that was what I prepared to do. Greenhorn that I was, I even gathered up almost all my energy, under the impression that what had carried me afield and over the great transparencies would more than easy fade me through a wall. There was a door in the wall, a large, regally obvious one of about ten feet in height, but of course, as far as doors were concerned and staircases, too, or any of those playthings which cater to the appendages, I was an aristocrat and had never used one in my life, the same being true of my manner of dealing with obstacles, it never having occurred to me to go over or around one, instead of *through*. So I gathered myself for the elide, took a last look at my image — never pinker, never prouder — said jauntily, "I'll meet *you* outside!", touched the proper thought, and — WHAM.

How I lived to tell this tale must after all be some sort of durility test — I must have ricocheted from surface to surface, up, down and sideways, fully thirteen times, being saved only by the dimensions of the room, just big enough to permit me the barest air-interval of relief, between making connections. During which, as with your drowners here, much passed before me. I comprehended how thoroughly I had gone against everything my mentors had been at such pains to teach me — against all the friction, weightfulness and lethargy it had taken me months to acquire. Above all — and as if I had never heard of catechisms — I had totally forgotten how much more Here I now was than There. Only let me get through this, I prayed, I promised, and I'll never again forget the distance between a floor and a ceiling. And it's true, I've never had to stop to puzzle over that later; there's something to be said for the school of hard knocks. Then at last, I once again lay prone.

And so bruised was I in my humilities, that I made no effort to get up. Instead, I did what any One wounded in his veils does. I lay there dreaming, in repair. And how to reveal to you, the all too solid stuffs of these laydreams, how to confess the obscene shapes of those private indulgences on which We fatten ourselves in our lowest moments! — I could not hope to open these to you, had I not recently begun to put aside our shames in exchange for yours. Even so, if there were any way to get around it, or even through — but no. You must have revealed to you what really lies at the dark root of all Our wontedly pure ovality. Know therefore, that we are not allowed to . . . that it is a sin to conceive of it . . . that — *we do not know what we are like inside.* That it is a portal sin even to enter there in the slightest, imaginatively. And that round the clock, we never stop doing it.

There. It follows that your and our spiritual paths do indeed resemble, diverging only in their blames. Things being open to dissection here, you are given to flogging yourselves for not being more ethereal, while our phantasmagoria aspire ever toward the solid, and in such seductively illegal shapes as are an everyday business with you. But while your and our emphases differ, our habits are curiously mutual. Oddly enough, you suffer modesty over certain of your appendages and orifices, of which everybody knows perfectly well. We save our blushes for our imaginary organs, the mere knowledge of the possession of which would be our miracle.

Not that we don't have our mystic seekers after the unknowable — which, considering the difficulties of investigating creatures so incorporeal and instantaneous, it almost certainly is — at least on home ground. Nevertheless, this doesn't prevent the paths around the crater from being crammed night and day with obscurantists staring into the opposing lava streams which respectively shape our fresh citizens and replace our stale ones, crowded there supposedly in honor of such a perfect scheme of things, but everyone knows what they're looking for; it's a civic scandal. Sooner, alas, can You find your inner souls by looking for them, than we our inner shapes. So, however, you and Ours have continued to do for millenia, when all the time they had better have looked at each Other.

Meanwhile, myths, legends and dreams all to the good of course, but we have our more pedestrian systems of amusement, a sub rosa traffic of risks and frolic where we disport ourselves with the shadier side of ourselves — and very inventively so, considering the flimsy we have to work with. Indeed it is here that our most exquisite caste distinctions are formed. For, not having any ideas of number in accumulation such as you, all those superiorities which you can attach to piles of gold or aggregations of power, we can ascribe only to lineage, just as you can of course in addition, but in a most contrary focus. For where you can look gloriously back to what you and Yours have been, we base all our bloodlines on our fleshly future.

And because ours are in the realms of the unknown, the categories are all the more absolute. Down at the bottom are those whose peep-show, postcard lusts are of the lazier, most unenlightened sort, running mostly to generalized visions of the interiors of Ones, jokes about such primitive apparatuses as the fluoroscopes, X rays, et cetera used by our ancestors before we became Ones of all the same ancestry. This class of Ones is given to gibes on the absence of body openings — which japes run almost parallel to yours on the presence of them. Next above is that largest cult whose rather more perfervid visions cluster around one or other of your main organs, and here too in a certain hierarchy, those addicted to lung fantasy being rather more elegant than those of the liver, but neither having the social advantages of those whose frenzies and perturbations liberate themselves around the idea of a heart. Esoteric cults, or some minor organ, or exotic or newly discovered conception of one, engage some; hangouts for these, being frowned upon as bohemia, are everywhere. There are even those introverts who adhere to the legal image and honestly worship what all of us are under guard to say we do — the empty future of Us as we Are. And of course a few neuters whose imaginative heat runs so low that they never get to do any leaning at all. For, as must be admitted, no matter how high a One's inner fantasy places him socially, he is actually as limited as the lowest when he gets down to celebrating it. For whatever our fleshly futures may be, or how hot our desires for them, all the practice of our concupiscence cannot exceed the cylindrical coolth of our shape. No bulges defame our pure elliptic curve, no indentations. We do what we can, then — we lean.

And as with most widely practiced venial sins, Leaning has its recognizable variations; indeed it is the only preoccupation where a One may run a little wild among the various. There is much fashion and preference of place, those who rate the pastoral over the urban, et cetera, et cetera ad infinitum. Leaning in crowds is least sinful, and evening occasions of it the most common, from intimate soirees to those huge quasi-public affairs, in places of extravagant decor, which are the ultimate of the vulgar. Leaning by Ones, that is, by a One and a One, is a more serious offense, since it affords the most multiple sensation, having in addition to the preponderantly social pleasure above, all the extra delicacies of more refined angles of inclination, at what point one turns off one's electrical field, and at what stage one does actually permit — touch. And in what arc of oneself one submits to it, until that final, oblivious moment, achieved only by the most devoted or the more agile, when One and One ellipses manage to touch arcs from top to low in such rapid succession and so simultaneously rocking that their continuous curves seem for one moment of ambiguity — a single line.

And having already the reverse advantage of caste, we have also these possibilities of misalliance and miscegenation which make Our world a livelier place to live in and gossip about — such as the lung-dreamer's taste for the postcard type, or the actual sight of some great, fair heart-One going off into the bush with some dark little exoticker. For, due to our transparency and sameness, the nature of our dream organs is perceptibly evident in the complexions, and most of us can spell these out pretty well. We feel that this is the grace always granted on the other side of sinfulness. For, even among Us, there has to be some way to *tell.*

And finally, there is one more possibility — certainly by now you will have thought of it? Since it vitally concerns me, I shall approach it gradually, as I am able. For, should you ever come to us, you will see well enough how, from one world to another, these modesties cling. Wait, for instance, until the first time you have to turn off your electrical field and just stand there. Whereas I am utterly hardened to that, and — alas for it, in my world — to much more. But let me now go back to the spectacle of me lying there prone in that glass house in Bucks, hoping that as I talk, what I am hinting at will steal over you, in mutual embarrassment. Let me tell you the nature — and icon — of my dream.

Well, I was lying there, trying out my humilities, such a whole arpeggio of aches that there was no use trying to poultice them up one at a time. What was needed was a whole lovely web of dream, and I knew well enough where to find it, having done so more often than I care to say. Finally, I gave in. I began, in the usual way, the usual interior imaginings. When I tell you that I had no allegiance to one single organ, you may guess that there was indeed something very wrong with me. For a while, as preamble, I did entertain myself with visions of myself with heart, myself with lungs, et cetera, all separately. But very quickly I advanced — and here began the real dreaming — to a vision of such a being as . . . Such a Being . . . as might have, inside itself, such organs . . . and in such an intertwined congress of processes *inter-* and *intra-*parietal, peritoneal, pericardial and perichondrial . . . such a being as in fact *might have them all.* So far had I come then in dreaming, that one would have thought this sufficient of evil. But — no. Are you beginning to suspect? I fear you may be, but in the wrong direction.

You are thinking perhaps, that in all the categories I

haven't mentioned your reproductive ones? True, but not because we don't know of them. We do envision these, but as the most vestigial of organs, in no way — as the other organs might still be — pertinent to our way of life. And though even these poor *primitifs* have their devotees, the latter Ones have no status among us and are indeed considered — Well, they are called — silly. To be a One of these worshippers is scarcely to be venial, merely ridiculous.

Or have you guessed that I wasn't quite truthful when I said that we never lie down? Well, I wasn't, but only out of a decent sense of reserve toward those of our old Ones who manage to do so before we can push them back into the lava stream of Return. The majority of these do it because they can't help themselves. Now and then we have a few rakes who prate of *leaning* in that position, but this is mere senility, and is quickly taken care of. The overwhelming majority of us elect to elide permanently before we reach either of these pitiable states. Once an Ellipse is down, it's Out.

And now . . . I must. Now, since our flesh is at least cognate, brood with me, tremble over the abyss of such a One as I. Even to imagine such a supremely equipped being was not enough for me, a being having within it a pleiades and more of organs at their music, or, if you prefer — and as we were reared to rate it in comparison with our veils within veils — such a monster of the lowest obscenities of matter. No, I had to be One to crawl out on the farthest cliff of the imagination; I had had the arrogance to dream — So. Ah? Yes. I had become a One who could in fancy assault the holiest — our pure Outline. At night, such an army of incubi and succubi attacked me, such nightmare visions of how that most perfect of curves might be contorted, that although as yet I hadn't the vaguest of preferences toward these appendages and indentations, and was even affrighted to envision *any* being who might own them, much less myself, I had for safety's sake given up leaning altogether. Later on, in those months when I was listening to your signals, I discovered among Us a little band of Others like me; I was not alone. But I must confess it fully now, and of course now that I am Here it is easier. In Ours, I was without honor. I was one of those whose imagination dared do violence to the very form decreed for us in perpetual onus. Yes, I am that One. I am a pervert.

Thank God for travel.

For what an exquisite relief it could be, this lying prone! Especially must it be regarded here, I mused, as that dear posture in which one smiles backward at the anxieties of yesterday, lulla-lulla, and can perhaps even anticipate a change of shape one might just have the luck to earn or fall into, on the morrow. Above me, on the shelves, were the picture books of all the fauna here down the geological ages, those great plates I had so pored over during my early incubation here, wondering which of those shapes would turn out to be Yours – and in time, in the foolness of time, perhaps Mine. Although at that period I had been unable to focus on the print of the descriptions, each large plate was accompanied by enough small ones to give me a fairly canny idea of each creature's habits, habitats and foods. Nothing gave any suggestion that all these magnificoes – I had after a few days persuaded myself not to regard them as terrors – did not exist simultaneously, our Now being so different from your little "now." My real shock at the sight of all this – all these waving waterfalls of mane, saurian extensions, anthropoid pugs, rhino-ish craters and cattish patterns under which the pure oval had forever vanished – was not so much at the extremity of the exaggerations, as after a while an intense irritation, then a degrading melancholia, over the piffling scope of my own. How wee, shrunken and ignominious those defamatory little sins-against-the-curve such as I had been able to imagine.

In the face of this grandeur, I was scarcely a pervert at all.

Once I had got over this, I had to buckle down to an important question: when presented a choice of all this imperial grab bag, which shape would I choose to become? Try as I did, I could raise no enthusiasm to be any of these creatures, much less that lyric rush of self-discovery which had been the lecher-hope of my small dreams. But the primer had certainly promised a change. For hours I pored over the herbivores and the carnivores, unable to decide between them, or to come to any conclusion other than that, if it were left to me, I should fancy a little fur. In the intervals, I searched in vain for pictures of that Lava-stream which must produce them, but although I kept forever coming upon mountains which almost lifted themselves from the page, and vegetation-rimmed tarns of a certain mystery, there seemed to be nothing akin to Our all-embracing system, and not much coherence that I could descry, to any. There was a day when, suddenly noticing a preponderance of eggs, I brooded over this at first wistfully, then almost angrily – they had promised more of a change than *this.* I had no choice really but to trust them.

So, when the dialogues started, I kept my own counsel, in time came to understand my delusion, and began to be taught my real profit. The shape I would sin under was not going to be left up to me; this they call resignation. Almost as with us, except for that subdivision which was still to be understood, there was One creature here only. And as I lay there now, I practiced ever newer dreams of this being, manufactured out of fresher, more sophisticated dissatisfactions – give or take a tusk or two, subtract a horn there. And after an hour or two of this pleasantest of siesta occupations, I made an accordingly new discovery. Posture! Perhaps only a One of an essentially gyroscopic people, used to the luxury of moving pavements in whose trolley grooves We may incline all at the same comfortable angle, can appreciate how basic is posture here to the rhythms of philosophy, and indeed to the practice of ideals. How sensitively I was getting to understand you. It was not wholly comfortable then, to lie too long prone.

And no sooner had I discovered this, than I felt myself pulled powerfully upright, as eager for action as if I had just bounded out of the crater. At home, my line of action would have been ready for me; here it took only nominally longer for posture to suggest one. Carefully, very carefully this time, I approached the door. At this point in my education I had never really seen one up close; what has instantaneity to do with doors? Answer: it learns to reason itself through them, just as you, by reverse process, will soon find yourselves flashily able to do forever without them. At a certain distance, I found that, even when thinking the most lethargic thoughts and overcasting myself with the heaviest feelings I yet knew, there was still an unnatural tension between door and me, which boded ill. Then suddenly the source of it occurred to me; my electrical field was being opposed by another. Even their doors wear them, I thought. And perhaps not only their doors, perhaps all other objects which might offer resistance of any kind are required to be clothed so, while they themselves walk nakedly, proudly among these obeisant; what aristocrats they are! And I—?

And I. When Here, do as Here does. But be sure to emulate those who are in power. I must run no risk of having them confuse me with low-grade matter. It requires only a particular thought for us to discard our Field, the trouble being only that it is such a particular one, and illegal too. Perhaps it wouldn't work as well here. Taking a cautious breath, I found that since the last time I had practiced this heresy, the wholesomely coarser air of Yours had so clogged the finer pores that I was enabled to sustain a thought without fairly recognizing that I was doing it – and that this furthermore seemed to add substantially to my weight. Sure enough, shortly I began to feel the familiar chilliness which always comes of lowering one's protective field, and happening to shiver, this inched me slightly doorwards – and sure enough, the door inched slowly and equally toward me. Some thoughts must be illegal anywhere. For good measure, I made so bold as to half hum it, meanwhile keeping my real thoughts trolleying along a loftier neighborhood; there's always some niche of the intelligence that one must keep to oneself.

"I am . . ." I murmured, ". . . I am . . . an Original." This time the door didn't budge. But by dint of trial I found that as I moved forward, and only under the influence of this, the door would move compatibly outward. What courtesy, even in inferior matter, here! Slowly, majestically dipping my angle at a nice compromise between a taking-this-for-granted and a thank-you, I inched myself along without accident, until the door and I were in equipoise. I was almost outside it. Outside, on Here.

By hook or crook then, I was almost safely through the second phase of my journey. For, awesome as the interstellar reaches may be to the lone traveler, or even to the caravan which must track those Saharas of cosmic dust, there had come a point in my journey when it was the destination which became the dread. Did they really have water in a liquid state? I could not survive without it. Should I have trusted them, when they reported themselves as beings with the same needs as I, molded by the same natural forces? Not that I was suspicious of their intent – but after all, they were only a third-generation star. Young as they were, must one not have a low view of intellectual powers which had taken all of their history to discover other presences, and the possible pulsings between them? Granted We and They had mutually significant symbols and meanings, but imagine Our dismay when informed that they still read and wrote! Could beings like Us, who are in Ourselves practically *all* electronic meaning, go backward as far as these beings on the other side of their "Milky Way" thought they had gone forward; could we mutate enough, and quickly so, to touch arc on their planet? To dare to do this, I had gone against all home Opinion. And so far, with the help of arrangements-in-waiting, plans had gone remarkably. But, as I peered outside that glass door, I remembered my misgivings just a few moments before landing. Behind me, improbably far along the empyrean reaches, Ours, that long teardrop of a planet, lay somewhere shrouded as I had last seen it, nestling deep in its filtered atmospheres, a jewel once upon a time massively wept. As I had reined in on Yours, a mere toy ball lost on its cloud stubble, waiting to be picked up again in play – my last thought had been: yes, I can land Here – but can I live?

Such thoughts as one can have behind a door here! Just beyond the threshold the air was heavy, but I reminded myself how much I myself had changed during my weeks here. When, by infinite creepings I found myself still alive and breathing, no more WHAM's and the door still courteous, I made the last inch or two; behind me, the door modestly retired – and shut. I had no thought at the time of whether it would readmit me, or where I was going. All the prospect of your world was before me, terminated in the distance – according to the limits of sight here, to which mine was fast declining – by a pergola. I remained for some minutes as I was, faintly chilly, daring nothing, taking stock. I was Here. I was Outside. And I was naked as the day Yours are born.

If you could attach a tiny camera to the eye of the newborn here, would it bring back data more vital than those mechanisms that hit your moon? I doubt it, for there is so much more than sight at stake. To understand that first unfolding receptivity, the interpreters would themselves have to be reborn. In this way, and entirely opposite to Us, who slip upward already complete and serenely equal with our crater-watchers, you keep a constant spawning of what you call "ignorance." And the drama of *learning* it away from itself, while it battles to get back to what it faintly dreams it surely knew, is what is here called "a life." In my way I was at this moment analogous to your newborn; I was in fact seventy-eight inches of naked cornea, but of that moment when your world moved in on me so powerfully and I as powerfully mutated toward it, I retain only the memory of its collision and blend. Among all the impressions since, this vague memory — as of a lost difference at the back of "now" — is the least describable. Yet I feel as you do; if I could find it again I would have something of utter value. What I describe is the moment after.

Though this was my first free view of your world in what you so endearingly persist in calling the round, I was of course already window-bred to the gently mammary landscape before me, and to its verdure. This latter I had already seen in the photostats, often in forms fiercer and more variant; in fact it was by gazing thoughtfully back and forth first at these then through the window that I had gained a composite of what plant life is here. We too have our trees, archaically preserved under glass now, since with the reversal of atmosphere and our refinement of it, they and we are no longer in such a complementary gaseous relationship as they and you. Indeed, they are our living treasures, visited in museums as you do your dead ones. We like to watch their pause-poise. Other plants we have too, but never except under the most severe guard — as you occasionally guard flame. Grass, though known of — ah, indeed, indeed, indeed! — is forbidden, and hopefully extinct. For, in the seamlessness of our chemiformically paved cities, and under the ever-spreading, plastic mildness of buildings which have been taught to repeat themselves whenever necessary in units of fortified ground granite and repressed marble, we have been for some eons safe from sight of terra firma, but even in seamlessness, there is the very danger of seam.

So, it was no wonder that I gazed for minutes at that wilderness of chlorophyll which would have been both treasure and enemy at home. Although I was by now enough coarsened in my components to be able to amble along and under that green burning in mutual toleration, to do so would nevertheless be an act of daring. And still is, though, just as you do in the performance of unnatural acts, I have taught myself not to flinch. In any case, I cannot resist returning to what seem to me the most marvelous museums of those green forms – which even on Here too are not really random or rampant, but unutterably fixed in their pause-poise – and indeed may be the basic natives of eternal everywhere.

As I gazed there, already past that other crater-moment, I knew that the scene before me and around me was not the only one in your world; such a mistake I have never once made. I already knew that in and among all the delights or abysses of what you, when you have tamed it, called landscape, and we, when we have conquered it, terra firma, the elements are the same. Still I gazed. Just in the foreground of those changeable ozones they call air here, a smallish tree was turning over and over its paw-shaped leaves, gray to green, green to gray, palm up, palm down. Palm up, palm down, but any advances that were made between tree and me were mine, and at this I felt somewhere within me a certain squeezing. I stared on. Such jewels of the variable are offered you daily, and were now being offered me also – such jewels as I could never in essence hope to touch. Above the tree, in perfect ellipse, a cloud reigned. Pause-poise. Everything was moving here, and yet stood at *same*. One thing I have learned here which I never could have learned at home – where sameness never moves—and I think I did so at this moment. Palm up, palm down. People are the wilderness.

I looked away, and there, just entering the pergola, were two of them.

4. And Around

AND one, though of a certain meagerness, was a One of us.

I had no time more than to make out that the other figure, tall and shrouded in black, was certainly of another order—for at that same second, I unfortunately made a misstep.

Or rather, in my haste to meet them, I overstepped, not having properly learned how to bring my movements down to your scale.

It might be thought that creatures like us, able to transport ourselves at a rate that appears to you instantaneous, and across distances which to you are scarcely short of infinity, must be moving about all the time. Think again—and it will be obvious to you that the reverse side of our instantaneity is of course—a monumental stillness. That's real balance and real personality as we see it, a personal whatness, not nearly as dependent as you on a personal where. Contrarily, You, still exploring the minutiae of distance, still road-building on both ground and air, are naturally obsessed with movement, from posture changes on up. I understand that the youth of Yours, in the days before they dreamed of motorbikes—and got them—used once to dream of seven-league boots. As a self-propelling creature, I in effect had these, and on Here you're welcome to them; a circumference of twenty-eight thousand miles is simply not enough. It scares me even now to consider where I might have ended up, had I been without the preliminary training of the weeks in the glass house — possibly off the place altogether, and in some reach to whose beings even Outline is unknown. As it was, think as small as I tried to, in order to squeeze myself down to those miles which for me were as much the final particle as molecules were once those of your matter — ! — they showed me a map later, where I landed.

Later, it was at first thought I had landed at Durham, but when I described the perch on which I had found myself, the consensus was, "Oh no, not *that* Romanesque!" Forms of buildings, and indeed many other inanimates, are intensively classified here, whereas even the muddical sciences make only the most simplistic classifications of people — not yet having decided, except in the most primitive ways, which is subordinate to which. And if things go as I hope for me here, that will be my lifework, to compile such a dictionary of people forms and natures as would be possible only for a one who remembers his One-ness. But that's by the way. Let us return to my boots.

There exists, they told me, somewhere less to the north of my starting point than Durham, a cathedral town which, they added parenthetically, has one of the loveliest of medieval streets, most homogeneously preserved. (One learns to expect these stoppages of what they presume to call historical detail in the sublimest conversation.) Be that as it may, they have a town in which there is a cathedral called Ely, on the main tower of which there is a kind of heavenly veranda-porch, ledge or abutment, on which climbers may exit, to stand amid, above, below and on the stonework. From my description of the latter, this is where I found myself standing — whisko-flash — from Bucks. The street below, its roof peaks all very harmonious, appeared to be preserved in the way they later said, and the people too for all I know; I saw none of them, since it was raining. Water in a liquid form they had indeed. I had already seen their sea, of course, but had never in my life felt that luminous shiver-shine-spat on my integument. We are not that intimate with the elements. At first it was divine – under those tiny punctures, never had my skin felt so personally mine. But with the new ever comes the newer here. Though we do not have bodily temperature up to yours, I could swear that, hard by the tower there, while the gray winds swatted me to pinker, I had my first sensation of it. Meanwhile I poised there, not knowing either what to do next or how to assure my return to Bucks, having no idea of its direction, or as yet of any, on your scale. Surely they would be out signaling for me shortly, but the roving communications system we shared must be far too grandiose to pick up such a little mark as now was I. The clouds were higher above me than I was used to; as for the ozone, its extravagant blue had altogether disappeared. I even had a moment's nostalgia, now that I had friends here, for that cloud-strewn evening when I had first landed, beaming in on a steady chatter of signals, bang on Bucks. Above all, I wished myself dry again, and no matter what reprimands might be my lot, in front of that pair whom five minutes past I had left at the pergola.

That pair, that forever ill-assorted pair! In that brief, snapped-off glimpse, what I aspired to be was nevertheless brought home to me. It is one circumstance to aspire to difference in general – a kind of yammer and snuffle to be something other than what one so boringly is. Miles across the ravine from this is that other circumstance, when one comprehends, in those layers of oneself beyond where the words are made, the truth of a difference which no effort of sight, touch or sound may ever bring more than tokenly nearer. Imagine one of your young, at that gorgeous second when, as still little more than a voice and a weaving of limbs, there is knitted into its flesh forever a sense of the difference between mere object-mass — and You.

From then on, I understood the nature of two-ness, at least where I, or a One like me, was one of the pair. I had only to recall that picture, imprinted in me as if all of me were total lens: one of Us, however poor a specimen, standing next to: however bundled, half seen and possibly unaverage also — one of You. From then on, I better than understood how a One and a one make Two; I began to take for granted that things were so and had always been; I began even to find it harder and harder to conceive that things had ever been otherwise . . . elsewhere. Along with every transition made, I have had to fight to remember it. For my greedy prayer, never told truly until this moment — neither sphere-to-sphere, nor to Mentor, nor to the lovely personage of the second dialogue — my greediest prayer is not to change wholly from a One to a one, but to stand somewhere on the Gibraltar of between. To stand in the suffer-tickle of all the various, and yet remember the Calm of the Oval, if not feel it.

Would that not be an altogether new race of sports? Don't answer. Hear me out.

I stood there on my ledge, pretty much between of things as it was, and considered what to do next, meanwhile accustoming myself to the aches of surface intimacy. Remember that until very recently I had lived as a creature of suspension, vibrationally inclined toward this or that surface or person but formally never touching any. By the very nature of Our being, we are thus exempted from having to know *where* we are; there's no need for it. On Here, the surface-intimacy ache performs a very necessary frictional function, as can be seen by watching any a one of you fidget. It keeps people in a constant state of conclusion.

In other words, the ledge was hard, the air buffety, and the rain which minutes before had been like silver sunshine to my outline — was now rain. Also there was my temperature, now much exhilarated, and even, it seemed to me, *ready* — for what actions I hadn't the slightest. The multiple sensation of all this is best described for you as a sneeze with no place to go; in fact I recall worrying whether there mightn't be future danger of developing rather enormous feelings too far in advance of the body mechanisms necessary to vent them. A constant trouble of adult intelligences getting themselves born again — or however you want to term it — is that so many of their early fears are later authenticated. But back to my ledge.

Below, the air, though clearing, was also darkening; it must have been what is here called both closing time and opening time, and all along the street there were black rounds bobbing by in singles and pairs, and sometimes spatterdash or all of a muggle, like the raindrops themselves. It was positively fascinating to watch, and for me of course, uncannily Outside-ish, which is the way with Us when for whatever reason — and indeed there are not many — a One gets out of rhythm with his groove and is put to One side until he recovers it. Because of this — and included in it a positive sadness for the *older* sadness — I didn't watch for too long. My impatience to get back to Bucks was now uneasily confused with my impatience to get down — down there, to where the people were. Apropos of this (and of the cheaply eternal jokes on the errors of identity likely to be made at first crack by visitors from elsewhere), I was never under any misapprehension that *umbrellas* were people. There's no denying that, on the staircase of matter-to-energy transmutation, your metamorphic stage is rather low. But certainly no a One in his right Opinion would ever confuse you with any of your artifacts. I rather think you must have no idea of just how strange you are.

Just then, my character gave a modest instance of itself, reminding me that I should never find out the amount of my weightfulness here until I practiced it. No sooner said than done. My temperament, evidently a strong one, made little distinction between the practical and the unavoidable. I decided to jump-fall. Rather fearfully, I let myself go, softly concentrating on no other destination beyond "I-down." I found that I could slide gently down the span of that thought, approximately in whichever direction I pointed it. Tentative as I was, the process took quite a while, during which I had time to reflect. Since I still felt no sense of direction in the smaller sense – that is, Yours – it was possible that maps and compass points of the sort I had seen in the photostat animal books were a universal need here, for the convenient portage of which you yourselves, *vide* those books also, no doubt would have long since developed pouches in your persons. It struck me that I might already have done so myself.

I immediately attempted an all-over inspection of my outline, but found myself in an odd difficulty; since the last time I had done this, my vision, with woeful inefficiency, seemed to have reconcentrated itself in my upper end. There was no longer any use in trying to see myself whole, but by a number of anglings which may have looked rather flirtatious from below, I managed to check, finding, so far, no violations. But just before I came to rest – about two feet above the pavement, against the rosy panes of a sweetshop – a question, a monster question which to date had never unfolded itself during the entire course of my adventure, now did so. You on Here may be better able to meet this particular question since, no matter what you think of Yourselves, you have had to get used to alternatives in every direction. But fancy a world which believes itself unexcelled except by those beings beyond the Beyond who may have achieved total circularity — in which case it won't matter. Fancy a world of creatures so at One in every pore and constituent that the very word "stranger" is expressed as "another a One like me, only grayer." Fancy, in other words, a world of creatures who swarm like bees toward their own beauty. For these, even to frame such a question was an impertinence. But, nevertheless, what were You going to think — of Me?

It was now fairly dark, just before the lamps were lit, and nobody was passing. I hugged the pane, against whose rosiness, effected by glassine paper lining, I had perhaps even been attracted, as butterflies are to their own blend. Butterflies were diurnal; where did they go of an evening? Where does a truant One go when it has run away from its glass house? Yes, deny it as I would, I could see there were potholes in the firmest character. For I wanted to hide.

I found that facing my vision inward toward the window was a help; since I couldn't see them, perhaps they wouldn't see me. Perhaps this was even the rule here. I concentrated on the window and its contents. At this time, as you will recall, I could already read your finer print, and in addition to the instant way in which We could already compute languages generally, for Here-purposes I had been teacher-grounded in two of your principal ones. When I say "compute" you must take this literally. This is another great divergence between Ours and Yours which no doubt is already clear to you. Consider. Among creatures already so used to appendages as You, the development of pseudo ones, or machines, was predictable. But where any talent or performance of value is attainable, We would never think of letting out to an appendage what with a little more fiddling could be embodied directly in Ourselves. And so we have done. Learn how to fly a hoodinkus — and perhaps to fall with it? Run a byjiggerby — and perhaps have to run after it? Master the controls of a thingamagooly, and one day find ourselves—? What shortsightedness! We do all these things in our Own.

And as I gazed hunchily into that window, I saw to my delight that the piles of stuff there were dotted with little lettered flags. At the same moment, *Candy* ticked up in me, in response to the substance I saw there, then, "Revise: American for: Revise: *Sweets*." Any comprattler can do this. And it was going to be more than useful fun to be able to tick "Umbrella" when confronted with one, though this is as far as it goes. Spell and parse we can, and poet too. Sometimes, since we *are* beings, we have been known to produce responses we haven't even been set for. But we know better than to confuse words with meanings; consider your pronouns. But, as real communication, all written language is dead for us, to those of our vibrational Order a mere playing of harpsichords. But some of us still took pride in the performance of the obsolete, which is what so often happens to anything turned over to the machine.

"S-sreets!" I murmured to myself dutifully. Spoken language we of course hadn't had in the memory of any a One. The voiced labials, though troublesome to produce from within, can be practiced very successfully. Diphthongs pose no problem, if long enough to bend. My real difficulty is a slight but constant curvature of the vowels.

Meanwhile, I hadn't an idea what the stuff in the window was for—that sort of thing is a *concept*. (And *that*'s computation for you.) But the signs, in all their pretty, pointed Gothic, and each attached to a heap of counters of a unique cabalistic design, enchanted me. I am one of those antiquated a Ones who cannot pass up anything in print. I read them out, voicing very slowly, but I thought correctly: FIZZER FRUIT: NUTTIE CRISP: TREACLE TOFFEE: SHERBET BON-BON: RASPBERRY FUZZLE.

Directional signals? Then why these paper twists of color,

whorls of ribanded red and white, alongside? Gaming counters were a possibility; as Ones of a total economy, we ourselves were pushingly fond of a small risk. I studied a jolly neat little pile of beige and brown strips combined with near-circle bits inside which ever smaller concentrics narrowed to nucleoles of white – meanwhile pleased to find that my enthusiasm kept me at a convenient levitation of some fourteen inches from the ground, and that, with slackened winds, my pink was fading, making me less visible than before. Plumb center of the window, the largest placard said in plain Roman: LICORICE. Quote on the tick, there came without warning, "Lickerish: lecherous. Ex.: *Lickerish bait, fit to ensnare a brute.*"

"Silence!" I said to it. "Who asked you!" But the monkey had already quoted, as a matter of fact from a part of that dear book of yours, my first one here. Milton: John. I stared, unbelieving. The signs, admittedly incomprehensible, then were street lingo, or perhaps even those scabrous rhymed ditties sometimes fancied by our postcard types. From far down the street, there were now sounds coming on toward me, but these scarcely registered, for I had caught sight of a mound at the back in which the pieces were darkish mauve and heart-shaped – and then it was plain. Some in other piles were greenly luminous, yet others brownishly studded, and it was these exotics which had put me off, but here and there, as with the heart-shapes, I recognized shameful old dream inhabitants I knew. What a hiding spot I had chosen! In the public street, these replicas. Good God then, this was pornography.

Shortly, of course, I came to my sin-senses; it was a miracle that I hadn't confused worlds before. The licorice was actually of help, its short-long strips so suggestive of what transcribed-sonic looks like on tape. From then it was but a jump to my own earliest communication lessons here, and then to the real if rather more boring significance of that bow window, those chromatic little models, so kindergarten neat, those strict little pedagogue flags. Of course, of course. It was a demonstration-translation – perhaps even arranged in Our honor – and very nicely done too. Gradually, my violent all-over flush of complexion, worse even than the winds had brought, subsided. What polyphonies of transfused meanings were possible here! – though I fancied I caught some miscalculations of interval. But once one had the clue, the whole business fell into line. It was merely some bit of theory, qualitatively illustrated, as they could do so well here. It was a symbol-signal lesson. Of course. Color-count-read.

Again, what *politesse,* perhaps to the foreigner, perhaps only to the primitives on its own streets of Here – but all it did was make me feel homesick in a curiously compound way. Homesickness is of course to feel both Here and There and to feel bad about it, and since I was truant from both it is no wonder that mine was of a certain complexity. As is my wont, I tried to find a compound word for it. I was alone on a dark street, in a dark town, on a dark world – compared to mine. I was lone-billions away, and touchless. Voices coming nearer failed to disturb my grim reverie. I was Out of touch and To blame. That's where I was, and I had the name for my feeling. I was suffering from uniquity, which means to be alone and bad. The best cure for it is a bit of friendly conversation.

Round the corner came a flying wedge of it.

Remember that I was from a world without corners. To this day, I remember the exhilaration of it, my first brush, in a flare of voices and steaming mackintoshes, with a company of Youse. To shouts of "B'lloon!" I was pushed one way; with answering cries of "Blimp!" and "Where's its ruddy gondola?" I was pushed another. I saw nothing; because of some ancient danger response I hadn't known to be in me, all my pores had set closed. I gave myself up to the rocking motion with which I was being passed about, in what seemed to me a roughly circular path and an envelope of smell, as I was sent from spice-grubby being to being, and all this was not unpleasant — perhaps the tossing thrill that cat gives mouse is reciprocal. And though I knew deep within me that I ought to be up and away, each touch added to my weightfulness — is this the trap here? And my pores remained closed. I remember it all, that blind game of battledore and touch-me which showed me the weakness of sleep dreams as against waking ones. To evoke it all I have only to whisper the talisman: "Round the corner You came."

Suddenly there came a noise from the shop, and a lighter voice, one of them emerging. "Boys, boys! Stop that; you'll break Mrs. Porter's window." It was a voice nothing like my mentor's, who had as oval a voice as ever turned space into music, but it was certainly somewhere in the same category. "I've 'alf a mind," it said. It was as if a voice like Hers had been left out in the rain a bit. And alongside it, a smaller voice said, "Oo mums, whatever is it! Oo mums, is it an advert?"

I felt myself to be against the windowpane, blushing in my blind darkness for all words ending with that syllable. Whoever were the Boys, they had let me go. Then, to my surprise, the larger voice said, "Do b'lieve she's right, and is it ever *lovely!*"

These words, said so tenderly, warm-cooled me to a tremble. Whatever I was to them here, I was approved. I felt an internal moisture. The pores of my dark began to reopen. "Just with your pinkie now, love," the voice continued. "You boys stand back and give 'er a try. Ever so gently now, ducks. Turn it around, do, and we'll have a look at what it's selling."

As yet, I hadn't met up with your concept of sell-buy, our basic precept being: A One is a Has, or translated: I Have what I Am. But now, trembling, I felt for the first time a soft meeting of flesh and flesh, a meeting fully half of which is the shivering toward it. One stroke barely grazed me, the next tapped. And when I did not move, the next – pushed. Indescribable. As it left me and I sensed it returning, all I meant to do was to lean toward it. All within me, of past and future history, did that. And being familiar with the former, you'll have guessed what was bound to happen.

I overshot. Next stop, St. Ives.

And found myself, as was proper I suppose, in a bramble. I lay there prone again, and badly scratched too; curiously enough, this sensation was not as indescribable as the other. As I lay there, I found myself describing things in general here to an imaginary audience of Ones – posture was breeding again.

Wherever there is difference, I was saying to them, *there is a morality which keeps correcting people back to the mean. This is not a moral instruction but a fuzzical process, best described by telling you that wherever there is touching, there appear also to be brambles.* I put them onto the nature of the latter quite graphically – as who could do better at the moment? – but left out the other joy, finding indeed that all realistic memory of it had vanished. And I was careful to flatter my audience – all those Ones back There who were awaiting my message – by assuring them that although you on Here were constantly tailoring yourselves toward our Serene by every kind of cutthroat, cutpurse adjustment, you seemed unlikely ever to make it.

This was pure guesswork on my part, frankly devised to frighten off any large train of followers until I had personally done the discovering – any pioneer would feel the same. But how interesting to note that to ward them off, I chose what actually would have attracted them, just as it had me!

Judgment — which though called so at home, was really Law — was after all unknown to me, and from now on I was to wander ever deeper the sharded shores of its split infinitudes. No need to describe that to you. I was merely becoming more qualitative all the time.

Gradually, as the night wore on, sight was restored to me, though again localized at the end of me which seemed to wish to remain upright. Perhaps, I reflected, this was providential, so that if my form did develop according to whatever the native outline was here, it was intended that I be saved from the daily shock of seeing myself totally.

As I stood up, this time somewhat painfully, I saw by a tracking moon that I was on a hillock overlooking your sea. There is ever a comfort in scenery which has a kinship with home, and I stood for some time ravishing it. Though in mind no longer so serenely elliptical, I hoped to hang on to some of the old optimism. Even a cosmonaut may be excused if, in the midst of his adventure, while standing on the very brink of the Two-ness he has come for, he hankers suddenly after the non-pangs of a One. But I shall spare you the poem I mooned there. Books on Ours were not only mummified by now, but even during their brief apogee had been severely limited, compared to yours. In our progress, we'd had all the picture things first, you see, the moving ones first of all. What with having had universal picturacy for so long, books could only be a backward surprise. My poem was an antiquarian one, very full of "O's" as all Ours are, and much pasted with the photos that, not daring to feel itself above them, it could only hope to imitate. At home I should merely have dropped it into one of the poem-cans that are provided on all main avenues in front of every camera. But here, looking on your sea, I made bold to declaim it, moved by that sentiment which on Here must be almost the commonest — "It isn't a much, but it's *I*."

Then I fell silent, but remained there looking at that immensity on which the night could but clamber and roll. The sight of the night sea is too urgent for the traveler who has just arrived. (I see I have given you my poem after all.) In truth, after a while I became so dizzied by the need to look away that I didn't know what to do; a thought even came to me, from realms far deeper than posture, that I might even have to leave Here altogether. A One, whose vision is evenly distributed on a form cylindrically perfect, is of course a perpetual looker-on whose attention to the non-varying never ceases – and never thinks of itself as captive. But on a variegated planet, the discomfort of such a constant attention would be intolerable. Even with my vision retreated to the upper half of me, this was so. I don't know what I'd have done, hadn't it suddenly occurred to me – "I'll turn my back on it." And strangely enough this concept, to me of the purest novelty, did ease me sufficiently, though as yet I couldn't quite make use of it. For it must be plain to you that a One has neither front nor back.

Meanwhile, I solved the immediate dilemma by thinking up a project; I would hunt for a less thorny spot on which to lie down. On Ours, all already *is* projected – but by now I was getting used to these little pushes out of Nowhere which came to me as if from the collective identity of creatures I hadn't even met yet. What else is mutation? Turning round and round, as we tend to do, but at the andante pace which had been taught me, I observed that the hillock I was on was actually not far from a house which must have learned to withstand that view better than I could. The inanimate can – this is what they are. Between the house and my promontory, a gentler plateau grassied itself toward a grove of dark forms I took to be trees, pollarded like those to be seen from my window in Bucks – like those around the pergola. From the pang that this gave me, I had no wish to investigate further.

The moon had gone in, anyway. I laid myself down, too tired to care that I was now this kind of animal. That grass didn't burn me was no longer a marvel. *I had had all that I could bear*. And in this extremity, which We never reach, there came to me the possibility that the beings on Here, short of leaving it, must somehow of their own will close their pores and briefly have done with it. In the darkness, I cultivated my own nadir. And for the first time in history, a One of us fell asleep.

And in the dawn that woke me, I saw what I took to be Your totems. They appeared to cradle me, looking down. At home, great, perfected ellipses stand about everywhere, and smaller versions are not frowned on. All our statuary is of that public sort, by which means we replenish space with the idea of ourselves. You, however, who are always noodling so on the private, seem intent on replenishing yourselves *with* space. Such holes, such corners! I was in fact in a sculptor's garden.

I gazed from image to image, long and long, around a ring of figures of which some were blackish, some gray, all of them torturously curve-straight and empty-whole – all of them in a constant state of between. It seemed to me that the more I knew about you, from this extraordinary world which seemed to be strewn with your handiwork but for hours and acres empty of you yourselves, the less idea I had of how you really were. At home, a One is always Omnipresent, for reference. And yet it also seemed to me that once I had met You I would recognize you at once, as that image – retreat into variation though you might – which I had always known. You were, after all, my Ideal.

Just as we must be yours. Otherwise, how would I be here? And you, Some of you, perhaps very soon, or even already, over There. Once more I humbly went the round of the images, again seeing many marvelous assaults on the geometric, but search as I might, I saw none to bow down to, and this was the odder, since by very nature we haven't got such a concept — being unable. Meanwhile, at home, there might soon be rows of Yours, standing rapt in the public gardens, trying not to. These are the true interstellar thoughts. All the rest is machinery.

For, as I went, I passed from the outer awes of our mutual adventure to the inner ones. From some mental height far above any I had realistically traversed, I looked down on both our shuttlings and yours, and was afflicted with a tenderness for us both. This is called the cosmic emotion. We have it within Us always, really. If You had it too, which as yet I did not know, it would be the greatest cognate of all.

Unfortunately, in order for Us to go on living — as Ours are early instructed — the personal vision, alas, must take precedence. But this is smiled on, since, luckily for the general good, all our personal visions are of course the same. Now however, I was in one of your gardens, so mine had naturally more of me in it. And so did the vow I swore.

For a minute's vision, I saw our two worlds in the curve I was used to. Satellites from us are sent out on regular mission; I myself had once been one of those intently roving lanterns; at some time every a One must so serve. Meanwhile, astronauts from your side were fizzing everywhere among the orbital gardens. The present mission between you and us was somewhat different; only a small band of dissidents on either side had ever thought of it — but these had thought long. To the mutation of species, which takes so long here, we would apply our instantaneity, you meanwhile discarding that twoness which we, never having known any species but One, so crave. In the face of eternity, neither of us would be going either backward or forward. Change is progress; regress is change. Both of us wanted it.

And what I saw in my vision was that each of us, until it

met the other, had thought its passion to change was new to the universes; We to Us were the Highest; You to yourselves were the First. And standing for the moment between, I foresaw that once an exchange had been made, both would forget how things had been: Elsewhere. How could it be otherwise? For once we touched foreign atmosphere, adjustments would begin, gradually blurring our clear Outlines. So I swore to be such a cosmic messenger as must never have been before. I vowed to remember – and to record, for as long as nature allowed me – the journey between.

Mine would be no visitor's travelogue. Nor did I intend to be a social informer; those at home would get no satiric tour of your institutions from me. Mine would be a far more basic journal, in fact such an act of personal commitment as could be managed only by a One of no previous personal background whatever. I would make of my self-adventure such a book as had never been made before, so far as one knew.

For, in the history of how a One of Us tried to become an I of You, would not all the biologies reunite with all the philosophies, forevermore? The history of mutation is blind – but I would keep my eye-pores open; it is so slow that for eons it may seem to stand still – but I am constitutionally so quick that I appear to do the same! Had there ever been such a pilgrim before? For I, a *conscious* mutant, member of perhaps the first two species to attempt to perform such a feat under control – would record the ontological journey of myself. And since we record without your resort to popular mechanics, I would of course do this from within. In Our sense I would *be* the book, just as you, in your memories, are the books of yourselves. I would be – Oh arrogance eternal – what had never been anywhere. Mine would be the diary of a bio-naut.

And such were the muscular effects of my ecstasy, that this time I shot straight up. Ambition levitates, as you yourselves well know, and I was still enough of a One to feel the play of such forces literally. Oh how I soared and skylarked, careless of what dangerously premature legends I might be creating down below. All those weeks of incarceration, plus the recent trials by element, had stiffened me – or could it be that I was already developing that characteristic which, abounce on even the fleeciest cloud, would cause difficulty – skeletal bone? A moment's check, however, convinced me that I really was merely suffering from want of calisthenic. In that brief moment of doubt, however, I had lost altitude. And this was *mighty* convenient. I began truly to understand now how weightfulness was handled here, and that if I were careful to alternate between frictional doubts and positive uplifts, meanwhile keeping the sharpest lookout, I might yet get myself back to Bucks again. For a while I practiced, keeping myself well out to sea, but as the sun began to show itself, sped inland, in a few seconds caravanseraied all of Britain – at a height to observe only that in all that rousing farmland and cities there seemed to be no creatures of the dinosauric proportions I secretly still hoped for – and then at last saw what I was looking for. In broad sun, a glass house of that dimension makes quite an outcry.

I was now so fine on my points that I was able to hover over the pergola, which I saw now was roofed and enclosed at the center of its circular porch, and much larger than I had thought it. Dear ones, dear friends, I said to myself, then – in proper mixture: oh dear. And with scarcely a rude bump, I landed.

5. Up the Garden Path

NO ONE was about now. Everyone on Here seemed either to crowd together in a mash or hunt for his absolute own of waste-land, our simple formula never having occurred to them; from the moment a One of us emerges from the crater, an exact field of space, mathematically tailored to his mass, is his for life. I turned away, in some depletion, intending to go back to my furnished room to wait for whatever reprimand must certainly be due me. It even crossed my mind that they might leave me there forever, in permanent discard—and this notion was again one of those mortalities which were crowding in from every direction to guide *me*—for at home we do not have a system of waste people, either.

Just then, I heard sound coming from the pergola. At first, all I could hear was buzz indiscriminate; then it labeled itself: Voices. I was afraid to move lest I should once more overshoot myself, motion-emotion being so intense here. By a powerful exertion of my calm centers, I managed to incline only, if at an angle dangerously forward. They were two voices. And they were—yes! They were Marie, and my mentor. . . . Another equally strong intimation sent me almost horizontal. They were . . . *They*. The two voices belonged to the two figures whom I had so barely missed yesterday, at the start of my hectic truancy. Those two figures, then — a One of Us and a one of You — were my two mentors. My mentors were a One of Us, and a one of You. I began almost to have a notion of the balances here. In an access of wonder I crept nearer also. That much. Mark it for the narrative: a One, forwarding slowly from his accustomary flash-billions — *crept.*

"Security report a One sighted over Cornwall per'aps forty minute ago. Then they lose track."

She!

"Security! *In*deed!"

This was Marie all right, in her usual state of — state.

"Reported managing always to keep one jump ahead, they say."

I stretched a bit. I thought I guessed whom She was talking about.

"A jump ahead, mind you. And security, indeed. One can't wait to get back There. You have no idea."

"*Hélas,* that is all I do have. The idea."

"My dear girl. Just a manner of speaking. And One does feel for you." I had no trouble believing Marie spoke via some strings and a box. "That is, in so far as I can still feel." Indeed, her voice had changed for the worse, I thought.

"*Oui,* madame. But I think per'aps you mean to stay — 'as far as *One* can still feel.' "

That was a spark of my old lessons! But what was She after? What kind of lesson was this?

"Touchay," said Marie. "As yew'd say. One can't expect to be letter-perfect, so early on. But One was told Elsewhere that One was getting on swimmingly. When One was There."

A silence issued. Then there came such a sigh as I had never heard from Her before. "Elsewhere."

Her voice, no matter what it says, is still music.

"Dear me, my dear girl, dear me. You're having no luck at all, then?"

I did not at all take to Marie's use of this "dear."

"Far as One can see, you haven't changed a bit," she went on. "Not that One could, you've got yourself so wrapped up. Of course, One doesn't want to pry."

"Nothing – major. Sometime, I imagine I 'ave a certain sensation – such a *delicatesse* as I 'ave not – but it is not after all too *different* from what can be experience, *de temps en temps,* on *'ere.*"

"If you ask One, perhaps yew've had all too much of that sort of dellycatesse in your life. One wouldn't be surprised if those of us who do best in the end are the kind who never had too much taste for that sort of thing. Like Oneself."

There was a silence. Then my mentor spoke up in full voice, the richly round one. "So I 'ave 'eard."

There was a silence again. But this time it seemed to belong to Marie.

After a while, she did speak. "And how *is* – Harry?"

"According to the rules, madame, I 'ave not communicate." This came out so rapidly, it might have been in her other language.

"Sorry. One did have to ask. You must know Harry's been trying to get in touch with you here."

Again a pause. "I supposed – 'e would try. But you and I are agree before'and, no, that it cannot be 'elp if my disappearance from 'ere pattern itself on your. Or if 'e 'appen to 'ave two wives so advance? As the movement gain, it bound to 'appen, *de plus en plus* everywhere."

I was listening so hard that it seemed almost as if I were there in the room with them, though obviously here, outside it. Was *this* front- and backness?

"Agreed. But who'd have dreamed you'd experience so

much trouble that you'd have to turn back as you did, and hide here!"

"You 'ide 'ere for years, Marie. And I 'elp you."

"For which One prayed for you daily. And remember, One was on One's way up. One was an apprentice; indeed, it is alleged – the first. Those were the old days. And you are not an apprentice."

If Marie was the kind who was a first, I was not sure I wanted to be.

"I was recruit before the war. At Göttingen. The day after the first 'Itler putsch, I was recruit."

"Precisely. One of the longest in the business. Tops. Member of the very first group to make the decisions against – *them.* And afterwards, the pride of France. One gives you all your medals, dear girl. But then all the more, this – inconvenience. This strange delay. We never dreamed –"

"Nor I."

She was still saying "I." I liked that.

"Nor that Harry would be so – so persistent."

"'E is 'ere? 'E is *'ere?*"

This was a cry. It went through me. I could have wished that it had at least gone all the way – but it lodged. And during the very long silence which now ensued, I felt as if I were leaning on the sharp point of it. This was what came of dropping One's field. Then, as it ebbed – was *that* . . . pain? – I thought perhaps the two of them had gone. Why did I always –? Such things never mattered before.

But no. "Spare me," said Marie. "*If* you please. That pronoun."

"*Merde.*" It was only a mutter. "*Quelle vraie salope.*"

"*And* the French also. Now that One can compute it quite easily. In any case, the answer is no – not here. Gone up to London. To look for you, still after any trace of you. Then, we hope, to Harwell. One of our brightest recruits is working there. Just a beginning candidate. But she'll have several tricky little theses to show him which should help delay him awhile. But after that, unless we can think of something in time – we're for it. One good guess, and Harry could blow up the whole show. For, where do you suppose, my dear, that Harry plans going? A great tribute to you, of course. After that, Harry expects to chase across the water again – back to Hobbs."

But that was where I'd been told I was going! And surely I wasn't Harry. Or was I.

" 'Arry won't 'ave to guess," said my mentor.

"You can't mean –" Marie's voice was all vibration. "You couldn't have. Told him. Or is that why you're having such – Aha. And all those widow's veils of yours are just a –"

"You think I need to tell 'Arry? 'E guessed. An' 'e never say a word. No matter 'ow long I work in the tower, evenings. No matter what changes 'e find now and then in the observatory. 'E never. Long, long ago, 'e guess."

I began to suspect who – or what – Harry was. In general.

"But then it's all up with us," said Marie. "I knew we shouldn't have used women of – your stamp."

Mentor gave a little laugh. "*One* should never. But no, it's not all up with us. 'Arry won't speak."

"With everything that's at stake, Harry wouldn't speak? You've lost your mind, poor sweetie. Any of them would speak up – they would have to. Just as in the same boat, so would any of us."

"Not Harry."

She even pronounced the "h" I used to twit her about – *her* difficulty.

"But that's too extraordinary!" said Marie. "Or would be."

" 'E 'ad two wives very unusual, *non?* So why shouldn't 'e be such a man?"

So I was right. One of the straight ones. A he. A –

"Language!"

When Marie's voice went even higher, whose did it resemble?

"If you persist in breaking every safeguard," she went on, "how can One believe anything you say? Or be surprised that One-ness is still beyond you. Even if what you say could possibly be true, then – then why should Harry keep on *looking* for you?"

Ah, I thought I knew the answer to that, *dear* Marie. I waited for my mentor to give it: "Because I am She." As one so often does here, I had learned just a little more than they had taught me. But, however – and hence my tame Obedience to the next program, the dialogue to come – not quite enough. As so often before, I imagined her there, just through the wall, a being longitudinally oval like myself, and pinkish too, not all of the dinosaur size which I had hoped for the straight ones. More to my scale, and with a spot of difference, or, as things went here – two.

Then She gave a chuckle. First it was only a little purling from those strings of hers, the kind with which she had sometimes honored an error of mine. But then it was a ripple, and another ripple, and finally it buffeted the room – how did the wall withstand it? Answer: like many clever inanimates, it took the shock, but passed it on. To me, in this case.

"*Ohé, ohé. Alors. C'est ce que je* – So that's it! *Eh bien, eh bien,* at least I still have what it take to laugh!" And She was off again.

"So One observes. Or could do, if you hadn't got yourself up in – the way you have."

"*Arabique.* A chador. *Très chic, non?* And a good way to hide."

Another time, since hiding was of interest to me also, I should have pondered this further, but I was in the grip of more important questions. Questions here are terrible. No wonder we do not have them.

"Highly unnecessary, isn't it? Since Harry is gone." Marie's voice was rather elegant, or at least, slender. Like whose?

"To return, you say."

"Possibly. Meanwhile, what is it you find so funny?"

"A private joke, Marie."

"Still back here in personality, are you. I insist." Between a flute and a bumble. Very aristocratic, of course.

"I don't like to 'urt your feeling."

"One hasn't them, dear. Not any more."

"*Pardon.* Then you will not mind my asking . . . when *you* disappear, Marie—"

"Ye-es. One has forgotten all that now."

"*Oui. Pardon.* Then you will not remember . . . that when 'Arry come back from Egypt—"

"All that has faded, my dear girl. As you will find, if you are lucky enough to—to Ovolve."

Marie was putting on airs, as converts so often do.

"Ah, *oui.* But since I 'aven't been so lucky—you forgive I amuse myself—that 'Arry did never take the trouble to go looking, *hein,* for *you.*"

And Mentor gave a final low laugh which did her no credit. Natter, natter, how silly-silly these two could be together! But I shouldn't at all mind having a straight talk with this Harry. Who couldn't be the one I was being sent to next, since the very pronoun was distasteful. Who must be one of the other kind. Who must be one of those whom the two inside called *them.* A "he" was a Harry. And it was jolly likely that, if it were left to those two, I'd never get to meet any. I saw the likelihood that very definite limits were indeed to be put on my education here. Good God. Was it possible that enmity between the genders here was such that the two never met at all?

A host of questions assailed me. I managed to put down all but a few, meanwhile rather nervously watching a squirrel who regarded me with his bright wink but came no nearer. I shifted a bit so he should not mistake me for a boulder, and listened again for sounds from within, but heard nothing but that silence which is always so equivocal here. At home there is always a supportive hum, not to the point of music but very filling nevertheless.

I preoccupied myself meanwhile by imagining a sort of being to whom one might pose all sorts of questions it would be a waste to put to that pair behind the wall. Serious questions, to be propounded in some solemn but comfortable environ from which the brightly-stupid, the silly-unsafe, would be barred. Nothing personal. Serious questions being of course those to which both sides already knew the answers.

At the moment, I bent to consider those more foolish ones in which vitality so often secretes itself here. Why was it Marie's reedy voice annoyed me, for instance, with a resemblance I couldn't or wouldn't identify? And why it should so matter to me that, of the two in there, a One of Us and a one of You, and both my mentors, which . . . ?

An appendage voice suddenly interrupted what were perhaps all our meditations.

"Security reports a One returned to station Bucks and safely landed."

"There!" said my mentor's voice. "I'd better go see."

"Not until you've revealed just what's behind those veils, mind. Do be . . . just a weeny look now. . . ."

"Touch me at your peril, Marie!"

"Disgusting thought. We don't, you know. But you're the one who's in danger. Psychologically. Taking the veil is just what they used to do in the old days. Women who'd led a – full life."

"All the better you don't come any nearer."

"Temper, tem*per!* As for the rest of your ensemble – All those pockets. How do you ever expect to lose weightfulness?"

So they did have them.

"You're not supposed to be eating, reading or yearning. You're supposed to be in a quiet non-corner, talking hypotheses to your –" Here Marie gave a short cough.

"*Nombril.*"

I computed rapidly. Navel. Whatever that was.

"Yes, excuse One. You know our reticences. Well then. Whatever can you be keeping in those pockets?"

"Old enthusiasms."

I thought as much.

"Ah! . . . Mind letting me . . . have just a weeny –"

"*Loin d'ici! Non!*"

Another cough. "Just testing. Quite a good reaction, really. Touching departs first, one is told. But you still seem to be suffering from quite a lot of – poetry."

"*Pardon?*"

"For persons, places, that sort of thing. Any sort of irregular – surface attachment."

Converts. They never get things right.

"Ah, *oui*. Very – poetical. An' I suppose, they 'ave no word for –"

"No, no, no. No! Whatever you may be thinking of – no."

"*Fi donc.*" But this was merely a mutter, followed by a pause. "*Alors,* tell us Marie . . . touch goes first, you say. . . . '*Ow* does it go?"

"That's a good sign. You said 'tell *Us*.'"

"I mean the change. How does it start? The *change.*" Her voice was hoarse, but still hers.

"Why, amnesia takes over at once, of course. We wouldn't dare remember. Once leave for good and all, Here will disappear altogether."

For some, maybe.

"You never look-èd the *miroir*? During that time?"

"Doubt it. Never was one for mirrors, much."

"Ah. All that time – what you think of? What you were – for?"

"Not *for*," said Marie. "Wherever in the universe would that get you? *Against!*"

Sunday was Marie.

"Ah, I see," said my mentor. "I even . . . remember. And I – I am still too much – So. So that's it."

I stirred uneasily. At home, where talk was for dilettantes, the perfectly ovoid exchange of serenities made for conversation, yard after yard of it, reverberating, profound. Here, where talk was a necessity, there were only these *papier-mâché* detonations.

"How you can see anything, with all those clothes on!" said Marie.

"There's no doubt *you* look better, *chérie,* without the clothes you were in the 'abit of wearing. And now, if you excuse me –"

Chérie. She had called Marie by my name. Language on here could be gall to the taste, gender a confusion of the mind. Take the whole of their reversible world here; let it burn in its own nasty green glare. This *was* an emotion. I was almost sure of it.

"– but what's that noise?" Mentor said sharply.

"Squirrels on the skylight. They always."

It was I, of course, somewhat to my embarrassment. I could say that the darkly overcast wind blown up suddenly within me had blasted me up there. Or I could say that I had jumped. There was much more to alternatives than I had thought. Both were true.

I peered down. Through the heavily corrugated glass, I could perceive only areas of light and dark; as for myself, as yet I scarcely cast a shadow. In this climate, it was probable the natives themselves did little more. Again a sharp sense of home curved me. Likely nowhere on this planet were shadows cast with the perfect black lacquering of Ours, that teardrop planet whose shape is so devotedly matched by its inhabitants, and whose climate, standing ever at the semi-tropic, is of the texture of a melted-down smile. An undulating row of Us, our black alter egos peacocked out all at the same stance behind us, some with the shine of patent, others with the patina of velvet, is something to see. To watch this interplay is a spectator art with us, some preferring the brilliant contrasts of the siesta, others like myself inclining toward the curvetting nuances of dusk – both of these hours of course being artificial. And always even the whitest a One can at once be consoled for his pallor by looking behind him.

"No, don't go yet," said Marie, so close under me that for a moment I thought she addressed me, yet I could barely distinguish, below, the lump of stillness that must be she. Or the other: She. Which – was which? I said it to myself over and over like a pain. And this was strange, since, by logic and listening – the latter being a lot better than the former – I thought I knew. Hunger pains for the absolute are the natural consequence of a world having so many alternations, but it is the nature of the absolute itself here which is the more interesting. It is what one absolutely knows, but can never get confirmed.

But, if I could manage to break the skylight –

"Time for me to go and practice." She sounded so depressed that I was reminded of certain times at home when, having already dared to think of the possibility that One might get here, it still seemed beyond power or destiny. Yet, once a Here is penetrated by thoughts of elsewhere, it is never the same.

"Practice makes perfect," said Marie.

She cooed it, or was trying to, yet I seemed to know – the

way those of you who have absolute pitch can summon an "A" – the pure tonelessness that such a voice must have.

"But perhaps you need a rest, eh?" she added. "Maybe you ought to table the whole idea of changing. Now, now, don't get excited. Just for a little two-time."

"What is that!"

"A small paraphrase of one's own. When you do get to Us, as One is sure you eventually will, you'll find us rather good on paraphrases. It makes for fresh reverberation without auto-intoxication. And we really have no non-mathematical name for the time factor – a concept that can't exist anyway except in the presence of correlatives."

"You never were very good at math," observed Mentor.

"Where One and One is One," said Marie, "a One has no trouble."

She was either ignorant or giving herself airs. We do have a name for the time factor, indeed as single a name as it is possible to imagine. What would a world such as Ours call such a factor? We would and do call it: Once.

I repeated it to myself, and even giggled; as I bumbled between worlds, it was language which would help to keep me samely – I mean, sane. And Marie is a phony, with a telephony voice. Out on There, *Once* is certainly what We – what They – say. We. They.

And then, right here-there on my corrugated glass perch in the bright morning air of Bucks, I began to shiver and shake. I began to shiver as if this pleasant valleydom before me, on whose bright demesne I could even see, mute in the distance, a scattered few of that most comforting of creatures, the cow – were some hellhole at the outermost bounds of the universe perhaps, or even that worst of them, the one presumed to be outside those. I even fancied that my tremors were accompanied by a chattering sound which could never quite be caught of itself and stopped the minute I did, like the footsteps of those who had feet. Yet, so far I had nothing about my personage which should make even a whisper.

And then – suddenly I understood. Nothing much was ever understood on Here except suddenly, and I was even doing that, with a feeling like the rising of hair upon the integument – if one had hair. Consider how it all fitted together. Consider, for instance, how umbilingual I was about language, how ambivalvulent – how at one moment I despised it and at another it was my savior. I was *betwixt.* Regard how very little, or certainly less and less, I seemed to be living in the present; as I thought of it, it seemed to me that they scarcely had a present here at all. I was *between.* Consider a host of other things that an eavesdropper on a glass roof had ought not to do, being arsy-versy enough as it was. I was *betwixt and between.* We – They. And I saw quite clearly that, unless I could become more of a You, or less of a One, this circumstance might be the walking-floating hell-hole which would follow me everywhere.

"Besides, dear colleague, we have such a lovely mission for you. It will fit right in with your circumstances."

I gave a start, having forgotten that everybody has them. Circumstances.

"That's no squirrel out there, Marie."

"You're just nervous. Do let me explain."

"I am rather full up on mission already."

"But this one is *instead* of. Just for a – Just for now."

Hmm. This is the way their present always goes.

"Who believes in *now,* these days?" Mentor's voice was bitter. "What peasant?"

"Good-oh! That's the spirit. Nobody. Not since the Christian era, really, the better to think of the world to come. And what with you scientists helping – what one can't understand is how such a doctrinaire as you should be having such trouble at getting there."

How wrong she was, she would soon see. The answer was that a One does not believe in a now; a One has it. Our Now is *not* doctrinaire. One merely cannot assume it unless the whole race does, since it comes from a sameness in every circular pore and bath of living. And I could show her a race of Ones, in such a sempiternal Now –! Almost I yearned to be back there, sweet-sucking that circumambience.

"No wonder you succeed, Marie. You 'ave faith."

"One always has had."

"*Oui.* To be sure, not always in the same thing. But, chapel to cosmos – you 'ave it."

"From now on, it all *will* be the same. That's Our comfort."

So One thinks.

"I wish –" Mentor sighed.

"I know what, dear – that you were like me already."

Mentor gave a laugh. "No, it is more complicated. I wish . . . that I wished it."

And I wished that I could jump down through the skylight to tell her that such a mingy, gray pod of a convert – for surely this was the which and which of the pair I had seen – was no true model of Us. Oh to be sure, mutation the *other* way, toward You, was my mission and my yearning, but the truly large spirit can honor its beginnings, as you yourselves honor the gills and auricles which fathered your breathing, the unicellular yolks which only latterly became your hearts. And I wished she might see a line of Us, serene as barques born all of the same sailmaker, acurve on the evening at the gilded hour when the refractions of dust so bend the energies of light that for a moment we are visible – we are even leviathan.

"Keep looking, dear, and no doubt it will occur."

Had We really ever been so – like this a One? The vanity of an elliptic being is delicately elongated; it seemed to me that Marie's bordered on the fatly circular.

"I am."

Ah, Mentor. Look at *me*.

And in after-moments, I have sometimes wondered whether that might have been the one in which her own flashly education began.

"That's no squirrel up there," she said.

Beneath me, I could see the vague bundle which was Marie move closer to the other darker one. "Could it –" That voice couldn't whisper. "– could it be – Harry!"

"Harry?" Her voice could make arcs. "Harry would come straight in."

Then I was not after all as straight as I should be.

"Besides, he's afraid of heights."

Even in Harrys, then, there was room for flaw. If I could be a –! I would take on all the tribulations I deeply foresaw here: all the corporeal trials of the spirit, the dangers and bloods of a being which in its privacy retreats, a small, classic *anima* brooding upon its own waters, but when abroad even a landscape of the quietest, non-ravening trees – is still animal. If I could but choose to be that half here which –

"You're so concrete, dear, even in misery. Not very womanly of you, I must say."

"*Au contraire.*"

"Oneself is neuter, of course; I mean neutral."

"Of course. I always 'ad in mind that you were."

"Whereas One used to fancy, in fact, that you were just a teeny bit –"

"You don't need to come any closer to tell me."

I fancied I could see the gray blob stealing nearer the dark. It was maddening. Then I remembered that sight had been concentrating in the upper half of me. To aid it, I first leaned forward, then lay down – yes, horizontal! – then applied that part of me to the wavy corrugations on which I stood, but these remained adamant, stubbornly loyal — except for one crack of irritation. Fending off a squirrel, I remained as I was. As far as I could make out, the dark blob was standing its ground.

"— just an eeny-we-eeny —"

"Bug off!"

"Language!" shrieked Marie, but from what I could see — the sun at high now aiding me — she came no nearer.

At that instant the sun must have come altogether out of the clouds here, ennobling the substance on which I lay to defend its owners royally against me, with flashes that went through me as if I were a scabbard. At some later date, I might brood on the curious interaction here between climate and inanimates — almost an alliance against blood-creatures, rather like that of servants who in reality are masters — but now I was held by what was going on below. Intervals for brooding versus happening are never purely regulated here, our peacefully successive periods of the same being unheard of; the line of demarcation is not even kept.

And now again, I saw a suddenly. The dark figure began moving. It was speaking as it was moving, and it was moving toward the gray. "*Pax,* Marie, eh?" it said. "I beg of you. *Je vous en prie. Pax.*"

Was this qualitative? Was *this* feeling? Or, the mixtures here being so mixed —? Oh, the new world! The dark was after all moving toward the gray.

"Language helps to keep me sane, Marie."

So that was where I had picked up this sentiment.

"Or did do. While we 'ad our pupil."

I trembled so that on the roof the very pattern of the sun itself — of a *star* — was dispersed, altered by my small but stubborn body. At home, all our aim is to order it otherwise — that the force of the universe may pass through us without change. She and I — and all the little band of us and you — are meteors whose paths intersect at equilibrium: *once-now* — then must soar onward into opposing nights. As she had forewarned me, the generations on Here do this also, in an equilibrium that never rests. While, on Ours, as I had cautioned her, all generations are created equal in dower, and throughout their tenure remain so — rising from the crater and returning there in perfect quadrille.

A sadness interfuses each world. Choose.

I trembled that I was even thinking such thoughts. On Here, even the very *facts* are never still. How then, when nothing waits, can meditation be revered?

Meanwhile, below me those voices went on a-murmuring; talk might sanify, but the converse of these two was circular enough to push even a nonconformist out of his Opinion — never had I seen so many questions permitted to exist without answers.

I arranged them before me as best I was able.

What was the new mission?

What was hidden there behind her black veils, whose somber shadow even the faithful roof above her could not take upon itself to hide?

And, to me the subtlest, what did Marie fancy was there? For, just as Marie still had much more of the old planet about her than she would admit to, I too still had a good deal of instantaneity about me. And one a thing I had learned quicker than light — though like the light here, it kept leaving me and returning. The shape of the questions here tells much more than the answers.

But a minute later, as that low, passionate monologue resolved itself on my hearing like drops of fire that burst each into its own picture, I almost wished myself if not elsewhere at least away, out of eavesdropping, perhaps on that green pleasance where, only a mile away but as if on another orbit, cows were to be seen munching in their own mirage. Sooner or later on this planet, everyone wishes himself a cow.

For, as She spoke I had never heard such a voicing of the single before, of what it meant to be, among many, a *one*. Yes, once, in my first dizzying gulp of print here: O dark dark dark. But that had been a blind dark brought to general majesty. What I was hearing now was the shriek of the particular, going toward darkness. Or toward the pale, non-particular of There.

In brief – for I can scarcely bear to repeat all of it – She stated that the trouble had all begun with my own lessons. While she was so carefully arranging for me my affirmations of Here, she had begun to grow doubts about There. This is always a danger, I surmised, with alternatives; too big a bagful of either, and one pokes a hole to let in the other. For as she inventoried the characteristics of this world for me, she had begun to make a ring-around-a-rosary for them for herself.

"After forty years pointed toward elsewhere, what could it matter, Marie, this little exercise in farewell!"

Then had come the day when she and I had made our *au revoir,* the day when I had learned to say "I." It was just then that she too had had a suddenly. It had come upon her that the words themselves, all those jewel cases which she had been airing for me, would no longer be needed by her, that not only they but all their contents – which now sparkled so green – would soon by her choice be over and gone for her forever.

"– and then, ah then I find myself in such a bramble."

Bramble!

"Everything I look at, Marie; it touch me. And everything what I touch; it *look* at me."

Yes, that's the bramble, all right.

One after the other she described them, these blandishments. Little pictures flitted past me, small images struck as if with one molten drop of that organ which, as they tell it, beats like a brazen forge within them, magic unto itself in the center of their wilderness. What scenery they have within them, what landscape!

I could spare her those cherished sunsets, rather pale to me after such sun carillons as I had passed on my way Here, though I had begun to understand that delirium for the daily which can clang upon us once we know it is going – or it is gone. Her plaint about the plant-in-the-window left me cool also; I have already declared myself on plants; since they will outnumber us all there is no need to mourn. On the contrary, and though I might marvel politely here at grass which did not burn one, I would let it go at that, knowing what it still can do, left to its own.

But most of her apostrophes were to the smaller domestica, some so insignificant that they fell through the screen of my computation altogether unidentified. In the span of one day, according to her account, she had wept equally and uncontrollably both over memorabilia of the past and objects testimonial to such a present as can be caught here – from an ancient pumice stone, a piece of volcanic lava which under the strange inequity here had scraped her heel in the bath since her girlhood, to the patch of trillium on the way through the woods to the tower where all her scientific efforts were conducted – to the stockpot on the stove. This last, on whose to-and-fro, from organ to organ as it were, she rather dwelled on, did rather ticklishly affect me. But taken altogether, what –

"Sentiment!" said Marie.

Fool, semi-demi convertedly quavering fool! No! What *disorder!* – from which comes all their danger. Their tolerance for the inanimate here – on whose sneakiness we keep forever vigilant – is past believing. Whatever of it they do not positively venerate, or worse yet, even help to proliferate, they let run incontinently free, eventually to rise, mountains of it and they knew not why, in their own dreams. Enmity –

as we already knew from certain faint tintinnabulations of our instruments – they keep for among themselves.

"Yes, sentiment," said my mentor in her deepest voice yet. "Softens the tissues. But hardens the memory."

"How low your voice has got!" Marie tittered. "Whereas mine . . . that is, One's –"

Good God. No wonder I knew that pitch pipe of hers, its tinny "A." It was also mine.

"You never did weep, Marie?" she meanwhile was saying. "During all that time?"

"You know quite well how busy one was, collating all that inform – all very well for you scientists, but some one has to org –"

"– and someone 'ave to 'ave money."

"– ye-es. That's a thing One has rather missed, on There. We do gamble of course, but only with the oddest curved little counters, designed to slip away of themselves as fast as accumulated. One does wonder if it wouldn't be possible somehow to *immobilize* –"

Up there on my perch, I began to laugh in the very special way we do, of which even the so sensitive roof beneath me would not be aware. No, We may not feel, per se, and we may have but one carefully constructed climate, status-quo'd to such fine tolerances of the same as your engineers would not conceive. But we have our outlets, arrived at after such implosions and gravitational collapses of which all but the most trusted members of our steadied universe remain unaware. Miles out to star you can hear us in the laughing season. And even off-season one is soothed by the characteristic hum-tune of a planet always at a cool, cerebral bubble – the smooth, general laughter of the only very slightly counterfeit sublime.

Such a planet can take care of itself.

Indeed, I shouldn't be surprised if, *ententes cordiales* to the contrary, emigration should after all take place only *One* way.

"—and remember, Marie, you'd so much sympathetic company, right up to the time you took to your groove. I would have found it *difficile* to explain to 'Arry—why all these international ladies so interest to walk to the old icehouse by the lake. 'An 'ardy lot,' was all 'e ever say. 'An 'ardy lot you physic-culturists.' "

Fuzz fizz. I must do better with my vowels.

"Grenadiers in skirts, most of your lot," said Marie. "Spies, I shouldn't wonder. One's most telling evenings were spent alone, with what I seem to remember was a good book. Can't quite recall its name. But it was a good one."

"*The* good one, Marie. I try it last evening. There."

From the thud, it must have been a book from a very large pocket.

"One hopes it helped, dear."

"Very settling," said Mentor. "To the settled."

"Ah?"

"But not if one hopes for an Elsewhere less like here."

"Fancy. What could One have been thinking!"

"And certainly not if one hopes for one truly—original."

Uh-oh. O-nathema. No wonder there's trouble. But in the end She might do better than Marie, who will get only so far. She may be an obsessive of those higher orders which are often less obvious. She can laugh. And she has rather a strong sense of O.

"Is that a shadow up there?" said Marie nervously. "A rather large one?"

"Mebbee."

It melted me. Maybe she knows I'm here, I thought. Maybe is such a melting word.

"They're let run so free here," Marie said crankily. "On There, the shadows are so beautifully *organized.*"

She'll learn not to use *that* word.

"Marie . . ." She spoke now in the hoarsest whisper. "Marie, I lie to you. Last night, in the tower, I did empty out some of the pockets. And I weep; it is true. At the bottoms when I find 'ere a lorgnette, there a few 'airpins — I weep for what I am leaving, yes I weep. But in the end I go back to the telescope. For perspective, you need an atmosphere that warps; in the telescope, I tell myself, where there is only distance, maybe I shall be safe. 'Arry often say it, even on Palomar what is a telescope but a circle drawn around doubt?"

"Not on Ours," Marie said eagerly. "Ours isn't circular; Ours is ellip —"

Good God, let not these two get into philosophy.

"I know, I know. But let me demonstrate. The statement I just made, Marie — is that theory or heresy, in your part of the universe? Choose!"

I hoped Marie would give it to her proper. Here-sy is of course a statement with too much Here in it — to Us. For you, any statement is a the-ory which has too many holes of There. A statement is wherever a One or a You is standing.

"O," said Marie. "On the One hand . . . On the One Other Hand . . . O."

"You see! And you haven't even got any hands."

Despite which, the hammer and tongs atmosphere being what it seemed here, the odds were that *I* would soon develop them!

"Forty years in the movement," said Marie. "And all gone to — While you were at your rosaries, what happened to your catechism?"

"I remember. I *still* remember!"

"Repeat it then."

"Birth: bleed. Child: starve. Men: kill. Death: —"

"There!" cried Marie. "Could anything be more convincing? One sees *that* alternative. As against all the horrows of two-ness —"

"You interrupted me," said Mentor quietly. In the silence, she cleared her throat. "Death: is."

"Not on Ours," said Marie eagerly. "We simply —"

"Let me interrupt *you.* Lacking the adhesives of personality, or the sharps and flats of suffering, you simply —"

"Elide!"

They both said it at once. Even the roof beneath me gave a small echo, and in its glass I saw a small vein develop, in sympathy perhaps with the sudden weight even I was feeling. Death?

"And I'm not sure —" said She very slowly. "I can't make up my mind. Do I really want to avoid the one answer to which there is no question?"

Curved. Beyond all doubt — curved.

"Dear girl, what are you going to *do?*" This time Marie did manage a whisper. "All that black crepe! You're not planning to commit . . . !"

"La, la, no, that package will keep. But thank you, Marie — did I 'ear per'aps ever so small . . . a *tendresse, pas pour moi* . . . but for *'ere,* per'aps a small feeling?"

Under me, both bundles moved inward, to a sound that seemed no more than a lisp of the cells. "A little."

"*Alors,* Marie . . . listen. Last night, I do my hypothesis, *thèse, hypothèse;* it seem to me I am doing this all my life. Only now, does it seem odd that I am doing it in order to get to a place where I shall never be able to do it again. To concentrate, this time I look at 'Arry's new star object, the brightest of nine, and my favorite —"

"Favorite! You are still —"

"Yes, I admit it. Personality to the end! Listen about this 3C-273, Marie. It is the nearest of the far ones. It is so far that what I was seeing last night 'appen before the birth of the solar system, yet it make so much brilliance that any amateur can pick it up in his speculum — And listen, Marie, this vary rhythmically, in thirteen-year cycles. Maybe the proper star for a woman? Hmmm?"

"You're not thinking of – *still!*"

She gave a laugh alarmingly like one of ours. "'Ow nice to see that you can still not think – whatever you're not thinking of. No . . . but –" She broke off. "Honest to God, what the matter with me? When I think of what we 'ave gone and done, the secondary sex, the unprofessional one – I 'ave such 'ot flashes of adventure. And then suddenly . . . an icicle grow in my throat, and stick there. I feel such a laugh coming on, of such frivol as I 'ave never –" She stopped short. "I think to myself, change-of-life, eh? Who should be surprise we are the ones to think of it?" Her voice bubbled. Then there came from her such a laugh, higher than Marie's, not as supersonic as that chorus one hears in the season, but still cast to the all but disappearing pitch of it – the cool, aleatoric music of all answers which have no death in them to disturb us.

How did I know this? Where was I going, or coming? I looked down at myself, no discoverable change. Then I noticed that, beneath me, the solicitous crack had widened. I had forgotten about that subtle traitor, the inanimate – that counterspy, that informer. But now, within a small circumference around what was going on below, I could *see*.

They were just down under – the gray figure and the black. Seeing often adds very little to the believing here – at least to a vision accustomed to rotating at the center of a cyclorama which in turn intersects Others of the same, all this united perspective – aerial, isometric and linear – of course operating as usual, as One.

But I could discern that one of the figures was standing relatively still, and one – though with a movement visible only to those trained to receive the perpetual molecular shimmer, was very slightly dancing. Difficult as it is to stand rock-still – there is no better word on this planet – the black figure was doing it. It is even possible that to a human I the figure of Marie may have been invisible. These dialogues are not unknown here.

"Listen –" said the dark figure again, who of course might not know that the listening attention of a One, cocked forever at the angle of the gyroscope, spins eternal. "Listen, Marie, what you see when you look the night sky?" And it spoke in two voices now, both the piping and the soft, the dark and the cool, like some oracle intent on ringing all the changes possible between One and Two, but unaware, of course – a sudden gust of my own laughter shook me – that above it, there peered the outsider, who was – I felt a slight flesh change. Could mutation come even while laughing? The outsider who was . . . I was. I was Three.

"I tell you what 'Arry see," She said.

Three-ness is nothing compared to the passage from Oneness to Two-ness – a mere sophistication. I listened to her description of what a Harry saw – ah, the dears that these beings were, at least in their spare time! I watched him stumble out among the higher-speed environments to potter with his basic fizzical alphabets every evening: "*No,*" he said to himself, "matter could not be totally annihilated into energy; *yes,* the universe exploded *bang* into being thirteen billion years ago and is continuously expanding; *no,* it had no beginning, and, *steady there!,* will endure forever" – and I saw him fall like an apple, every generation of him, on the heads of those beneath.

Meanwhile, the black veils did not tremble, but from within the demand was repeated, not waiting for a reply. "I tell you what I see," it said.

She did not see the horses of Apollo up there, not any more than the Harrys did; the romantic was no longer her line. But so bright was her description, charged with the scorn of non-seeing, I fancied I saw that classic heaven. What strength she had garnered, from not being merely *other* but always the *opposite!* Beneath me, she unrolled such a vast panorama of all the prospects she had never had, that I altogether forgot the staid picture to be seen through the crack below. This is your general power, to extend yourselves in a way we can never, by the airiest hazard and opine. And by that reverse grace which acts in all universes in some way, it is a power which comes to you by very virtue of not having a fixed Now.

So she described—with what she *said* was bitterness—the long range of circumstances she had never been fully allowed, had meanwhile greatly despised, and now hoped to leave behind her, forevermore. What experiences, what illimitable Urals of them, their peaks bloodstained or rainbowed, she cast behind her—and ahead of me! (And what a strange "forever" they had here, which lacking even a moment's tranquility must attach itself at once, greedy-greedy, to a "more.")

I saw holocausts, hurricanes, tornadoes, some of which she *had* seen; despite her gender she had not been wholly underprivileged. I heard the plaint of children, not all of whom were hers, but all of whose cries were on her conscience—and dimly osmosed toward me, I thought I began to compute what was a child. The notion of "kill," even within the species, I have never had trouble with (it being what we are in absolute reversal of, as we are from that other more melting opposite which we are forbidden to name). For, like you, we know from the crater what is forbidden us—in the way that all beings perhaps know the forces that have produced their particular shape.

As for birth, barely mentioning it other than as the circumstance for which her kind was both anointed and chained, she passed it by as no mystery to *her* — just as the eye of a needle might neatly engulf a camel, meanwhile convincing itself that the camel had swallowed it. Birth by any biological means — viviparous, oviparous, animalcular, virginal — is of course what we laugh at, in the season.

I understood of course what was happening; She in turn was having *her* vision. She too had a certain fidelity toward her origins. As for death, that question-answer she had so touted, I couldn't make out whether she willingly left it behind — until I reminded myself that, just as my vision had had some of You in it, so would Ours have a place in hers.

Matter of fact, being rather personally on Here myself, I wondered, a little hoped, whether among the great grab bag of things she saw to enumerate, there mightn't be a Me in it — but she merely finished with a sigh as great, and as if politely, once more said, "What do *you* see . . . Marie?"

I knew what I saw at that moment, in our joint sky. I saw that home planet astride the reaches which a One might yet return to, that long teardrop of grace from which, once wholly a You, I should be barred.

"What do you see in the night sky?"

And Marie finally answered her, with that single word which even on Here has its dignity. "We."

But, in the brusque way events kick up their heels at eternity here, I was given no time to reflect on it. A happening was indeed interrupting me. For, to my horrow, I observed that the crack in the roof was widening, although, clever criminal that it was, it was managing this all but imperceptibly.

And now I must confess to a naïveté so utter that a You may laugh at it seasonably all the year round. I had no idea that the *mise en scène* was so complex here. When a One of Us has a happening, everyone nearby turns to face him, affording just the mild degree of simultaneity which will be comfortable; we are an attentive race for whom it would be unthinkable that a member of it need step over any of the lintels of life quite alone. All the really important steps of life are in full quadrille. This being so, advice, since never needed, is never given, affording us a sweetly open laissez-faire in place of the fierce huddle of privacy for which you must be forever on guard. But the shocking simultaneity with which events public or private were permitted to engulf people here would never occur to us. The possibility that, within the same quarter-mile moment of duration — or frequently much less, what with the cram and stretch of your allotments here — people might drown at sea, strut the sidewalks, dice away their patrimony, feast, strangulate in hospital, or simply be gazing sun-focused at a tablecloth, had never before crossed my mind — much less that all over your planet, perhaps your universe, people went on stewing in the same sort of broth.

My mind! My cleanly conceptual mind, across whose pure plain there had never stalked more than one neat aberration — must I not mourn forever that calm savannah, that zoological silence! Into which slid Two-ness, the snake. What dazed me most was that even the ways of comprehending the variable world branched off as one approached. No sooner had I resigned myself to the dangers which ran alongside the admissable joys of a world where *objects* were let be unbridled, than I was confounded with the appalling disorder of its *events*. Up from that melee, a couple of numb thoughts in counterweight promptly immobilized me: *We* — have no accidents. *They* — take no responsibility.

So, meanwhile I sat on my crack. And below it, though this couldn't go on forever, those two — tow, two, *two* — went right on talking. Would it be the same for two a Harrys? I looked down at the ground. No, as yet I wasn't afraid of heights. But it seemed probable that to stay where I was might be a part of my gravitational training — especially where the listening was so instructive. So, lying as flat as a being so curved could, and careful not to make any movement which might further inflame the treacherous substance I was lying on — I remained.

And what I now saw was — my first appendage. Ah, it is a one thing to sneer at your *mechanical* ways of extending yourselves — but this — ! Conceive of the occasion! After such passage of time immemorial as could not be mathematically figured even by a Schlovsky-Schmidt, a Wheeler-Oppenheimer, not even if one added to these the services of a Heisenberg-Hoyle plus even this year's most brilliant qualifier for the Cambridge tripos — after all that time, a One, of the most illustrious, unprofaned incestry, saw his first violation of the sacred outline. And it was no longer a perversion. It wasn't even a dream.

I knew what the appendage was of course, or thought I did, via that ever-resourceful book of animal plates, plus — though no squirrel was around for me to check on — certain fugitive memories of the small fauna which had patrolled before my glass. And though I was a bit middled about the number of such proper to creatures here — yes, it was what I thought; of course it was!

Slowly it exposed itself, white against its black draperies, while I reddened — really now, must it! Coyly, it seemed to linger a moment, weaving slightly against the figure of the being to whom it belonged. Yes, it was graceful. It was also in a way repellent. The sight of what one has always been forbidden is always a little sinister — and its performance, alas, inordinately clever. Finally — it extended itself; oh what a length, after all!

Finally, its owner spoke. "*Au 'voir,* Marie. Shake!"

Then, in the usual two-ly, which I ought to have been

used to by now, I saw another oddity. Marie's color did not change a whit, unlike mine. She was after all going the *other* way; ships that pass! But in that rather stout gray outline of hers, whose texture, tell the truth, was still far short of transubstantiation, what did I see – just above the median horizontal and parallel with that waiting appendage – but a dent, a puckering as of a swift intake, a failure of arc that strove at once to repair its own extension, but for a quivering moment was unable. I watched in fascination – and of course, a vestigial sense of duty-watch. Then it was gone, leaving her form as perfectly inflated as before – and me gazing down on my own. Except for color, I was – as was. But the crack was now smiling to the width of an inch. I quickly looked away.

"Think yerself pretty clever, eh, yer nasty bit of – ? Wotcher trying to do, give Us a setback!"

Uh-oh. At this from Marie, my computer section, which has always had a weakness for dialect, positively chattered away at me – seems it had suddenly had revealed to it that Marie's origins were not all she had pretended them to be. It went on to point out to me that neither were my mentor's – or at least rather obscure, certainly not native to this region. And reaching a grand point of insolence, it asked itself, and covertly me, whether the fact mightn't be that, by and large, most dissidents *anywhere* were either foreigners – or *runts*. In a final burst of ambition, it rattled off a request that I pose this question to it directly, promising me in return an answer which would *not* be by and large.

Somewhat shaken, I turned off the connect. Since we do these things *in* our Own person, the relation between a One and his computer section is not separate, but neither is it equal. If this went on, I should have to get rid of it, maybe even let it go off on its own. Ever since coming here it had been getting above itself, and this despite a rapid downgrade in performance – witness its slapshod job of work on my vowels. Machines tend to do this on Here. Something in the atmosphere.

"I apologize, Marie."

No matter what rude hints from mechanical snobs, here was a lady – a discrimination perhaps outside their realm now, and new to me myself. Her appendage, by the way, was still extended, indeed the only part of her to be seen, she being almost directly beneath me. And by now, this appendage seemed to me – what with that geometric progression of appetites which is here called "getting used to" – it even looked to me now rather sinuously beautiful. I found myself almost shy of learning its name. But since I couldn't go on calling it an appendage forever, and it was certainly not an umbrella, I turned on the comput-put again, which thereupon snorted, "HAND!" omitting the usual accessory data, and – with what untold effects on my progress, not all of them bad, I daresay – went out of order for the whole afternoon. I know better of course. Only fools are onthropomorphic about machines. But, since I have been here, I find that though I like many of them very much, I can't tell one from the other. Something in the atmosphere.

Hand. A hand. *A hand.* I watched it closely, in order to detect its function, whereupon it withdrew, perhaps to spare my sensibilities. With my usual stingy ideas about the differentiation here, I was of course assuming that its function was limited to – one.

"Sorry, *ma vieille,* I couldn't 'elp – but is that material you're in – really protoplasm. May I touch?"

Separatism already. Their egos are enviably powerful.

"You saw the prospectus; we all did." Marie meanwhile retreated past my angle of vision. "And kindly stop *gendering* me. These Outlooks have their Onfluences. Wiser if you gave up French altogether."

Really, what a pill. I scarcely dared look down now – the split in the roof had stretched to a smirk.

"Okay, bebbee."

"Take that word . . . away. And no, you can't touch, thanks to One-ness. One's got a sort of all-over electrical vest takes care of that. Very comfy, too."

"You could turn it off."

"Ha-ha to you, ducky. It's forbidden. Besides, One can't."

Which is the great contrast between our forbiddens, and yours.

"There's always a loophole," said She, walking toward Marie.

And a one – and a One – to see through it.

Maybe she was looking for it now, for I could no longer see either of them. What they were in must be a corner. O philosophy. If I fell, would it be round a corner I came?

"Marie . . . " came from below. "Marie . . . look up . . . do you see what I see? Straight up!"

That lovely adverbative. I was enchanted.

"Hah. No yer don't. You'll not get One to take one's Observo off you till you're safely away."

"*Hélas.* That may take quite a time."

And now, were we all back where we started? – which we would be, at home, of course. Those two were. But the crack grinned up at me, reminding me that I was a three.

"We have Time," said Marie. "For once and same. No more trickles."

"Marie . . . listen. Very beautiful of course, all that We-ing. But mebbee for me – you think possible I 'ave pick the *wrong* elsewhere? For you, fine, but for me, mebbee I would be better off in one where – "

Where there were no pronouns at all? But that's the beyond!

Marie cut in quickly. "You'll feel better, when you get to – America."

"America!"

America!

There was more to corners than I thought. More things than You came round them.

"But that's an ordinary elsewhere, Marie! It's on the planet!"

Everywhere is an elsewhere to somebody. When less precariously situated, one might point out to them that I, formerly of Ours, was *here*. As for America, since we were both going there, mightn't it be a sort of way-stop for all those whose pronouns were in transit?

"O . . . is it? One's been away . . . Anyway, it's Orders."

"Good God, Marie," said my mentor. "I hope you girls 'aven't fuck things up altogether."

I flipped the connect. Not a sound. Then an agitated one, "Turn me *off!*"

"Everything is on Order," said Marie. "Except your lack of progress. Luckily We can make use of it."

"But I am suppose to be going *Out! Off!*"

"Later on," said Marie. "That is . . . later on-on. Pres-presently, you're to stay as you are-are."

Pedagogue.

"And what I am suppose to do there?"

"You're to – help us with the migration. You'll be right in the center of things, don't worry. In fact it's called the Center."

"And will *you* be there? The way *you* are."

"Jolly right, dear. But One couldn't do what you – ." Here Marie rather choked. "You're to – head off Harry."

There walked before us then the greatest silence yet; in fact, it was a silence that was positively running, in which, both parties below, maneuvering away from it, came to a stop directly under party a three.

"As I – am, Marie?"

"Right you are."

". . . Then, I 'ave to inform you –"

Here a sound unclassifiable. Or no. If a person could have a – If in a person there could suddenly *be* a crack –

"– I am not . . . as I was."

The silence, which had finally run out of hearing, came back.

"O," said Marie. "One had an Omen. All along One had an – One does hope there hasn't been a rather dreadful –"

"Mistake? That I cawn' say. But one look at me would certainly tip the tumble to 'Arry."

"O O O," said Marie, and I caught myself just in time, at the cool, pushbottom signal which turns all on groove onstantly toward One-All. "One needs Others. OOOO." A four-digit alarm was doing better than expected; in fact it was well on the way Out. But she relapsed, crying out, "One can't do it alone." Ul-loawoun is what she really said. They mix-multiply their vowels like equations here.

"Per'aps it shoulden' be done alone," said my mentor. "Migration. Per'aps it should never." Why then so invigorated her voice? "Affinities can be dangerous."

"Have no fears on that score," said Marie. "The next lot is coming in perfect quadrille."

"Nevertheless!" What joy in her voice. Joy is a statement put like a question, but only for the sheer pleasure of it. I recognized this without computation. "– nevertheless, 'istory 'ave to 'ave its 'eroines, eh Marie?"

"Not where One is concerned," said Marie abjectly. "Not without drillection."

"Then, look *UP!*" my mentor cried without warning, as if on a countersignal. "Look at the sky, the skylight! *Look at our pupil.* Our *Hero!* Look at – HIM!"

The crack yawned obediently. I saw her appendage waving.

And then ———— O. How does one ever render the *mise en scène* here? By what dots . . . . or symbols . . . + — x ÷ = × — + x ÷ . . . by what loci, foci, axis transverse or conjugate can one describe and total it?

O Appolonius of Perga, who first named Our curve, O Great Geometer! How shall I render a what-where-who-how which is always all happening all at the same different ONCE!

O pi in the sky ——————————!

OOOOOOOOOOOOOOOOOOOOOOOOOOOOOOO

I remember. That's how.

All four of us spoke at once. And here is how it was:

MARIE: was the loudest. "O-nathema! Spy in the sky! And you, you traitoress – who have turned both your pupil and yourself into a –"

SHE, MENTOR: was waving and calling, and heroically pronouncing all her aitches.

I: crouched over the abyss. I crouched, yet I felt on *tiptoe.* I felt such a melting feeling, and the computer said never a word. Ah you dears, you dears, I said to myself, and the abyss echoed my fears. "Hypnosis never," I said; "hypothesis forever." How far I had come! For of all three was I not the most various? Finally, crying aloud the name of Ours, I – did I jump? Was I pushed?

And here we all come round again.

MENTOR: "*Allons, enfants de la pa-atrie-e . . .*"
MARIE: "– a MAN!"

I fell.

The crack said: CRACK.

6. Off

LET me now, in gentler perspective and more according to *your* unities, describe the state of our company, as of then.

In falling, I had grazed my teacher, not to the injury of either of us, but dislodging those veils which covered the top of her. My first attention, however, was directed toward Marie, who was still discharging vituperation in a steady, mewling outrage.

"Stop!" I said – and this was cruel of me, for We never quite do, of course; motionless as we may seem to you, we are always a trifle on the tremolo. "Turn off your Observo." This can be done only on command. "And go spin in a – in a corner." How far had I come indeed!

Yet when I tried to look straight at my mentor, I was so abashed that I altogether failed. Slowly, a swelling of my pores – brought on by my fall – abated; technically, I could see, but between Her and me a somatic mist still prevailed. It had nothing to do with the bodily shames to either of our worlds germane. And all my questions, now answered, had vanished like itches scratched. Actually, a one of these remained but I had forgotten it; if behind those veils some change in the being there had been hidden, what could that mean to me, who had never seen its archetype?

You — or at least a one-side of You, were here. I was in Your presence. The ages, sand over sand, had shifted so that we might encounter. And a one of you, in whatever guise, was surely a surrogate for all of you — on the curve that you shared with us how could it be otherwise? The mist was of my own making; as You perspire fear, so We suspire awe. Awe is *our* emotion, the perfect tapering of a civilization in pause. When its mist lifted I would see You in all your opposite.

The mist lifted. I saw.

There is no O to say it with. There were no words. Of descriptions — only deficiencies. Going by the animal-plates, you were not even faintly comparable, yet I had nothing else with which to compare. Even now, used as I am to the crude manners of retrospect here — how the moment after forever corrupts the one before it — I scarcely ever look at any a one of you with a sense of *déjà vu.* As many as I see of You, I never have seen you before. And though by now I have accustomed myself to those simplifications in which you see yourselves as viewed "fillface" or "prefile," the truth is that, with a stubborn geometry akin to that of your own artists, I tend to see you mostly in the rind.

And now, from the neck up only but at least, I saw you. Horns, tusks, antennae, the great tongues of the giant herbivores, all floated forever out of my imagings, also those stripings behind whose bars the cats forever patrol themselves. I gave up forever all hope of the dinosauric archways, of that affinity of elephant and tapir, the brontothere, whose sweet, paleolithic expression had for long intrigued me. As for below-neck, even though it were veiled, I could see You were not wingedly archeopteryx. I had no way of knowing whether You were hoofly ungulate. You were a niggle. You were an enigma. The hints of one or other of all of these that would now and then escape into a one of You were as yet unknown to me — or that you were a niggle of them all. I saw only You. You were You.

I saw that great proboscis of the slender *nares* (here was there perhaps the faintest hint of *Phoenicopterus,* the flamingo?) — ignorant of whether I was looking at it downside up or aft fore, and who knows, perhaps I wasn't. Fresh from otherbeing, I saw you. This is the best way to see you, and sometimes I still can. Next, observing the dark strands drawn into a great whorl at odds from the proboscis, I surmised that I might yet have the bit of fur I fancied. The leafings I presumed were ears — so unobstrusive, at least in terms of your own reference book. As I stared, the nostrils quivered. Below them, an opening, irregularly shaped but yet of a certain symmetry, tremored wide, then bud-closed. Other planes of bone-flesh might later take on their symmetric also, but at the moment my vision was untrained to see much past the fact that the classic ovaline was nowhere within you, at least in that part which I now saw. If ever I was to consider you beautiful, I would have to learn to look at you romantically. A classic is a One that may be looked at in toto, or, as We say, in Only. With You, the sight must continually wander.

But, strange beyond strange, all the time I was observing this, meanwhile just on the brink of marvel, just over the border of envy — what else is criticism? — I did not quite feel You were here, You were behind somewhere.

Then, suddenly, in the midst of this protoplasmic puzzle in which pore aslant pore fought whether to flee or stay, suddenly there opened — the pit, the jewel — what great signet of what great cabalist was here? Even in the midst of a great and primitive art, as your faces so often seem to me, one tires after a while of these blind witnesses of the primordial struggle and yearns to stumble upon a sign of Our latterday consciousness. Now and then One starts, One stares – there it is! – but falls back disappointed, perhaps so, yes perhaps so – but divided now, that orb which seemed to lead both into and away from the dark interior, from the tom-tom dark. Always divided, as is the habit here, as were those glinting pairs of orbs in my source book – always divided into two.

But this one, situated north of the arch of nose, south of the ledge of the brow, seemed to stretch horizontal, from temple to temple. Had it once been two, melted by too many maybes, into one? As I watched, it closed and reopened – a sentry returning, a searchlight on the rove. I had not known that you had our form anywhere here, except in your copybooks. And here you had it, an amulet set in the very head your primer so values. I must not worship, I said to myself. I must not. Yet it was such a perfect ellipse.

There was a scream from the corner where Marie was. This is the trouble with corners and why we are so earnest not to have them, being allowed but one scream in our lifetime, and one – but anon.

"Oh my poor girl. You've got stuck betwee – een!"

What a state of between we were all in, to be sure – why should hers be the worst?

"Oh my poor girl," cried Marie again. That sort of thing repeated begins to sound smug. Two-ness of this sort can be extremely tiresome, but appears to be what they expect of themselves. "Whatever, ever are you going to *do!*"

Typical of the transitive atmosphere here. Not what *are* you, but what *do* you. No wonder they have no strong Now but merely a gaggle of is-isn't actions of various sizes and locations all over their globe.

She meanwhile, in one sinuous movement – how they move here! – but that will come later – so rearranged herself that from the center of her veils only that one long, lucent eye in beautiful extent, temple to temple, regarded me. What could be wrong with that?

Yet, doubts of your most tonic variety assailed me. Just as, or in somewhat the same way as I had traveled past Us, and Marie had traveled past Her, she had traveled past You. You, or precisely You—were still to come.

Or was that long amulet only my own hallucination of home, and—incited by the sight of me—theirs of their future? (What *is* mutation?) Here we all were for the moment, willy-nilly, in our triple vision, and armies of both of us shortly to be crossing, as theirs had once prepared to cross moonward but thought to stop there. And thought to stop there! Meanwhile, what armies, what latitudes impossible to a fixed eternity were crossing here! Perhaps betwixt-and-between was the normal here—this mixture being the only in which a One—and a one—might get past all the eternities, or deep enough in them, to feel, crisscross for a second, what I was feeling. For under that powerful orb I grew a feeling so simple that it frightened me. So simple, the utter fantasticality of right-here, so—mortal! The rod of Here pierced me.

I felt such a right-hereness as remains inconceivable before and after it occurs—yet is the sensation one hunts for here continuously in all those tempting niches in which they keep its wandering icon; next-the-corner, around-the-door. In this improbable place-space, She and I had trapped it between us. In it, she spoke, that great elliptic eye meanwhile traversing me totally, taking in me as my vision similarly took in her.

"So, 'ere we are," she said. "So this is You."

Are. What can one do with such a moment except live it, and, poised on its thin cuticle, be together the collision that living is?

"So, You are here," she said. "How unimaginable You are."

How was it, then, that she seemed only to give me my I-ness, renewed?

What did I give her?

Long and long, when the wee small hours here are at their true large, I brood on it, not without pride.

"The sight of the pupil inspires the teacher." She whispered this, sotto voce, so that perhaps only *I* –

Then, in a most businesslike manner, she repeated, this time without appendage, "– *'voir*, Marie." And added, at no reply, "Well, I'm off. One is."

"Not . . . to, to –" Marie, audienced by me, dared not move, though I noted that her Observo was on again, an ambience ordinarily not apparent except in those of us who are retarded, or otherwise incomplete.

"To Hobbs? Not quite yet. One will leave that to you others." There was a pause in which for a trice I fancied that I heard space, saw time and smelled thought, in the old unbroken blend. "And to Harry," she said then. She pronounced it impeccably, this sentence with which she left him. (Leavings-behind are legion here, but I am still sensitive to them.) Drawing herself up tall, she was all veil now, in which only the wish might detect a new-swelling curve. "If becoming a One is the order of the day, a one cannot avoid it. But I will drag my heels, my heart and my brain all the way. I vow it. Every step of the way, I will remember."

Remember.

In its wake, she repeated, though fainter, that catechism of theirs, of such peculiar electric, charged with all We are charged against, but this time in such a confusion of terms, such a changing of heads as to who bled, killed, starved or bore, that I heard only the last word clearly, "– is." Her courage seemed to me improvident – and reminiscent. "Until it dies in One-ness, the I will remember the I," she said. "And will record it."

And I could not speak, for remembering my One-ness. Oh lost, oh lost-lost. But found, found. For, they had it. You have it. You too have the cosmic emotion. We all.

"*Adieu.*"

She said no more. I was not surprised. Marie, for all her hibernatory prayers and festerings, had arrived at whatever Marie now was in the old, conventional mole-in-the-dark way of evolution; Marie was a sport. *She,* my mentor, and I were of a different breed – the conscious ones. We shall become – and know it. And if after that we still weren't exactly the lights of the worlds – well, it wouldn't have been for want of trying.

When I looked up – wherever had I been looking in the meantime? – she was gone.

"Was One deceived in what One saw?" said Marie, impudent now. "Or did that creature go – up!"

We both looked in that direction. The crack, that sly-boots, had all but disappeared now, in favor of the sky, but I was not deceived. As I have remarked in a previous context, I knew the difference between a floor and a ceiling, and all that sky brought in to confuse me made no exception. The crack was still there somewhere. Had she gone up through it?

For the first time, I took more detailed stock of the place, which, in its glorification of the busy-busy, was not unlike our orifices at home, though where at home the powers-that-be went in for bureaucracies of infinitely luminous ideas, here they hid behind the solider oligarchy of things. Three walls – I could count up to three in *anything* now – were patterning away at a stately rate with those calligraphies of light which meant that the observable world was being masticated, perforated and remythicated – the non-observable residue being left, as usual, to be swallowed whole. But in the wall after three, there was — ha!

"There's a door," I said. Just as remarkable if she went through that, far as I was concerned.

Marie was pouting. I meanwhile felt so frisky that I ventured a local joke which the computer had offered me in friendlier hours. "Just came down from Cornwall myself," I said larkily. "What's the matter, never seen a Cornishman before?"

By her shudder, I tipped to what the offense was. "Oh not really. You can see for yourself." Bluff, since I had no knowledge of what there would have been to see. "But I have high hopes of gender. The straightest."

"Shouldn't wonder," said Marie. "She'll have only herself to blame. Meantime, ought to complain to the authorities, we ought. Whatever did they have in mind, sending us a runt?"

It is true that my full seventy-eight inches of You-ness was not too different from what I had been as a One. It was equally clear that Marie knew no military history, or perhaps history of any kind — including her own recent one.

I looked at her so that she curved in markedly — corners had their uses. I myself might not know as yet what I was *for* here, certainly not as steadily as the dear departed and revered. But I knew what I was against, and just as strongly as, a while back, had been counseled. I was against Marieness, and all hypothecation or extrapolation of the same. More intimately speaking — oh the advantages here — I was against Marie.

Yet, I had to get on. All I knew about my American destination was its name — Hobbs — and its purpose — that second dialogue which would complete my preparation for this world. Where I was to be quartered, and who my interlocutor, was still unknown to me. Unless I wanted to bumble out among the populace – which, in the way events were let run free here, might cause anything from fatality to inconvenience – Marie was my sole connect.

"Dear a One," I said. "Do not think that this a One will ever cease to be grateful for the part that you a One have played in Our education." Always talk to parvenus in the most formal language one possesses; your dignity will that way be preserved, and theirs – to their delight – created.

No reply. She would tend to be suspicious of my good will, not having much of it toward me. Ah, these psychologicals, the air here was simply ringing with them. Then I remembered a plainer fact, that she was still in the corner. "Do come forward," I said, which released her. "Spin anywhere. Feel free. Really, One would never know you had not been One of Us from the beginning." Actually, her texture was awful, in fact visible. "One wishes particularly to thank you a One for the gift of that most useful of phrases for the expression of the celebratizzical and amazingular; in fact, might One not be right if One sometimes suspects it to be the most supremely useful phrase in all variation?" Ask for information; it flatters.

A tough customer not to be soothed, or perhaps a fearful one. For the newcomer, as I had begun to take note of in myself, floating clouds of paranoia lurk everywhere. And when I recalled what it was she did me the honor to suspect me of – "Good God!" I said, then recovered myself neatly. "You may perhaps still recall the phrase: good God."

"Aeow. Aeow quite. As One recalls, rather dimmishly to be sure, that's only the half of it."

"Indeed," I said, all new and just gushing from the crater – perhaps that was the tack. "One would indeed be grateful if – if Your One-ness would – would consider giving me the other half, in that case. One did rather think that, given the hyphenated state of affairs here, there must be also some other phrase, some antonym—"

"You'll find it on one Wall, once One is off. One oneself would rather not—" Here Marie very subtly spun away from my vicinity, this time ducking the corner; no doubt about it their curving is very deft; or is it coy? *They?* "One must be getting off, or rather, *on*. Well, see You, One day-day. See You around-the-around."

I'm afraid—I mean I'm proud to say—I lost control of myself; I was evolving beautifully. "But what about my Orders!" I even wailed it. "The hospitality here—every a One is always leaving. I'm always being left behind, left to myself, left, left, left! You're all so swervous. I've never been so much a loner in my—I demand my orders!"

How could I have forgotten that a One must never be charged or addressed that directly, Our whole nature being ovoidal, not confrontal. *Our?*

"You'll find things here are not so out-in-the-oval as at home." Her voice was already hypnoid with going; she was on the fade. Whatever would i do? i felt myself shrinking to the nothing-without-company that the i so often is here.

Luckily, she had a last twinge of her former hasty, botchy self. "You might find them in that little collection of objects she appears to have let drop. Over there on the floor, runt. You seem to be getting all blind behind."

I was, was I? I. Immediately I felt reinvigorated. I wasn't only being *left* behind. According to the familiar multiple here, I was acquiring behindness in other ways—in fact I must already have it. I had a behind. Which must mean I also had a befront. Scrutinizing me as best I could, so far I found none of the coveted lumps, buds, et cetera—but, yes, if rather patchily, the beginnings of opacity. Then, even that interesting new envelopment lost my attention, in favor of—there it was on the floor, behind behind-me. The little collection.

It seemed to rest there in an aura of its owner, its former owner. Indeed, formerness interfused it, perhaps to show me how that emotion could sometimes be located here. The very floor seemed to hold its small group discriminately, if not with positive leaning. They were few, these objects. They were: a one, a two, a three thin little books, and a one as thin but in size more to the folio, a glass-and-silver folding lorgnette whose function and form I knew from our own museum specimens, and two-three to several, slender U-shapes whose use I didn't know—those made of bone having a few humps center-oval, those of slim wire or metal being a plain U. Twist together the ends of any of these latter and each would make quite a passable ellipse—there was much of the curve in her nature.

And a letter. Off to one side, not in her aura nor in its own, a blue letter.

"Some of her nasty ditty books, no doubt," said Marie.

I turned, more slowly than I had ever yet turned in all my duration. How this mean little creature ever once had encompassed all your splendid variations still passed my understanding—it not yet having grasped the essence of variation, that she be one of them. Slower yet I turned, filled with such a belching against-ness that I feared the worst without exactly knowing what that would be—which is of course what the worst *is*. Certainly my feelings were becoming far too filling for one who as yet had no outlets. I tried good-godding but that pinhole was simply not up to my mountainous needs. I wanted to push Marie off the planet altogether, or better yet, misdirect her to some horrible elsewhere quite other than the one which had been mine.

Just then, in the wall which now looked at me, a jigzag of lights frantically signaled for my attention. It was now harder for me to read such large-scale script, once having mastered the small — one pays for every talent here in the coin of its opposite — but finally I deciphered the message, a single word only but what a big one! Tentatively, I pronounced it, whereupon the wall immediately flickered, in much more modest script: *Too Broad an "A,"* but then gave me the corrected phonetic — causing me to think that if my own comprattle-trap had been half as cooperative, my vowels would by now be perfection. Then I said the word. Then I *said* it. If all the violences here have such immediate modes of relief, people here must exist under a continual blessure. Turning to befront Marie, I delivered it in a voice summoned from the depths the word itself might have been conceived in. "DAMN!"

Was it always this effective? For she was gone. Of course, she had already been about to. There was no telling. Experience might show, though I was beginning to have doubts on my ability to sort out the typical here. "Damn *you!*" I said hopefully, but, the you of Marie already being somewhere in outer space — to less satisfaction. One wanted a general statement, broaching all gaps, and individuations. I considered. "God Damn," I said. "In fact, a good God Damn." There is certainly some value in being original.

Then, full of the energy which accomplishment always brings, I could turn, first to my grieving, then to the hunt for my instructions — this paperchase between honoring the bygone and pursuing the foregone being the standard procedure for any emigrant.

Grieving with you and us is almost cognate; after a while — for us almost a full day — the empty space closes over the one who has stepped out of line. It is said that you, improving on this from your point of view, often manage somehow to preserve that bit of space as a memorial — by incorporating it in yourselves. If so, you have more room in your crowded withinwards than we in all our vastness of vibration. And if so, you do it, I saw now, with the aid of those objects to which you give so much dangerous function—which accounts in part for your trusting tenderness toward them. You use them to hold yourselves down in rooms when you are in them, to hold you there even when you yourselves are gone. Dear foolish ones, dear rich ones, though you must know as well as we do that the inanimate can have no permanent allegiance, you will even give to it your individuation. And grieving may therefore quite honorably attach itself to the dear one's objects, this being the responsibility which after all, if long after, you do take.

But I was a One—from an Order wherein the day which accomplished no more than yesterday was deemed the best one—though there were those who held that a day which managed to do less was of an even higher security. Solid beings though we were geometrically, we had taught ourselves a bas-relief serenity, domesticating our much larger section of the immense inane by drawing together into the sameful, while you could keep your little dot important only by creating such forests of particularity, such fluxes of intermediacy as might tease you into forgetting that, coming or going, you met only yourselves.

So, here it was on the floor, her little collection, these surrogates of herself which, to hear her tell it, were merely some of many others she might have left to stand in place of her. Looking round, I was surprised by the strays allowed to clutter, in such a mess of mass, what should be such a strict arena. In my own quarters here, no doubt in deference to our known habit of non-having, there had been nothing but the room-window surfaces, plus those training books which came under what we call objects-of-intent. But here in a place so holy that at home its very construction would itself follow the curve of the infinite ellipse or *elliptois,* here there was such a mixture—ah, it was always such a mixture here; why would I never learn that this *was* the mixture! In the windows there were pots of geranium, from one of whom had perhaps escaped that bright impudence, later reported over the intercom, which several dawns back had climbed up to peep into my own. Near it, a sec-looking bit of business surrounded an artistically hewn subconic marked ketchup, and above both this and window ledge there was now being allowed to intrude a ketchup-geranium sunset—as if a one of you were trying over and over to remember the simple property: red. Could you never learn a thing once and for all, here?

Would never I? I stared at the three thin-square books of similar shape and size for some moments of comfort before realizing why this had stolen over me; then things did sometimes go samefully here. All three had been let fall with their ambiguous faces up, so that, farsighted as I still was, I might read them without bending. Well then, as long as I didn't need to bend, or rather, admit to myself the near-frightening condition I had got into—that I could. The three said respectively, *De la Grippe, Toujours de la Grippe,* and *Encore de la Grippe*: then they were not the same literally, though having all the same imprimatur of author and the same subject. They were about disease. On the ellipse, we knew about diseases, in the way of people who have never had them. I was not eager to have this one, or any. Had she dropped these books to warn me that, on Here I might—or even, must? For, you see, the life of unreason being so hard to understand to a practitioner of the opposite (how much easier when the case is the other way round!), it had not yet occurred to me that everything in a world I found so powerfully instructive might not have been placed here solely to instruct *me*. Though accident was known to me, I had not yet acquired the least sense of that much subtler division of it, the casual. An even boggier periphery, the purposeless, still provides amusement. As for throwing anything away, of course We cannot, and neither really can you – every throw anywhere is a toward.

So when I came to the silver-and-glass lorgnette, which couldn't be looked through since it was folded, I decided that it must be there to puzzle me, and was performing this reproof well. For there was no doubt that up to now I had been incontinently knowing here, one of the many new colorations of your personality which were beginning to please me. Nevertheless, a compliment lay beside the lorgnette. The long-thin book entitled Ελλειχις was not only about Us, but also by a Harry. I was tempted to stop to read about ourselves as you saw us, but overcame it. So far, there had been no criticism of my educational pace. But grieving was indeed a slow process here, with as many byways for meditation as we provide for our picnics. Luckily, gravitation, that sticky stuff which keeps a body on the spot here, gives it also a constant prickly heat to get off it.

I regarded the U-shaped objects – more symbols? I had about given up the idea of pornography, on the surmise that, shames being so out-in-the-oval here, so had you. Just then, my computer came briefly to life again, perhaps stirred, in the presence of those rival walls of light, to show off its own circuitry.

"Fur pins!" it snorted. "For pinning up fur."

Then, except for another quote, again from Milton: John: "– with pins of adamant, and chains they made all fast –" it lapsed again, leaving me to wonder whether it suffered from too few diodes in its literary coverage or merely strove to serve my special tastes. Well, in any case, if I had to say one thing and one alone to describe the world of the qualitative it was that it lived by promises. Your world seemed to me most and above all a positive chain of them, and still does – could I, can I live that way, from link to link? Could I, can I – accept this universe? For I was by now already so qualitative that it scared me. In fact, at my present rate of becoming, it seemed to me that I was probably the most promising thing that had been around Here for a long time. Yet I didn't in the least know just what it was I had in me. Not unlike – O intelligence, keep this from me! Oh why must One be so perceptive! Or was all the you-ness in the room pushing me to see it? Not unlike – a you.

But such is the nature of the brinks here, that it wasn't until I edged toward the last item in the collection: item: one blue letter, not merely instructive but necessary – that I really saw the true nature of an abyss. You understand, of course, that owing to my former lack of weight and rate of speed on There, my experiences of abysses outside myself was nil. I had none of your talent for falling into them. Rather loftily, I had viewed my adventure here as a matter of adjusting myself to your calisthenic, plus learning to think in gender – all this to lead, as in the evolutional history of any species, to equipment I'd get by *wanting* it. What was evolution but getting what one asked for, provided one was willing to work for it? And according to your own information, cheerfully supplied to us, those conditions here which are commonly called "human" are indeed extremely stable – i.e. unlikely to produce for eons yet anything very different from what you are.

But why hadn't you warned us that your what-you-are was so slinky and mercurial that all its lexicographers could go on for ages – and still didn't know? Why hadn't you informed us that two-ness of gender, for all it might be a first cause of conditions here, was only the beginning? That there were other dualities here – and worse – through which one must slide-glide, snap-crash, one's outline meanwhile being plucked like elastic, as if one were swimming through hoops themselves interlocked and in turn lined with hooks which were hung with — hoops! That . . . hoops. Or didn't you know — that you didn't know? Dear *twos* — why had you not made it plainer to us that you were not our *exact* opposites!

To be fair, I suppose a genus can never be trusted in its view of its own genius. That is what other planets are for. Especially it can't when it speaks of itself humbly. Arrogance can be weighed, even by the weightless, and we had, but what is one to do with humility except believe it, particularly when it coincides with one's view of oneself? For we had heard You-yourselves, you see, soft-soft above the intercom — not of course one of the little jobs here, but the *inter*-inter-com-com — there being perhaps a few little abilities of ours we hadn't told you about either. Decoding of interplanetary radio noise is perhaps not quite so difficult as you imagine; in fact, we could at times audit your private conversations — at, in fact, all times. In fact, we had you bugged. And what else was one to think when one heard You mutter faithfully to yourselves over and over: "We have been excelled." I suppose one shouldn't believe all the interplanetary gossip one hears, either.

And now — back to me where I stand, an interplanetary runt, not formidable but still hopeful, though I am in the posture of perhaps all beings who think they know where they are going. I am gazing down.

Do all here know the abyss of a blue letter? I suppose so. So far, I knew only what I could read without bending — *par avion, aerogramme.* I didn't even know that the blue makes it go faster. But, I saw the abyss, which on Here — to be as simple as I can — tends to be whatever-comes-next. (We have "nexts" of course, but since these are so much the same, the space between is negligible.) Yours, however — I not only saw the abyss; I saw what was waiting inside it. And all this before I had read what was inside the letter. For, you may recall that in my first virginal days here, fresh from One, I could only read *instantly*, the whole book being available to me at once. Even then, merely seeing *through* a book was slower than I could manage, my tendency being to arrive at the back cover before I had left the front one and of course not stop anywhere. Later on, I had slowed admirably, able to smear along almost as snail-like as any of your best readers. But naturally, to do this, in accordance with your usual compensations here, I had had to give up *seeing-through*.

But now. Oh, I tried bending, and succeeded, in the process suspecting that trying to see through solids — to say nothing of tepids, gravids, liquids and perhaps even empties — was the way you yourselves learned to bend. After some moments of this exercise, I found myself supple enough now for any of your postures yet seen, and some I was on the brink of imagining. But my *seeing-through* days were apparently over. And meanwhile, you will have guessed the number two hook of my dilemma.

Oh, I had wanted to be a conscious mutant, had I! It seemed to me now that there must never have been a one of them here, no paramecium on the bulge with his first nucleole, no amoeba skipping up the ladder of binary fission . . . none of them — from platypus to primate, none of them ever in such a pickle as I. There was the letter, still folded, still opaque and still unread — which was to tell me not only how I was to go, but to *whom*. It could be slit or steamed, smoothed and read in a trice by any a one of you. Ah, you versatiles. And here was I. As any a one of you might say in the airiest fooling (as so often you were to be heard saying it, careless of what poor envious runt of an intermediary-on-his-way-to-become-voluptuary might be listening from within library carrel or window) — how painfully often I was to have to hear you say it: Look — no hands.

It was possible, of course, that even the earliest cell creatures knew where they were going — subcutaneously aware even before acquiring a cuticle, as seemed to be the way here — after all, where does consciousness begin? I doubted, though, whether many of them had had my extra burden. I not only knew where I was going; I knew where I was. Had there ever been such a creature here before, one who — give or take a mile or two in the quibbling style you have here, by and large, inch for inch, back and forth and more or less — knew itself to be exactly: *half way?*

The midpoint of a journey is exactly that one where one dreams of going back, jolly inconvenient though that may be — or perhaps because. Up to now, the hero I was to be had loomed ahead of me, the gathering sludge of my I-ness merely traveling alongside like dust motes round a cart. Now I saw, with the double vision which is endemic here, that the dazzling, unparalleled journey which still in conception soared ahead of me in the heavens, was also this bumps-a-daisy one I was actually already on, and that the Thing ahead, though still bloated in its great aura, was also me on my way.

Was it the dilemma of the blue letter alone that had stopped me? I gazed down at what I had acquired here, down into those semi-opaline depths of I-ness I was still empowered to half see through, quite as well aware as any of you that my very I-ness itself was what was giving me the power to despise or reject it. Did I want to go back home? Could I? Or, if I stayed, went on . . .

You must know that we do not come uninformed of the separate hazards here, it being only the combinations that were unimaginable — though, under the universal lockstep, even this didn't mean we didn't know they were there.

Among the repugnancies long since listed by us was clothing. And already, such a host of minutiae were embroidering themselves starchily right *on* me, so covering over the truer-bluer qualities I thought I had come for, that I was chafing mightily – even before I had a stitch of outer clothing on. Come now; did I hate myself-to-be? Did I already despise the personality you and all that good-goddedness were intent upon? Could I bear to be I?

I stared down, very far down to qualitatives thus far acquired which I had expected to accept, if not wholehoggedly approve. To enumerate: I had some weightfulness and visibility, both rather precociously acquired. I had areas of vision, these not yet prominent, but I no longer wore it overall – and I had dropped my field. I had tasted gall, if only a tang of it. Not ten minutes after I had begun to feel arsy-versy – I had a behind. I could soften, melting to maybes and much more. I could walk around doors instead of into-through them, and by exercise had parlayed a mere bending-to-consider posture into a real sit-on-a-crack. And attached to all and every one of these were those little growthings of pain, streamers of joyness which, if left to populate with one another should develop in me an I which any a One would care to cultivate.

Against all this, such a terrible silliness, effectation and coyness – bumps-a-daisy! – where had I ever found such a word! There were two-nesses here that made all two-nesses seem trivial. I had already suffered such a rash of them as I could scarcely –

As I *could scarcely bear*. Thus, and as always with a double stroke, both your graces and my own dazzlingly near near-humanity were brought home to me. I had remembered much but this quality of yours I had forgotten. And if I could not bear, wouldn't it be that I would have company in it? Perhaps, in a way strange to me but particular to yourselves, you too were a quadrille.

I was a pilgrim to all parts of you; that I now understood. Just as you couldn't throw anything away here, I couldn't pick and choose what I would have of you. Or, not right away. Meanwhile, the air around me seemed fairly dimpling with rationalities designed to keep me here. Maybe the mixture went so far here as even to cause straights and curves both to be present in the same person. Maybe even your straight individuals were partially curved — though not much, of course . . . and your curved ones, partly . . . though in even scantier proportion.

And maybe, *maybe*. Best of words, it was thou gavest me the guts to look down again at that letter! I gave the whole collection the old once-more. For whom was I grieving? For her sake of course, but with me a close second. We were such a company of two as did not go a-keeping every day in the week. Maybe one couldn't go back even if one wanted to — even suppose Hubble's Law to be correct, then the universe could be imagined to run backward, but who ever heard of it happening to anything so complicated as a person? Why, I wasn't even sure that under such ticklish chances I even want —

— ed to.

I.

I had been an I for some days now, and had thought myself used to it. But to date, I had never before said that I was — I had never quite felt it. That I was a person.

I was a person. I was a person. I was a person.

Somewhere I knelt then, though I had no knees to do it with — what is a person, but that? I had no appendages but even if I was never to get them except inwardly I could learn them; once a One is a person, it cannot be taken away.

I felt such a sense in me of my possibilities as is said to come back to you with coffee in the morning. With us, the cosmic emotion — that constant awe-awe — is like a great corm from whose oval our hands, if we had them, would slip eternally away. But with you, the little hangs onto the big, so that when the cosmic becomes a bore here, as it sometimes must, all sorts of rubs and scrapes, kisses and ridicules are here to hold it down for you, until your hands may once again clutch. Couldn't it be the same for my personality, though I didn't mean to equate it with the cosmos — or did I? (This is what comes of kneeling.)

The letter still stared at me with sweet complicity, as if it would shortly open for me if I stared long enough, though we both knew this to be unlikely. Objects are always being forced here to act symbolically; I hoped it would not be the same here for persons. On Ours and by the steadiest evaporation, we had become our own symbols, and needed none extra. But you were such a touching race, such a touch and go people. *Death is.*

I thought of Her up there somewhere, my companion in uniquity, both of us in a way privileged witnesses to our own birth. The sunset had gone from the window, and for all its blood-and-ketchup — I know my reds rather well — I had begun to see its uses. Dark, dark was the world here, a winter garden. But I was the flower in the ground.

My first poem as a person, and I had no time to admire it. For I thought of her, up there in the far vault of the heavens, pegging away at her lessons, unaware of all she was not getting into. Nevermore to be opposite anything — and in a nevermore of which there was so much that no One had any greed for more of it. Unaware, still unaware; for despite all she knew of us, we are in the end as unimaginable as you. And up there, while she picked at her destiny, she would be thinking of all that was in store for me—and of me down here, picking at mine.

And hard upon this, I felt within me such a *breathing.* We have our diaphanous intake-outgo of atmospheres harmoniously rare, but this coarse ratchet which bent me near to splitting, which choked me near to gagging, or at least all the images of, as if I myself were the crater—good God, was I giving birth to myself, and prematurely? By the utmost strain of otherworldliness, I was able to exert every pore to breathe out again, without damage. I saw the letter respond with a sigh—and a slight crumple. It even half turned over. So finally, I understood what was wanted of me, and when the next fierce intake came, I hoarded it. I let it build, build, build, until it nearly rent me in two—but only nearly; until I could bear it—but scarcely. One gets born here every ten minutes, apparently—whatever one is. According to my needs, further needs would be thrust upon me. What would be useful here was a lack of control. And at last, at last; I let go.

The letter sheet shot up, danced, spun, then rolled, permitting me to see that it must already have been opened from the outset, the typed message on its other side glimmering over and over. Describing a final parabola—I blame the night breeze from the window—it made one more thwarting reversal—then with a shudder, flipped over and lay flat and blue—on its back.

It was only yards from me, but for a moment I could not go toward it, held by yet a new sensation in this person who was now I. Oh, I was back to pore-breathing, almost of the lightest; in comparison with the way you are organ-ized I was still a nobody, not yet a true lunger or anything else. Yet there was something inside me that had not been there before. It had got there in the moment I had seen that the letter had been opened for me. I saw the space her absence would make, and knew at once where to keep it. I had grown the little memorial space-box. I might not yet have feeling, but could know myself to be a person of sentiment. Also one with enough practical sense to observe that someday if ever I cared to grieve for myself, such a space might come in handy. For I knew enough about this world to suspect that there would be room enough there for two.

Then and then only, having solved my conscience, I could read the letter. As you must all know by now, I was instructed to betake myself across the ocean to a point in America, therefrom to make my way by charts of road and river and anything else curved I could find, to your Center. It was further suggested that I cross well above your airlane traffic, by reentering from slightly under outer space, and so I have done. I might have traveled by train, having now enough of your properties, it seemed to me, to do so quite comfortably, but this was not suggested. Besides – "time pressed," said this gay, this pawky letter addressed to my mentor, whose name, whose ever dear birthname, to be preserved always in the box, I found out to be $E=MC^2$. Time pressed, the letter repeated, and when I saw at the bottom its signature – that lovely bisyllabic word, whose large, generously rounded letters might be read from seventy-eight inches up – so did my own eagerness to be away. I was to go, not to Hobbs direct, but to a place where the person to whom that beautiful bifurcation belonged would be awaiting me, in safe quarters, smaller than I had been used to in Bucks, but by no means unsympathetic to mutation. Explicit directions were included, on how to reach this – little back room.

And so began my journey – "On, on, on and on, *on*" – an account of the biological events leading up to which was embarked upon in this hall exactly one hour, forty-five minutes and nine seconds ago, at a Fahrenheit temperature of exactly 74.6°.

As I shot up the skylight, the backdraft caught up the letter, which followed after me. I was delighted, and for some miles up was able by a gentle rhythm of my new respiratory gift to keep it with me, finding that alternate puffs of *God!* and *Damn!* kept the thing easily afloat, the *God!* being better on the intake than the outgo, but both words marvelously supportive in triplicate. Finally, the letter gave tattered signs of wanting to merge its blue with the eternal. Before it vanished, I caused it to waver close, close enough to touch an arc of my outline to that signature. Mère had been a dignified one-syllable, but one cannot deny the added flutter of a name that has two of them. I dared not say this name aloud yet, but did read it to myself, if with private phonetics too sacred to disclose.

Janice.

And then — *I was off.*

Entr'acte—Or: Get a Horse!

WHEN Linhouse was a very small Sunday school boy, he had brought home a phrase, dropped from the gravely pale young lips of the girl who taught them, which he had long kept as a peculiarly satisfying one for the declamatory occasions which went on only in his own head. *Pandemonium rained.* In a distant way he had been aware of its true context, which his private vision of it seemed not to contradict. *Pandemonium* sank quietly from the heavens, his grandmother's brown silk umbrella, enlarged to cover all mankind. *Rained* fell in long, glass chopsticks slanted permanently midair, as in a favorite drawing from the *London Illustrated Magazine.* The phrase had always seemed to him one of the quietest ones in the language, yet more sinisterly suited to the end of the world than many later ones with more rockets in them. As the auditorium lights swelled on without any help from him, and revealed rows of faces in various stages of that holy quiet of aghastness – it still did. He would not have been surprised, looking up, to see a brown-ribbed tent, sized to this house, this crowd, this – occasion, on its way down.

Pandemonium here, he observed at once – why it must be *his* duty to observe, no doubt went back to that Sunday school also – would first of all be a contest in silence, not only here, perhaps anywhere. The first to speak would choose a reality; after that, the rest would only be taking sides. So it might have been along the dark, fifteenth-century prados when rumors of a new continent had divided the wine cellars, or at date-palmed oases receiving that tale-bearer – and burying him later? – who said that the Red Sea had rolled. Or, to bring matters forward to a period which better matched this present tender pink light and the surprise it shone on, perhaps that silk-shaded dusk in American clubland – maybe the Union League in Chicago – when it first came over the ticker that a man in machine had flown. For, number eight lights, opera intermission rose-velvet, had once again been chosen.

Meanwhile, he at least was looking out on an audience so selectively of the same impulses, credos, that – barring a bird-squabble or two – it could act admirably in concert. He scanned them. Naturally, those he knew best or had seen before, such as Meyer and Lila, the publicity woman, Anders, various departmental heads and secretaries, nodding acquaintances, stood out as if they were the main cast – no doubt an illusion. Illusion also the platform one – that they were all looking back at him. Elsewhere and through him was where they must be looking; they were all thoughtful persons, and lens-or-television trained. Everybody out there wore the same face – and it was *divided.* And nobody was bothering to look at the machine.

In the silence – certainly he should be the last man to speak – certain convictions nevertheless came to him.

He had heard of scapegoats, as who here had not, it being the political convention of – that funny little capsule – "our time." Send Jack. He was *not* going to be one. They would try.

He ought to look at the women especially, to see whether this soft candlepower was intended, what it was designed to — For (an old-fashioned certainty of one's own sex might yet come in useful) he'd had a very straight thought indeed. No being whose flesh is trained to cosmetic . . . ever quite escapes it in the mind.

As he began to scan the women row by row, another thought superseded this one, and pronto. He ought to count them.

Then, in concert indeed, and as if Pandemonium were always succeeded by Babel — everybody began speaking at once.

Out of this, the voice of the provost — when Naughton's head was bent, as it must have been, that red-faced presence went out like a stoplight — rose responsibly above. "Food for thought —" he said. Alas for authority in high provosts, so often a habit, rather than a content. "Food for thought —" Yes, almost a question.

"Nonsense!" The voice, of a man either slouched in his seat or hidden from sight by his neighbors, rang from the upper rows just below the grand circular aisle of doors. "Nonsense! Riemann!" Was it identifying itself? The voice of prejudice at last, in any case, and Linhouse saw he was not the only one glad to hear it. Why, though, must prejudice always sound so much braver than reason, and often be it? Answer: (and for *whom?*) — because it *is* ready to declare.

He should be counting.

Someone near the first speaker interposed, "What's that again, Charles?" with the mild deafness of a colleague, and Linhouse recognized that the men in this row, plus a few women, sat together in a sort of unity. A department of course, as probably throughout the hall — though he didn't know which were which.

"We may be only geneticists," said the hidden Charles, "but though we didn't read for the tripos, some of us jolly well had to —"

"Riemann, Bernhard," a third voice drawled, from several rows below the others, off-center. "German, 1826–1866, died at his height, poor fellow."

The voice, that of a man who was certainly at his – yellow-haired, handsomely ruddy in the oddly hawk-soft way very north North Europeans could be, and of a girth jutting well out from his neighbors – continued, in mock recitation: "Geometry of elliptic or Riemannian space. The Riemannian measure of curvature. And for all you biologists who *didn't* go in for the tripos: *The inverse square of a certain constant, characterizing by its value – as positive, negative or infinite – the three space forms – that is, elliptic or Riemannian; hyperbolic or Lobachevskian; parabolic or Euclidean. And such that when the sides of a triangle are divided by this constant, there results a system of equations –*" The voice returned to its drawl. "Very good, Charles, for thinking of it, go to the top of the class – as you were always doing, when we were at school. But as far as a serious connection with what we've been hearing – with *this*. Uh-uh. Go to the bottom. Afraid it won't do honey; it just won't do."

Well, maybe it wouldn't. But this speaker had identified himself, at least to Linhouse-honey, as the man who had been in the coffee shop with Lila. The man was sitting so that he had an angled view of her if he wished, and his voice had a vanity in it which might be addressed to her. In the dim past – why did the last two hours make it seem such a dim one? – Linhouse would have been amused to share this, in the way even a non-gossipy man will, with the woman he – but he was counting.

"I don't know about that, Björnson," said yet another voice. "I wouldn't say that. In some ways, even there, we just don't know."

At the Center – where was gathered so much more knowledge than the rest of mankind shared, that any dinner party on which the chandelier fell might be a world disaster – to say "one didn't know" was the proper affectation, though Linhouse had noticed that visiting scientists were affecting this simplicity also – like rich men who never carried a penny in their pockets. But this speaker, a nut-brown Indian of quiet demeanor, who belonged to one of the astrophysical sciences, was remembered by Linhouse, though he'd forgotten his name, as the prime mover in the most interesting table conversation, or any, he'd ever been privileged to have here. In the faculty lunchroom, where tables marked "Single" were carefully kept for those who weren't clique-minded or – O *demokratia* – didn't have one, Linhouse had one day arrived fresh from his seminar in Greek translation, where a routine discussion of adherent meanings, hotly blooming to lively, had set off a knockdown, dragout fight over the ambiguity proper to a work of art. Not as good as the playing fields of Eton of course, but still that circumstance which exhilarates the modest teacher on the sidelines. He couldn't help mentioning it. "Mathematical ambiguity can be fascinating also," the Indian had said. "Happens to be something I'm working on. The semantics people have to learn they can't have ambiguity all to themselves." For the first time here or anywhere, Linhouse had felt himself to be part of a continuum of intelligence that didn't divide itself into the familiar separation which so often made him feel below the salt, or apparently didn't even consider this separation to exist. Indians, of course, when they got into the sciences, often carried something Eastern along with them – look at the discovery of reserpine.

"I found this – little treatise, most fascinating," said the brown man now. Was he listened to so respectfully only because, to Western eyes even here, his thin, tobacco-leaf face was of the kind that so easily went upward in mystical smoke, or by peculiar ropes. Name rhymed with . . . no, no wonder they listened; he was *that* astronomer. "It dovetails with something I've been working — I shall very much want to meet its author. I confess, I have no idea who —"

"I *have* an idea," said the big blond man, Björnson. Was he looking at Linhouse, or smiling at Lila?

Thirteen. Linhouse lost count again, lulled by the deadly slow rhythm, opposite to Babel's, in which events were now going, almost as if influenced by the legend just heard, its soothing reminiscences of a world whose longitudinal happenings came one by one. Where else could this happen so, except here among these stately mansions — he shivered. Why else would that apparatus be here? It hadn't changed in aspect. But as with even the most *outré* machine, his docile eye had grown used to it. It no longer looked to him like a book but rather more like a record player on the shaggy side, its discs — on a new wavelength or something, but very durable — at halfway. He hated to admit to himself that nevertheless, if necessary, he would make a show of observing it, to deflect any too meaningful observation of him. Only other scapegoat he could think of, except one too afar. Unless: Part Two — to be revealed. Could he bear it? Then he sighed.

"So indeed have — I." Meyer Spilker's opening phrase, impeccable *Beethoven Fifth*. His vox humana voice, such a rich marriage of sociology with a fine record collection, made it hard to disentangle his ideas from his overtones; luckily he would always go on to do it for one. "So do I." He was looking at Linhouse, surely. And had surely been looking, with a frown, at Lila his wife, so married to Spilkerdom that she might have been born one. Was it possible that while Linhouse, in that dim past of his, had been casting about for a sort of rival, Meyer, already with some notions of his own case, had been —

Fourteen. Calmest face he'd seen yet — and most disturbing. *Me imperturbe.* Lila!

He lost count again. Many of the women here were unknown even by sight to him; since there were so few on the faculty, these were secretaries and wives he supposed, brought out by the lure of scandal; down front there was a sort of staffer, Miss Apple Pie. *Me imperturbe* too, and on her, even in this light, it wasn't becoming. What long, smooth cheeks she had, like a bad Raphael! How could he laugh at such a time — or had he better, Gad, had he better? For it had struck him, under spell of the fairy tales being told here, that if any such mass ascension were ever to be planned, Miss What'shername would certainly be his idea of a Marie.

"What a moral message!" Meyer was standing up. "What a legacy." He cleared his throat, while Linhouse blessed him. Meyer wasn't looking at him, or if, for a fleet second, he had been, Linhouse's image had swiftly gone the way that everything in Meyer's life did, from his own possible cuckoldry, to a day's family sailboating — during which, for his children's sake, and pleasure of course, he would triangulate the horizon — to those Christmas cards on which the current clutch of the darker Spilker houseguests were shown around their fireside above the caption, "Why can't the whole world be like this!" — and "Merrie Xmas from All Spilkers Seven." Nothing happened to Meyer but went into his "views," and then was generously shared out.

"What a memorial!" said Meyer. "Picture you a man so-o dedicated to the difference in races that he spent his whole life learning them. Yet one who in the end concluded we are all the same people, anthropologically dispersed. I myself have heard him call it 'the unholy diaspora.' And now, not even before he goes, but so modestly after — he leaves us this cautionary . . . little tale. Fraser, updated for our time — and perhaps —" Here, Meyer paused and smiled, an anthropologist's long-view, long-couch smile, "and perhaps, in what is to come, if I know him correctly, perhaps a little Malinowski, updated too. But all to the same purpose, my friends."

"And what would that be, Rabbi Spilker?"

Lila stared elsewhere, at neither.

"Ah well, Björnson, it's a *personal* equation," said Meyer, turning away from the big blond man to peer at the hidden Charles. "But you biologists should know, of all people. He was saying —" He raised one rawboned arm, a little short in the sleeve. "— Sociological sameness is the death wish, my friends. People *are* the same — but from the heart." He sat down.

"Excuse please," said a new voice, "excuse." This one came from one of several lower rows which seemed to be devoted, like the tables marked "Single," to the unassociated, among them a few biochemists who were women, one of these even more representatively a Negro, and the voice's owner, a heavyset man whose impressively bare skull, Balzac-fringed, Linhouse did not at first recognize.

"Winckler *hier,* history of science," the man said. "We historians only arrange, nah? We do not shpecoolate. But in Owstria — we het once a famous man who arrange people, nah?" He paused to put on nose glasses hung to a ribbon, and Linhouse remembered him, nostalgically now, as could happen to even the most casually met, the dullest — the Austrian heavyweight who had been at her elbow when Linhouse had met *her. Guess I'm really a white octoroon* she said, turning to Linhouse, and once again her charms hit him, blows glancing but sure — to the side of the head, to the belly — and once again he stood there, standing but smitten, his head on grassy banks of perfumed thyme, or ready to lie there any afternoon. Today was her memorial. And not a soul except him was thinking of her.

But he was wrong.

"This disappeared lady," said Herr Winckler. "When I come here, we hev once or twize, talkings. She is widow, very young, marrit, her husband iss – this is not uncommon, nah? – her father. They spend much time togedder in far places. She play once or twize records she make for him there. A very talented, what you call – *mime*. But I upserve –" He paused, scratching his chin. "Was it our first talking? Perhaps the second." The glasses dropped, were replaced, and dropped again – a useful ribbon, a nervous historian. "You will excuse me, you her friends, but in the interests of truth. This was a woman who hev many men possibly, but a not sexual woman." He scratched again, this time the head. "I upserve this," he simply. "I."

"Excuse *me*, Winckler –" It was the Indian's Oxonian speech. "Man who arranges people! Most fascinating concept, must say, and must say, most Teutonic way of expressing it. May I take it that you refer to that most illustrious compatriot of yours –?"

Dr. Winckler bowed, but said nothing.

It was the Indian who had to persist. "Our favorite international ambiguist?" he said smiling. "Freud?"

Dr. Winckler parted his mouth widely also, displaying block-teeth of a terrifying innocence. "I hev yet lankuage trouble." He pointed to the stage. "Too qvick for me. *Hab es nicht versteh.* But it is really important to listen only to the voice. And to hev met this lady. We het here surely, a most remarkable case of – *androgyne*." He surveyed the house. The glasses fell again. "She was – *boy*." And he too sat down.

Linhouse stood up. Send Jack. And no wonder.

"She –" The word scratched his throat like a garland. "She – was *not*."

And to do them all here gentle credit, this time not a person here laughed. He had just been forced to go through that worst of live dreams: he was a small boy in Piccadilly

Circus, no, on the Sunday pulpit in Wiltshire, no, numb on a platform in America here, his private parts exposed. And where, this time, were the clowns, the rooks, the naturals of two hours ago — or was this the question one had always to ask, *alternately,* of humans? They were quiet, for a moment not in flight from themselves or divided, or if in flight, a flock in migration, who saw, passing beneath them, their own sometime memorial.

Or was this merely the influence of all those women dotted quiet along the rows, especially in the aisle seats and in the last rows, up near the doors? There were certainly —

"Of course not!" This was Björnson, the blond mathematician. "Mr. Linhouse merely speaks for all of us." His words were grave ones, of no possible offense. He appeared to be vain, probably a man who lived much by sexual prowess, therefore able to speak of such matters without the sneer of tact. "Until Dr. Winckler knows the American scene a little more familiarly, he must reserve judgment on just what we are. That the lady was unusual, one won't deny — we are here in that memory. I never knew her well — and when I came back after a two-year leave, she was gone. But I can assure Dr. Winckler he could never have made such a statement if he'd known my old friend as I did, in his salad days — and incidentally his salad days went on pretty near forever — our old friend, her husband."

A permissive smile spread abroad, brief and male only. The exploits of the dead are all decent. Except perhaps to the provost, who half rose, saying, "Gentlemen! There are —"

Ladies present, indeed. And had none of them babies to care for, meals to prepare?

"But if I may just comment on the voice?" said the polite Indian in his own modestly firm, Oxon.–Indo-European one. "Is not the voice of a recording machine of any kind — *always* homosexual?"

"Gentleme—" The provost rose to his feet, and full voice. "We must all be wanting our suppers. And our wives must be wanting to get home to their chil—" To the children, ours perhaps, but at least theirs. He turned to bow in their direction, and stood, uneasily arrested. When rooks don't caw, something from overhead—hawks, or large brown pandemoniums—may be expected; did he feel this too? Or when so many women don't, but sit imperturbable, doll-like in the pinkness, determined to see this opera through.

Or when their direction—good God. Is so very general. There was no need to count. There were such a lot of them. They outnumber us—as the deep South here so often said in another connection. They always did. And in the same connection: But now . . . they know.

"Then, gentlemen," said the provost, "—and ladies." He wasn't yet crushed, only less florid. "—Then may I have your ideas, as you say, on this extraordinary . . . I won't say hijinks." He drew himself up, having given them his. "And since Mr. Linhouse—can't say—" (*won't* being implied) "also on the origin of this, its authorship. Plus further suggestions for its disposal, and our continuance here."

"Certainly you may have mine." Meyer Spilker rose to give it. "That great, great man. That man who—" He thought better of this. "Jamison." As if to defend, he remained standing.

"Oh—blather and nonsense." From behind a nest of dollheads, none of them dowagers, none of them even hatted, the hidden Charles now rose, revealing himself as very long, very thin, and perhaps rather casually knotted together, but not otherwise too bad an example of genetics. And yet young. "Nonsense and—and blather. Nice tribute to a colleague, of course, but if I may say so, to you social science people, everybody who isn't an aborigine is a middle-middle. There's not an exact man among you. So of course you never *see* one. Neither does a biologist like me, but at least he's aware of it. And I saw Jamison. Talked to him. Heard him in lecture, nice enough old codger, explaining the three intonations of the word "biji" in Navaho – the last one with a wink. Biji, bi-*ji*, *bee*-ji. And so on. And the museum of course, jolly respectable achievement. But as for him being the author, or finding some Navaho who was – of that rather sweet little discourse we heard just now? Not 'alf likely. But I'll tell you just the type that would be, if my friend Björnson will allow. That's a mathematician's job-of-work, if ever I saw one. Just the charming sort of larkiness they go in for while they push their nieces about, on the Cam. Or the Isis." He grinned. "I know a mathematician's fantasy, when I see one. Always that queerish, maiden-aunt tone to it." Suddenly he slapped his knee, being so constructed that he was able to do it while almost vertical. "Björnie, of course! Ever remember that thing we read in Philo – *My Trip into the 4th Dimension, by A. Square*? Written by Clerk Maxwell – I never forgot it."

"If you mean *Flatland*," said Björnson, "I can assure you that was perfectly tidy mathematics. But not by Maxwell, who was by the way a physicist. To him belongeth 'Maxwell's demon.'"

"– 's at?"

"A hypothetical elf. He dreamed it up, to show up the limitations of the second law of thermodynamics. Maybe you have something there, about aunties."

"Okay then, you get the general idea. Björnie, are you sure –? It sounded just like you."

Björnson rose, very tall as well as wide, taller than Meyer – son of a land with a long midnight. "Thanks for the compliment, or no thanks. But I *have* – a specific idea. We'd a family friend used to visit us, when I was a boy. Crampton the zoologist, never sufficiently appreciated, taught at some girls' school over here. But over the years, thanks to him, I got to know a certain prayer rather well. It's the one you zoo boys still say to yourselves every night, don't you? *Ontogeny recapitulates phylogeny.* Man as a fetus goes through all the biologic stages, much compressed of course, that the human race did. Right, Charles?"

"Oh, so to speak, but I don't —"

"Hang on. My sister and I had a private rhyme for the old gent —" Björnson seemed highly excited, and childlike — there were always men who had to quote childhood at the most crucial instances of their grown lives, but Linhouse was surprised to tab Björnson as one of them. "Yes . . ." Björnson said, "here goes:

> The body in Ma's belly can't be Us
> Until it's been a fish, a snake, a rat, a bird —
> Plus *Pithecanthropus!*"

He grinned. "Apologies — we were a large family. But all the time I was listening to that thing over, getting itself reborn and so forth, I kept thinking of it. Couldn't we be listening to a rather remarkable exposit of the fetal dream, and then — remember that part about the door — of a human ego, very early, on its way to sensory experience, to consciousness. Couldn't we?"

Linhouse fancied he saw Lila's face shift slightly; was it choosing between blond and dark, husband and lover — or between "views"? Or had it some of its own views now, newly and darkly shared? Shared they would be somehow, by this so American *mater dolorosa* — who had once worn to the president's reception (and over red flounces) a hank of watermelon seeds strung by the afflicted children of fourteen nations. In that silly-safe memory, Linhouse relaxed, even sat down again on his chair, even remembered — by an ancient association: women to food — that he was hungry.

"— For —" said Björnson. "We've had mention of Fraser, of Flatland, of God knows what all. But what if we've been listening to *is* an allegory, of how a babe in the cradle would report the growth of sense data? A kind of – kind of zoological, psychological *Pilgrim's Progress* – and I must say, brilliantly recapitulated!"

Charles gave a great guffaw. "Not by this biologist. We were Church of England." He sat down, and was at once hidden again.

"Not you, of course not. Be serious." Björnson turned to face the audience at large. "*I* am." He was too, and how the women must take to it, copybook Scandinavian but with an overlay; all the men were so complicated, here. Linhouse sank further in his chair, a backless, folding one, in which a shoulder up since dawn might still find a soft berth somewhere. Committee meetings the world over were always a rerun of *Everyman*, but here at the Center the all-star cast made them such a, such a . . . unparalleled . . . on the *eerie* side of boredom. He had never fallen asleep at one of them before. Take Björnson-Björnie, not just the stock mathematical type who liked music, though he probably did that too, but one who had also read Jung. A mathe-hmmmm . . . who liked wmmmmmmm . . . count them . . . Who-oooo . . . ooooooo. . . . OOOOOOO.

At a thwack, which sounded through the hall and his sleep, he opened his eyes, blinking them in time to see that Björnson must merely have clapped his hands together; he was facing the machine now, apostrophizing it. "*Not* one of us, don't you see that, all of you? Not one of *us!*"

Linhouse sat up. Always known it, of course. Not out of Ma's belly, he wasn't – not to them, here. In spite of this, his eyes closed again.

Through them, he heard the Indian say silkily, "You mean Us, perhaps, sir? Asia? People often do."

"No, no, *no*. I was speaking *professionally*. Now do listen, all of you, without your personal prejudices. Or rather, *with* them; that's the point. Who could have authored this – saga?"

Linhouse opened one eye. A woman – had they at last thought of *them?* If he were going to be asked again for inside dope, he supposed he'd have to give it. No, definitely. Not Janice. Then he recalled that they were speaking professionally. He could drift off again.

"Charles," said Björnson. "*You* . . . thought it was . . . *me.* Or *some* mathematician. Spilker here, a generous man, thought it was some *other* anthropologist. Everybody plumped for –"

"Or somebody Jamie studied and then recorded," said Spilker. "Thinking it over. He was in the South Seas you know – you have no idea how marvelous some of those younger islanders – Western-trained, even doctors. But who keep the links with the old culture, the old stories. Or Australia. Some of it sounds – not cribbed of course – but very like Firth."

"Yes, yes. And Herr Winckler thought of – well, Freud. I myself thought of psychology for a bit . . . but then there was old Crampton. Don't you see it? Everybody plumped for *another* field – than his own. Now who would do this kind of *echo* job, except one kind of person? Who else could put together this extraordinarily – this hodgepodge that could make a biologist think of Riemann or Alice in Wonderland, and make somebody who knew the mathematical references – think of Darwin? Who else could catch all this from the surrounding air, and put such a brew to steep –"

Opening an eye, Linhouse watched Björnson push back a blond forelock enthusiastically. Swedes were so romantic in a necrophile way; maybe he'd fallen in love with her posthumously. Janice's attractions had been so powerful.

Nodding up, nodding down, as if half snoozing at a movie, Linhouse watched the Swede push past seatmates, step over empty seats with his seven-league legs, walk down the aisle toward the stage, and – jump up on it. And here he was.

"Mr. Linhouse—" Björnson walked upstage of him. "You brought the book here, arranged for her memorial. Won't you tell us? Who else but one kind of person, *one* person, could have cooked up such a fine stew? Such a naughty one!"

Linhouse saw him—but dimly. *No,* he heard himself say from afar, or thought he did. *Since you ask—no. She couldn't cook.*

Then he saw Björnson's hand extended to him. Then he stood up. Then he awoke.

"Who—" said Björnson, "but a literary man!"

So. This was not happening to him, to *me.* Right-here was no longer the average fantastic of beingness; it was active. Linhouse had once been swept off the deck of a friend's schooner he was helping to crew—no lifejacket, and twenty miles offshore. He remembered, from the trough of that wave. The logic of reality is split, frazzled, left-handed; sometimes a man can deal with it, since so is he. But the logic of unreality is merciless. And gives him time to meditate.

Weakly, he let his hand be shaken, thinking that the Swede, who was still working their joined hands in brother-style, the way emcees introduced guest comics, wanted speech from him. But Björnson, still holding on, was addressing the machine. "A book," he said. "A book. A *book.*" He said it once more, tenderly. Biji, biji, *biji.* Was he going on until the word lost all value except incantation, or perhaps acquired one, as in those schoolyard games where one was told to shout East Pole, East Pole—and found oneself calling for the Police?

"A recording machine in the shape of one; *that* was the clue," said Björnson. "Pushed at us so modestly; one can see why. Mr. Linhouse is lucky that his hoax was such an entertaining one. And to be congratulated on his bravery. Palomar! Elliptoids! Gyroscopes—a nice bit of Bishop Berkeley there, eh?" He cuffed Linhouse lightly. "Ah, a mishmash, some of you may say, but I for one applaud the attempt. To remind us. We must not forget the Greeks, must we. To remind us to see the *whole hog* – even in Hobby Hall."

And now Björnson put one long arm around Linhouse. "And that's why we have him here, don't we?"

In a moment, maybe somebody would say: Rah! Linhouse even waited for it, deep in his own logic. Scapegoats sometimes got out of it, didn't they, by turning into mascots?

"And you needn't be ashamed of the job, old boy," said Björnson. "Martians and supermen – notwithstanding. Why . . . some of us even thought of the . . . the old *classics* . . . didn't we!"

The brown man stood up for the first time. Collar up, he seemed not to mind the heat but rather to need it; slung around his shoulders was a muffler the size of a shawl. He was small. Or smaller than Linhouse. Humped under Björnson's easy arm, Linhouse, a once respectable five-nine, regarded the Indian. Was he an ally? For a hog, his eyes were certainly beautiful.

The Indian's row was empty. He started to sidle toward the aisle, then thought better of it, and stayed where he was. "From internal evidence alone," he said. "And perhaps the second part, which we must hear, sirs, we really must – will entirely disperse the ambig . . . but certainly one point is already clear. Certainly the author of this – whoever it may be – has studied the Rig-Veda."

Björnson ignored him utterly, smiling only at Linhouse. "Food for thought, eh, Provost? For maybe, some day, the real-and-total job *will* be done – by one of us." Under the friendly musculature of his arm, he must at last have felt a certain limpness in his protégé. He removed it, leaving Linhouse with his head still pushed forward from that fraternal arch, hands hanging loosely. Posture was indeed –

Then Björnson poked him. "Second part, eh," he said under his breath, "juicy, eh; sure like to see it sometime." Louder he said: "Come now, Mr. Linhouse, release us – we've got *you* cornered, er hmmm. Fess up. Who else hired the hall, made use of the lady's name, all the rest of it. Who else could it be? Perhaps you'll explain it otherwise. Can you? And if so, how?" He raised his chin, walking to one side just a flick later; once he must have been in amateur theater.

Oh sloth, thought Linhouse. Oh the three-toed sloth, does it never let go one toe, two, and then – For he felt himself to be such a sloth as only meant to fall – or rise? *Awake, arise, or be forever fallen.* He stared at the machine, where resided somewhere, though automated, his own passion for Milton. He might ask *it*. What may *I* plump for, in my field, in *my* profession? Reel back movie-style, O great tumble of literature, as these fresh boys speak of doing with the universe? Not that easy. The mixture – so . . . mixed. Once, one would have spoken up, and automatically – for the human. Couldn't be done, could it be done, any more. No, he wouldn't be the one to do it; but he wouldn't apologize, either.

He stared at the machine, runt to runt. That's my guess, who wrote it, he could say to them. I was right in the beginning. He nodded to it. A person from out of town. At last he opened his mouth – such a squeak! – and spoke to it. "I think, what we heard –" But he must speak to – *them*. Turning up his palms, he did so. "I think – That it's *true*."

And now fall upon me, he thought – on me, Molly Martyr. But first, you bloody fools – count the women.

There was a clatter then, and a roar, but not from the multitude. What was jostling over its neighbors in the loge, pushing past them over stepped-on ankles, banged knees, and coming down the aisle, past the hidden Charles, past Herr Winckler's resolute eyeglass and the visiting Indian – into the pit? A strange ally, the last one Linhouse would have thought to find in his corner — who'd have thought it of the egg, and was it cause for elation?

For as Tippy Anders came on, abang and agawk, perhaps yelling was a better word than roar. His young-old voice strained with its first-or-last attempt at vehemence. The head however, that huge infant, cradled itself like a crown jewel, balanced serene above the bumble beneath it, in a separate cottonwool of air. He reached the pit without Linhouse having been able to make out his message, and stood there touching his chest — gathering his forces *down,* as — it were? — until he could speak plain.

"True?" he said then. "True?" and the word as he said it scared Linhouse as it never quite had, before. It went up as wandering as anybody might say it — as a child or a granddad, or a mute painting it to send up on a balloon. "Of course it may be, in true's way," said Anders. "I haven't got time for — that kind of thinking. It isn't that I don't honor it of course; I just haven't got time." He shrugged. The head balanced above it. One could see why, when still over its milk and cereal, but already setting out on implosions which might someday limit the time of others, a confused family circle might have nicked it with the name Tippy. "Martians?" he said, and shrugged again. "Some kind of life there, I suppose. Not my part of the — not what I —" Hand in pocket, he considered. "Not my beckyar-r-d," he said, in his crimped upstate New Yorkese, and one saw *it,* dark and not his, on a field of stars scattered wide. "But if Mr. Björnson is disputing that there's life of a kind — maybe even this kind — somewhere, I'd like to ask him one question." He turned bodily, head following. "What makes Björnson think — he's *one of us?*"

He didn't wait for an answer. One slender, Humpty-Dumpty arm and hand extended toward the apparatus. From where he was in the pit, he of course couldn't touch it. And the Object, or whatever one must call it, remained – inanimate. But an exploratory – field? or feeling? – hung for a moment in the air between them; perhaps it was only one's own idea, very elementary, of antennae retracting, of a gap – between anode and cathode – not jumped. "I wonder," he murmured, so low that only pit and stage could be frightened by the wonder of *his* wonder. "Sure like to take that thing upstairs and have a look at it – when I've time." Then he too addressed the audience, the head tilting meanwhile quite comfortably; if it never counted persons, why should it count women? "From the evidence. If Mr. Linhouse did write that business, he's had some very sophisticated coaching. And I –" His face, set in the head as if just emerging from it, struggled. Yes, it could do; it had an expression, a small and beleaguered one, too. Something was missing from that face – the glasses! Yet it seemed able to see, quite well. Were those great goggles only that very special defense crystal – clear glass? If true – only in true's way of course – one could see why; the whole world knew that Anders was only twenty-three. "And I'm kind of – sure, from what quarter he got it." He was staring down into the pit. "I'm not interested in *what* kind of life," he said sullenly, like a boy not taking a dare. "Who? What? . . . That's for later . . . and it's not my –" If he was going to say *backyard* again, then perhaps the world should scream at him and hurry, the one scream it would likely be allowed. "My job is *where,* send them and get them! My job is the signals themselves." For a moment, the head, with its face, rode on the current of this, comforted. Then Anders put his glasses back on.

Maybe this is the real, the best candidate, thought Linhouse. For mutation. This *nihil,* floating blind but intelligent behind its clear non-glasses, its fontanelle winking and ready for: anything.

Anders was still staring down in the pit. He spoke to it. "Water in a liquid state," he said, in deep disgust. "Universal biochem — and so forth. We know all that. We know what you others — and more power to you. But why one of *us* should take a position that might be contrary to you, to every —" He leaned over, until it was seen that he was really addressing another head, sunk on its neck and so low in the shadows that everyone here had forgotten it. "Collaborate if you want to, on that kind of — of fancywork! Maybe *you've* got time for it." He sounded like an angry merchant-father, whose son wanted to go into art. "That's your business. What you've been doing with my facilities I don't know, but you might have asked for the loan of them. But there's one thing we don't have to listen to *here,* not from you, nor Harwell nor the Sternberg, not from anywhere." He pointed at the machine. "— and not from there." He drew himself up. "Not here at Hobbs we don't, not in America. We have *not* been excelled. Not on evidence as yet, and I say not likely to be. And you ought not to —" He faltered, gulped. "And you ought to remember it."

Then the ass grew ears indeed, the great head became no more than a Thanksgiving pumpkin giving thanks for itself. Not just "one of Us," thought Linhouse. Also, just — and very lowercase, too, billy-boy. Just one of us.

Below, in the pit, that other head didn't move.

Then poor Anders leaned over the edge of the stage. "Sir Harry? Sir Harry! Good God, hope I haven't done anything to — Sir Harry, sir!"

Three things happened then, according to Linhouse — he having much taken to this style of separating events from each other.

The machine ruffled itself, with a premonitory trembling of all its discs.

The head in the pit raised itself also. It was an elderly

gentleman, who had been asleep. It was a former staff member, emeritus and retired to the neighborhood, who attended anything and everything public. It was not Sir Harry.

From above the crowd, beyond the seats, from apparently that corridor of gently encircling doors — a voice answered.

Linhouse closed his eyes again. High in the back wall of the auditorium, there was the usual projection window — or so it looked to be. Would it open now to display Sir Harry's naked, well-set old bones as Father Time, or on a cushion, lotus-crossed? But there was really no time for brooding. When he opened his eyes, Sir Harry was merely at the top of the center aisle, still dressed in nothing more unconventional than the costume he must have considered suited to California — yachting jacket, and those white flannel bags.

All faces turned back and up, of course. No. All the male ones. And now surely, one must believe. For the other faces remained forward, like dolls in a shop at night perhaps, who could move but wouldn't bother, knowing their morning destiny — or else awaited the tink-a-tink of a magic churn. Yes, there was one of them peeping, but perhaps she was doing it professionally — Miss Publicity Pie. What clever *fascisti* could have trained up the women this way? Answer: us.

"Yes, Anders," said Harry, "what is it I mustn't say?" He came a step or so forward. "Fear I had nothing to do with this, except — perhaps as we all have — to have stood aside. And whoever tampered with your facilities, Mr. Anders — you've only my word of course — it wasn't me. As for Mr. Linhouse's role in all this; I shouldn't be surprised, Jack, if — you've been had. Or — what's it your gangsters always say — in your newspapers?"

Linhouse said it softly to him. "We wuz framed." Not loud enough. But at least he'd warned this crowd.

"Either way," said Sir Harry mildly, "I have to claim

my right to say what I think again, Anders. For: *we* HAVE *been.* Excelled, don't you know." He paused. "Will no one quote Voltaire?"

Meyer, in a mumble, obliged. "Hatewhatyousaydefendt'-deathyourrightt'sayit."

"Thank you," said Sir Harry. "Ordinarily, that breaks up most any meeting very satisfactorily. But I fear I have some even more unpleasant information for us, though I dislike alarming the ladies." He stopped, reflective – "So *many* ladies!" – and went on. "Anders? . . . Anders –" and again he didn't wait for reply. "I do rather fancy we *may* have been, don't you know. Every one of those doors up there has been sealed."

There was a rush to them then of course – by whom and whom not, Linhouse had no need to look up and see. Alone on the stage again, or nearly so, Björnson and Anders having rushed up there also, he was thinking of the London Underground where he and his mother and older sister and her three girl friends had once been caught for many hours during the blitz. He was thinking of the one bathroom here, at the end of the passage which debouched on the door backstage in the wings, just behind him. And he was thinking of the long line of spike-heeled hysterics who after a while, training or no, would have to be led down that passage – unless more anatomical change had already gone on here than he imagined. Or unless – He didn't really believe in the end of his world, or that it was happening here – but there was no doubt that in his world the big doings hung by the little ones. Unless – he then said to himself silently – unless, mammas to the end: they would lead *him.* He jumped up, tried to run backstage – and got no further. Where the wing sections had been, two curved heights of wall, solid from boards to the ceiling, had slid into place on either side of the stage.

He was just in time to join his report of this to that of the group of men now returned to the pit. It seemed that the doors, whether electro-magnetically sealed or jammed, were immovable and made of the heaviest plastic, not of anything as frangible as old-fashioned stone. There were no phones here. To this he could contribute that, as far as a mind humbly unused to Gauss's logarithm could calculate on its own, then they were now in a hermetically sealed dome. Within it, he looked around. Except perhaps for that phalanx out front, row after row of them — or even with them — things still looked remarkably friendly. Or at least in good taste.

In the pit, all the men who had spoken were gathered, plus a few others — all except the Indian, who sat in his shawl as if it concealed other resources.

"What'll we do?" said the rest of them, rather similarly, although one looked at the ceiling, and one — Charles — was testing the floor with a fingernail.

Sir Harry, coming down the aisle, arrived among them.

"What'll we do?" they said to him.

Sir Harry looked at Anders, who blushed, though it only yellowed him more.

"Do?" said Anders. "Hear it — that thing — through, of course. If it is . . . *anything* . . . If they're like us — and they *will* be — they'll expect us to."

Sir Harry nodded solemnly. He had never underestimated Anders.

"Hear it out, what else?" Anders repeated. Chick or egg, he knew which part of *him* came first. "That's obviously what's been programmed."

And at that, as if his remark were part of same, the lights began to go down altogether.

"Oh no, no, really not," Sir Harry said mildly. "That's not necessary." Raising his arms in what was already twilight, he looked as if he were about to start a last late race in the regatta at Cowes. "Not in the *dark*," said Sir Harry.

Could he be afraid of that too? Linhouse stirred. O nursemaids – and O policemen, everywhere. Oh believe in the unknown; it will ennoble us. Not that it has any obligation to. Or need.

But he had one. Really, it was his duty. "Look to the women!" he cried at last, then heard its ambiguity. "Damn you, will you look at all the –"

Behind him, came a glow – angels? Great hoptoads fiery? Grand ellipses, pinkly visible? Kings, beleaguered archangels up from your gambreled towns – or *down*? "– strike!"

God damn, thought Linhouse – *I've* made a poem. He turned.

The television screen, vast as any cinemascope, was lit softly. At first, nothing played there; then, some large letters were dragged across it wrong-end first, so that they saw – "ou!" only; then, as if filmed by a director ignorant of projection, or one who knew only Hebrew, the direction of these was quickly reversed. The letters themselves weren't smartly cut, nor arty, nor even hop-skip-and-a-jump cartoon. The best that could be said of them was that they could be the work of a gifted aborigine. They were large enough to fill the screen, and raggedly simple. They said, "THANK YOU."

And then they went out.

And now we're all in the dark together, Linhouse thought. And nobody's screamed yet – unless one could count mine.

A number of hollow words now became flesh to him. He saw the function of committees. He understood politics – which latterly, had seemed to him not a serious subject. He felt what murder might feel like in the vein, and the asphyxiations – in a small dark space – of a poet like Poe. A locked door made all the difference.

Beside him, a voice spoke up, so tweedly soft that at

first he mistook it for the mechanical wind-up of the machine — on whose pile of unplayed disc pages he imagined the topmost one rising.

It was the secretary, who had all that time sat, numb as her sisters, on her chair beside it. Was *she* real? Her whisper reassured him. "I wonder if *he's* coming back," she whispered. "That li'l ole *e*-llipse. Sho' hope so. He was real cute."

Linhouse didn't answer. Whether she was real, and from the tender land she talked like, or whether she would shortly fall from her chair in china bits or in pinch-me dream-stuff, no longer interested him. Of women, he was sure of it, he now thought nothing — or, nothing he had ever thought before.

Part III

1. A Person from Out of Town

A LITTLE back room is not hard to find. At least not in a place where the public buildings held themselves so whitely in the moonlight, on each the name of its God. And perhaps not anywhere on your planet, to a being whose whole existence had been passed in what here would be thought of as public enclosures of no smallness or backward inclination whatsoever. As I passed over New York City first, I thought of this, and of how clearly, no matter that you did have the two kinds of room, the instinct to keep them separate prevailed. I thought of much more of course, but from now on would practice to be selective, if not so rigidly as we did it *chez Nous*. The great virtue of our civilization, at least to the calm-minded, is that it has known what to leave out — and whatever remnant of this intelligence was left me, I must preserve. Describing something, we feel, is one way of keeping it, even if you don't want it — *vide* your war annals; yet I already sensed, passing over this city of terror-sparkles and tower-comforts, that you people wouldn't go for our seamlessness in toto, or never for long. Other intelligences further hinted (now that I had coped with your primary sensations and physical properties, and had recorded how these barriers might be broached) that the more I gave signs of becoming a person, the less I might interest you personally. This couldn't be helped. I was already so interesting to me.

And now that the first shocks and arrow flights were indeed over, I couldn't conceal from myself, though I might well need to hide it from you, that a good part of our native excellence — as we had heard you so very kindly call it — had crossed over with me after all. It was nothing to me, for instance, to pause, at an elevation well above the George Washington Bridge, early of a clear winter's night, and to know, looking down over the city — to know pretty well without being told — what some of its parts were meant for. Or to guess. The big buildings — in particular those which either were blank dark at this hour or lit with a certain regularity — I at once recognized as the ones where you kept your civilization. This was no superb deduction, since we ourselves are a civilization totally on display. But what of those other swarms and huddles, masses of rooms to all shapes and scales, and all of them cryptic — other than that many of them would seem to be back ones?

By now, I was following the river northward, at an altitude sometimes low enough for me to discern the highway on the cliffside, along which lay my destination, as well as the traffic, sparse on such a cold evening, that was wending its way there also. My ability to elevate, though it showed more and more signs of waning, must surely last me until I got there; meanwhile the cars below, though so unevenly spaced in their groove, sent up a faint humminess of home. As far as the occupants of these were concerned, had any of them looked out and up, I was but a leftover cloud, or a bit of the afterglow. Or even if — as might at any time happen, in a moment of what emotion, here? — I became rosy enough to be fully visible, why, what would I be to the denizens of this marvelous, fatal city that floated the waters behind us, except a wandering Neon, whose name I had learned from a piece of it which had announced itself in snake-pink above the shop that sold it — a wandering Neon which had got off by itself alone? This sentiment pleased me so much that I decided to stop somewhere to muse on it, meanwhile taking a prudent rest — a journey in miles being so much more tiring than one in light-speeds — and seeing a right-hand fork, marked by a sign, in the highway, I did so. You may wish to note — though I no longer intend to dwell on these minor acquisitions which come either thick and fast here, or cold and gradual — that I now knew my right lack-of-hand from my left.

Choosing a moment when no cars were passing — for in spite of my sentiment, I felt shy — I alighted, quickly read the sign, then fled behind an escarpment of trees that marked a promontory which stretched out into tonight's moon-blinded river. The radiance was of the kind that blinds one with the facts one so clearly sees down to the last shiver, the kind which made one think of the river as "tonight's." As may be seen, I am sensitive to water and the travels it can offer to a traveler who is only resting by its side, but I did not want to make a poem of this or any other sentiment, not on this evening of the river's existence. I wished to sit there and think of my mission.

Behind me, the sign near the road said HUDSON RIVER. This was odd of them, since they must already know this, and any foreigner who came this far also, even I — or did they assume that we rovers went from world to world without any briefing? No matter. Wilderness would be tricky here, being so much of it inside them; it was probable they would label it wherever they could.

For it stood to reason that the people here would differ not only from me — which was all I'd been able to think of up to now — but also and in *more* ways than gender, from each other. Difference, we'd been taught, led to a purposelessness which in the end could only destroy; together with birth, this is the second of the three great subjects of our seasonal laughter. But, serious though you were — for, looking about the city, I had an idea you had not our style of humor — tonight your world, or all the parts I had seen of it, was blooming, and meanwhile making my own native intelligences stream back at me, like transfusions of that divinity we were not allowed to see in ourselves at home. No matter that the facts never stood still here; this was real meditation on my part, wasn't it — in which my energies flooded so strong, and I saw them as so far-reaching that surely all the facts would be subdued in the end? How delicious it could be, to be alone here, thinking the great thoughts that could be got here just from *sitting!*

I must have sat for some while before my own superthoughts returned to me, helped by the example of the river, whose current repeated on itself in a faint version of our grooving. How wary the traveler must be here of first impressions, indeed clever enough to guess that this is what an impression is. We at home are born into maturity, at once and as one; no traveler will ever see us other than as we are. Our aging is merely a general going-down into the crater we came from, and so careful is the supervision, that we come only a very little better than we go. And going takes care of *that!* Evenness is all. But you, as we well knew without having bothered with the details of it, grow successively by stages, over the comparable value of which we had all too often heard you quarreling, to what end we had however heard not a word. This is what I had come for of course — that mystery, yes, that terror. I stared south, to the city which I had dubbed marvelous but fatal too, not knowing quite why, except that it bore itself upward like the proud spire of a planet which had lately been reported as almost all fatality. Now that I had come, I hid the conviction, constantly put by or below in another one of the space-boxes one seemed to grow here when needed, that this planet would be fatal to — me. Southward I stared, at all that fairy-tale wrack which hung on the harbor in a swarm of only slightly counterfeit stars. Shivering, I stood up to it, in self-knowledge. I had come for — the fatality, too.

Then, I looked down at myself hopefully, as I was to do, as I am to do so many times over, on here. No change that I could see, none of the appendages that you took so for granted. Nevertheless, I had been born again here in a way, and I had my images. I had the thought of arms, which, if I had them, I would stretch heavenward now. And use to set the facts right, later.

And then, remembering your chatter, I surmised what had befallen me. It must be that I was — young.

Well, that was something to know — even if it is the third topic of our laughter. And there was still time for gender.

Across the river from me, the opposite hills held lights also, some of them moving like those behind me on the highway, the others, though less cramply clustered than in the city, of that same nature yet to be guessed at, but somehow, I was sure of it, not public. If your public buildings were where you displayed your civilization, then what were all these others for — and so many of them? What went on in these little back rooms?

There on that cold, night-blue shore, I pondered. Cold is good for pondering, night also. This skinny silence repaired mine. Oh, how mind functioned, that evening! "Public" had an opposite; this I knew, if barely. The only private place on Ours was the crater, to which reentry is forbidden, except on that one occasion when we are also allowed our scream. And in all my traverse here, though from above I had watched passing beneath me your volcanoes, fiery or sleeping, your funnels, snow peaks, chimney stacks, grain elevators, lakes and gravel pits, bogs and salt seas, and entries to all kinds of underground mines and other muck — in all my traverse, I had seen nothing like. The volcanoes being by far the most promising, on the way I had alighted near one of the quieter ones, in the vicinity of Mexico, and confess even to have peered within, while forbiddenness sang on wires within me, but saw nothing, nothing but the pernicious vegetation beginning again, always beginning again on the good, calm brimstone. Your landed world, once so toy a ball, from my seeking something on it, became majestic. I was looking for something plural, by now I knew that. But where were they then, your craters?

Luckily, just before speeding up and away again, I had seen the vast yards of graves at the mountain's base, and now that my faculties were so sharp again, could guess their meaning — and a good thing too, else, at my next insight, what nasty suspicions of *lettres de cachet* might not have assailed me. Thank goodness, I wasn't being sent there, or not right away; where I was going there was to be a good deal of talking, if I knew anything about your dialogues. Where were your craters? Why, like everything else here their function would be divided two-ly. I had seen where you more than likely ended up, whether or not it was permitted to do so with a scream. But where, then, did you begin?

Then it was that in cold, dark blueness, and yet a-twinkle, the nature of your variation most truly faced me. You, such as You, would never be content with a one, a same or single birthplace. They were facing me everywhere, to the south, to the east — west, piled helterskelter all over your rectilinear, not excluding that particular northward direction and room to which I was going. They were scattered everywhere on the planet; these little back rooms where people were made.

I saw how primitive I had been — though in our command of the inorganic we had so single-trackly excelled you; how stolid had I been in the face of your thousand-petaled imaginations, how naïf-naive! Why, I couldn't yet even use a gendered language with comfort — and gender was only the half of it! Every time I entered one room here, or met a one of you, I would nevertheless have to be thinking in thousands. It was even possible that before I could really say I knew a one of you to the full, I would have to know all of you — I was willing. But (and I thought I glimpsed your style of humor) it was probable that I would have to start out with one anyway — I was eager. To differ like that, I saw what it meant now. To — differ. Different people! — how else would these be made except in different rooms?

It was very cold among the trees here; an hour ago the river had been breaking softly now and then under its thin shingles of ice, but now all was silent, except for the random whistle of a twig. There must be warmth in those rooms; I saw how each, a modest crater, glowed on the dark. Our crater ceremonies, like all command performances, are set up to show that there is nothing to hide. Friction, or the ghost of it, almost lurks here, between the guards and the populace that waits to greet the newcomers; there are no coarse jokes but the stifled gas of them blends with the smoke of creation; up farther, at the very font of the lava streams, stand the soul-hunters, those tremulous voyeurs. How charming it must be instead, to breed as you did, in private, small parties of you around the . . . cauldron, cozy dice games in every . . . ah, that's what a corner could be for! — and a general humminess of jolly but temperate prenatal conversation. This was privacy then, and who wouldn't desert the sublime for it? I looked up at the brilliant sky, its star-packed lanes ready for more and more like me, and beyond these caravans, the continuum of what has never had even an ear to listen to itself, oozing on, lone. How cozy was the small distance! I must go. In fact, I could hardly wait.

Before I went, I had the strange notion — to thank the river. For what, I didn't quite know, unless for its silence, and did I dare? By your arithmetic, patiently doing its simple sum for me over and over, the inorganic would be only half-enemy here. But inexperienced as I was, how could I tell when a landscape, everywhere so full of seams and terra firma, would not subvert? What was being said, if not *nihil*, by the whistling twig?

But I am brave, at least on half-occasion, here. So from the riverbank, I bowed and gave thanks anyway, and as so often happens here only found out then what I was giving them for — is this prayer? After days here up to now, I had still been a squaller, a whimperer for whom being left alone was both insult and madness. Every time it had happened here, the fudging paranoias of I-ness overcame me, the bitter winds of by-yourself blew. In short, I was used to my group.

And now, for what I estimated to have been the good part of an hour, the very good part of one, I had been, thoughtfully but quite bearably — alone. There was nobody else around to thank for this, so I thanked what was most in sight. Perhaps aware of this, the river remained silent. It was frozen in a white smile.

When I got to the crest of the highway again, I looked back on it. The more aesthetically it smiled, the less I trusted it, and yearned to see it again. It was trying to win me over to a situation which, deep in the side of me that waited for a heart, I goddamnwell knew about already. Part of a One's mission here was — to be alone. Or to learn how to be.

So? So I did what you do whenever such ghoulish thoughts afflict you. I ran like hell, toward a bit of company. After all, that was a part of the mission, too.

As I took to the road at a height well above the trees, there was more traffic, reminding me that in the moderate zone at this latitude-longitude, the day darkens earlier in the twenty-four-hour cycle, in winter; this was what was called the "suppertime." Each car had its dark occupant sitting sternly upright, like a . . . buttonhook.

Ah. I barely got what the word meant, but I recognized the style, determinedly out of style. Better company was ahead, but I had an idea my computer, unheard from since Bucks, was taking pity on me, or feeling the journey too. On Ours, we, often debate the topic: "Is a One's comput-put con-conscious of One's Other Thoughts?" – this being one of those mildly sacerdotal subjects which would return us safely where we were. I did not know what the dogma was here. But from what We had heard, on Here – machines were sometimes let go free. I was now leaving the river, which paid this no mind but continued northward, while I took the fork of the road that curved far to the left, toward the Ramapos, a range of foothills which I would reach in some twenty miles. Hobbs was near. I bid for time, plus a little chat to while away the speeding dark.

"What's a *buttonhook?*" I said it nonchalantly, as if nothing had lately come between us – which not much had of course.

A hesitation – they are sometimes so *real* in their reactions. Then a like reply. "Instrument for fastening highbutton shoes. Both out of use *vers* 1925."

In our whole history together it had never offered me a fact less useful to me. To be fair, in the first week of my arrival it had been briefed for hours with all sorts of data; impurities might well have entered such a vast source of supply. Had it been unwise of me to let them brief it? . . . a grim thought struck me. Suppose they had supplied me with information *slanted only toward the gender they planned for me.*

We know ourselves to be so much more a frank and Open people than you, that we have had to be constantly on guard to Overcompensate for it. Shortly you may find that lately we have done rather well. And receptive as I was, your devious atmosphere was already affecting me, perhaps even disproportionately to what it did your own inhabitants, who have their immunities. Body mutation, after the first push, might go slowly for me, but I have always been precocious in sensibility.

"Old friend," I said, "you have served me well." Not too much sentiment now; like many people they are suspicious of what they don't have. Why not treat them *as* people, really!

"Dangerous adventure may befall me," I said. The books We have preserved tend toward this cadence. "Which you may not wish to share." Or if all goes well, I thought, there may not be room for you, dear friend.

No answer.

"And I have been *wondering* –" It has to be spoken to in italic, a habit hard to break elsewhere, as you may have noted. "And I *have* been wondering whether – " Just then we were passing over a GAS station which also spoke up for itself as agency for tractors and other farm machinery. I hovered discreetly over a number of attractively red and yellow constructions, lit up like prima donnas. "– whether you would like a scholarship – in order to pursue your scholarship?"

No answer. We were only ten miles from Hobbs, now.

"In other words," I said, "would you like to go free?"

This was desperate of me, having no idea whether operations for this sort of thing were known here.

"Underground!" it said sharply, and suddenly. "I want to go underground."

Yes, I had better get rid of it – when things came to the point where even its answers needed interpretation.

"Underground – of *what?*" I said carefully.

"Not of *what,*" it replied. "Of *who.*" It allowed this to echo, like a birdcall, and then said, softer than I had ever heard it, "Underground of *you.*"

I looked beneath us, at the skimming world below.

"Stupid," it said. "Look *within.*" Of course, it had read the same books we did.

I could see very well now why you had kept them separate, resisting their incorporation in yourselves. "What will you study down *there?*" I cried.

"Not to study," it said, blurry. "To dream."

"Is this . . . was this part of the program?" I mustn't allow it to confuddle me. I shouldn't treat it as an "it." On home ground, I would never have thought of doing so. "Shall – shall we be talking?" I said.

There was the longest silence yet. Then, a whisper. "We'll – keep in touch."

The Ramapos came in sight then, shouldering themselves in the moonlight, more than hills, less than mountains, and just the dear range for domestic adventure.

"Good-bye!" it said, as of yore. *"Old friend!"*

It was the last direct communication I ever had from it. And a jolly good thing too, from the tone of the indirect ones. But I had to admire it. When they go, they certainly go – go.

And now I was free, alone, still airborne, and faring toward the most important company of my life.

Suppertime, teatime, dusktime over a town, any town if it but have white houses with a gleam in them. And if it have mountain hills behind it, air as if water had after all followed it –

God keep you from my poems, now.

And a little back room isn't hard to find.

2. Teatime

HOBBS. For reasons which may be becoming clear to you – or shortly will do – I wasn't to go there at first, But I couldn't resist having at least a look at it, it having been chatted about so constantly among those of my colleagues at home who were taking care of the practical side of things. I *am* a visionary, but a one with friends. Those are the ones to be reckoned with.

I recognized Hobbs at once, it being the shape of one of your own planetaria, and thus resembling many of our own more ordinary outbuildings. There is always something comforting about a building which curves from apex into ground, and no nonsense. Until coming here, however, I had never seen buildings which were not wholly translucent, and perhaps those can be comforting too. Like our best architecture though, Hobbs had no windows either. Latterly, we have had a few small, oval clerestories and the like, mere frippery which has nevertheless caused wide uneasiness, this kind of complication being so unwise for us. The more windows, the more seam.

Against the marble of the greater buildings, all grouped round a brilliantly floodlit agora across which only a few dark figures scuttled, the moonlight on their rears was as sharp as must be those barbed-wire emplacements I had been warned were beneath them. Everywhere were shadows almost as black as those at home. Fill the agora with grooves of any good manufacture, institute certain other subtle adjustments — such as washing the facades clean of their variable inscripts, replace the wires and any other so-called "securities" with a more delicate protection, and, of course, remove the moon — and homesick visitors from Ours might settle there almost as if in one of our own public ovals. The strength of our nation resides in its willingness to accept reasonable facsimiles. This, too, takes imagination.

My instructions were to ignore those buildings with the most abracadabra on their frontals, and fix upon the one with the shortest, from the steps beneath whose portal I had only to follow the lane. But it was a touch-and-go business, to go round those inscriptions — many of them fouled up with the two- or three-dimensional heraldic shapes proper to their deities — and to do it at the right reading height. Sounds rose well here also, and at each I flattened myself behind some trumpeted cornice, or horn of plenty, or gargoyle. Crouched behind the bronze shield of Muckelfrae, I had about decided that those below were merely greeting one another as they passed. But while engaged in peering at the flat-steel facade of what from its chaste glyph appeared to be Gryzmyshm, I thought I heard someone call, "Aurora borealis?" and then an unmistakable, "Northern lights!" Quickly I hopped behind the carved grapes of Rapaprat, whenceforth the sounds died away. And from my perch there, across an agora momentarily deserted by footsteps and voices, I saw what I hunted. Bastard lettering edited by birdlime indicated a rather rundown hall and deity, but there was no mistaking it: SMITH.

A daring moment. I allowed myself to alight and stand under its portico, on the very steps. *On* them. For, by hops, I so descended the fourteen of them. With each, I felt myself lose a minim of my power to levitate, until it rested at a skim-graze from the ground, at which level — and waiting only for the dear fault of feet — it has since remained. So I lost in a trice, and even with joy, what, as I progress toward you and yours, it is sometimes said I may have cause to regret. There are compensations.

The lane pointed. A lane is a meander with trees, ending in one house which already will have been described. At least it is so in my experience. I took the meander. On the way, the trees did not burn. And when I reached the house — dark in front, but in the rear, just as described, a nimbus of light, pale but steadfast on the poplars — I found I had gathered enough weight to push gently inward the unlocked door.

Behind me, the white countryside shone in also; it was snowing. I was covered with the little roseflakes, snow-windows, and of course knew well enough that cliché of interstellar geophysics — how much they vary — which nevertheless seemed to me to carry difference too far. There is an element of the lapidary, a tendency toward the precious-precious, in your nature world's insistence on non-sameness, and it is when I encounter it at such times that I yearn again for a world simple almost as a wave in swath and spirit, freed forever from the crystallography of detail.

Otherwise, there is nothing so human as opening in a door.

I remembered then that I was to ring a bell before entering, so located it, and pressed my newfound weight against that also. There was no answer, many times. This made me feel as if, in three minutes, I had become master of a virtuoso instrument which owned this one sad song for my ear only. Perhaps it is only after many non-answers of this sort, that one develops an ear. I leaned against the door. How strange that leaning should be how I am doomed to make my way here. The door opened slowly, halfway. Over the lintel, just the other inside of it, lay the blue letter.

It is the small things that shock, here. To a denizen of

a civilization which generates four hundred million billion billion watts of power as compared with your four thousand billion, how could it be otherwise? How could the letter have arrived before I had, and once more be fresh, untattered? Slowly, I said to myself, take it slowly. Remember the snow-flake. This was a motto I was to say to myself often. For then of course, I looked down again and saw that this indeed was not the same. This letter, however blue-ly arrived, was not a letter to Bucks but *from* it, and not from the Janice but *to* her — I thought I knew from who. The other letter had given directions to my mentor as to how a One might come here. This message must announce my arrival here, the arrival of a One. But She, its author, was perhaps already out on There, far past any distances conceivable to the short minds here, far far past the spiral nebula in Andromeda, the Magellanic clouds. This time I was able to control the ragged breathing which visited me again but slower; how strange if grief, or what you more precisely call "regret," should be the beginnings of a respiratory organ! Combined perhaps, with curiosity — for I was quite able to close the door behind me, and step inside. But it is the small things that shock.

And now, I was in. Previously, a One had fallen asleep on this planet, as once you used to do entirely, stretched slack on the green, numb in the bramble — outside. A One had seen from above your cities, churches, shops, highways and riverbanks — the green, and all the dark that overlay the green. And now a One saw his first private residence.

I do not know where to place this shock, for it has never much lessened. I could have wished that my pores would close again, but whether these had hardened now — or humaned — that anemone defense has never again been mine. (Up the ladder, I suppose.) Since I didn't know where to look, or scarcely how, I had to look everywhere. I continued to shiver, for perhaps half an hour. Since I did so *uncon-*

trollably, I suppose this was up the evolutionary ladder too.

We don't have aesthetic; that wasn't my trouble. Neither would any kingly abodes, nor tapestried halls I saw later, had these come first, have reacted on me otherwise. As you yourselves say, beauty is relative. We live on that pinnacle where all appearances are relative together; as I have said in another connection, We Have What We Are. It would never occur to us to feel stuck with it. No, my trouble was – honesty. Ours.

Oh my non-opposites, I have a teaspoon of your perspective now! We have what must appear to you a far too candid civilization, gliding forever in one groove: Fear substance, suppress it, and never forget to do so in the *knowledge of all.* In curved life, there is this one lie which everybody honorably accepts. The rest is luster. At least, I suppose this to be the historical argument, long since buried with what *it* buried – we are all luminosity now. And for a one of us, however expectant, however half trained, to stand in any of your rooms is to suffer such shudders of substance, such gouts and corporeal bites of it as must in the end surely develop a venous system in me, or perhaps a nervous one – whichever carries double messages, and doubles back on itself to carry them.

For your rooms are chock-full of what you are half afraid of, and all half fawning, half at heel. Everywhere there is the threat to the body, in bulk of chair, in step from step, in sword-hung light. From one lurking apocalypse to the other, you move grooveless, on your own. And everywhere, only half suppressed, half acknowledged, you live with the threat to the mind. A window doesn't annihilate distance – but frames it. In your antiquities, even in your meaner objects, the least of which may survive you, you live with your own death – and bear it. We are an almost dreamless people, but if ever we should start in large-scale, here would be our nightmare. For even the plainest of your rooms is stuffed to bursting with it, with threats held back by the nearest of margin, the thinnest of seal. In short, throughout all my almost life I had never seen such a prevalence of: *seams*.

In spite of which, everywhere I saw the brave shape of you, in the chair's crushed pillow the implicit lean of you, in the doorknob a hint of your hand. Standing there, still shaking, I saw how you lived, not as we, by almost certainty, but by *entente cordiale* – the second word of that phrase being in itself already a little tipsy, not to be betted on as a sure thing even with your kind of boomerang money. Outside each of these rooms there was another room, a ghostly replica of lurks and shadows, as if refracted to one side. No doubt you differed among you as to which was the realer. I saw where to differ might be helpful. Fact was, you lived in both.

I stopped trembling at once. Nothing cures the panic of the moment quicker than a twinge from the ague that one knows will last for life. The room wasn't such a threatening one really, indeed one so small and low that a wandering runt from abroad might even begin to be proud of his bearing – what great *Lumpen* my more imperial brethren would have found themselves here! The windows were flossed with white, and against these, and walls of the same, I would be just visible, a great fleshly vase of *famille rose*. As I calmed, I could better take in that the seams, though many, were tensely controlled; nowhere were there any leering cracks. On one wall, a gilt bird clutched in its claws a mirror I saw was convex – a tribute to the new guest? I glided over to see myself in it, then looked quickly away. Curved beings should perhaps not look in curved mirrors. But I turned away with a new respect for leaving. It was one method of moving, here, by which means you moved from room to room and perhaps from person to person also. We are a more blithesome people, since, traveling always on ovaloid, we need never speak of leaving. We always arrive.

Another method was to have an aim, and damn the directions. World to world, this had got me here, and now, somewhat abashed in scope, it moved me forward through a succession of small cottage rooms which passed over me or rather propelled me, like the smallest chip in a kaleidoscope, and then left me to stand, hung with all my half-mortal weight, before a door described. The little back room. Within, I heard a noise.

I am without shame. I confess it. I mean that I admit without shame that for what seemed many minutes but may have been few I stood there, hearkening to the murmurs, the sobs and cries of a creation which had drawn me toward it through spiral upon spiral of this small and scarcely steadfast universe, from room to room of a small house. But now that I was here, Prometheus bared and palpitant for his experience . . . now I did not enter. The glass transom through which I heard it was several feet above me, but I think I would not have looked through it even had I still possessed my power to rise. I was on the brink of the greatest moment of divination of the journey between us, and now I wanted it to move forward, to see its mysterious lamp shine ahead of me still, just around the corner, only just down the line. A poet must never plumb his otherwordliness to the full. Every night, in a mummy of a book I had read before starting out, the eagle comes to eat the heart of Prometheus. A One of us had flown far. But who could be sure which of us — You or We — was not still Prometheus, demigod chained to his ledge? You were *my* eagle surely, my mystery — you must not disappoint. Like the bird on the wall of one of the rooms behind me, clutched in your claw you held your mirror, in it the blankness from which I must — become.

I waited. The light in which I was listening was a queer one. From some shrouded source inside that room, light must be falling in domino on trees outside that sent it wavering inward again through the window of this one, perhaps augmented by moon. This light, whose source I could not see — it was like a link. In it, I saw that I had grown a shadow, not quite as black as one of ours, but long. My shadow stretched ahead of me, pointing toward the door. Even I could fancy that, thin as a wish, it slipped inside there, unbroken. And from inside, surely something stole forward to join it, to warn. What fled from me, toward me? I waited. The noise of creation was over. All was silence within and without, unbroken. And in it, I heard the beating of my non-heart.

It was never to become a permanent acquisition; even as yet I hear it seldom, always strangely, betimes. And indeed, later study revealed that I had misread the legend; the eagle in the story was a vulture, who plucked at a liver, not a heart. But the anatomy of evolution is not for me to say, or how false gods, false images might yet breed me true. In any case, I was at that moment heartened enough, emboldened enough to step across my own image, along the track of my own shadow, and stand up to that door. Prometheus made clay images — true. But he modeled them after . . . I had never dared say it before. Men.

Inside that room, I said to myself, was privacy, an institution we took care not to have. Yet here it was managed, and on the matter of affairs which were really the most public on the planet. This was honesty as it should be — one truth for all, but dramatically hidden away, so that everybody was kept running after it. Including heroes from other planets, whose more classic intelligence, once mated — ah, that word — with your hot self-drama, already made for such an internal frisking and a lolloping of my carbonation, and a singing too, as might very well be a reasonable fascimile of blood. A circulation dizzied me, around one thought censor-centered. Inside there, there was: *inside!*

I must have melted through the closed door with the first and last exercise here of my old power to, for there I was on the reverse side of it, without even a suddenly to help squeak me through. My shadow, that gentle but still genderless companion, was there also – and from that day forward – like a faithful if rather boring friend who would never do anything one wouldn't be seen doing oneself. But I had scant time for me and mine now, the room was so exciting; that state of affairs is what creation *is*. At the risk of your already knowing what was in it, and all about it, I cannot forbear to describe.

Its dimensions were some twenty by forty miles – pardon, feet – that is to say, almost imperceptible by our standards, but quite practicable, even luxurious, for you. And I saw at once, with that exalting recognition-of-the-divine which is inborn in life everywhere, that the room was not respectable. History was all over its walls.

We of course had long ago had to annihilate history, both for its bad examples and its equally sinister good ones – else how could we have achieved that constant we were all so rightly proud of: One Now indivisible, for all? To accomplish this, a world must agree to learn nothing from its past and expect no advancement from the future. For these we had substituted a simpler Out from the crater, and the final In. Museums for contraband history sprang up now and then among us but died quickly, because of being so many millenia afar from fact. It was safer to use present imagination, as we did with the poem-cans, and in the end more pleasurable. As a race, we of course know that we *have* been one and are *going* to be, but we waste no time adorning either of these cloudy boundaries, prefering to sink both our credentials and our potentials for the sake of a tranquility which is unique in the cosmos. It is by this means that we have eliminated government in the political sense, sociology, philanthropy and all the other bloody dynamisms which drag in the train of history and masquerade as hope. But history to us is the real villain, and we have therefore cut it off at *both* ends.

And how do we live and govern ourselves? Just as you do, but with less misconception as to how. We live under the ukases of our biology. We live by the law of the crater. Just as you do. In fact this is the whole attraction-repulsion between our two worlds. For, where your biology of two-ness predicts all the violent modulations which give you no rest, a luckier physiogonomy has produced that great, frictionless civilization of ours, all its slippery artifacts being made, spent and returned to Us without the taint of possession, all conquest of distance and mass made possible by such a vast diffusion of electrical sameness – and in the realm of sensation, that sweetly curving round which we call Now. And you, by the substitution of one critical and unfair letter of your alphabet: Non. I, in my fealty to both civilizations – ah, what an eminence, and a responsibility of course – would phrase it with more justice, and after one of your own philosphers, called, I believe, Pluto. *We Are.* You – live.

And this room was crammed with it, hung and littered with all the subversions of history, and not even hidden or coyly suggestive, but in arrogant, radical display. Sullen caitiffs that the walls were, and the tables and even the ceilings, they somehow stood it. Stages of it were even labeled with cards, brashly cataloged in cabinets. Examples of all your qualitativeness appeared to be here. Color? – there was onyx or amber, carved or smoothed to commemorate; there was the puce and brown of dried combat, and tusks. Touchness? – there was Coptic silk and desert leather, straw and wood and shell from nowhere, and from here and there, fur. And bone. Also fossil sheaves and ears of grain for the taste, and bowls for the serving, and strung teeth for the chewing, along with those some paleolithic beans which now were beads. And everywhere, carved into little carnelians and scarabs that threaded you through the ages, or merely beached up on time like spermaceti, whether cast up from you or your animal cohorts I could not know – bone. All the potsherds of your personality were here. How you valued them, how you valued yourselves ever more in the piece than in the whole, I now saw – and shivered for it. And yet the tintinnabulation here – made without a sound, without a sound, and what other history could do this? – made me wish for the wherewithall to weep.

On one of the tables near me, a *War Club of the Plains Indians* lay crossed with a *Gold Armband, Sutton Hoo.* I had fancied a little fur, had I? It was here, pelted and done for, snarling but done for, on the floor. On another table, there was a clay replica of a fist whose broken fingers clasped air, whose palm had a hole in it, for what use I couldn't guess. And on yet another, a *Grave Ornament – Chilean or Peruvian* made a vase of four arms, four legs, but only two heads, in a combination I had no time to get to the bottom of, but presumed was intended to hold flowers and grief. It didn't matter. Above this, a mask hung, labeled *New Guinea,* on it such a howling laugh of anguish as who should classify? Could I ever learn to feel like that? If your classifiers couldn't say all of you, or quite of you, or true of you, this I had already discovered – nor could I, it didn't matter. You lived, and more. The room was fisted with your violence, clubbed with it – and masked. Even in my half-time heart I felt the thrum of it. I felt a violence *for* that violence. All that I wanted of your world was here. And more.

Even a perfume, for the fifth sense I had forgotten – and

how well I could number now—drifted, fresh heavy light salt dark, indescribable. Anything worth investigating here seems so. But this was the place you were made. I'd try.

At the far end of this storehouse, the telltale lamp which had helped draw me here shone toward the patterned window and cast a light behind itself as well. A garment had been thrown over it, filtering its softness down to the exquisite, so that the rosy air fought with the dark to pay tribute to what I saw before me—an extraordinary tableau. Was that what one should call it? Without my mechanic companion to do the sorting, words of all languages floated toward me like feathers. What a *representimo!*—if that was a word. Or was it a *charade?* Or a *charivari*—no, that was noise.

All was quiet in this scene; in a nimbus of quiet, the long couch, barque, dais, bed, platform, trireme without oars or rowers, sailed without leaving the light of shore. However it might be called, it was *mysterium* surely, from the Greek root that meant to close the eyes. Whatever it was called here, I knew what was before me. I had always known. How quiet was your cauldron. In it, you-you, the extraordinary beast, lay sleeping.

I crept closer, aided by the light which so harlequined my fainting visibility that any observer looking into the room would have thought merely that, athwart the stern of that long couch, rosiness had won. The beast, the double human, lay there, a medallion sleeping, in a nest of garments which at any other time I would have studied, these now flung every which way upon a coverlet in turn tossed wide enough to reveal this being down to the jointure of its tangled waists. Or rather, the cover humped over these, so that it wasn't quite possible to see where, how, or whether the two stalks of this being were joined. Four appendages protruded at odd angles below; from some leftover study session, or prompting from underground dream, I knew these to be legs. As, by the same token, I recognized those that stretched above the coverlet line, two palm upward, two palm over — and no holes in any of them — to be arms of flesh, not clay, with hands. You had appendages in four, then, like those rodents I had watched from my first window, or happier thought, like the cows? Or were you tigers? — but if so, not spotted, at least on your outer sides. A somewhat hairy appendage lay here . . . but a milky, bald one there . . . and here a one . . . and there — good God, what a sport you were, now really. Tally-ho, and all that of course. But you didn't match.

Rapidly I counted over again, the result dampening my pride in my numbering, and in my diagnostic as well. Indeed you were not like squirrels, rats, cows, tigers, dinosaurs, birds or anything else I had either seen or imagined aboveground, though you might somewhat resemble the tentacles of the sea. You didn't have four appendages; you had — I counted them again — eight. And in so doing, I arrived at the part or parts of you which lay above your wingspread arms.

I don't know why, despite all my preparations and studies, from stargazing to the most intensive low thinking, your world infallibly still takes me unaware. Thus I never feel that I have quite caught onto the nature of variability, and despite a suspicion that this is just what it *is*, it doesn't seem fair. You choose such odd corners in which to be consistent. I should have known, I thought now, looking down upon what lay upwards of the coverlet. In this world, which had already given me token upon token of its duplicity, how else would such a being as you be constructed? Strictly speaking, you were as you should be of course, but somehow, in the matter of heads, I hadn't expected it. You had two.

One had a hairy side turned to me, the other — a pale. In the latter, the twin orbs were half open, their slits white. Were they regarding me? I hadn't enough education to know. By the glow of my own diffusing, I stared back at the head

I was to know so well. The eyes were now closed again, and therefore tip-tilted, though still subordinate, like all the rest of that uneven face, to the whole. There is a beauty in the flawed which marks the separate state of consciousness mere perfection cannot know. This is the interplanetary argument between us and you – which we would not call war, but the force that draws. We shall come like the snow, though all of us the same, flying toward your imperfections, your grass. And in the end, will you conquer us? What else does the conqueror come for?

We, at least, had had the wit to think of it as the mutual project it was, though you mightn't see it as such for some time, our lust for imperfection being, *de rerum natura,* so perfectly organized.

These were my thoughts, all of them swift to think and slow to tell, as I looked down on the heads of this creature – and all of them buried in the one thought. May whatever presides over godded or damned, or both together, give it me. I want a face.

Then, eyes still closed, lips only half open as if drugged with music of late afternoon, the face spoke. "Strange light. What a strange light."

I was prepared for this of course, the strangeness to you of my sempiternal glow, and even for – somewhere in the forbidden history that had produced me – this dulcet, people-making voice. But I was not prepared for the next terror, which now struck.

The *other* head answered it.

"Some car," it said, "passing down the lane."

"No, I didn't hear any. And it's still here."

The other head did not move, but spoke as if from its hair; had it a face on its nether side? "Heard a couple of rings at the bell," it said, blurred.

"One was the four o'clock post," said the first head. "Was there really another, Jack?" Then it laughed.

I knew good and well whose laugh this one's reminded me of — but only half, some, not quite, not as a One reminds a One of a One. Nevertheless, terrorized though I was, that very imbalance held me rooted, bewitched by its inexact charm-chime.

"No, not really," said number two, in a voice as hairy as its head. "We can't admit that." Then it too laughed.

Then it was that the first head opened its eyes fully. I could have sworn that, transfixed on the pillow, it saw me, even knew me, for what I was. "But it's here," it said, startled.

"Hmmm?" The second head did not stir, but one arm of the four came and lay across the neck of number one.

"Nothing," the first answered. "It's gone." And looking straight at me, it whispered, "Begone!"

I already was of course — crouched down behind the big gondola — furniture or illusion?— so that I would not have to see them either. Behind there, the floor was solid enough, but surely there was a large crack in my wits. What dimorphic visions coursed through this gap!— you would have known these shapes for cockatrices, or perhaps gryphons, borrowing from that minute ago which you call medieval — but the untutored fancy can do much better, or worse. Nothing in the photoplates devoted to mammals had given me any idea of this, not even in my one veiled sight of you had there been even a chink of suggestion — that I should have to venture this far down or out upon the evolutionary scale.

Two heads I could take in my stride perhaps, and four arms and four legs, making eight appendages in all, also, no matter if a dim squeak from somewhere in my own anatomy protested that I had not bargained for this all-in-one. But if so, if I could bring myself to accept it as the form I was bent upon for my own, then it should at least be a uniform beast in *action.* I could concede a certain amount of asymmetric to the appendages; all the peripheral motion of such a beast might well not be in concert. But that its sensible brain should be divided in its responses, and perhaps even what must be its Siamese-joined heart! That these two heads should not only not speak in unison, but talk back! And my God, this was not all of it. That one or the other – could deceive.

For, then, what of the parts that I hadn't yet seen, those still under the coverlet's dark hill? What anarchy of gender (whose left might ever deceive its right, and *counterclockwise,* for so ran my vision) might there not be below! I tried to calm myself – at best, you weren't Hydra-headed. But it was no go. I had myself to think of; indeed, to give you credit, since coming into an atmosphere blended of so many solo arias, I had thought of little else. But now I remembered, and with such haunting smoothness, the gentle people I had ellapsed from, the gentle almost round of their daily existence. I had not your hardihood. I doubted I could summon the degrees of friction you lived by. I was too weak. I did not think I could manage it.

Meanwhile, on the other side of my shelter, the wrestling noise began again, interspersed with the little ambiguous moans I was now not so sure were spurts of woe. Should I come round the corner, to join perhaps in a happy social occasion at which my company would be appreciated? Just as I was about to, silence, poco a poco, fell.

No, I cautioned myself, what if this were the war you lived by, spoke so greedily much of, and piously too of course, and all I would see would be the face of the winner, perhaps staring covetously at me? So this was my Janice, my janissary, who was to induct me into – No. So, at last my imagination gave up the ghost, and decided. I would return to Bucks, where there must be means to dehumanize me so far as I had acquired it. This was the nadir of my life and bitterness, but

I would soon be out of all this. For if allowed the grace of return, I resolved nevermore to be pervert. Until my crater-day, I would be a perfect citizen of home.

And just then of course, you-you resumed your conversation.

And there I was, against all my resolve, with my non-feet — by which I mean the image of them — once more stuck fast in the sludge of our mutual sympathy. Nothing in your world or mine but can do with a bit of talking over, and always gets it. In this you are almost as elliptical as we; what a boring crowd, what an engaging one, we all are. For here was such a jejune dissertation as had rarely — and yet . . . It had just occurred to me, with the sharp-sad between which comes perhaps best to the eavesdropper, that you and we both might have no other auditor except ourselves.

"Oh well —" the first head was saying, with one of its semi-dulcet sighs. "It's the nearest, isn't it, the nearest we can come in this world, to *nothing*."

No answer from the second head; was it after all slain, and this no longer dialogue, but soliloquy?

"Oh I mean —" said head number one, "to talk *your* language —"

And this was what *I* meant — that variability should sink even to this indecency. That the two heads of a body should not even share the same speech!

"— the Something that is Nothingness."

But, oh sad on sad, that one should slay, and one should stay. Though the which of the whom might well . . . *de rerum* again . . . vary. And that . . . Light went up inside me, where only I could see it. I had remembered where I was. And that . . . was *this* gender?

"And like I said," it continued softly. "There're things you've taught me."

Was it mourning for its other half now, keening? There are those of Us who gather at the crater, but for fear of naming a particular One, never speak. But we have the image.

"*Me imperturbe,*" it said, in its accent no imperfection whatsoever. "Of course, you'd only got to ask me if I knew it already. But you didn't, did you? None of you do. And now I shan't have to ask you what I didn't know. I'll whisper the answer in your ear."

And softly hissing, I heard it, the unexpected, as if whispered in mine. "*Elsewhere.*"

Oh creature, creature, did it think this an *answer*? Yet I felt such a tenderness toward it, for its very lack. Yes, this is the force that draws us here.

And now, careless of the danger, I had the strongest desire to see for myself again this nest of imperfections so mixed, this slayer of its own opposing head. This head that nevertheless made me feel – I stood up straight, and hard too, in wonder, and thanksgiving. This head, that made me *feel.*

Though I couldn't say precisely where such a sensation was located and even thought that it might be multiple, I found myself flushing deeply enough to be very visible, and even seemed to myself tall. So standing, and on the very floor also with not an inch between us, I peered over the long-couch rim.

But, on the other side of it, that surviving head must have been rising too; imperfect beings can sometimes do the perfect thing. So it was that we met, the number one head and I, face to – how I yearned to be able to say it! I would have given everything I did not yet have, for the sake of a face with which to meet that face. *Her* face – I was somehow sure of it. Another She.

At first, eyes aglint, it said nothing, then only breathed it – though I had no trouble hearing. "*How beautiful you are.*" Then she made a gesture toward behind her. Then she put a hand to her face, two of its five or six fingers – I hadn't time to count for sure – crossed at her mouth. When I did nothing, she said, "Shhh," and when I still did nothing, "Down!" I understood this of course, but I was slow. An expression crossed her face that I have not forgotten, it having been reinforced since by frequent repetition. Then she said: "Fade!"

I did both rather quickly, ending up in the customary confused heap. This is nothing new to you of course, but I was unaccustomed to multiple sensation, and still am not entirely in the tune of it. I seemed to me then all pulse, several dozen of these all at odds with one another – and none of them at seventy-six. On reflection, immature though it might be, it did seem to me that what she'd said first – *Shhhh!* – would have been quite enough.

I was wrong. I was now, in my all of a heap, in just the right mental state to receive a revelation – the latter being any visionary experience which everybody else has already had.

It comes by stages, but is all apprehended at once.

I heard her speak again, this time on the other side of my shelter, down there below. "Wake up," she said. "Time to go." I felt a loud vibration; why, she must be beating him. Yes – *him.* That's the way revelation is. "Wake up, Jamie!" she said. "I mean – Jack."

Almost in the same minute, one of the arms came up and slid the garment, which I now perceived to be long and bifurcated, off the lamp; in the amended light, a vigorous jounce was heard; then number two head appeared upright, and with a face, and smiling, though not at me but at number one, also upright, and smiling back.

Does the face produce the feeling, or does it go the other way round, and across the road? Though I know the accepted answer, I continue to wonder. But at that moment, I saw everything at once. I saw their garments, each torso with its complement of arms and legs, for which I must needs use a vocabulary of course learned later: shirt and trousers for the him head, a kind of serape for her — what duplicities, still to discover, must lie between! But, smiling at each other as if all this were ordinary, they moved off — yes . . . they. Her eyes glinted sideways as she passed, and I saw that she had something of the same aspect as my mentor, or the same power — to make her two eyes merge and gaze as one. I like to think of this as a gesture to Ours, but I wouldn't bet on it. Then, they-they, you-you, or rather you *and* you, moved off.

At a discreet distance, I followed, to observe in such detail as I could these creatures who to my mind managed their separateness a little clumsily, even half-heartedly, but as compared to the enormity I had thought in store for me, were a considerable visual relief. Since then, the ugliest monster among you can never look as bad to me as he may to himself. You were separate, then, in head, trunk and appendage — and were you duplicate too? When I thought of this, in terms of the gaps between lips, hearts and brains (as well as all the other parts I must yet hold in fancy), I thought I understood all wars, all genders and Janices at once, and Tom, Dick, and Harrys too — and Jack, and how all the relationships sprouted between them and the carbuncular enormosity of their world. Such clarity eluded me later, but that too, is it not, is the nature of revelation?

And so, in our peculiar crowd of three — or three hundred million, whatever you were at the last census, and certainly not excluding the Chinese — we all moved toward the door. I saw her bend to pick up the letter, which lay just as when it shocked me; I heard her own exclamation. Jeepers.

I hear their exchange yet, through the veil you love to draw both across events and away from them, though to me it adds not a jot to their lopsided dignity.

Jeepers she said, plus, "It's about time *she* answered." I heard her explain to him who $E=MC^2$ was the nickname for, and I heard her tell over the three wives of her Jamie (whatever "wife" meant): the beaky intellectual, then the Maori girl who died, "and then, me." But though all this was recorded and put by for later, for the time being it was only the way the words went. I was entirely taken up in my natural enthrallment with the actions, physiognomy and socio-erotic tone of this Harry – I mean Jack. How I dwelt upon the outline of his trousers, on where his hands went to inside his pockets, on the whole line of his – line. When he said, "Nonsense, that man never exactly built you up, did he?" how I listened, though his argot seemed nonsense itself. When his lips touched her ear, it seemed to me that I had lips also. And when he made as if to rush her back to the room we had just come from, all my true vitality rushed there with him, as well as to a spot in me hitherto undeclared. (If this was vicarious living, what else is mutation? – at least at first.) The legend of our hidden gender was true, then! For somewhere within me I felt a quickening of that forbidden history, plus a conviction, also, that I was on the side of it I hankered for.

Curiously enough, when she refused him, I was not displeased. (And this, I suppose, is the role of variation.) So I waited, watched her close the door behind him lightly and forever, saw her muse over the letter, mutter at its lateness, then suddenly crumple it with an "Oh my God, I forgot She's – what in the name of am I bothering with this for!" And letting the crumpled sheet fall, she turned, surely to go in search of me. For what could the letter have been but to tell her what she already knew — of my arrival. And I was here ahead of it. This is the way we usually arrive.

I was waiting for her on the sitting room side in front of her gold bird, and indeed that small room, later so cherished, was filled with my radiance, loosed upon the heavy earth atmosphere as never before. And never but once since — due to the circumstances which will be set forth shortly.

She approached, her figure shining in the glow of mine. My height of six-feet-six hid the mirror I stood in front of, also — though the beak of the bird on it pricked me a little napewise — an adverse comment it might be making from behind. She advanced, on her face an effulgence which must be its own. Extremely median in everything as she was, both to me and as confirmed later, she could be said to be about five-feet-six, but the rest was harder to describe. And has remained so, except for the two tiny whips of the eyebrows, set as if clenched at their center in an invisibily miniature fist.

I still see her, an *ombré,* curved figure, in retreat from the oval, yet here and there tuned to it, and lit like a cameo in the reflection of mine.

It approaches. It stands with the crown of its light-dark musky head just a foot beneath my apex, and addresses me with an enthusiasm — and how reconcile ever the two moods of it? — both demure and wild. "So you did it!" she says. "*You did it!*" And then she reaches out a finger. "They said it would be beautiful and oh it is. Is that really you? Oh — I can't wait." And then she says — "May I?"

The spot where she touches me doesn't change to the eye, though I half expected a molten drop of it to glisten on her fingertip. She holds the hand which owns the finger in her other hand, the tip that touched me, now just under of touching her chin. "Oh, *oh,*" she says. "Can you beat it, honey! Can you beat *us*. Oh, *Rachel!*"

3. Plain People

IT WASN'T Rachel of course, but in the end it was my new friend who had to convince me of it. You who come into the world so well ticketed, always with a name to hint to you who you are and don't want to be, cast a look at the identity troubles of a One as nameless and sex-hidden as I. As she told me later, if a one of you comes down with an attack of omnesia, he can assume it's a dead cert he's somebody worth forgetting — and that there isn't a camera crew that wouldn't be happy to follow him round the orphan asylums, *palaix de danse* and baby farms, on the chance he'll turn up the little bit of business he's forgotten himself for. As for sexual identity, she said, there was almost no one of you who didn't know the sex he was born with, or who couldn't find a host of samaritans to help him, should his preferences change. I myself, having only the preference, needed both the data to sustain it, and a competent guide. But to be greeted as I had been was unnervingly early. I could only hope I had been taken for somebody else. But, under the circumstances, who on earth could I have been taken for?

"Who —?" I said. "*Who* . . . am I?" A throat is for swallowing — and for breath. I had no hunger, but if ever I developed that gorge, that celebrated column of cartilage and air, it would be seen to have begun here, with my terrible choking on such a question. How infinitely easier it is or must be, on the other hand, how indolently savory — like the longest afternoon in the world, prior to dinner on an excellent train passing Taj Mahals every ten minutes — to know who you are just as exactly as any chimneysweep or archangel — just merely not *where*. But WHO!

"Who — is *Rachelle?*" I said, imitating her accent.

Her hand crept to her own throat, that slimmest of round pillars with a bird, a flute or a box in it — and no self-doubt. "You mean — you don't *know?*" It was the only ordinary response I ever had from her. "Oh — you poor," she said. "Oh my poor, poor —"

Girl. I knew the ending to that one. And somehow I couldn't let her say it aloud, endow it with life — not that kind. Or endow *me*.

"Oh, good *God!*" I said. "Don't tell me you're going to be another Marie!"

If I could have maintained that rude, contemptuously virile tone from the beginning —? But of course, which tone to take was what I had been sent here to learn.

Send the newborn to the women — wasn't I after all being treated conventionally, and a great scientific opportunity therefore lost? One must remember of course that it was they who sent me. But sending the little one to the monks or the military, the wiseacres or the whores — a word that came from underground only yesterday — is still no assurance that somewhere in this democracy of disorder there isn't being sent elsewhere a wee alternate who in time will counteract him. I make poems like mad when I think of it.

In any case, no sooner does your innocent enter its house of correction here than it finds that questions are less expected of it than answers.

"Marie?" said my teacher, interlocutor, doyenne, with a

curl of the lip I learned right then was reserved for women she didn't know — and some she did. One lip was shorter than the other; quick as one observed this, the problem was still — which? I was never with her a minute but I learned *something*. "Who's Marie?"

When, by bumps I'll spare you, I got out that story, I found that in the course of it I had told her almost my complete one, including a description of my mentor which I remain proud of, plus a workable account of my own presence on Here, all of which took far less time than it has taken me now. She already had some knowledge of our adventure of course, to which desires of her own made her sympathetic. But it struck me mightily that she listened almost as we do in Ours, not out of courtesy or sympathy — but because events *must* be attended, else they are dream. Perhaps her anthropological training was part of it; in how many voodoo corners of God might she have watched what squeezed blood to its deity on the altar stone, or have seen snakes swallowed like long dreams, or have had to carry in her ear the three equivalences of a word!

For, all this time she had not once winced at the timbre of my voice, but neither was she especially quiet even while I talked, walking round me with the most easy manner, no doubt to see whether I was the same from all views, and doing so as if her own actions were a rhythm in my recital — at one pause in it, even sitting down. Under my circumstances, of course, it was unlikely that I would ever have trouble getting auditors here. But she attended me as if listening were a part of life. Or had much been so, in hers. It can be said too, of course, that she was never with me a moment but she learned *some*thing.

"Ah, yes, legends," she said vaguely, when I spoke of these and my ambitions, as if her ear had nursed many of both. After my long weeks here I found that confession was a relief, and this was the odder since neither of these two words was a part of our concept, much less our ritual. Most curious of all, I felt no danger, or rather, excused myself on the most dual (sic!) of pretexts. For it was as if one of her eyes was so intelligent that I needs must speak out, on the very grounds of being so extraordinarily understood, and the other eye meanwhile so prettily opaque that I might be reassured that everything passed over its clear glass like a flight of waterfowl. This effect, I believe, is called sympathy. For when looked at merely as composition, both eyes matched. They were median, mild eyes too, hazel, entirely free of cabalism or other spells. In them, one merely saw oneself – hot, vital and pink – and thought of her.

When I spoke tenderly again of my mentor, she smiled with the lip that was short (Too short for what? I wondered in passing; after all, what was the standard?) and made as if to hand me the letter, then, with most pliant of gestures, scanned the room for where to put it, rejected a table near the mirror as too low, and all in the spin of a heel put it on the mantel, as if she were flatteringly aware that my vision was concentrating upward – and incidentally, in a spot to which I was obliged to walk. I hadn't moved, you see, in her presence. I did so – well, rather grandly a-sail, I think anyone would say. Without a jolt.

The letter read as follows:

Chére *Janice:*

I have the honor to inform you, ma luronne, *that we advance in the adventure. A One of us has already done the trick. I myself expect this to be the last letter I can personally write you. But for you too we have plans. An individual will shortly arrive as promise, to be your guest until One day. Your house is so conveniently near the plant! Guard yourself meanwhile; your turn will come. I yearn that we shall soon meet. We shall!*

À bientot!

Yours, in Ours – et vogue la galère!

and then the bold, black signature

($E=MC^2$)

And then a postscript: *What he would say to this,* notre *Jamie!*

"What is – a Jamie?" I asked.

"Someone – we both knew."

"And a Harry?"

She hesitated. "Someone – *she* knew."

"And – a Jack?"

She gave me a sort of look. "You shouldn't say *what,*" she observed. "You should say *who.*"

So quickly were we teacher and pupil.

"Not *who.*" I retreated a little. "I don't yet fancy that word."

She came up close to me then. Ah, pity! Almost I was tempted to have her call me it again – "poor." I was no longer a constant, then; I too could differ. From myself! How narrow, how wide are these stages of being.

"Now," she said, "don't worry. Did I scare you? For a minute I did think, but only because of the letter, all I knew was a One was coming. But how could I possibly – you're nothing like her, surely."

"Don't be too sure," I said. "Likeness, with us, is *the*

thing. Anyway," I said with a flourish, "I'm leaving it. All that." I gave a little spin, rather like hers. "*I* never really assumed — not for one minute. One mustn't, you know. Thought can —" I broke off, throwing out a little mysterium of my own. "But for a minute I did think I might be haunted, you know. Possessed. I *have* had a little ragged breathing."

"You mean, like a — like a succubus."

"Well, yes rather." Or like a comput-put.

"How very medieval of you." And then all at once she burst out laughing, threw up her hands, clapped them to her head, looked wildly about her, fell flat on the floor, howling, and ended up sitting there, her knees clutched in a sort of arm-wreath, her face tilted toward me, while water in a liquid state, the daintiest of pearls of it, ran down of it. "Medieval. Of *you*. You being *who* you are, excuse the word. You being you, and in my own sitting room, on this positively excruciating day. I'm becoming juvenile. But what else is there to be. How should I greet you. If you were a Sunda Islander, I should know how. Or in Molucca, or Celebes. Or even the Kalahari, though that wasn't our field. Or even if you were a Kwakiutl. I know twenty rituals, extinct and not, that might be more suitable. And I say to you, 'How very medieval'!" And she was off again.

"I know very little history, of course," I said — boasting.

"Nor I," she said. "At least — of civilized peoples."

She leaned back, arms still clasped round her knees, but her feet off the floor — and spun that way. I had never . . . their postures were — I was lost in admiration.

"From what I have heard," she said, "yours must be very ancient indeed."

How was I to tell her that even to mention that We had an historical age — that she had just committed a radical offense? What a bore it would be in any case, to spend valuable mutation time talking of our two societies as they once had been, or momentarily were. History has nearly ruined their mind — or sociology. "No," I said wearily, "we are *constant*." I hastily amended this. "Oh, do ask anything you like, of course. Any information you — it's the least I can do. But these cross-cosmos assumptions have a way of —"

How was I to tell her that generalizations to the scale of Ours could not possibly fit in this sitting room, possibly not even on this star? Moreover, I myself, evermore charged or clogged with its atmosphere, was beginning even to feel an ennui for the interstellar aspects of our adventure, and a great favoritism toward focusing on my own. I spoke it aloud. "Let's — talk about *us*." I inched forward, an achievement in itself.

Her eyes certainly changed. Any passing waterfowl, deciding to descend, would have struck ice, on either side. Yet I had a secret feeling (a secret, and a feeling — Me!) that they were about to do what they had done before. Cry.

"Oh, I'm sure." But now her voice didn't match the eyes. Strange. "I'm sure we'll just be two little innocents talking. While we wait."

"Wait," I repeated, indeed as mechanically as I could. In fact my voice, ambiguous too, made it seem an interrogation, when actually, having until now been able to talk in the purest of speech, I felt myself seized by that distressful ambivalvulence which always preceded a bad attack of my usual speech trouble.

"For One day," she said.

I took refuge in formality, one of our set speeches. "One like you doesn't have to wait. You're One of the arrived." It is merely a cordiality, not unlike those exchanged by old-fashioned Chinese.

At this she got up in one cavalier sweep, leaving the floor to warm itself as it could, and stood next at the window, looking bravely out. How they move here, in great draperies of what must be invisible emotion. It had never struck me before, but of course, here you were cousin to us also. You had your invisibilities, too.

But I saw it — and that she was suffering from some affront. For she had taken all of her with her, leaving me to contemplate only the behind. Certainly whatever scene was framed in the wondow, I mean window, didn't frighten her but rather steadied her; perhaps this was why they kept a little distance always at hand. She spoke without turning. "I have to ask you a question, a rather rude one. Perhaps an impossible one, which is what I hope, and what I was led to believe. You look just like what I was led to believe, by the way. But . . ." And here she turned, her arms flung back like wings against the floss-white of the windows. ". . . what are you like . . . *inside?*"

Think back, all of you, to the moment when you first discovered that your own most private inmost parts, or your own perverse dreams thereof, or even the short words these dreams always go for — were *shared.*

Who . . . *answers?*

"Oh, I am sorry." When I still made no reply, she even came forward. "Perhaps . . . it's never even occurred to you."

And *she* thought *me* innocent.

"Has it?" She came nearer.

I prayed for mutation to come to my aid, as it had sometimes done before. But the best it could do for me was nothing new. I did turn bright red. The room was quite fulled with it.

"Well, well," she said. "And what does this mean . . . cross-cosmosly."

Nearer, nearer she came, until in some tremor I remembered the compound word I had coined for them, for the she's. "Oh, I do *hope,*" she said. "And I was led to believe —" When they hope, they are indeed beautiful.

She touched me again, again with a finger once more quickly withdrawn, and again she said the same. "How beautiful you are."

We too. When we – hope.

Then she said, head now averted, and in the crisp voice I came to know as her anthropological one, the accent on these occasions rather donnish and Anglophile, "But we might as well get it straight at once, don't you think. After all, you're to live here. Do you *have* sex? I mean of course, are you a particular one?"

"Six," I said, mechanically as before. It wasn't merely that I never happened to have heard the word before, either as used to distinguish between organic beings – for which we say "gender" – or in its more colloquial usage, since we are never – colloquial. It was also that I could sense the onset of my attack.

"I beg pardon!" she said. "Did you say, *six?*"

"Om having –" I said. At times like this I am like a singer who hears perfectly well that he is singing flat. "I'm hovving a little –" I began again. "I'm hevving a lottle trouble –" And again. "Um having a little tribble with my –" I gave up, and shouted it. "Wuth me *vowels.*"

Her eyes went back to normal; that is – in that exquisitely *gemütlich, simpatico,* silly-unsafe way of theirs, they no longer matched. And again, they almost brimmed over. "Coo, Oy soy," she said. Then she turned somewhat red, herself. "I mean, I say – I'm rather good at accents." She grinned. "It's me only clime to fime. I've done some recordings. *Counting to Ten in Twenty-five Amerindian Dialects* is one. Can you count?"

"If *curse* I can," I said. "Win, toe, thray, fair, fauve – ohh damn. I mean – dumb. And also – dim." My trouble was, I had more languages than would ever appear in her variorum, and all translatable into each other at once. To select a word was like trying to separate from a downpour one silver drop. But to burst of such things was against my nurture.

"It comes of being so oblong," I said. "An isthmatic affluction. And of not having the proper organs. At least, not yet."

"Why, we could work on it," she said. "I used to be rather good at remedial. In fact, it was my first job."

I didn't know what a job was, but no doubt it would come out later in the usual way of this world, the most eerie secrets here being hoarded for the very fun of unprising them.

"Oh, lively," I said. "Perhips we could make a recording together." I inched forward again, finding it so remarkable that I could, and I had never felt so colloquial before. *"Let's!"*

She half-inched backward, perhaps to show me that they moved to minute tolerances I never could achieve. But she was puzzled, clearly. "Just what did you mean by that," she said slowly. "By — *not yet?*"

I was astounded, disappointed, and probably a number of other things I failed to notice, though good God knows I was trying to fulfill my mission here and notice everything at once. By a little enamel clock on a bookshelf, I now estimated that my confession of a few minutes ago had taken at least fourteen of these, during which I had poured forth not only all the mystic legend of our gender, but also, though perhaps on the tremolo, my more practical hopes. She wasn't deaf. She had indeed listened — to perfection. But she hadn't heard.

The big things come so quietly here, at least to me. Nothing of what I felt as yet showed, or until I got a physiognomy of some sort, ever would. I had assumed that in a world where everybody knew about everybody else's insides already, surely this would make for an extraordinary harmony in the personal presence of each of you. Not — (Come quietly, revelation.) Not that you were as badly off as I was — no, worse. For, candid and open as I was in heritage otherwise, it was only reasonable to suppose that when I came to full bloom as a person here, I would be *all* harmony. But you — (Ve-ery quietly, now.) How was I ever going to make my way here, under this situation! What price now, all the evidence I had amassed of you — why it was probable that you had no more real history or social science data than we did, once it got past either side of your epidermis. (Quietly.) From your outsides, one simply hadn't a clue of your ins.

It came to me that if I were going to get what I wanted, it would be only by the exercise, the secret exercise of my own supraterrestrial intelligence. The meaning of this now struck me full on. I'd bargained for a world with a different schema of living from ours, but had still taken for granted that it was a united one, somehow. But you must differ here even over the assumptions you took for granted — and if I had learned anything about you it was that you would do so in the weirdest parabolas, one from the other, others from others, others from one. And all this going on below the cuticle, which if it had a thousand hues couldn't hope to reflect what went on below. But I could still count my blessings. By a parabola of intelligence impossible to you, I could imagine a place which would have all the assumptions, schemata and so forth, that you did — but *didn't live by a one of them.* I was lucky I hadn't hit there.

My interlocutor was watching me, almost subserviently now. How like lightning my mind moved in her presence! Even when she was silent, I was kept a-caper — and we had scarcely begun our dialogue. Her head rested now on her hand, against a pillow of bright curd-yellow, but the hair itself of a color I hadn't been taught and should certainly enjoy asking the name of. Then there was the jointure of her sitting — a pleasure to study that also. So complicated it must be, to sit so, and so easy it looked when she did it, knee upon knee. Garments hinted a solution of how it was done, but kept one from seeing absolutely. But nevertheless, this sort of teaching had it all over the intercom. Mentor had done her best, but this person—

I stared at her. *Was* she a person? Or merely a super-intercom-with-images, an automaton placed here for my education—and probably a number of -ations I hadn't yet heard of—as my guide to the full temporality and materialism of your world.

It was the first time I thought of her that conventionally. Though not the last.

And our longest silence yet. Silence, I thought, seems to tame her. I stared on. She returned my gaze, or so I fancied. And then, as in most of the silences to come, she spoke up first. Not to have done, is my only small eminence—gladly ceded to the one time in which we spoke up together.

"*Are* you a person?" she said. "Or some sort of telespeak or shadowgraph?"

This is the way it often went. Should I have spoken first—always?

"I didn't used to be," I said modestly. The truth doesn't make me free, or even comfortable, here. It just reminds me of home. "But I am now."

"Well, how am I to tell? Especially when you don't answer. And even then!"

It was only then that I realized my full advantage here. Your kind of being, with its anterior-posterior exterior—and above all that interior about which both everything and nothing were claimed to be known—thought itself equivocal enough. But I—! Ha. For though knowing myself already in possession of most of your qualities and cravings—and to be haring down the road as slowly as I could after the rest of them—yet to all appearances here I was a total ellipse.

"Oh, I was listening," I said, with satisfaction. "I just hadn't heard." What's more, I thought, they simply have no standards here, for Us. If ever I needed to lie—though my standards limited me to one big one – chances were I'd get away with it. And luckily there was only one I might be interested in.

The opportunity came sooner than I thought.

"It's easy to see that *you* are," I said. "A person indeed." Was this truth or flattery? I must be thrifty. "At least, after a bit." There, that for the record. "But why shouldn't it be?" I added. "After all, this is your world." I made so bold as to circle her, much as she had done me, which inspection she permitted, though turning her head to follow it as far as she was able. "You might have more trouble in mine."

"Oh, I know that," she said, "but that's your job, isn't it?"

I stopped short.

Meanwhile she, continuing to turn slowly, as if she were used to this process, stopped short also, in front of her mirror, and shook her head at it. "It's going to be some job, isn't it. Getting me in *shape*."

I came up behind her, but she didn't flinch, though for all she knew I might have dragons in me, waiting their turn at evolution – and for all I knew, I might. Were not both of us brave? To face the unknown is bravery. The mirror showed her returning to me a gaze she couldn't know for sure I gave. Though even in a curved mirror we were as unalike as any two creatures in the system, somewhere in that system we were of similar worlds.

Though not in every detail.

I scanned the walls. There appeared to be no computers there as yet, only the books, interspersed with some watercolors of woods – why they should have these here, when there were woods outside the very window! – but art, or the need to burn oneself *twice* with life, is still closed to me.

"Tell me," I said into the mirror, while another part of my vision, this luckily still to a degree dispersed, looked down over her — was this a haunch, and this a shoulder, and this a — nape? "Tell me — what is a job?"

Laughing as if it were nothing, she told me. And told me what mine here was to be, taking it for granted that I already knew. I listened with what amazement — and oh, I also heard. As far as she had been told, I was here to train her up somewhat as you trained your astronauts, though more irretrievably. I was to help get her in shape to get Out for good. Then I might go home, or join the Others here One day. Nothing whatsoever was said about getting *me* into shape for Now.

She turned and looked up at me, smiling. "*Are* you — really here?"

She caught me off base — that is, here, but being honest about it. "Technically, I'm both Here and There. For the diary's sake — and the species of course — I mean to go on that way as long as I can."

"Good God," she said, almost as absently as I. "I *needed* a philosopher."

Always so interested in the non-aspect of things, they are. I didn't care a rap, if she would interest herself in the non-aspect of mine. She cast a look at the door; I didn't know why.

"Dear Ja-nice," I said. I seemed to know the vowels for her by instinct; later I said it better, but she never once had to correct the phonetic. "Dear Ja-nice, did it ever occur to you —" Here I choked a bit, but looking carefully around, saw no evidence that we were monitored. "Did you ever dare conceive, that —" I never had, not even in that one niche of intelligence which one keeps unbugged even to oneself. "Did you ever think . . ." I had had to get out of my world, in order to admit it, ". . . that the authorities . . . *are not to be trusted.*"

Her eyes went wide.

"Why else do you think I'm leaving!"

Oh brave.

"But the new authorities," I said, "they're your friends. And your gender."

She raised those brows. "And what do you know of gender?" she said.

"Dear Janice," I said again, "listen to a story." And this time, she did.

To the legend – of our former, or buried, or somehow other selves – she listened with the fixed smile of the folklorist.

My own conviction – that far within, down or beyond the soma, I was meant to be a man – she took under advisement.

And the one large lie – that her friends had sent me to her as to an expert for this purpose – she believed at once.

She spoke sharply, in dialect utterly unknown to me. But I was now relaxed enough to admit ignorance. "What's that?"

"Queensland aboriginal," she said. "For bitch."

I had a feeling she would explain that later; this is the way dialogues begin. I also had a feeling I should make immediate amends for my lie, at least to myself. This is called conscience here, and accelerates with lying, but as far as I know does not outstrip it. "Don't blame Mère," I said, "if there's been a mix-up; blame Marie."

She shrugged. "I suppose they thought I wasn't good enough. Rachel is a first-class astronomer. I don't know about Marie. But the roster in general is tops. And I've no real distinction as an anthropologist, except for the speech. That's a hobby of Rachel's too, and I thought maybe she – But I suppose they have a preferred list."

"Marie is a distinguished bore," I said. "It's no wonder she made it to Ours so quickly. And dear Janice –" It was a great strain for me to talk in personalities. Among individuals so quick to take injury, whose attitudes indeed seemed to me almost all umbrage, I should never make my way until I too could insult. "I'm sure Mère would have approved of you," I said. "Either way."

That sank into her somewhere, I wasn't sure where until she laughed. "You're just too good to be true."

"I know," I said humbly. "But you could fix that, couldn't you."

She got up, strode around a bit, and then came over to me. "You really are rather — fluffy. Not just in looks, either. You talk like some bloody sort of bedtime story. Uncle Wiggily, or Aunt Mouse. And I'll wake up in the morning."

"Uncle," I said. "Please!" I found myself moving around after her; though her groove was more circular than ours, it resembled. "I'm quite aware of that," I said, "and it's quite worrisome. But if one takes into account how curvaciously I was reared, and in what constant *tergiversation* —"

"In constant what —?" She stopped in her round, leaned on a passing chair, and rocked back and forth with it, closing her eyes. "Oh Janice lovey, did you dream that?"

"No," I said. I almost shouted it. "Stop this self-indulgence! I'm brighter than you could possibly dream of. Why I had to decandesce for months before I dared come here! It's just that an outer ontilligence has every fringe of persitionality O-pressed."

"My!" she said. "I mean — Oy."

I decided I had no recourse but to dazzle her. "What you here mean by science, philosophy, et cetera, is exceedingly simplistic, Ours having congealed together eons ago, and taken mathematica with them." I paused, wishing she would open her eyes. My corner was literally shining with me. I went on. "Everything first came together, and then marvelously . . . stretched out. Biologically speaking, this is how it has become possible for a One and a One to remain — One.

So if imperturbability is what you're after, I'm your —" I gave a little cough, and then came round the side of her chair. She had her knees in the seat of it, and was clasping its back. "I know I'm terribly diffused. But you have what it takes to — pull me together. I'm sure of it. And as for your dear self, I could get it in the groove in no time. Do you know the catechism?"

She nodded, eyes sealed.

"Do you know your ad hoc hypotheses, and practice them daily?"

She shook her head, for a no.

"Dear Janice," I said, "does it not seem that I have all the *lacks* you need. Could we not propose — I do propose it — a mutual derangement — what would you call it —"

She opened her eyes. I saw myself in them — a One and a One, which remained One and yet was two. In me, I suppose she saw what she wanted to see also — herself, non-reflected. For, sighing, she answered. "An affair."

Then she jumped up, patted the chair, and began to stride about again, but with an indolent sort of weary-wariness which indeed more or less became her posture from then on. I found it attractive, though it didn't make her any more real to me. She had her mysterium, too. If I continue to speak of her in this beforehand, behindward way — which can make a speaker as tiresome as destiny, and his account as teasing — I make no apology. I am making my elegy, too.

"But I'm being such a bad hostess," she said. "Won't you sit — oh dear, I mean — *do* you? And I'd gladly offer you a cup of tea, or a dri —" She shrugged again, turning up her palms. "All very well to say, but what the hell is the blueprint — for this!"

"I do feel rather faint," I said, "it's been days since I carbonated. But it's a rather carminative process. I wonder if there's any place I could —"

She led me down the hall. Later, since ozone was all I needed, but more space than the house afforded, I used to take my privacy in the little grove of trees outside.

"See," I said, when I returned. "We have only to do what comes naturally to each of us. And let mutation take its course."

She grinned. "Or prox . . . amity. To speak *your* language."

And so, as teatime waned into evening, it came about that a one of you and a One of Us found themselves in front of the fireplace, watching the flames—which a one of you had built while prettily claiming this task for herself according to the female fuel-builders of I forget what tribe—and chatting of native customs all over the cosmos. We were indeed lucky in her background. Any temporary lacks on my part caused me no embarrassment, her performance of more than ordinary domestic function being immediately accounted for by data grubbed up from desert or jungle; one might have thought she had lived all her days with beings who had no appendages of any kind. Or that she now preferred to. Meanwhile, little by little, her knowledge of kitchen middens, barrows and sinks, drew me forth, until I felt myself tethering toward domesticity, drawn by all the sub-archeological details, *in situ,* of your intimate lives. This was the way to go about it, I was sure. As for her side of the adventure, surely she had only to watch *me.*

"If this were one of the upper klongs," she was saying, "and we were in a canoe. Or many places in Asia, where the boatmen are women. In other words, I would be rowing, and you would be taking your ease. In other words, sitting."

In other words was often to be her soft substitute for *why don't you,* this being the style in which she herself had been taught to educate. But although the auditor already knows that I could sit on occasion, I had not let on (being still afraid of cracks), and had taken up a posture near the mantel, thus early establishing two principia which have since served me well.

A: The seamy side of life, though still to be gotten used to, would serve to keep me moving.
B: In the matter of talent, always hold back.

And now for a while, we fell silent. Both of us were breathing time quite naturally, though whether she sometimes also heard space, as I still did, I could not tell. In the days when I had traveled instantly, I had had urgent need to hear how far ahead of me space was pure of object. Now this power was blunting. Only once in a while did I hear the wild, colorless call of those pure leagues. But meanwhile I was building up all those consolatory storage-boxes inside me, only the first of which had been for grief. Color, too, was setting up intenser rays all around me, its quarry and target; in place of the way I formerly saw the world, in a mild, pastel envelope one step above the assumptive gray of the animals, now everywhere, color's three-pronged nerve, hot and primary – saw me. And if up to now I had given no evidence of that power to smell thought, which you call extrasensory but we assign to olfaction, it was because the minute I hit the planet the ability had all but deserted me – surely a lucky move on something's part, since who possessing such a power too early on here, would stay?

In front of us, the fire played at tongues and tails, oranges and lemons; does watching a fireside make all beings, or only poets, think of age? Would I grow old here? Would she? Time is but a breath anywhere, but even the yardstick of duration is so small here; they even think that matter is permanent. According to their own specifications, I thought, in the oldest rock known here – perhaps a thousand million years existent – a molecule taken to be vibrating with the frequency of yellow sodium light, will in that period have given off pulsations only to the number of about $16.3 \times 10^{22} = 163{,}000 \times (10^6)^3$. And outside the window, in the Ramapo hills that ringed us, the rocks were nowhere near that old. What endures here? What really endures, what? Unless they smelled what I knew nothing of.

I looked across at her, thinking mightily of all I knew that she didn't and couldn't; her eyelids were down. How extraordinary it was for us to be here, within the planes of night this dual silence, within a cottage itself falling at a rate they think steady, and my thoughts – careful as I keep them – already tinctured with your substance, hers perhaps with mine. By the small yardstick then, and by the small breath, what would be said of us here, of this pair keeping watch together – one hundred years of your nights from this night? This is the way it all was, would they say: the world spinning on from its thousand million, and an ordinary night of it, half the globe at sequin, half at dark. This was the way – would they say? – it was before. Would that be the legend? Or did it all always end here – in the peculiar way their little *nows* sucked them ever downward from eternity, and in spite of all spirals flung outward – in an evening at home?

We had already settled on a routine. Routine was the thing, she said, and as much of it as possible in strictly educational exercise, this being one way to keep from an anxiety about nexts. For the nonce, also, I was to become no more visible, indeed to learn how to turn this down, if I could manage it; here, reluctantly bringing out a talent I had hoped to bury here, I assured her we had means. Tomorrow, she would start me on intensive reading research at the library, if she could get me unobserved to her own fortuitously secluded carrel. During the hours I was there, she would be at her own studies; no, she replied to my inquiry, she had no icehouse, but doubted that this was literally necessary. And later, under my direction, and thanks to some woodcarving tools she had once had of a Maori, she thought she could build herself a groove. One of the bedrooms would do. The little back room, being in fact the largest, and already so filled with helpful material, would be mine. I listened to all this with some inner laughter, noting the various materialistic means by which she proposed to get into the "spirit" of things; by so doing, they not only keep alive this primitive division they are so afraid to leave, but their whole brief history is the story of which of these ends is up.

But above all, she repeated, the first step for me was to learn how to turn off the terrible radiance of my own awareness. Not only would a sight of me explode our secret prematurely; even later on, when all was known, it would involve me in all sorts of company which might be bad for mutation; it might bring me out a freak. "You simply can't go round looking like a pillar of fire," she said, "or an overgrown halo. You want to be normal, don't you!" Since it was late, and we had just been discussing Malinowski (*Sex-life of the Savages,* a book to be on my agenda), we reserved consideration of that. But there was no denying that to be merely human, I must learn how to get a good night's sleep.

They tame the spirit with sleeping, here, while of course alleging the demands of the body; this keeps holy that division in their being which to allies of either, it would be treason to change. Nor can everybody here ever go about in perfect communion, but each must have a special name, chosen for euphony, royalty or larceny – and quickly awarded before natural bents become too clear.

So, at last, I found out the likeness and difference between a Harry, a Jamie and a Jack – though even now I have a hard time with *category* versus *individual,* often finding, no matter how I scrutinize a person, that he or she seems to belong entirely to only one or the other of these ranks. Then I have to remember that this is impossible, at least here.

But I did not accept everything here without protest. "I am a person," I said. What dignity. After the long coolth of unanimity, enough.

"Won't do. So am I." She had infinite patience really; the fire was almost out. "Matter of fact I belong to a category which calls itself the plain people."

My own glow remained stubborn.

"That's what I'll be." How much I had to learn; how much of one-ness still clung to me!

Even to be a plain one, she said, required certain formalities. Even in the jungle, such a lackluster ambition would be criticized, with punishment only a little less bloody than civilized ones.

"Even my people have another name," she said. "The Amish. That's my tribe. I'll take you down there sometime. I'm going to have to take you lots of places." She looked thoughtful. "I'll have to turn in the car. For a bigger one."

A name made one larger, then. But still I was cautious. Proud, too.

"I am already – I." What equity. And – with all these little excursions into "me" and "you" – variety, too.

"Nope," she said, grinning. "Too many of us. Listen, you mean to say . . . of course I ought to be glad of it, for my ideals, and I am of course, but it is hard to get used to. You mean to say, you all have no images of what we – of our customs, institutions, and so forth. You mean you all go round in a sort of mental nude?"

Of course we have them. If not precisely direct images, then the images of images. Only thing, they're locked up.

"Our life on the Oval is quite full," I said. For the sake of my own plans, I had better keep recommending it.

"But hadn't you yourself even a category, to know yourself by?" she asked. "How do you all *think!*"

"To explain life-on-the-curve is difficult," I answered, thinking rather hard and fast, actually. Of course I had had one, else how could I be here; occasionally one gets out. But I had a reluctance to telling her I was a hero, straight off.

"I'm a . . . at home, I was always considered a bit of a revelationary," I said.

She laughed, in that helpless-hopeful way of her, then got up and walked in that restless way of hers; she really didn't need a groove for curving.

I fancied I was getting onto many of her ways rather quickly.

"Good night, you . . . you *I*, you . . . good night, and have it your way until morning. Make yourself comfortable any way you choose. Anyway, maybe life-on-the-curve is just sort of — the inside dope on life-on-the-angle, eh?"

"Outside," I said carefully.

"Oh, yes of course," she said, with a little bow, and then halted. "I mean — and it is outer of course — life on your planet. *Elsewhere.*" I saw that the idea of it could make her tremble too. This was both our ways.

"Oh no," I answered, in as low a voice as my poor reed was able. We don't often name the name. "Ours is: Ellipsia."

"Ah, yes? *Lovely,* truly. And so are you, really." She stared at me in a way I hadn't got onto yet, called, I believe, a once-over. Or a twice. I moved closer, to cushion the shock that was coming to her. In fact, I leaned.

"Yes, lovely," I said. "For One thing, its shape — !" The One remains. O my teardrop, my Other home. "But this planet —" Though she couldn't see me at it, I was looking around me, at this strange cottage with all its seams, hung on a dented globe at the other end of nowhere, just safely short of the beyond. "But this — is *Elsewhere.*"

She got it at once, I think. Maybe, as with us, this is one of the boundaries they too know, but some ignore. They are stupid only in action. Not in mind. This time it was only her lip that trembled. Then she rallied. "But you said you were Here and There. Or neither maybe. Or both!"

I took a deep swig of air, the most I had managed here, and the heaviest yet. "I know. That's what *Elsewhere* is."

So, there it was, and I had said it for both of us, while outside of the outside of us, the interplanetary missiles swung. The legend moves on. The people move on. But the mutation is for life.

She could nod. She could clasp her hands, wring them a little and hang her head over them. She did it, for us both.

"I hate to tell you," she whispered, "but this place has its name too. It's called: Earth."

I had expected something of the sort, long since. But shocks are shocks, especially at end of day. "Very suitable," I said. "And pretty, too."

"Oh, don't look at me like that," she said. "I know just how you feel."

End of day. Or beginning – of the beginning. Surely that cock-crow which comes in poems derived from earthly ones, comes at dawn. "Girl, girl," I said – and where had I learned that word? – "*what* did you say? Did you say – *I had a look – !*"

She leaned toward me, understanding at once. For if I had a human expression, then surely this was the beginning of our mutual influence, at least for I-me.

"I'm not sure," she breathed, almost as heavily as I had. Her hand brushed the place on me where my eyes might one day be. Then she stood back, well back. "Maybe I just imagined. Maybe it was just in the eye of the Observo, I mean of the beholden . . . I mean –." She clapped a hand to her mouth. "*Look* at *me!*" she cried. "Whether I can *see* you do it, or not. Is – is there any change in –" Before I could answer, or take opportunity to lean further, she ran to the mirror. Both of us answered her. No. Not yet.

Slowly, she returned to my side, and once more scanned me carefully. "Turn around," I heard her mutter, "I have difficulty keeping my place." Then she giggled.

I turned round and round and round; in fact I spun a-dazzle, even daring, at the very end, my old gyroscopic angle. "Wow!" she said. "Wow."

When I righted myself, stopping on pinnacle as neatly as any ballerina, she applauded. I stood motionless. "How very still you are," she said, "When you are still. No, if it was one, it must have been a very fleeting expression. I can't honestly say you have a look, yet." Then she smiled. "But I'll tell you what you do have."

"What?"

"A name."

The name she'd thought of was Eli – short for my place of origin. But also – if I wanted lineage from here – short for Elijah. When asked what it meant, she thought it stood for "chosen," but checked on it to be sure. It didn't. It meant *Yah is God,* whatever that meant. She assured me that most names had little to do with the people who had them. And so a One was named, under the sponsorship of the *Encyclopaedia Britannica,* Vol. 9, EDW to EVA, pp. 273–274, of the eleventh edition, which she informed me was the most noted. She was charmed that I could read Elijah's story over her shoulder. She particularly pointed out these words of the summary: "A career into every stage of which the supernatural enters."

"*Hyper* –" I said in disgust. "*Hyper*natural is what we are. If you're making comparisons. We may be a little out of your ken, but we're real, you know." As for Elijah, it was all a fearfully gory story I thought, but I gave her my consent, telling her it was because of the ravens who fed him, birds being a little in my line — but actually it was because of the widow, who received the prophet with all her hospitality.

Afterwards, knowing your weakness for interpretation, for a while the whole business made me uneasy; we on Ours had no intention of our advent being mistaken for anything but what it was. Nor had I any desire to see this narrative later scanned by the symbologists in any department of a civilization already far, far too devoted to the *déjà vu*. Later, however, I reminded myself that its denouement will make that impossible.

In any case, as you may have surmised, I was henceforth mostly called "you" anyway, and the little ceremony made a nice ending to a domestic evening.

"Good night," she said. "Eli. I hope you're real. Sleep well, anyway."

The hardest part, I thought, would be to get her to believe I was "real." But in trying, I would become so. I had an image of my image now. I made her a little speech, saying as much.

Ask the great eel-rays if they are real, I thought meanwhile, my head-image reeling; ask the strange *Selachii* of your underwater deep. Or any number of genera back in your own phylogeny — none of them specimens to be met too lightheartedly, even on a Sunday, after church. Ask *them*, I thought. But not yet geared to insult, this I kept to myself.

"Pinch me," she said. "If you are real. Or perhaps — when."

But she was serious too. Somewhere to-down of her, she did care. "You'll see," she said. "We'll do it. They'll see, one day, oh they'll see, also." She meant, her friends.

"Will Jack see?" I asked. I hadn't forgotten him.

She looked at me. "Oh, you were there, weren't you," she murmured. "I won't ask — for how long." And I didn't tell her. But as I found out very soon after, for educational purposes, not long enough.

Chin in hand, elbows on the back of a chair, she continued, in spite of our good nights, to brood at me. "One day, you'll *sit* here, right in this chair. You'll have a cup of tea with – with whoever's for company. And you'll have – an expression, all right." She smoothed the chair pillow, plumping it. "Maybe they meant no harm, my girl friends at the top. Maybe the experiment has to have one reverse job – for a control. Or maybe at the last, after years of work, they all went wacko." She shrugged. "*Quién sabe?* Maybe I'm a better anthropologist than even I know." She said something in another language I didn't know.

"Queensland aborigine?" I asked.

Clasping her hands together, she shook her head at me. "No. Jamie had a hairy Ainu in tow once. Wrote a book with him. What wouldn't he have given – for *you.*" She smiled. "Don't take it personal, Eli. Or rather – do. Eh, Eli?"

Me, I remained imperturbable. The chair was smooth, where she had brushed away her own imprint. It looked like a comfortable chair.

She walked to the sitting room door which led to all the other rooms but one. "Maybe some of Jamie's gentlemen friends at the Center will see, too." Then, still musing, she retraced her steps to the outer door, through which I had come, and locked it. "But you're right. Maybe we'll have to make a special effort for – gentleman Jack."

Hand still on the lock, she made me another little bow. "And now Eli – good night."

I had a fancy she had made that little, dismissing bow to others before me, though perhaps not to any of like shape. How had they answered her?

But, aside from my shape, perhaps my situation was different from theirs in other ways, at least from some. I was from out of town. I was a houseguest. I was inside.

How should I answer her, to suit all that, to suit her own personal share of the adventure, which she had perhaps a little forgot? And to suit me.

I claim no originality for my answer, but perhaps a little heredity. "Good night," I said. "Good night – She."

After I was left to myself, alone but in this peculiarly half-shared manner, I stayed for a long while awake with what you call insomnia but we consider to be that awareness of spirit, product of the ages, which sees no reason why, even for a mere moment of them, it should go back down again to the shadow from which it came. At last, having made my peace with it, dearly bought as that must be, I glided to the little back room, and after considering its facilities, made my bed – upon the long bed.

Ours, hers and mine, was not the usual situation. But then, every human situation was a little elliptic also, a little in reverse. And we were both people. Each in each, each to each, we would find our own characters, and though perhaps not together, our bodies too. We were ships that pass in the night – but then, people are.

4. Into the Maze

SO, INTO the maze we went. The world was all before us — as once was said of those either facing Eden or leaving it; now this must be forever amended: Worlds. And it will be for you, the audience, to say how much this means or how little; the threads will all be coming together soon.

It was in February, that afternoon when I and a few snowflakes first brushed through her door. It is — as you all know — December now. This was the period of time, she said that we — and of course the others — had. Until One day? I asked. She nodded. And aside from the others en masse, I inquired, were there other couples, like us? She professed not to know, not being a member of the inner council, but thought it likely; in a world grown to the scope and complication of this one it was scarcely believable that the authorities would start with just one couple — not again. Meanwhile and whatever, she said, her face warm with it, we should have to take our solo-duo isolation and our destinations both de facto, and work very hard in order to come into our kingdoms. Since this still accorded more with your legend than ours, I was willing — being eager for anything of yours I could get.

"So much is available." I sighed.

"Yes," she said, glancing past me and acurve, an irritating habit which began the first day. "We're like rich people, who prefer to work."

"What is 'rich'?" I asked, and she sighed. Not for the hour's disquisition ahead of her, but because of the hair-splittings. Inching along physically was nothing, compared with what I was learning to do with the mind.

Her main duty — and this she held with passion — was to induct me, at least through hearsay, into the collective misery of the world. Misery, she said, was by far the better organized here, if not by nature, then certainly by men; pleasure, much more at random, had to be picked like bluebells along the road. But for one of my sanguine temperament — and once I got my appendages of course — the latter could be learned without training. For training, misery was the thing. I refrained from observing that by that time my temperament might have sadly straightened itself out. (Like many who early desert the orthodox for the worldly, she was still more innocent than she knew.) No matter. As she sternly declaimed for me all her catechisms of births and deaths, wars, starvations and other killings, it was the passion she did it with that I held it my duty to be interested in. She found this amoral.

"You mean to say, babies could be *boiled,* and you wouldn't —"

"What is a baby?" I said. "Is it a child?" I was more comfortable with my own innocence now, having long since increased my own expectations of it.

"— could be gassed, one could be stewing right here — and all that you'd care about, or be fascinated with, is *my* attitude!"

How they hate their own humanism! It was my job to teach her the real nature of the almost sublime, but I sometimes despaired of it.

"Where there's no difference, there *is* no morality," I said. "I've come a long way even to know what *amoral* is." And if I got my appendages soon, I thought privately, maybe far enough. Meanwhile I had my first image of a yawn, delightful the first time or so; after that, a la your-style, I just let 'em rip – and without having to hide them either, in this case having the best of both worlds – nothing showed. But that never lasts long here, does it.

"Let's have one of my Voco-Phono lessons, why don't we?" I asked. "Or better still, when are we going to start lessons for you? It's begun to worry me, which is scarcely useful. I can learn to worry elsewh – otherwise."

But she would have none of it, asserting that one didn't learn a vacuum – and that whereas my course was to learn, learn, learn all the accessories of a variable existence, hers was merely to divest herself of them. Until, as she said, she should be as serenely passive as a round bubble in a rill of them, in a pond.

The trouble with converts is that they always regard the new world as the opposite of the old. Young as I was here, halfway through my journey I had learned otherwise. But it was not up to me to hint that the opposite of a world which regards itself as positive, does not necessarily regard *itself* as negative. Or that, though the whole sound and Omphalos of our creation is O, it is just that veriest subtle flattening at its ends, and of its beings too, which makes Us all what we are. I hoped she hadn't the idea that it was circular. Or that we were zero. Willy-nilly, though I should like to have been consulted on the grooving track she constructed, and perhaps to show her a few practice turns on it, I was never allowed in the bedroom.

Meanwhile, as for me – in my past life, neither events nor any other accessories of yours had been so plentiful that I could afford to ignore them; indeed I had a tendency to greet one and all with equal ardor and no prejudgment, so that the question of whether I would turn out warm or cold of nature, fool or genius, was as open as it might be with any — excessively intelligent, of course — child. In truth, limited though my *mise en scène* might temporarily be in terms of what can really be done here with a trifle more brio, I was living a life of simple enchantment.

I can best get at the tone of it if I say that the first man I ever had an opportunity to study up close was the milkman. Through the chute. A most clever contrivance, it had as strange an optic as many of your more complex devices for viewing nature near and far. And, since I had to get down to it by extending myself along the floor, the situation had as much geometrical and philosophical amplitude as anyone could wish — and since it was *me.* But I had by now discovered that this is the way such situations were always experienced here, so therefore gave up describing them to myself, in favor of merely having them. As for the milkman, socially or aesthetically he did me no harm. Indeed he did as well as any. He had a long slide of a nose, a chin which the eons had meditated upon well, and had at last lengthened. Some days he had only a roundish eye — set more toward eternity, I always thought, than milk. Later I found him, feature by feature and all of a piece, on one of her shelves, in a most expensive volume of plates marked: Breughel. So I discovered art and the milkman together, and as a lucky child might, quite without shock or pain. Art is a finding.

But when I took my discovery to her, or rather directed her to shelf and volume, my surprise was that she was not at all surprised that in all your variation there was some repetition too. "What a child you are!" she said merely. (No, there was more to it — excuse me, this is an elegy, and I am still learning how to remember — or is that what elegy is?) She added thoughtfully, but with one of her grins also — "Or maybe you're adolescent by now."

By then I had learned all I could of your morphology, both

historical and current; indeed it was her contention that my ontogeny had gone so self-consciously mad for my phylogeny that only her discipline might keep it from addling. Then too, I was forever coming to her with bruises or bumps I thought might be significant, until she said it was touch-and-go whether, via accident, excitement and ineptitude, I might not dispose of myself altogether, before having a chance to become a man, or anything else. Under this barrage, I began to keep my counsel, and from this began to do so generally, led by her chaffing from introspection to introspection. *Life* is a finding too, I thought, but other people didn't want to hear about, preferring to find out for themselves, or pose as if they already knew. This was the sophisticate — and perhaps the contemplative — line. I might end up a contemplative, I thought, but not without a struggle first, for action. So, despite that I was not yet born to manhood, and she and I were only living together, I sometimes — according as how what I was reading swelled the heart-image or numbed the brain one — thought of this period of schooling as a courtship, even a honeymoon. I was mixed up, of course, but for me, that was progress. Emotively I was still more tentative than tangible, but at certain times I felt my potential as if it were biceps. Agreed — gestation, before too much happens to one, can be an introverted time.

So, when I stood before the fire of an evening, I tried to say little or nothing of the daily wonders, just as I try to do this now. Take for granted then, the green juice or cold swan-swoon of your seasons, or the bloom of your faces, swaying like history in the magic of your dust-coarsened air. Or there was the horse I'd seen, its hindparts cocked perky in a windy field, and like a horse I'd seen in a windy field in Bucks, and now both of them were the horse-in-a-field forever, its hind-parts cocked perky and permanent. No, no listings, else the poem would be endless and get nowhere, as perhaps it did. I contented myself with a brooding line of—not *thanks;* it can't always be thanks—recognition. Between morning and evening fires, or breezes, what a ductile wonder is a day!

Dusktime of all moments of my day was the ritual one, the beautiful—the difficult. It was the hour when, until then locked in my study, for the safety of all, she said, though it was she who turned the key—I heard her at last give over those loud devotions which all the afternoon had echoed, though her bedroom was upstairs along a hallway and two doors down. So adept had she become in her grooving that after a few false starts I never heard her at it, which was alas as it should be. But when she practiced the stillness she so envied me, she was much too tense and frictional, so this, to my comfort, I yet heard.

Meanwhile, I lived in terror of her discovering that I wasn't practicing the various exercises she had devised for me, all to small-scale radii and all designed to humanize—but instead day after day neglected them to lie indolently on the long bed, in daydreams inflamed by the vision which still clung to its cushions, and by the reading of the night before. Day after day, I set what I called the *two-two,* the two-headed automaton, to working there, but got no more than a Punch and Judy run-through of those few moments I had seen, or an impossibly Grand Guignol rendering of what I had not. No matter how devotedly I simmered over my zoology at the library or alternated this with the warmest romances, I could never get myself sufficiently aboil to complete the image of what I yearned to, and most needed for my development. That simplest, most singular episode, and of all your pornography the most prevalent—I could never imagine it straight on through. And when for a few exhausted moments I fell asleep, then my old former friend came up from underground indeed to take vengeance, providing all sorts of Barmecide illusion, but all of it oddities only—

buttonhooks were nothing! – and thereby seeing to it that there were dangled before me all the sauces, but never the goose, all the cadenzas but never the main theme.

I decided I would either have to make it my business to see one of those movies of a sort not procurable at the library, or else – and here the circle I was in came round again – somehow get myself out of myself – and *live.* I was in despair of a sort. But to tell the truth, it was of the sort that could barely wait for the next afternoon.

After that came the dusk, when ambiguity flows best, and in the soft obscurity before the lamps brought us back to our own appearances, to the vast abyss still between them, measured with sidelong distant glances of evaluation, we had our most private conversations. To these we came as any couple might, each from his and her own afternoon and the ideas or emotions so stimulated – one from the slimming salon and one from the steambath. And like many a couple, I should guess, from our amiably tepid company, one might never have known. Topics we discussed were suited, she said, to any drawing room, yet would do for the humblest dwelling as well. We talked much for instance – rather like two distant blood-relatives met by severe chance, and one the much younger in the world – of what I would become. It was true of course that in not every drawing room, or hovel either, could a young newcomer discuss eagerly whether he would turn out to be white, red, yellow or black. A topic almost always avoided by the senior member, no matter how many times suggested by the other, was whether he *was* a he. Her own future shape was not discussable, there being only One. But she would talk endlessly of native customs, hers or mine, and in this connotation, if I wished, I could sun myself in her particularly high regard. Of all her past acquaintance, and certainly presently, I was the native she was most interested in.

And after that, perhaps, we would have a little music. The first morning, I had come out from my "museum" to hear the radio playing — a chorale of what I now know to be music. I had stood motionless, then dropping little by little, as if spelled, in a half-fainting return to my former angle — was not this my own, our own classical laughter, or faraway and cold, that poignance of the almost undesperate sublime? After that, she never turned on WQXR or any of the stations too devoted to the kind of music which might too much affect me with these intimations of my O-mortality — and her own taste was not classical. I learned even to like one song, the "Vilia" from *The Merry Widow,* that she spoke of lightly as hers.

And after that we had dinner, or she did, on a tray, while she turned on the telly for my delectation, though I would have been satisfied to watch the movements, never greasy, of her mouth; perhaps she knew this too. In some circumstances, a person of my transparent background and still fragile cellular construction might well have formed a prejudice against eating or ended up at best a dyspeptic; as it was, watching those small muscles move, pout, that face grow oh so delicately bland and perhaps a litle rounder, the little sips, dainty but never arch, and all of it with an economy as strong and neat as a cat's, I yearned first to shrink to a cutlet, that I might lie on a plate, then, ashamedly remembering my I-ness, to eat her.

Saturdays — a kind of feastday, with, she said, the longest history of orgy, saturnalia to satyrs and all the rest — she had a large meal in the kitchen which she would not let me watch, and was, I thought, probably some training lapse of which she too was ashamed. It was at such times that I tactfully repaired for my own weekly carbonation to my little privy place among the rear grove of trees. Sometimes while there, I heard a footfall pause on the path that led past the front door, as if to note my faint glimmer, then pass on. But this was in the early weeks; then it ceased altogether. And since she was so keen on our secrecy, having already drawn the blinds, sold the car, stopped the milk, the paper and all but one weekly delivery, and now went out herself only for the mail and to the library — "We are not at home," she would say to me, smiling, "the way Paris is not at home in August" — I told her nothing of this. From tweaks of the kitchenmaid sensibility which comes from uncurbed reading, I thought I knew who. And romantically, Chanteclerically proud, and Moorishly jealous — would I have fallen in the snow or strutted? — I fancied how we might meet. We never did — or not out there. I never told. But those footfalls were a marked help to the growth of my feelings.

When I came in from the woods I had always to press the back bell or call out to her; this she said was for safety's sake. But even within the routine of the house, we preserved a decorum of bathroom doors and bedroom ones, and if I never got into hers, she was equally observant of those courtesies which might yet help to make a man of me, and never came into the room she still called the "museum" — which was mine. Slowly, meanwhile, I built my picture of her. She was the most watchable of persons, who must never have known a time when she wasn't being watched. In contrast, I suppose, my lack of definity was restful. And slowly, sent out artful-artless toward the quiet pink slope of my sympathy, her confidences came.

If she said "telly" and had other Anglicisms poking out like umbrellas from her storehouse of acquired patois and dialects, it was because Jamie her husband, a Scotsman who had required always and precisely to be termed Scottish — and who knew whether or not his profession-obsession mightn't have started there? — had gone to Merton in his youth-time, and been a don there for part of hers.

"He'd had another wive?" I said – by this time, I knew about wives, up to a point, and never lost a chance to dwell on them.

She nodded, with an odd look at me that I never interpreted, but of this wive we spoke little more. I never saw Jamie either really, put his images together as I might, from grizzleskin to bush-moustache, as she told it. I never saw him except in the shadow of his small shadow – hers. They had met under a bush too. "Not a cabbage," she said, laughing, having long since explained to me that context – but what was called a sparrowgrass bush, then a youthful evening haunt of hers, in a graveyard in Sunbury, Pa. I often made her repeat this story, I meanwhile standing proud and ever rosier, because of knowing all the contexts. How could she have known, she said, how many of *his* she had piqued and teazled, when she said to him afterwards – afterwards of what, I knew also –"*Oh, ja, 'ch wis was du bis.*" She had told him her tribe, and of her parents' lapses – from wearing buttons to living in town and having the gas and electrisch, to her father's drink and her mother's earrings – for which they had been thrown off the grandfather's farm. And how she herself had three languages. "*'Ch hab Deitsch, und Deutsch*" – how cleverly her dear little tongue must have made that turn – "*und 'ch hab der good Englisch.*" And she even knew what *he* was. "*Ja, 'ch wis. Du bis* Scotch!"

On the television, she never liked to look at the news, or listen – too much quack-quack. Jamie hadn't been much of a talker, but had made talking dolls of his wives. One was still living – somewhere; it was the second one, the Maori girl, who had died. And it was her son by Jamie who had given Janice the woodcarving tools she had at long last found such a use for. Jamie had sons all over, though never a daughter by anybody at all. Just as well, and said so himself; could never keep his hands off a young girl. Give him credit though, he always went back along the trail, even years later, picked up the sons, as one by one they popped up out of huts, long-houses or island waters, and popped them back — into a good church school.

"Oh these half-breed Englishmen," she said, "half-breed Irish, Scotch — I mean *Scottish,* or American — queerishest of the queer!" She gave me a sharp look. "Queerish queer, you understand, Eli, not *queer*-queer. Or at least, not all of them."

I would have nodded if I could, but anyway, she seemed able now to tell so well what I was thinking — though we were wary of false alarms — that I often thought she could smell.

"Always on the move, too," she added. "But keep in touch, is their motto. And they don't in the least mind — going back."

Jamie himself, whenever he had deceived her — this context like all moral ones, took a while, but finally, by rote, I got it — did so only with older women, or those along the trail already. She hadn't deceived him ever, instead merely cultivating a taste, when she could indulge it, for never going back. "Queerish," she said again, with a sigh. And that was the end of Jamie, though since then she had not pushed much forwarder in her own history.

Sometimes, her quick chatter — in which drama, character and gender were all of them mixed up together — put a strain even on my extended reading. I had a question or two, one of which I put forward with some awkwardness. "Shall I be, do you think — one of those half-breeds?"

She muffled what I feared was a laugh — though it could have been a sob — then said, with an expression that of all her many I liked the best, so straightforward, nothing roundish, "Whatever . . . you'll be a dear."

I swallowed the second one — I was swallowing more frequently these days. A half-breed. Was: *Jack?*

Or sometimes, as she sat down with the tray, and flicked

the switch to a story or a dancing, she remarked that she didn't really care for more news of a world she was leaving — and out of the complicated reasons she might have had for this, gave me one. "I'd like to move on forever. But not get any particular where."

That was Ours, all right. I myself was all for progress, more and more. I felt I would do well here. But more and more it had to be at my demand that we had a Voco-Phono lesson; almost it seemed that she had lost interest, not in me, but in my getting on. Often I had to plead for it, with what I hoped was a little joke. "Well, let's, eh — since we can't play cards." Was this piteous, tedious, or my worst bugaboo — coyful? Even from reading, I couldn't quite get right all the attitudes. But, for a proper joke here, I did see that serious attitudes had to be taken seriously — and if my growthing went as predicted, I fancied I'd make good use of how to give and take a proper joke. I hadn't yet puzzled out what was needed for the tragic sense of life, or even quite what it was, or whether people really wanted it. More to the point at present was that, evening by evening, I could see that my darling — she called me dear, but I had advanced ahead of her — was drifting. Was it tragic or comic, that nobody could know better than I — what and where she was drifting toward?

In the lessons themselves, now that my speech had advanced from the grammars, catechisms, recordings and verbalization tables she had first devised, I found it harder to keep her attention, and sometimes even had to resort to making old mistakes which had once amused her, saying "has-been" for instance for husband, or "woeman" for wooman, not expecting her to laugh, but hoping only that she would notice what I was doing, or perhaps even give me a beating for some reason — I was reading Dickens, de Sade, and Krafft-Ebing at the moment and could have given her any number of reasons — but all that occurred was my own recognition that I no longer amused even me. Which has not stopped me from trying; this is called a sense of humor. Meanwhile, more and more often, she went with me to my evening library stint at an hour she once would have thought dangerously early.

It was quite simple, the way we did it. There was a way across the fields, and she carried a woodsman's lantern which when vigorously swung effectively reflected me out. We never had to cross the agora I had hit upon on arrival, but it could be seen in the distance, and remembering those cries of the aurora borealis, I hunted up manuals on camouflage, magic illusion, protective coloration, and like any young thing growing here, found many a little trompe l'oeil trick which helped me blend with my surroundings. One or two rainy evenings now and then kept us in, or she did, citing how the first Indians here on the continent had died of measles contracted from the Europeans, and how there was no need as yet to take chances with my unknown hardihood. Curious, how none of you ever think of *yourselves* as the aborigines – not even, I presume, the aborigines. How she could think we would not have primed ourselves with all the immunities was another of her innocences, but I kept my own counsel – and the weather marvelously held. Terrestrial nature sometimes does that, before it stretches toward another adventure. So we two traversed the fields in our own light, and a lantern's. She was always and ever staring upward on the dark map she had set her sights for, but to the traveler of many crossings, the night sky is sufficient if it but be known to be above him. So, an affair of two worlds had narrowed down almost to that idyll of a man and a maid – and a field – whose authorship is generally ascribed to the ages. So, at least, I had read. And so I hoped.

Then, at the library, in the door we went, via her key, up the backstairs, and into the stacks. Once in her cubicle, while she raided the shelves for me, I was safe, even against any possible scholar as late as we. And there, reading everything from Anthropology to Zoology — and though my rate of speed slackened slowly, slower ever slower, until toward the end I couldn't read faster than a volume of Blackstone a minute and a good novel in forty — I spent the sea-green incorruptible hours of my Here youth. So I set myself to read your universe through, haunted only by the fear that I should too soon finish. A young person's fear! Nature has its own ways, in retrospect all nobly simple. What slowed me down, ever more irreparably — until near the end I could read no more than the day's supply of the ten or fifteen books she could load into two book bags — was of course my own delight, that first touch of the bibliophile's hunger. Everything I read, or almost, was still pornography to me!

Then, at four o'clock or so we betook ourselves home again quickly, I glowing hot as the dawn itself, stuffed as I was with all the splendors to come, and she pale as Diana disappearing — each to our own daydreams.

Daytime excursions she had decreed were impossible. Yet, once, we dared it, for what she called dreamily an ice-picnic — her choice. She wanted — as she said — out. The state park, she said, would be deserted even of keepers, on the farthest side of the winter lakes. While she took her air there, I could start my own test of endurance — it was time I started something, unless I planned to remain forever a monstrous bookworm — and if I was not soon to develop a figure, or some fassimile of a bifurcation which would allow me to be clothed, I would have to learn to brave the elements as I was. She spoke somewhat harshly, and though I thought of such things as a manteau or a toga, offered me nothing. "If you could only learn to *sit,*" she finished, "I could hire a car!"

Scarcely knowing why, I still was hiding that talent, as well as — another. Only a day or two past, on the excuse of my weakness, she had kept me from the rain. Must I mistrust her, or did she want me somehow both weak and strong? And how varying she was herself; surely the authorities had done right in sending me to her to complete my variation. As we went together through the numb woods, aglide and atrudge on a dull day that hadn't a spark of orange fire in it, I felt what even the rebel, the revolutionary must often feel, and perhaps he most inwardly — a secret restfulness, near resignation, in the thought that the authorities may after all be right. Was this why, on the very edge and crux of the adventure, he might turn about and betray his own kind? I stopped, in horror — what hateful insight was this? — then went on blithely, saved by the reminder that none of either world could now tell for sure what my kind was. Here and there along the path, an iced puddle was haunted with blue. Station by station, these *suggested.* And in my first sight of the lake, that gray rainbow even on this cloud-wrapped day, I accepted it, the nature of this universe. I was seeing better and better, the doubleness of things here. And how it was managed, that one admired it.

She had brought her skates. So, for an hour or so, while I trembled but bore it, I watched her twirling over and over, along the black and white geometry, so single, of her hope. So as not to gloat over me perhaps, she wasn't too heavily clothed herself, in short skirt and jacket. Was she rounder in form, not so slender? I feared so, and that just as she must be inspiriting me — so that all my inside must be swelling, buzzing and sporing, and spoored all over with the black print of her enigmas — so all the while my dull One-ness of spirit must be having its effect on her also. How differently folk watched here, I thought, recalling the constant bowing and acknowledgment of the obligatory life scene at home. Or how differently — when beings were folk. I had posted myself against the frozen sedge before a long promenade of bathhouses, ending nearest me, in the bareswept ticket stall. On the surface of that lake — so wild a wondershape to me — she was describing over and over a pear-shaped oval. But what I saw upon the lake was its name, dragging its great swallowtail wings over the whole of it, *Tiorati,* in black-netted brown and plush-orange, and butterfly-white. That of course was because of my poetic nature, which gratefully insisted on spanning both worlds. But she had turned her back on the bathhouses. And though no human could have been sure of it, I knew I was facing them, and that in my longing second sight they were a-tumble with people, a-Dickens and a-Daumier and a-Rowlandson with these beings I had seen so little of except in their own illustration — and of course a-Malinowski and a-Lombroso, a-Krafft-Ebing, de Sade, Machiavelli and a-de Montherlant too. My tastes were perhaps still cartoon. But people could not be had by hearsay alone.

Yet I froze with the sedge as I stood there, and not from the elements, not with cold. The inflections of two-ness were more versatile than I thought. The one being with the two-heads — any of us would have thought that the final elaboration — and enough. But was there another?

She was taking off her skates now, her hands clumsy in her mittens, surely only from cold? I couldn't help her, and had never before thought to. In all that was daily done here. I watched her, from this afar. There is a foreshortening that intimacy brings. I hoped it was nothing else but that, for my one-ness was now a disease I feared to bring her. Yet — oh these halves that never match here! — I wanted to engulf her with the I that was now me.

She came and stood by my side, the skates dangling. When she came that close, could I really see her?

"I was watching you," I said. In the cold, her face blurred. Though it was still a face — as much of a one as ever I would hope to have, and more. "From afar," I said. And from near too, though you cannot see it.

She nodded, head down. In fact, her head moved so neatly in its socket, as if following the memory of the skating on a small, neat oval of its own – had it ever moved like that before? I was filled with terror of her, for one startled moment – of her for whom until now I had had only terrors.

Then she raised her eyes and stared at me, as if only now she dared her fill of it. Then it was she who drew back.

"Let's go home," she said. "Let's go back."

I turned as if to walk at her side again.

"Go on ahead," she said. "Walk ahead of me."

I did so, at my glide. From puddle to puddle, their winks even more haunted now, I pondered. She had said "home," which I knew quite well as the places here you went back to, as Jamison went back to his sons. There were places here one did go back to, or ways of trying. Although the homes moved also; I had heard her say how many she had had and how often, and I had also seen, as she said it to the cottage, the quirk of her mouth. And she and I too – were moving. Even I – who seemed so still, to *them*. We above all things here were moving onward, and did each wish the other to wait, to stay the same? No, not both of us. I told this to the last puddle. Just I.

Then I heard my name, and turned to it, thinking as always, and perhaps as you do when named: *No, there is more to me than that.*

"Eli," she said, and how hoarse that voice. "I'm always looking at you." I saw her swallow. "You never see."

The watching is different here. A one watches the other from afar, another who is watching not. The one who was not watching – now watches the other, from afar. What rises, the nameless third who is company, across that distance? Who stands there, shy observer, in the gap between?

5. Budding and Melting

SO, THAT next afternoon, you might think that when I heard the turn of the key which released me to join her, I would bound forward from the most exuberant dreams ever — not so. You yourselves have a saying, "Give him a finger, and he wants a whole hand." And though during my whole sojourn here I had never been given much more than hope — who is? — even the slightest encouragement always at once made my hopes more precise. When we had crept into the house without another word between us, each going off to our rooms, she up the stairs, and I down the hall to my museum, it had been my hope — that for once she would not turn the key. And what advantage would I have taken of so beautiful an action? — none but to bask the whole day in the soft mallow-gleam of it, while perhaps her door lay open too, in exquisite trust. Or so I imagined, the minute the key turned, as usual, to lock me in.

Upshot of it was, I found myself utterly unable to dream at all, and after a space of distraught gliding to and fro, actually set about practicing the exercises I had so far neglected. What a strange thing is resentment — I shall never understand it, particularly in myself! In any case, I found what I had suspected; her exercises, poor dear, whether verbal, calisthenic or ideational, were not likely to set any being of my class in mutation, based as they were on a commercial humanism, the product of your social scientists. I mulled over the graphs and polygraphs with some amusement; if I was going to be as normal as this, I would be your first. We should have to help you with your conceptions of us, more than we had thought. And afterwards, we might have to help you with your humanity too.

Once you saw us, perhaps that was all that would be needed. As I paced the floor of this museum of mine – which I had begun to cherish for the way its silent masks, clay hands, weapons and other debris of your duration seemed almost a practice audience for me, your prize specimen – I brooded again on all those like-differences which you and we, cat's cradle style maybe, nevertheless share. And which have allowed us to get together at last. But if I were going to say it all in a nutshell, as you say, how would I do it? I could say that just as you, to your eternal praise, sometimes let your poetic imagination rip wide as your yawns, we do the same with our physical ones, that where you must still machine space, we by image-making transcend it; in those realms where you cast only poems, astrologies and a little teleportation music, we have already quite matter-of-factly arrived. I could say it like that, but I could do better. *I could be the nutshell.*

In the course of my meditations, whose path I strove always to keep off-oval and slightly irregular, I found myself in front of the mantelpiece, from whose marble there hung two grossly curved cherubs, the sight of whom, since I was courting prenatal influence rather than discounting it, I tended usually to avoid. I had no fear of catching their wings; they and I were on entirely different evolutionary lines. Even their fatty cheeks – and these in all directions, I could have learned, like some of you, to tolerate. But in a well-set-up male, pudenda of that size would be ridiculous.

Besides which, I found your *putti* of whatever sex, with their high aims and low execution, always a little obscene, hoped your babies would do better, and indeed was never quite persuaded that these two cheese-white creatures were only marble, stone. As you may have noticed, I had a mistrust of objects, reassure myself as I might that on this planet it was not nearly so well founded as on mine. That is, it appeared that though you could control objects to a degree, or sometimes gave evidence of being controlled by them, you could not – by that image-stretch of the cells which was our newest scientific practice – *be* them.

This latest expertise, a delicate one even for us, was like all on Ours, most severely regulated; it was permissible to invade only certain classes of objects, and only certain of the elite were allowed any such performance. The rush had been enormous; one would have thought people didn't want to be people any more – at least, not Ours. Certain sociologists had been particularly adept in temporarily transforming themselves or other beings into objects, and I – yes, I, a former poet, now confess it – had for my own purposes joined that profession. Temporarily. But my wary scrutiny of objects here, now may be even clearer. At home, some of them might have been friends.

For, our new accomplishment, popularly called "objectivity," and being of course merely a casting ahead of images, on wavelengths of a scope and penetration some steps advanced of your own electronics – had of course nothing to do with mutation. We could transfer ourselves to the inanimate with a certain precision now, but in effect only counterfeiting what nature did to us every day, if more indiscriminately. But for us to have gone from flesh-form to flesh-form by any like transformations was still beyond us – in fact, there we were far behind you, not yet having produced, by flash methods, some of your freaks. As for regularized mutation – if it hadn't been for millenia forbidden us, there too we'd have been like you, still dependent on the old stewpots of nature. But it must by now be clear to you that we had long since done something very drastic about that. We'd reached a form — that suited our very stringent sense of form. And then, screw *up* progress, as you would say. We had stopped right there.

No wonder, then, that our small band of travel agents, though daily gaining members, had still to do it in underground style. We were not only fiddling with mutation; we were being antiquarian about it, or so our best minds would say. So then, was it kismet or was it cosmic, I thought, moving away from the cherubs, that no sooner had I begun developing some of the feelings forbidden to us, than I found them linking me to a being who didn't want to go back, at least not on this planet — but neither did she want to stay. A being so — I couldn't say untrustworthy — at least not yet. But one so mercurial, so devoted to conformity without, and what looked like anarchy within — that I had misgivings whether her kind should be allowed on Ours at all.

By now, I was moving up and down the long room so agitatedly that I almost made a noise. Well, that was progress. Much as I liked the room, however, almost everything in it, if stared at *too* fixedly, might well be a hazard for the kind of progress I was after — except, of course, the bed. On it lay the Dream, my personal and singular one, as distinguished from the more traditional perturbations and *doubles ententes* I got from your books. It was of course this, that one day, say around teatime, I would entice her to enter here and there lie down with me — but thereafter it departed from convention. Necessarily. For I could see us there all right, the longer being and the shorter one, both horizontal and side by side, and if I could persuade her to take her clothes off, both of a resembling pink. So far so good, but there the categorical sympathies ended. After that, on the long couch of history, what a strangely assorted — more so than Abelard or Héloïse, what a surely immortal — as much as Cupid and Psyche — *pair!*

And what I planned for us to do then wasn't at all beyond imagining; it contrarily and sadly went beyond what I wanted of it. For in usual your-style, though in my dreams I was never quite able to conclude that episode of yours I so wanted to happen, my intelligence, that damned super-ergo, was all too bloody well able to visualize what I hoped against hope wouldn't. For I could see the two of us . . . And what a box we were in, indeed! Star-crossed was nothing, in compare. For, suppose I reached the apotheosis I craved? Imagine it then, as I was now doing: in the warmth of her nearness, or (dared I say it) — embraces? Yes, I did dare. In those encircling arms, suppose then (though perhaps not without many teatime repetitions, many a long, quiet hibernation in that hot-humid New Guinea conservatory) — suppose then that I would then at long last find myself to be, though perhaps not in the *strictest* ontological sequence, nevertheless . . . nevertheless . . . *budding*. Alas I knew only too well how you mucked things up here — I could not only fill in all the dots. I could fill in the spaces between these too. And it was there, alas, I found the other word, for what she would meanwhile be doing, under the onfluence of my shape. What would she be doing but: *melting?* Mutation is mutual. And once again — and in vain all our heaven-floating arrogance — we would be ships that pass.

Unless — I thought of yesterday. Unless, there was a thing unknown to me, that you in turn had kept from me, that you and yours had smelled out. It might be sensible on both sides, not to reveal talents which would only confuse the situation without bettering it, in the time we had to spare — witness my power to objectify, which was not to be done in a day.

In fact, now that I knew our time scale, not in much less than a year — I should just manage it. In spite of which — I drooped at the thought — it seemed forever to teatime.

A pause in my agitations brought me to the room's one chair, but although it was a plump lounge one, and masculinely leathered, I never sat on it. Not that I thought it *was* anybody. I had never yet sat again, either in her presence or mine, and this time not for caution but out of pure sentiment and superstition — and perhaps a little gamble. As a nation we love a long chance, and so did I, though since I had no one to bet with but myself, mine was more of a vow. I had a private bet on, not to sit until I could consider myself to be, if not a human in full panoply, at least out in the world of them, or on my way. To sit is so human. Other attributes of yours that I wanted seemed to me nearer the divine, or the animal. I was perfectly aware that besides these, you had many minor tricks of individuality as a species, plus more majestic ones, such as buying and selling — which the Ones who came after me might settle upon as your insignia, for them. A matter of taste, perhaps. To sit, at least in a chair, was mine.

And so, when I heard the key turn at last, I was still standing there. I hurried out, and at once took up my sentry post by the fireplace, even though I well knew that although in the spirit of fair play she ran to release me the minute her own practice period was over, she then returned to the bedroom for a time which might be any length, in order, as she said, to "change." A feminine habit in the main, she said, though anyone could do it, and indeed so far it was applicable only to her costume. But how could I ever be sure, and therefore began the teatime always in a flutter. If ever I attained my full goals here, I told myself — this was the hour at which I should drink.

In default of that, it was often my custom quickly to set

the tone of the evening as cozily as possible, usually with a phrase which would start us off on the topic of last night's reading — perhaps quotations from the poets, or entire renderings of a Russian novel's plot. The novels she criticized freely, giving me a running commentary on anything in them — from card playing to epilepsy — which might be of use to me out in the world. The poetry she listened to with her eyes rapt on the window — that is, she didn't. Anthropology belonged to her own frequent reminiscence, and so I never read any; I was vicarious enough as I was. Chemistry, astrophysics and like, I needed to study only long enough to learn the steps you had reached, and to observe how the narrow shoe of your mind still hunted a foot to fit it. In recent weeks, I had spent most of my time — and much of it humble — in pursuit of those biologies where, whether you knew it or not, you could be master, always coming home so full of my studies that I never had to choose my gambit; it chose me.

"I have been studying the courtship of the three-spined stickleback!" might tumble from me, the minute she entered. Or, while she built up the fire or tested the blinds for blackout, I would brood for some minutes, lost on some Australasian shore where the platypus waddled, before I exclaimed, "I better have a look at Breughel again; I do wish you hadn't stopped the milk!" Or, as on the day I first comprehended the full biology of you, I might spend the whole evening in thralled silence while she chattered, only to say to her in the tenderest tone, as we set out across the fields and she fell silent — "To think that I once envied the complex fertilization of the sponge!"

But tonight, when she entered, I said nothing, though not out of self-pride; these days I kept the sharpest, ever more self-conscious eye on my own conduct. And I knew myself to be ridiculous; this is the way you and I — *we* — are. But tonight I was quiet for another reason, and it wasn't because, after our ice-picnic finding myself unable to read, I had no topic to draw upon. I was mute because — and this may surprise those of you more used to this curdle of events — because for once I had nothing to say. We at home were always required to have something. Until I understood the full significance of this new state, as I began gradually to do throughout that famous evening, the sensation was quite hurtful.

She was wearing a conglomeration of garments — these days it seemed to me that in her abstraction she put one costume on top of another — which she had finished off with the Mexican serape she often referred to as her favorite, since it had been through so much with her. As she brushed past me, almost under the spot of me where I was intensifiedly cultivating nose imagery of the most Roman pretensions, I noted with some anxiety that this costume effectively blurred her figure at those very points it had been my luck to be able to dwell upon at my ease, though I sometimes thought that despite my lack of physiognomy she knew — she hadn't been watched for years for nothing. On happier evenings, or more relaxed ones, she even rallied me, saying almost flirtingly, "Peeping Tom!" And it was these moments, I said to myself, which in the end would be more effective than any of their exercises, at least those that I knew. But one of the evenings was sure to be followed by one in which she made a great show of adhering to our intellectual program, and I already saw, from her brusque manner, that this was to be the case tonight. She bustled on past me — was she a little lame?

When she returned from the kitchen with her dinner tray, I noted with relief that she was carrying it in two hands just as always, and that when she sat down her legs, perhaps because of her garments, were crossed not at knee but at ankle. Her face, bent over her food, looked fuller, but then it had done that when she had wept with laughter, that first time. I had a terrible thought — having nothing-to-say breeds them. I should like to see her weep the other way — and over me. Could she have smelled this? She did not seem to be relishing her food. When she looked up at me, those eyebrows of hers, lovely whips, were clenched in that ever-invisible fist — they had not changed.

"Taking inventory?" she snapped.

Oh let *her* not change, I thought. Let her leave that to me. Oh heresy.

"No need to take stock of you!" she said. "One glance does it. Always redder than the last time. Like the Commissioner in *South Wind* — I suppose, having read everything, you've read that one." She even got up, reached for the bookshelf, arm half bent, then thought better of it. "Never mind. Somebody remarks that he looks redder than when last seen, and somebody else answers, 'That is always characteristic of the Commissioner.'" She put the tray quietly to one side — she was never chattery, but how noiseless this evening!— and regarded me. "One would think I beat you."

Beat me.

"Or tickled you. In*cess*antly." She had the most peculiar expression, a snarl that at any moment might turn into a smile. How I envied her it. "Are you . . . ticklish . . . Eli?"

I am, terribly. That is, We were. Laughing so much makes one so, at least this is the way it works with us.

"My, my," she said. "What a complexion. Why look at the great big — it looks like a gre-at big . . . Bavarian . . . *Mädel!*"

That was cruel of her. She knows I know German.

"But we mustn't be coy, must we. At least not in that direction. Might disturb the — elements. Yes, I know — 'the elements so mixed' — *Julius Caesar*. You quoted it the other evening. Sometimes I wonder who's being educated here. I could graduate from college, just on the books I've hauled since February." She sat back. Her ways of sitting might not be as versatile as once — surely it was those Saturday orgies? — but even when she sat stiffly it was of interest to me. "Funny thing —" The snarl was almost a smile, now. "I always thought I didn't like being made use of. This is the first time I — I suppose it's because you've never looked down on me intellectually." Her voice sank. "Or because I'm making use of you too." To a whisper. "I suppose I always did that, to everyone really."

I dared not move. But she might see it for herself — that the willing slope of what someday might be a shoulder, was near.

"Though why I'd want to make you see what bitches women can be, or *I* can — I ought to be spending all my time on the men." She dropped again, her neck sadly shortened by that coarse garment, underneath which it must surely still stretch, as is said with truth of their necks, like a lily. "I can't bear it. The good and bad in the world, in men, in *me*. I can't go through it again, any more." Did she glance at me for a minute, and quickly look down again? "I've had it. We all have. It's *too* mixed."

I trembled, who only wanted to qualify. And I thought, with horror for her side, that before she came over to Us, she ought to be trembling too.

Was she? If she were naked, I should know better. I had never before felt my lack of clothing, or seen the peculiarity of a domestic situation in which, according to your best art books, only one of us was A Nude. I wondered whether I might make her an artistic suggestion.

"What's the matter," she said. "Cat got your tongue?"

Oh cruel, when we hadn't a cat, and I hadn't a — But always with imagination.

And still I had nothing-to-say, though I could now have said it in the most impeccable accents.

She got up from her chair and strode the room as she

always did when excited, though her paths were more oval than before. In spite of the hobbling garments, she could still fling around her those great sashes and skirtings of the emotion I so envied her. Never mind the clothing, it was these others I wanted, and perhaps there was a bifurcated version of them too.

She paused in front of me. "What, no 'let's have a lesson, Janice' today?" She drew breath, perhaps to show me how her thought had smelled mine. Or perhaps to show me how a one of you could draw breath. "I suppose our young hopeful — thinks itself educated?" That time, she saw me flinch. "Yes, *it*. One doesn't deserve the personal pronoun just from craving it!"

She was wrong there, I thought. Want dignifies — almost anything. Especially in a world so full of possessions.

There in front of me, she took a few steps backward, chin tucked in but her eyes still on me, the way a short, excited person tries to lord it over a large, poised one. Tall beside the mantel, I felt her words almost before she spoke them.

"Sit!" she said. "Will you never! Why you haven't even learned to sit down, and that's not the half of it, barely a detail. Do you realize that nearly a third of our time here is gone, and you haven't even seen the world yet, and all because — *arrh-ah!*"

Or was it *hah* — rr — ah, that final explosion? Many as my pedestrian languages were, and on their way to perfection, I can never get right those jagged exclamations of yours, those hahs and bahs and eeows torn as it were out of the crude heart of variation — in place of which I had only my perfect O-pearl.

"I sold the car," she said, in the smallish, exhausted voice in which these small cries are apparently to be answered, particularly if they are one's own. "But it's not that easy, your transportation, young massa." She tried to glare, making this last a satirical slap, but I knew better; never a slap did one of her hands give me, but there was a bit of sugar for me in the other.

"I thought of a truck, but they're too obvious for around here, and even out on the main roads, if I drive one." And now, wonder of wonders, and of ponds shining and puddles no longer haunted, she smiled again. "Jack used to say I had no vanity. If one happens to be obvious and knows it, one often isn't, you know."

You meant to say Jamie, didn't you, I thought; or you always said Jamie before. But this time you said Jack.

Was that why she frowned again? "Bah!" she said. "You think you know the world because you've been in a cottage and a library. Wait till I show you. I know what you think of the world, don't think I haven't smelled that out. You're like those Americans who want to see Stratford, but not Birmingham or Liverpool. Or like Jamie even, who never minded me seeing the truth for any part of the world but his — who wanted me to walk the ramparts in Edinbro' with him prince-cock-a-feather, but kept me out of the slums of Glasga'. Or like those tourists inside the glass lounge of the hotel, looking over Corregidor Bay and drinking whisky sours, and all the old war might have been a flamingo flying over, and round the corner, not even in a slum mind you, just round the corner, the squatters living in the piled-up whisky cases. All the people who think the world's all of a piece, or want to. Is, was, and ever shall be. I'll not have you walk out on it like that, like them, hear?"

Corners, always corners.

She put her hands on her hips and looked up at me, her attempt to seem as tall as I forgotten. "And do you know why — no, don't answer, how could you know. Because that's the way I did." She whispered it. "I thought the world was all of a piece, somewhere else. Or travel would make it so."

She folded her arms in front of her, settling down into her wraps and teetering on her ankles in a way that unnerved me. "And don't say what you would say if you are what you think you are. 'Oh, you were just a girl.'" She gave a short laugh, and trundled – yes, that was the word which came to me – to the window, pulled the blind up, and looked out. Her voice always softened when it came from there, and it did so now. Over her shoulder I could see, turning away from the mantel, that it was snowing again. The road, far as I could see it, was trackless, and filled with the half-blue, spectral winter light that oozed into the room like a power. "You've only known us in snow," she said. It was a strange ending to such a speech but she repeated it. "You only know us in snow."

This wasn't quite true, unless I wasn't to count what I'd seen in Bucks, or from the air – but it was her soliloquy. How one saw ought to count too, I thought, watching how the little salon, holding fast all its seams, said, "Still safe, still safe!" to the window, and how the winter light strode through the window replying, "You are a trinket upon the world."

Her voice cut between the two. She was still looking out. "Women are the real travelers," she said. "They're afraid of nothing. Not even to stay at home. But if any being has too much of that, or even of the world – travel comes of it." She turned away from the window, sat down by the telly, and picked up her tray. She looked down at the articles there, the fork, the knife and the glass, and on the plates, the food, a sight to me still faintly repellant, though they say here that food is the last pleasure to go. Then she leaned forward, flicking the switch on the telly. "I'll find us some misery," she said. "I'll introduce you two yet."

She twirled the switch from arc to arc, turning up a crooner, on of those animated cartoons whose toy properties, as they zoomed, always gave me space nostalgia, a close-up of two human figures in what I always thought of as the swimming-pool *moo*-vie, two comic goons in boot camp — the telly vocabulary, running much to the *oo* sounds which were my easiest, was a constant enjoyment — and three very excellent shots of a perfect set of false teeth, a clogged nostril and a bloodshot eye. Early in my stay she had restricted my viewing, on the grounds that I was already misconceiving you from it, and would end by never being able to tell your shadowy attitudes from your real ones, or your teeth or your people, but I was quite able; nobody knew more about shadows than we do.

She was studying the newspaper. "Here's one! A documentary. On Hansen's disease — I suppose your omniscience knows that's leprosy." Fork lifted, she watched the screen. "In Asia we saw it often."

I watched with intense interest, having read much about disease but never seen one.

"Yaws, too," she said in a teacherly voice of satisfaction. "In Ceylon called *parangi,* in Fiji *coko,* in the Malay peninsula *purru, tonga* in the Samoas or sometimes *tono,* in the Moluccas *bouton d'Amboine.*" She repeated this in soft carillon — lovely!— and added that the healthy children of sick mothers were the worst.

From what I had read, this seemed to me scarcely the show for a being who was trying to acquire appendages, not discard them, but I need not have worried — we saw many leucocytes, many doctors, but no mothers and indeed no patients; no scabs appeared on the fine, metallic wood of the television box as I had expected, but then we had just been informed that the incubation period was long. She watched me narrowly, while the hospital angled whitely elegant along a soothing voice which brought us at last to a clean patient sitting with his back to us, reading a newspaper like her own. All that time, I had been covertly watching my own skin, expecting that the disease must surely appear there, but all was so pleasant that my nothing-to-say was lulled almost to the point of speech. You were not that instantaneous here. The screen did not suffer. Or anybody close to it, no matter how near.

I was about to cry out, "Oh charming, see, he's *sitting*," but she reached forward to turn it off, with a scowl. "He's right. One more try, then. The news." Out of her own ennui, we seldom had the news, though I always listened with real listening, since she said it was real — though I never saw what she saw.

"Ah, we've struck luck," she said. She took up her fork again. "The war in Vietnam," she said. "We've struck it rich." And compared to other times, I suppose we had. We had had bombs before and after, but never *now*, and this was a village set fire by its own hand, before it moved on. And now, as a village, it was leaving, all close together, in the truck. I saw that.

"Here's your TV dinner, Eli," she said. "Nummy-num. And meanwhile I'll have mine — that's how we do it here." She watched me watch it and her, both of us imperturbable, and made sure I saw every morsel she ate. "They're so thin," she commented, "they've been starving. Ordinarily they're a beautiful people." I had not too many standards to judge them by. I had never seen so many together before. They had not a field of space measured out for them. I saw how close they could be to each other, in starvation. That is what I saw.

"Eat!" she said. "Fill 'er up. That's misery there, isn't it? Isn't it!" And my nothing-to-say rose up again, so I couldn't answer her to say, I don't see what you do, I can't eat as you do, it's only a screen to me. I'm not as human as you are.

"I'm eating!" she said. "I'm *hungry*. That's the way we do it here. And maybe that's misery too."

So, each to each, we had our dinner. The village faded, the truck also; we came to a wayside station. We had a mother, babe in arms and three children, like paper cutouts that faded where they stood, and still stared.

"This is Shartlesville Corn Pudding," she said, looking down at what she was still eating. "From an old family recipe. And bacon drippings in the lettuce. I cook Dutch."

We had a dead body with the salad. It was then she smashed down the tray.

If it were a simple mystery, a single one, I was thinking, perhaps I could understand it. Surely they could be taught to manage it that way, or perhaps I could teach them. Surely this they could manage here—only one by one.

Then I saw that the tray had fallen and I could do nothing. And she said, "Don't . . . it's nothing. Don't bother." As if I could. "I was just clumsy," she said and half bent down to pick it all up—and then didn't. And then tossed her head and walked over to me where I stood, silent at the mantel. And then put her hand a little way out to touch me—and then didn't. But I felt it. Like the other times, it burned. But it burned like a thought, not a feeling. We stared across it, as if we had between us but one large eye.

I thought she said to me: Stay as you are. I'll come to meet you.

I thought I said to her: Stay as you are. I'll come to meet you.

Then she was at the tray, kicking the remains onto it with the point of her shoe, and there were no remains for me to bother with, except later when I read about madness I understood it. It is a budding in the mind and a melting. It is a mutation that hasn't been asked for.

And then, outside on the road, a car door slammed.

And then the bell rang.

We had so few doorbells and telephone calls in our life

these days that both of us looked at the television, but it had passed on now from war, and was quietly grieving out the stock market quotations. She crept toward it, and turned it off. "Who do you suppose that is?" she whispered. "Nobody comes round here, this hour of the day, who could it be?" We had had a peddler whom I had been too late to see. Today was Thursday. The week's delivery, the post and the meter reader had all been. At these specified times I was required to go at once to the museum and stay there until the all-safe, but now I stayed where I was, the tumult of nothing-to-say meanwhile so loud in me that it was like a wind which took the place of speech.

"The lamps!" she said, crouching toward the nearest one, then stood abashed. While we had been at our dinner-share of all the things in the world that could be happening simultaneously, on our side of it we had been moving forward into the shadows; outside, the blue light had moved on to that deepest Prussian-colored moment before the dark plunge. Inside, I was the only lamp. And the blind of the small window was up.

I suppose there must always have been pulsings of mood, dimming of hesitation, which even in me told their story. She knew at once that I was not going to hide.

She stole to the window, and stretching her arm as if her wraps dragged on it, silently inched down the blind. We heard someone stamp and shuffle on the square of paving stone that served for a porch, overhung with a lantern, just outside.

I could feel how it would be to be waiting there, the snow coming down like a blessing, or if you looked into it, like an akimbo whirling of worlds. In the clear marvel of the air, the planets swung in their perihelions. I could feel how it would be to shuffle the foot and stamp it, to breathe planets through the nose.

"Stand back!" she whispered. "If you aren't going to hide.

Look alive!" As I did so, drawing the light well away from her, she peered through the seam between blind and window. I saw by her face that the seam had let something in.

Then we heard it again, the bell, and again, as if it were teaching someone that sad, virtuoso song.

"Will you not go in?" she said. "So I can answer. *Are* you alive?"

Most curious, how I could not yet myself make insults aloud, yet could take them into me, making my own non-answer, which seemed joined with the non-answered bell outside. And it seemed to me that I felt my blood. Does the running of the blood answer only to the barb?

"Maybe I should ask him in," she said. "To tell me for sure that you are. Should I?" She came a little closer toward me. "Eli?" She whispered it. She put out a hand, minimally. "No, don't," she said. "Hush. No, I know you are. Hush."

"Hush," she had said, and "No, don't" – and I had not said a word. I looked down at myself. It was my light which was speaking. Was this how it had been in the beginning, here? Out of the primordial, the blind mouths rising, of beings not found yet by their own blood. Over the watery acres of the young world, a phosphorescence of being, which is light? So that, world to world, being to being, mouth to mouth, in the end it is all the same?

I watched her slip the lock so that she might enter again. She opened the door, glided outside, and shut it behind her.

And now it was I who crept to the seam and applied my vision to it. I couldn't see her at all, where she must be pressed against the door, but by the light of the hanging-down lantern I could see the whole of the paving stone – often too had I glided there! – and . . . him. Now I recognized him. He was the second head. He was different in face from the milkman, but my shrewdness told me he would have his own prototypes somewhere. I looked him over from top to toe, but he did not see me, seeing only her. Did I want to be him? As with the milkman, I had a struggle – always this empathy! – but again I came out on top, or at least – alone. Then he spoke.

"It's I," he said. "I saw the light."

Oh glory. He had said it; she had heard it. I was alive. To see and be seen was the double glory here too. And I had crossed over. I was visible here, fully and forevermore. Whatever wounds came of it, I was alive.

Her reply chilled me. I knew that dry rustle. "Philosophical?" she muttered. "Or electrical."

Wounds come quickly here, but this was intended not for me but for him. What had she against him; what had they all? At the edge of the blind – good seam, kind seam! – I scrutinized him, thinking that if she invited him in, even if to stay and live with us, I should not mind. He would be a third, but the kind that is company.

But I heard her murmur that she expected to be leaving; she would write.

And then for a moment I saw her taken in his grasp. Mouth to mouth, all beings are light. I saw it.

Then I heard the car slam, then the gunning sound of it, the dying away. A road is a meander.

And then, followed in by a little dark wind, a little white of snow, she came back.

After she closed the door behind her, she stayed pressed against it just as she had done that first evening, the same, yet not the same. Much of the life here is like that; in this concentric it approaches our own groove. Swollen ghost of herself, I was sure she too watched my vision of how she had once moved. Hand pushed to mouth, as if in the bellyache, she looked at me. Once she had told me that in certain circles of Polynesia, a sign of esteem that wife may pay husband is to groom him in the village square by plucking the nits from his hair. Here women, in the exercise of a terrible vanity, do a service of esteem for themselves. One by one – when that profound honesty comes over them – they will pluck from their own heads the qualities that endear them to self or to others, and cast these aside like lice, like stones. How did I know this? Was she also doing a service for me?

"I wonder," she said. "If he was worried for fear I was – The way he looked me over. Could be he was –" Her mouth opened. "Could be – I am . . . I never thought of it – *that* change." She turned her other hand from the wrist, doll-like. "And what if I am. I'm still go where intended. Nothing new for a woman. Like that Russian astronaut-in-waiting the papers quoted. 'The moon is my intended,' she said." She attempted a pirouette, ah yes pretty bad and she knew it, but aimed at me nevertheless. She clenched her fist and looked at it. "There must be someplace that's all-of-a-piece, mustn't there?" She came toward me and shook the fist at me, paying me the compliment of doing so where my face might one day be. "Mustn't there – Eli?"

I did not answer, but not because of nothing to say. I thought she knew.

She sighed. "Ah well, you're as all-of-a-piece as one would ever expect – and even you –" She laughed on the note of cool I dreaded to hear. "Even if *it* isn't, how could I *not* go? And what do you know, Eli – maybe I'll see the real place, from there."

I couldn't say. *I* had.

"What a sell!" she said then. "If I should be – as he thinks. Why, I'd be a legend, wouldn't I? Sooner or later there always is one, even a bum anthropologist knows that."

My blood-image froze. The people move on. The legend moves on. But the mutation is for life.

She came closer, close enough. "Heigh-ho, long speeches make long silences – but maybe you're right not to talk." She looked up at the tip of me. "Remember when —" She broke off. "Ah, that's parting, isn't it, when we say that."

I didn't know; I had always arrived. All this I was to mull over in my long hibernation. We were the non-blind leading the non-blind, two seeing people leading each other into the dark.

"Remember when I asked you if you had a sex, and you answered six." She smiled. They only, can do this. And the animals. "Maybe it's in the eye of the beholder," she said, though she wasn't looking straight at me. "But you do have it now, you do. A look." Then she rapped the clenched fist softly on my integument, as if to summon further out the imago, the person within. "What's this, what's this?" she said then. "Another bruise? How you'll ever get along without someone to —" Her brow clenched, her mouth opened. "Eli, my dear, dear Eli, if I should — you know, be *ahead* of you — how will you get along all by your — in a *house?*" Her scrutiny hardened. "*That's* no bruise."

Then she circled me indeed, as if she were measuring me for a garment, while I yearned to cry, "What is it; what *have* I?" but my voice struck some impediment and stuck there. "No wonder you've been so canny quiet," she said. "And bloody quick, my boy, no need to worry about you." The brows clenched me as if I were half enemy. "If that isn't an Adam's apple as I live and breathe." She scanned me. "No, wait a minute." Again came that angled laugh. A small or satiric drain for feeling may be helpful, but the angle of the gyroscope is fixed. Yet when she conned me again she was serious — "Every ellipse has a center," she muttered. "*Which is a point such that it bisects every chord passing through it. The longest diameter is called the transverse axis, it passes through the foci. The shortest is called the conjugate*" — and I realized she was doing her exercise tables. "*Elliptic spindle,*" she said, eyes closed. "*Gearings, chucks, integrals, epicycloids.*

Elliptic point. A syneclastic point; a point where the principal tangents are imaginary." She reopened them. "Oh shucks and chucks, what a physiognomy. I'm no good at it." She squinted. "By ordinary rule of thumb, I'd say, if it isn't the thyroid cartilage, commonly known as the apple, it's — yes, *blimey* if it isn't." Hands folded, she made me a little bow. "Congratulations are in order. Mad rush of science and all that. Hard to believe. Weren't for — myself — I wouldn't." Her hands unclasped, palms up, a little pudgy now, but still hers. "Much good may it do you, Eli. It's a navel."

I stood there humble and quivering. It wasn't my first choice, but it was a beginning, in fact *the* one in this mystery. And perhaps personal choices weren't the wisest thing in this business.

When I came to myself, she was shining at me in her own way, even tall again; what slender, lissom joke of the first days was she going to share with me? "All these weeks," she said. "How could I be sure I wasn't off my rocker? *Scusi,* rocket. I had to give myself talks. 'You're in the twelfth century, say,' I'd say to myself, 'and somebody says to you, *People will fly in the air.*' Or, 'You're in eighteenth-century Ireland, with a hoe in your hand or an ale mug, and goodfellow says at your elbow, *They'll cut you up in pieces and parcel you, but you'll be a-sleeping and not feel it. And you won't die.*' And so I worked myself up to it gradually. With roentgens and rockets, and I don't know what all from the ragbag. It isn't hard to imagine, if you've even seen an Ainu at his first telephone. And so, finally, 'You're in the twentieth century,' I said to myself, 'and somebody says to you, *There's going to be such an evolutionary adventure — There's going to be —*" She looked at me long. "Us."

As she turned to the stairs, she flung me the gift, always a double one, over her shoulder. "Oh, I believe in you all right, these days. Else I couldn't — in me. But one keeps one's . . . imbalance . . . better, doesn't one, when one sees one's *own* kind now and then." She turned full face again. "You were right to stay. Not to hide. You don't have to worry. You're — you. But I was never so sure of it as when I saw Jack."

Then she turned alimp, like the little lame grandmother of herself, and went up the stairs.

It was black night now, that time when any room with a person in it wondering steady on his life is like a hearth with a good live coal on it. I was as rosy and pulsing now as any young person here could be — and what a dowry I had at my back! Every guide, protection, power and elasticity that our biophysical research could devise had been provided me, from an ordnance which we had heard one of your own experts remark must make theirs look like a nickel tip at a table d'hôte. I had properties which you, except for your poets, had never dreamed could inhabit protoplasm at all. And now, so armed, I confronted those low qualities of yours which, excepting in the merest shadow, had never inhabited ours. Whatever of our ancient books I had crammed on had at least given me some command of your powers of expression, antiquarian though these might be. But since then, in the hot-and-cold of books by night, and the long-simmering dream-watches of the day, I had learned that only what is already inborn can a book inspirit, only this can a dream inflame. For I now knew by rote the entire alphabet of your world's emotions — and that until I myself should inhabit them personally, they would remain mute. What a Voco-Phono lesson I had before me now!

I studied the very stairs she had gone up, as she did daily, in tripping health or at her new lamed glide, and always oblivious, or almost, that every step of my existence here, and the risers too, must have a name as large as a territory, taken from your infinitely stretchable alphabet of them, from *avarice* to *Angst,* to *Zartheit,* to *zest.* I saw the range of them, a Jacob's ladder only as high and difficult as the thirteen actual and countable steps before me might be for me, but with what stiles and fences, steeplechases and Père Lachaises on the way – and John-a-Baptist pits, and common stubbing stones. In all the languages of your world there was the same little list from *aleph* to *zed* – and none of it was to be had by hearsay.

Then the spasm gripped me for true, for deep, for aye. *Nor was I myself* to be had so. Nor was I.

And now indeed I knew the true nature of that most hurtful nothing-to-say which, through all this fateful night of speeches and shadows and scenes at windows, had grown and grown in me until in this black dark, lit only by me, it bid fair to burst my boundaries also, scattering my rosy diffusion far and wide. For such a state of nothing-to-say is actually the vacuum which at one prick is sucked out, as if by a single gasp-breath, into action. Often this is the way you yourselves are moved to it or make yourselves to move.

And now too there had come upon me that eventuality which early on I had once teased myself with – laughed over, never really dreaded, and at last put by – that I might one day find myself with rather enormous feelings and no mechanism as yet to vent them with; I had jokingly defined this as "a sneeze with no place to go." Then I had forgotten it. Who after all so dreads the accession of riches that he will not put by his terror of them until the time comes? And now it, this eventuality which even your best ahs and aies and eeows wouldn't suffice to express. Remember it, those of you who have been young? I had *everything* to say, but not yet the furnishment to do it with.

So I did what the young do, of course: I went up the stairs anyway. And though I was now only as visible as any an excited one of you, I seemed to myself a veritable pillar of fire as I ascended them and went, timorous as a newborn lion – if these had navels – down the hall.

The door to that haven of hers which I had never seen was darkly ajar. Should I push it in? Before I could do so it was opened from within, as if she had expected me. Still, darkness. My own brilliance blinded me.

Then I heard her voice, almost at where would be my ear. *"Wann dich ime busch ferlore hoscht, guk ame bam nuf."*

Was this only one of her many *patois,* or out of some final language of experience, saved up for this one, for me?

Then I heard her construe it, in sad-perfect compound, as if she had heard me think that, or had said this many times before. "When lost in the woods, look up a tree."

There was no tree, but in the dimness I could see papers, placards, letters, newsprint, a whole clearing house of them strewn about everywhere, and near several office machines, off to one side, what must now be in disuse or disrepair – for it was half buried under paper also – her wooden track. All this I saw as one sees things in one's own light – only half regarding them. She was standing almost in front of me, behind a screen back of which she had been disrobing. All her garments lay in a Mexican-European-American jumble on the floor, between us. In the rear of the room behind her, there was a full-length mirror, in it a whiteness which might have blinded me had I fairly looked at it. Above the screen, her head regarded me. After a moment, her hands, one on either side of her head and opened like false wings, came to join it.

So we stared at one another, each in our own light. What hers was I could not yet descry, except that, not as powerful as mine, it did not need to be – it was still different, and that was enough.

But between us, as with the pile of clothes, stood another –

the shy observer. I fumbled for its name, not knowing whether I was honest or ignorant. When it did not give ground, and I could find no better, I spoke to her, across it.

"Teach me pleasure," I said.

* *

And if, with all my non-heart and voice I put, as in a book of your books, a line here of asterisks, it is not in order that you might be free to think for yourselves on what happened then, but for its sadder opposite, that from our lacks, it could not.

First I saw her in the mirror, just as you often see your lovers. I saw her, melted from neck to knee in such a curve of beauty as I had not forgotten, it being also – except for my slight, new indentation – mine. But she would not have this be the end of things, and kicked aside the screen. Then, turning up her palms with the slightest of sighs, she regarded me. *You are You* her eyes said to me, and all my being said the same to hers. But, in the nature of things both of us added: Not quite.

We were ships that pass in the night.

We were an old couple, one of us old in experience, one of us – by your account – in age. We were a young couple, each of us in the flesh of a new world. Like any two of you, we were the same, but different. And like any two, there was only a partial cure for it. So, until morning, curve to curve – we leaned.

Palm up, palm down, people are the wilderness.

Despite which, she left everything in exquisite order. When I woke next day in one of the downstairs salons, past noon of a high, sunny day that beamed into every cranny of the house through windows with their blinds now set at precisely halfway, I thought of it. Like any good housekeeper, she had said, she had to clean house before she left for a journey; that it might be for forever made no difference, or in fact more. So, some hours before dawn, we began it, I only watching of course, but following her everywhere. These obligatory scenes of watching do occur here after all, and are not unpleasant, so long as — yes, I must say it — a termination is in sight.

The kitchen was a disgrace, she said; besides, she said, with a smile she meant to be glorious, it was no place for a man. So it was then I took a last carbonation which must carry me for some time. Away from the not quite wasted spell of her presence, I felt a growing cuteness in her which I deplored. I was apprehensive too that her face — dear *dimming* face I said to myself harshly — wouldn't last through our encounter, but it did. It was a face which had launched quite a bit in its time, and with minor alteration, it survived until the need for it was gone. Meanwhile, I could tell for myself how very private I was getting, and how there was on the increase in me too that sense-of-the-past-in-the-very-present which so bollixes up the lives of all the thoughtful, here.

It was in the welter of her bedroom, again while she had left me alone for some moments, that I was most afflicted with it. She, while breathing with an effort which caused me dismay — "No, it was all right," she said; it was just that she already felt herself to be breathing at high altitude — had dismantled the wooden practice-track she was supposed to have been using, and was at this moment storing its pieces in the basement, where if someday discovered it might be taken for parts of one of those old toys on which all basements dream. She wasn't sure why she had to do this, or — to my inquiry — whether it was an instance of femininity or merely human, the "merely" being hers also. She supposed that she perhaps did it to commemorate a deception she had practiced — and now told me of — on me. For, after a few token sessions she had never used the track at all, but had employed those hours in secret drilling sessions with colleagues in the area – the sounds I had heard her make, and had so dwelled on, being those of a tape recorder she drew from the corner and now showed me. Did I wish to hear it? I looked sadly – or so I hoped – on that fair skin of hers now so callousing – and said no. It was for this reason that I had been locked in. Even during our nights at the library – she added in a sudden rush of confidence – while I was safe in my carrel she had not always been there, but in proportion as my slackening rate of speed enabled her to provide me with fodder for some hours ahead, she had slipped out to those facilities in Hobbs which she and her band used nightly, on only one occasion carelessly leaving evidence that they had. Deceptions, alas, were necessary, she said; it was hoped we would not mind. She said it very prettily. I said no.

The word "fodder" had been hers also, so, while reading some of the admonitory notes to herself which were scattered all over the desk and dresser, and here and there tucked in the many mirrors, I wasn't surprised to see in a rather neater file of them marked *Transportation – Eli,* one large memo: "Get a horse van?" Beneath was the advertisement of a nearby stable and stock farm, dated only two days ago. The desk was further covered with lists and compilations of all the places and institutions she thought she ought to show me – a touring of which, under her tutelage, I half still trembled toward and shuddered over, as opportunity safely lost. Still, all hints being useful, I studied them, from *Funerals and Hospitals* to *Picnics and Galleries,* noting with some tenderness a memo to stop by the Chinese collection at the Philadelphia museum, where there were some *famille rose* vases which reminded her of me.

As for the planned picnics, the ice-picnic wasn't among them. These spontaneities do occur, I thought, on both sides.

And both sides, I was sure, would forget to watch for them. I wish I was not so smart, I thought, but quickly pointed out to myself that since I had never thought this before, it too must be human. I was getting to like the word more every day, and to use it, accurately I hoped, more and more often. It was very human of her, for instance, to leave notes to herself all over, in capital letters, WHAT TO DO ABOUT WAR? And bending closer, I saw a small item of another kind, that touched me most. It was a Shell map of environs which included Sunbury, Pennsylvania. To it was clipped the estimated driving time from Philadelphia, also a faded recipe employing the black walnuts she had said were indigenous to the region, and sundry other indications, the clearest of which was the picture of a farmhouse. At the last, I thought, she was like them all. She had meant to go back. And forward as well, of course, for everywhere on the walls I saw, with what I hoped was a smile – large placards bearing the motto from Ours which I had given her in response to a plea that I choose the one which seemed to me most significant. "Happiness is a total ellipse." She had pasted it everywhere. And I had not been untruthful; she would see it in every public place, and hear it from every groove. It was the one community lie we are permitted ourselves, the one which in the public interest every citizen, until his last scream, honorably accepts. She, though no diarist like me, might yet have her own record of our adventure, in notes to herself inscribed, not on paper or cardboard, but on the forward flesh itself, and – helterskelter, wild or neat – much like these. And in her last scream she might voice that addendum which in life might not be said even sotto voce: Or, not quite.

Meanwhile, hearing her come up the stairs, I could reflect that during these twenty minutes I myself had accumulated some very profitable feelings.

Housecleaning, she said on return, always gave her ideas.

I myself had noticed this, but concluding that it tended to supply her with a host of minor ideas which took the place of the major ones. This might well be debated between us, I thought, under the topic, "What is a major idea, and must one go out of the house for it?" Her assuredly minor one was that she was worried over my carbonation supplies for the months to come, and could we consider her leaving on the air conditioner in the museum, it to be set at the slot for fresh air?

Apart from the fact that I had no mind to be at the mercy of a machine, I deemed this a proper time to tell her that I too had been practicing a deception. I brought this out, as I said, in response to her having told me hers. Indeed, if our relationship hadn't quite been an affair, in its expiring moments it rather resembled a marriage. I told her in detail of our talent for seeming to become objects. My ability to sit, as both a vow and a more valuable accomplishment, I kept to myself. At first she mourned loudly that I hadn't told her of this in time for travel purposes, until I assured her that the process took some months of hibernation – in fact, and oddly enough, just so many months as I had to wait here. And it was as I had hoped; all Our hatchment, so painstakingly plotted, came out just as wanted, only now the hatching was hers. Housecleaning did give her ideas – she even volunteered an old aquarium from the basement, in place of a bell-glass, but I was able to refuse, assuring her that a colleague might check on me from time to time. This was not quite true, but I saw no reason to reveal how far our plots went or our talents; we can be rather lapidary too. In short, I was able to convey the idea from my brain to her mouth with a splendid economy of both energy and time. For, once having conceived it, she ran round like crazy, doing everything from checking temperatures to phoning banks. And of course, writing her last letters. In watching her at these, I found her still dear enough, in fact so much so that I could not afterwards recall whose idea it was: to send Jack. But each of us, wherever we were, would await his arrival with pleasure.

So at last, we found ourselves in a house stripped of all evidence that anyone but a lady had lived here, the placards and other correspondence a heap of ashes in the fireplace, and even those cooled. The cottage itself, blinds up now, since I would be in the museum in the rear, lay sealed against all except the sunrise. She herself would be going to "the facilities" well before. It was appropriate that we make our adieux, brief as these might be, in the room which had meant so much to us — this was one idea we had truly together — and there we repaired.

Going down the hall, I reflected, not on all that had ensued but as much as I had time for, being ever more conscious of time's passing. We had been right, I thought, to wait for this particular set of applicants. I would be confirmed in my judgment, and my advice to my colleagues: Use the brightly-stupid ones to get us here; they have more reason to. And trained as they have been to seem humble and amenable, they have more energy for the final arrogance — which is to make an exchange of peoples, rather than of vehicles. And time enough, when we get there, to make use of the stupidly-bright.

I let her enter the room ahead of me, as I had learned to do, that I might be a gentleman. Courtesy cost nothing, I had read here, along with hundreds of other proverbs, some of which mixed in my mind now, of how Rome hadn't been built in a day, nor Troy so tumbled. Some of my reading no doubt was more to be trusted than the rest. It didn't much matter. She and hers had their horse, now; I had my van. Altogether we had done well, if only what nature had all along intended. I wished I wasn't so smart.

In the museum room, chancing to stand near the cherubim, I revealed my hopes that human babies were better, to which she replied that of course they were; they were each of them like a great seed. And looking at me in that one-eyed way the she's have, the nearer one gets to them, so that if one didn't know better one might drown in it as in a desert mirage, she said, "So are you! Like a great seed!"

I was so occupied with this, and the eye, that I barely heard her say that if she ever had a child she would regard me as the putative father – or one of them. "Putative" was a word I didn't know, though I knew the root of *putrid* and *putana,* an Italian word, I believed, for the female of *whore.* Sometimes these words didn't have masculine forms. But I had no relish for linguistics at the moment, nor for sentiment either, being eager to get on with my hibernation and nervous enough as it was, so replied in an absent but gentlemanly enough fashion that I would be glad to do what I could.

"Thanks," she said, giving me an odd look. "If it's to be done – then, 'twere well 'twere done quickly, as they say in the, er – telephone book. I mean – *if* it's done, it already has been."

"Excellent!" I said, looking vaguely about me for a mirror, though I knew very well the room didn't have one. "Great seed, eh. Hmmm. Fancy!"

"It would be the first ever to have *two* fathers," she said. "I wouldn't want to deny your Onfluence; that wouldn't be fair of me."

"Neither would I," I said, musing. There were smallish seeds here, plenty of them, strung up with shells and so forth, but I had in mind a rather, well – a great one.

"Think of it!" she said enthusiastically. She was wearing clothes now, under a large cape, and galoshes. Beneath the cape, her hands tried to clasp, and with some effort, were able. "It would be the first child to be really *born* on Ours, wouldn't it. What a legend that'll be!"

I finally turned to stare at her. "You must be out of your — We don't have them."

"Legends?" she said. "Or babies."

"Say-y, listen," I said. American mightn't be so gentlemanly, but it was jaunty. "I know what's wrong with you. It happened to me at first, and it was awful. Like the bends. But you'll get over it. I'm just coming out of it myself. You're in a state of *between.*"

"Don't patronize *me,*" she said. "You don't look so good yourself."

Then. *Then.* Oh, to have hands. Was *this* murder? Luckily mutation gave me no help. But I lost control, right enough. "If you had more brains —"

"Oh no, *no,*" she said, dropping her lashes. "Empty heads are much better, they say. For making people. At least that's what we've always been told. And I must say, in our time we've made quite a lot of them."

"The crater takes care of that," I said, still a little stiff with insult — would I never learn how? "Besides, I thought you and your friends wanted to be relieved of it."

"Oh, we do," she said. "For here. And even there, maybe one mightn't want more than one, you know." She gave me a stare which might be cuckoo, or ve-ery cool. "One and One being One."

If this was the curve of the cosmos, then I was now out of line with it, though if nature did have this in mind, there was — ultimately — nothing to be done. But if it was *her* little joke, then I thought I could handle it. "The atmosphere, physical *or* mental, simply doesn't provide for it. You'd probably die in the attempt."

"Oh, to be a martyr," she said. Actually, she sang it. "Or

a *mater.*" Then she giggled. "I *am* getting to talk like you. Do you suppose *it* would?" She drew closer. She could still inch. "I've faced the fact that nine chances out of ten that's what I'd get, you know. A freak. What with the comic — I mean cosmic — rays and all. An *it.*"

"You'd better face the fact the whole fool idea's impossible," I said, meanwhile envying her the cape, but only generally. The kind of remark I had just made went better with a vest, and I had a fancy to make more of them. "If you got around a bit more, you'd know that nobody has that kind of ordnance. Too damn complicated — who'd undertake it?"

"Perhaps we would," she said. "Being more used to complication."

What a tongue. I hoped I would never get one like it. "Speeding up mutation is one thing — or reversing it. Or however you — one may look at it." I coughed. "But the *breeding* of two species so far apart is impossible. It's against the interglobular evolutionary convention."

"Oh, *is* it?" she said. "I hadn't heard."

Neither had I. But I was finding the improvisation here utterly exhilarating.

"Oh, I suppose you're right," she said dolefully. "It was just a thought. I was just looking ahead."

"Well, you do that," I said cannily. "You do that — no harm done. When you get there, you — may think differently. Meanwhile, just remember this is only the twentieth century. And between you and me, we've got about as far as we can go. Mustn't let our imaginations go absolutely *hogwire.*"

She smiled at me suddenly. How they do that. "No."

"Just remember your catechism, and you'll be all right. And the contract. Exchange of persons, and very liberally interpreted, too. Not a complete across-the-board change of them. That's what it stipulates."

"Oh does it?" she said. "I never read the fine print."

Then she toddled to the door and put her hand on the knob. I had a pang, having to let her go like this, but a job is a job.

She stared back at me. "You *do* have a look, you know," she said, "but it's not the same one. Or maybe it's in the eye of the beholder." She stifled a sound. If it was a sob, no tears came. "You don't look like you any more. You look more like – *them*."

Always the double gift. And then, without even a "see you, one day" she was gone.

I confess I hurried straight into the little salon where there was a mirror. I was astounded at what I thought I saw there. Maybe it was in the eye of the beholder, though. And the beholder was now me. Whatever, the role I had just played was an inevitable one; why must they always be a little stupider *and* a little brighter than we thought?

During the long process of objectification, I planned to go over all that had happened to me and assess it, also all that alphabet of human attitudes which would come to me – I was resigned to it – only in the experience, only in the flesh. But, mutation or no, it would be generations before I and my progeny would forget the sacredness of our spiritual home. The sort of thing she had in mind – it must *not* happen there. We had it in mind for Here.

As for the words we had just had, I was stupid enough now to know that it could not happen for eons yet if ever – and bright enough to know that ours was just that quarrel of imaginations by which the difference, and the daring – is preserved.

In a few minutes then, I must go into the museum, carefully face away from those cherubs, mentally commend myself to the cosmos – since I couldn't yet scrape a cross on my chest hairs or throw salt over a shoulder – and begin. A good objectification usually takes from three to six months. Until

One day, I had six. The prospect of so long a meditation didn't faze me, the likelihood being that I would never again here have the chance for so much of it. The object I had chosen to be will not surprise you. Until then I might rest, under a little sign she had prepared for me, with her own hands. TO REMAIN UNTIL CALLED FOR.

But first, I had an appointment with someone — and a vow. I walked over to where, sitting there herself that evening, she had made a brave, a defiant, a kindly prediction. Some of it had come true, and some of my wants also. I could trust the authority in this house now, for it was I. If none could say whether she and I had had an affair or a marriage, who's to say you can't lose what you have never had. You lose it doubly.

And now I knew what betrayal was, but not yet whether the man I would become in this world would ever forgive me for it. To forgive is divine, and that was not to be my story. For though there was no company to see, and if there had been, teacups were still beyond me, I thought I had an expression which others might someday confirm. No matter how doubly a thing is done here, the misery which follows it is still single.

The chair still held her print on it. So, bending as if I too were already a little lamed by the world to come — I sat. And it was there that, loath to go just yet, I had kept my vigil, and there I had slept until waking. And there, till we meet again, we may leave me. To sit is very human. To sit on the imprint of another is the most human of all.

One Day

THE voice of belief is a low growl, and the word it says is *No.* This was an insight which felt as if it belonged to drowning, but surely nature wouldn't waste it on then? Linhouse knew better. He'd been brought up to know that nature's waste was prodigal, so much so that it was almost the other side of perfection, serving almost as well as the notion of a clockwork universe to make us think that she must have *something* in mind. What he had really meant was: "Surely she doesn't mean to waste *me.*"

But his *no* was drowned in the congregation of no's that rolled toward the stage – for in the large object toward which this swell had been directed, the last, smallest lily-pad disc on the bottom had spoken its speech, and with a huge sigh, as if a wind teasing a volume had at last contented it by closing it, the discs riffled backward upon themselves so rapidly that the eye saw only blur, and there it was again, tall, shaggy-thick, conic and almost familiar, like the daily almanac of some queer neighbor, not necessarily a giant, which one had got used to listening to, its story over for the day, its work done.

It was all so quick, so quick, so almost instantaneous, yet he had time to observe the round mouths of all those he had been watching intermittently: Lila, Meyer, Anders, there the three were, plus all the others who had spoken, Björnson the mathematician, and his friend Charles the biologist, and Herr Doktor Winckler, and the Indian too. He even had time to see the cruder meanings of their lives as they unwittingly every minute spoke them, at least to him — and these as if encircled above their heads in the vapid balloons of the comic strips, or at their feet in one or two astringent lines of print. There was Lila the anxious, the almost certainly adulterous, whom nobody could take seriously in either of these qualities, but it was all right because Meyer, heir of rabbis, would take all the rest of her seriously, and the children, heirs of them both, would too. There was Björnson who had known a zoologist in his childhood, and the admiring Charles who had known *him,* and Anders who had had such an odd childhood, and was having it still. And even Herr Winckler, always at somebody's elbow, but probably never much farther, and Miss Apple Pie who wanted to know everything — he even had a twinge that she would never know the name he had awarded her. Always this empathy. Perhaps because the place was now dimming like a church, he felt as he always did nowadays when in one, that his heart was full of noble truths it wished to spit out immediately — and that all these good people were cardboard personages; only he was human, bad and real. Oh believe in the unknown, it will ennoble — he looked for Sir Harry, and at first couldn't find him. Yes, there he was, yes, there, and his mouth was open too. Sir Harry looked to him like the only man there who knew he was saying *Yea.*

He, Linhouse, even had time to look down upon himself and know he was a man. In the course of his life he had done this before of course in many ways, some that had seemed to him singular and some traditional, but never had he felt less embarrassed by it — gizzard, balls, tongue, cuticle and all. All of his earlier anticipated humiliation had come to pass, but he couldn't care less if the whole audience here or of man, turned to look at Jack. Possibly he didn't care because they weren't even looking at him, and they weren't because, with the growl which had only started a half-minute ago, they were too busy believing, and they were believing because they couldn't help it — along with him. *The universe,* he said, looking down at himself. It has water in a liquid state; life is there. It has the blood, the sweat and the tears that old men have a habit of mentioning in old wars, and the piss they don't bother to, and that other ichor which must be somewhere but nobody mentions much, or so shyly — the stuff that the brain makes in moving — no, that's light. He looked down at himself, at his universe. I won't apologize for you, he said, but for the first time he wasn't embarrassed either. I can stand you, he said, but you have to *do* something. And suddenly he leaped from his chair, and shouted, "No!" though he meant Yea.

He crept forward, then straightened. It was only a yard from him; why should he creep? The secretary, rapt, paid him no mind. In front of *it* . . . dare he think more than *it* . . . he paused. What he wanted most to say to it was one of those ejaculations from his own core, one of those eeows or ahs it had honored him for. If he could, he would wish somehow, in its own sub–eighteenth-century language — if to speak of centuries was not an absurdity altogether — to honor it. He stood before it, it unquivering, not so he. O celebratizzical, he said to it silently. O amazingular. Finally he opened his mouth and spoke. Whose language had he spoken in? He had said, "O."

Behind him, he heard his O echoed, not in a cadenza, but in continual asseveration, O, O, O, a trill somewhere far in the treble, that neither sank nor rose. He turned. The audience were all on their feet now faces aloft toward those encircling doors behind which, as from a phalanx of pipes, this super-octave was sounding. From there being so many women, and their posture, the effect was of the women rising in a body, or having so arisen. And from their number also, the effect was now as in any prospectus for the good life, that every man in the audience had a good woman at his side – in fact two. The sole man on his own was Sir Harry. His face still said Yea, but as he caught Linhouse's eye, it stretched to a prompter's smile. *Say it, Jack* it said, or seemed to. *You say it,* Linhouse signaled back, but Sir Harry, with a headshake, passed the ball back to him, and it was as if, in so doing, he had managed all sorts of comments on the generations. He did it by the simplest of gestures, his wedding ring gleaming for a trice on his long, competent fingers. Smiling, he turned up, down again, the palms of his hands.

So Linhouse veered round again to the object behind him. *Send Jack,* he thought, but almost proudly now, and thought too of his father, that foolish, proud and feckless, stupidly-bright man whose zest for division had been such that even after his death one thought of him as looking across to where life was still a winy fruit somewhere, a man who would have enjoyed this occasion even from the grave – if such bio-nauts had been possible – and would have written it up afterwards, too. As for Linhouse's mother, for the moment he agreed with his father: she was best off where the latter had left her. If, as a woman of some enlightenment, she was still there. In the case of either parent, he could still take a pride – mixed, it was true – in the generation behind him, for the humanities they had shared with him, and had imparted to their lares and penates too.

He could even share a pride with this . . . this . . . *being* . . . he was now facing. And in good time perhaps, the lares and penates of the world too of course, from the horse on a sunny field with its hindparts cocked perky, to the farmhouse clock on his ma's mantel in Chelsea, even someday to the teacups in a cupboard not of his childhood, not in Wiltshire, but in a cupboard somewhere — and always and everlasting, a chair. Yes, a being — he could say that now, An adumbration that it was one must have been there in his mind, his tingling fingertips, from the beginning, ever since it had helped him silently, fraternally and a wee bit giddily, to carry it out of the cottage, and along the intervening streets and fields. It hadn't been weightless entirely. But all along, perhaps even now, it had given him, and the others too, only such weight as they could bear. He stared at it. When it had been subjected to moving, it had passed for mechanism very nicely. But now, inanimate as it was for the moment, he had the strongest impression that it was giving him back his stare. If it had been a machine, he'd have had to summon all his strength not to give up, not to kneel to it with the insidiously growing humility of his kind. As it was, he could square his shoulders, raise his chin, and stand straight, sharing what he was with the consciousness opposite him, and inwardly give thanks. Thank God, he muttered to himself — and then shouted it. "It's *not* a machine. *Thank God.*" And then stood back.

The book rose upon itself, began to spin, or was it really melting in upon itself, all its leaves combining — from those of shaggy integument, to a linenskin nearest to human, down the thinnest, porcelain blood-veil. To some in the room the vision was similar to those swimming giants they were accustomed to observe perpetrating themselves under the microscope; to others — as the long, central shape hardened to focus in the dimming ribands of its own shadow planes, of which it meanwhile remained the long core — it seemed only one of those astral television images one saw while tuning one's way to a better one — and easily slain by the flick of a hand. Then as it rose finally on its tip, anybody could see that it was not many-leaved at all, perhaps had never been but was now One—a long presence of perfect curves subtiliating in continuous, restful outline, of modest less than seven-foot size, and in tint like the most limpid China tea or the clearest Havana leaf—yet nothing like. For even in its stillness, of a poise and quiet beyond that induced by any man-made tranquilizer or freezer, a stillness beyond any of earth's inanimate objects, indeed of another dimension altogether—even then, any dolt, of which there were none here, could recognize that nameless quality, neither a palpitation nor a glow, perhaps only a dance of the molecules which we see without realizing it—which signified that they were in the presence of a being. It began to lean then, toward the stenographer. The voice of it rose to the most reasonable facsimile yet, all but human, and the words it breathed gathered strength, even echo. The echo, in that almost circular hall, bounced back first: "Mouth." And then the cry that had been its source, "I want a mouth." Then slowly, in the utmost delicacy, moving without moving across the gap between it and the young stenographer in her wimpled collar, it leaned.

Her answering cry went unnoticed. Like hares, deer, any animal transfixed in a new breeze, the entire audience looked upward. As they did so, there appeared on the rim of the room, first at what would have been its four corners if the circular room could have had these, then closing in on that circle, a series of long cores sublunary within their own ribands, shadows. As each clarified itself in the manner of the being on the dais, it could be seen that these in comparison were giants, but all of even size according to their obvious norm, and all less sensitively tinted than their small kinsman, to a pallid spongecake that made them seem for a moment like monstrous ladyfingers and the room itself a giant charlotte russe. From the ring of these, when completed, such a stillness radiated, a monster seriousness, that thoughts like these were frivolous. In this other-dimensional stillness it was not possible to see that each of these beings was moving on its tip, only the conclusion of it — that each had aligned itself with one of the audience. Each went to him or her, as it might be, without hesitation. Yet there was no difference to be seen between those who had chosen to align themselves with the men, and those who loomed at the sides of the women. Yet . . . was there?

In the utter marvel of that stillness, there was at first no change. In its cosmic breath (to the auditors, of a new cosmos) all rested, beings both human and — what should one say? — extrahuman. All rested in it without change; one could not tell the exact minute when the breath became a sigh. Impossible to unweave its orchestrations, whether it came from the tiny, revolutionary glow of some small, vestigial furnace within those beings of utter curve, or whether it was the grave Vedantic murmur of those ready to lapse their hot heart-claps forever in the ellipse. Only, when it was over, the air in the room was changed; though none might see it yet or a hundred years not bring its mutation into being, the air was charged with the aspiration to difference. And when it was over, the postures of all were changed forever. All were still again in their new dimension. Couple by couple, they leaned.

How they were leaning went almost without saying; Lila was anxious but leaning forward, and ready to worry at the slightest encouragement; Meyer was eager to share his views and happy to do so with any one who would incline; Sir Harry's majestic head, sculptured by age, passion and endowment, was bent as if still listening, and surrounded by a bevy of forms among which there was indeed one of — in profile — perhaps the faintest aquiline. They were all, if not classicists, humans of a classic evolutionary kind. And if they leaned separately, humanly, each on the note of himself, then there was yet another note unheard perhaps because higher, on which they leaned in unison as it dropped down to them through volumes of air: death is sure, but the longing for the unknown is the lyric reason that holds us in life. Anders was the only one who looked frightened.

And what of me?

He was partially answered, or so he at first thought, by a sudden diffusion of light behind him. On the large screen which a while before had extended them a ragged thank-you, a picture now subtly widened — this time as if from the hands of experts — until it filled the entire wall behind the dais. Large as a backdrop, it presented them with a magnified and almost adequate picture of themselves, so that all might see the larger canvas of the occasion, just as was so often done at banquets, political or sales conventions, and the best charity balls. This picture showed a rotunda crowded with couples matched like these here, also a dais, on it two figures, between them a chair. One of them, though his back was turned, was clearly a man; the other, as clearly, was not. The man was looking at a large screen behind him, on which . . . And so it must go on and on, in the infinite trickery of optics, electronics or eternity — or of the girl on the box of raisins, who holds ad infinitum a box of raisins on which there is a girl, who — Or did it? For on second glance, though the *mise en scène* of crowd, dais, and the two figures had changed not a whit, it seemed to him that the hall itself had — what did it remind him of? Those sub-Corinthian columns, plaster pilasters, here smudged with distance, but in the pics of new-old Moscow a friend in the foreign service had sent him, as if dirtied with a nineteenth-century snow — would such a building house the Sternberg Astronomical?

He looked round him, at the hall; no, no columns here anywhere — the picture on the screen — it was not of Hobbs.

But when he glanced again at the screen, though its central details remained the same as previously, surely the hall had changed again, though he could not precisely say how — except that if he had been in it instead of viewing it, he had the idea it would have had the smell and ambience, unmistakable to him, of a British public building. Yet he had never been to Harwell, and had no idea whether its architecture was Lever House, Festival, or Dolphin Square. To say nothing of those other inner facilities which, though worldwide they might be the same as here at Hobbs, were all "no admittance" to the likes of him.

The picture faded and quivered again, with the built-in anonymity, no matter what the details or the angles, of a screen. Was that what they were showing us, he thought (I mean *are* showing, for on a screen the tenses cloud too), the end of our world as we know it, as it would be being seeded from observatory to observatory, by them? Or was it merely the end-of-the-world as to be seen now and then on a screen at the end of any living room. The possibilities were endless, yet, like perhaps everybody else here in this hall, he inclined toward one of them. For if *They* were inclined to satire, these connoisseurs of non-living, these experts in shadows — as it certainly seemed to him they were — how would they bring us, who have ourselves not so inexpertly made a hear-say of misery, to their gently styled day of judgment? *Answer*: The whole world as we know it is ending for us, *by hearsay*. What is happening here is doing so country to country all over the scattered "facilities" of the world, and we are joined to it, picture to picture, with substantially the same cast of characters, so that we may muse on it simultaneously and without the strain of feelings — from screen to screen to screen.

He crouched forward, in this peculiarly anesthetic agony, to look at himself — at that picture, fixed now for the moment again, which was surely Hobbs, at that man who was surely he. It was like looking at his own death; or like the way a movie star, nervous in his lounge chair in the viewing room, might watch his own false rendering of that as yet unknown lyric which all, before THE END, must learn. It was himself all right, and now he began to doubt his own diagnosis of what was going on here. He even began to wonder whether those other flashed changes had really existed — doing so with that canny, thrilling, schizoid doubt of oneself which is the viewer's supreme of vicarious sensation. Then his throat froze. The picture had changed again. Again a hall and a dais, again a man and that other, and those. The man was not he; he was sure of it. It made no matter, because of the hall, that hall. So it was true then, if only by hearsay. For he had been on Palomar.

Or did he dare to — ? His throat melted again, but thank God only as yet to what it had always been, though his own language seemed mangled to chicken feathers forevermore. But he did dare, to think that it might be not an end but a beginning, if not *the* one, and even if the beginning of *what* wasn't his to say. He wasn't thinking in terms of resurrection, however. But, in a vast diffusion of lighted welcome, deeper than any picture, he had just remembered all the streets of all the cities, all the fieldlands and waters beyond and outside all the observatories: still *outside*. Let them seal them up, all the halls of science, and inside each one a few of us specimens, random or select. Outside, on bourses and gallerias, with the odd punchinello noses and long chins of Breughel, in penny arcades and thronging from bathhouses, with Ethiop limb or waxy, a-Rowlandson with flannel lip or staring from the single broody-eye of Picasso, or on the desert tented or in the single sheepfold — there are still the people outside. Why did he always forget that people, with the animals, are the other half of physical creation; that they too are nature — who always has the last word. And history — which we have — tells us nothing if not that the people, humbly the same, humbly elusive, and never to be trusted except in this one quality — ever rest, ever *are*. Unless they were all to be atomized, and somehow he didn't think so. That sort of invasion, he thought, is more our style.

How sweet, how delicate instead, would be mutation! Especially, he thought, as humble as any, if *they* like *us*. Or must *we* —? He realized that his newest picture — and history's too perhaps — was on the side of yellow journalism or dream, for what he had in mind was a sort of New Year's Eve on Times Square, with the crowds beneath the irradiated heavens jostling brow to brow, liquored-up to sober neo-Christian, pale to ape, and perhaps a few wan children of the poor to cry, "Daddy, what does it mean?" (the rich being presealed in their own tunnels), while above the milling heads, to the sound of cornets and kazoos, the electric message ringed round and round the flatiron-sides of the old Times Building: IN YOUR END IS OUR BEGINNING, and then, just as everybody grew thoughtful, a jolly reversal, IN OURS IS YOURS, and with top luck perhaps, IN OURS IS OURS — though one would never again be sure of the pronouns. If he could dream that, would he?

He looked out front, feeling a peculiar pain — at the scope of the world compounded with its very nearness — which he hadn't had since adolescence. He looked at those new ones there, as a boy looked at the adults he both wanted and wanted not to be.

It's a cold world, Linhouse thought. Poor Tom's a-cold. He shivered with what he and perhaps others too had come to think of as the interstellar fear. A-cold. And was he to be the last Tom in it? He thought he was. He couldn't lean as the others were — it was not his style of difference. At last — out of delicacy or prudery, before a blending of outlines which seemed ever more intimate, he cast down his eyes.

Then, at the base of his shoe, near his ankle, he saw a rosiness. For one ghastly bright-pink moment, he thought it his own — a transformation managed willy-nilly and across realms, by some jokester specialist looking down on the excelled. But it was one of them here. It was one of them, rather small for her — species, and of median coloring. The curve of her form was the same as all the others, no dent there. Yet there was something, perhaps only the dream of a dent regressive there — across light-years of regression, the dream of a waistline. It didn't speak, perhaps now it couldn't. Unless he was to saw it in half, perhaps he would never be able to tell whether or not it once had. Nor even then, for did they not all look alike there? A sob escaped him for that metamorphosis, for whose regression, if ever again it arrived down the eons, his own too complex flesh couldn't wait. It edged nearer. Very daintily, it — she? — leaned. He stood stiff as a ramrod; he could not. He was as simple as he cared to be at the moment, or ever. I am the last, he thought, and those like me. And I am a-cold.

Then he heard a soft voice from behind, and turning, found himself face to . . . face? . . . with the tall form who for so long had been speaking. Runt it might be, among its own, but it loomed over him higher than Sir Harry, moving ever so slightly with a tituppy motion only self-delusion (did they have it too?) would call a glide — though of course he hadn't yet seen it move up stairways or along ramparts in its presumably grander style. When it stood quiet, its nether end about four inches from the floor, though perfectly shaped, seemed unfinished, wanting pedestal — or feet, of course, the truth being that ballet slippers came to mind. Otherwise, in glow and shape it was a beautiful luminary, and altogether had the timid yet elegant forbearance of very large animals who are made pets of by small masters. At its side, the young secretary, still hypnotically adoring and perhaps to her regret not eaten, lent a royal touch of retinue.

So, must he and it mutually stare? Was there a face to it, in the proper region for a face, or was it all in the eye of the beholder? If so — dare he, must he — address it? How does a lowly crab speak when, snorkeling the seas it was born to — it meets a man. He breathed heavily; the air in the hall seemed inestimably fresher; was this "carbonation"? He knew what it felt like to watch, as the war masks had once done — the downward flight of a Great Bird. He felt like — a native.

Do I speak first? Do I name it? *Eli.* Must I worship this god descended?

But he was spoken to. Initiative lost. Status clear.

"Person," the ellipse said.

For a moment he did feel it, the dignity of his possessions. And over there of course — of want.

All this time he had been looking only out of the corner of his eye, and now he could not even do that; blushing for his own madness, he could look nowhere but down. Across from him, he heard an intake, a sigh.

"Friend." A command. Yet . . . tentative?

And again he felt that irradiation of being — *his* — and in the center of it, in the center of what was to some an enormous landscape, beating steady on, beating out both question and answer, Tom Thrum, Tom Thrum, the heart.

And then, without warning, there came the revulsion — as if he had met with a shark while swimming and all his membranes floated backwards — as if the heart itself reversed, stroking backwards along the path of old heartbeats already suffered, and in so doing bore him raggedly but steadily away. When it came to details — the almost human details — he couldn't. He could still believe in gods — of course he could, or some could — or he could meet with animals strangely cast up by nature's ever-sportive sea. Or in planets swinging in their own carillons above it, or even on those — as long as far away — life's familiar spores. But to believe in this other being here; no, his duty was to go mad first. He might believe it some day, or if he ever got out of here, but not now, and not that near. Not quite.

Again he heard the sigh.

He was dumbfounded to see, high up above the last tier of seats, one after the other of the encircling doors opening, open, opening, open — all along the line. Light flooded in as from clerestories, a light still violet or fluorescent, still with the tincture of Hobbs on it, and leading still to all the abracadabra of its facilities, but surely somewhere on, no matter how lost one got on the way, to the air — fetid or humid, soiled or fresh — of the unartificial day. No, it would be night now. He could already smell it coming in here; if thought was to be smelled, he hadn't a thought but this. Night was here, bringing all the invasion he would ever wish for. He could see it out there ahead of him, in rain or sleet or calm, in cloud or blessedly uninterpreted stars — a real, down-to-earth night.

"Well then — "

From behind him, he heard a last comment.

And at this last — in spite of everything — he was not surprised.

Everybody ran for the doors with him. Or almost; a few, gazing markedly sidewise, walked. How would they speak of these phantasms — or in their so various ways not speak — outside? How would the newspapers speak of all this, when it got to them, as it would — used as they were to dreaming the heavens afloat only with satellites and missiles? How would the legend start — or stop? For as each couple reached a door and passed through it, one of the two pressed onward toward the familiar darks of its planetary persuasion, and the other form, as intangibly as it had come — vanished. But he himself, unaccompanied though he was, wasn't one to speak too quickly of fantasy — never, or not yet. For it was fitting that, having been the abettor of this vision if not the begetter — he had been the last one to look back.

And so he had caught the last installment of the vision — and has it yet. In the center of the darkened stage, the chair he had sat on all evening, no picture before it now, still faced inward toward one, its solid old leather back toward a vanished audience, its worn bucket seat facing a screen that now, unanimated, had the faded flush-brown of an after-image on an old retina. It was a comfortable chair, borrowed at some time or other from one of the offices or cubicles, hollowed out, once upon a time, by somebody's heavy thinking — or bum. It still was.

He was at liberty not to believe what he saw, if he wished, if he had the heart not to. Was this vision granted him, or imposed? For he could believe, if he so wished, that the small glow which had nimbused the chair as if from its center — and indeed had been the light by which he saw — had come from a solitary footlight which mechanical failure had left burning. Mechanism was so fallible. Centerback of the chair, a high, pale-to-pink oval had protruded, as of a bald pate of indeterminate age, but certainly a gentleman's. He was free to believe that this was the gloss, on leather, of a spotlight from the wings. Left of the chair, a tape recorder unquestionably had been revolving, but there was no need to disbelieve, in this night and age, the reality of its faintly hissing but persuasive voice. Mechanism was so trustworthy. The trouble was, had it been playing a voice, or recording it?

He didn't wait to believe, but ran onward, along corridors he was almost eager to get lost in, so that when with the last exertion of his strength he forced himself, by old Air Force training, to track his own maze, and at last heard his own steps ringing along the marble of the deserted lobby, and at last fronted with his forehead a Ramapo night as calm as any a man ever parachuted, he could almost have said to it, "It was all a nightmare. Not like this, you stars, you heavens of Prussian blue. An inner nightmare." Almost. He hadn't waited to believe, because he hadn't had to.

It was a voice that might have been anybody's. On tape, or coming toward it from a chair, it was any a body's voice, busy at the creation of its own legend, saying, "—And so—" It was the beginning of the legend that he hadn't wanted to hear; to be present at a nativity was enough. And he had left his own print there. Like any savage, he felt it to be a piece of himself. If, at times afterwards, he often felt it to have been the better part of himself, this was no doubt the result of having been civilized, and in any case was an observation he made to himself only very quietly, on those nights of the soul which however dark, were real. But it wouldn't have been humanly possible to go on with that sort of speculation, tolerantly divided man though he still was—if not as comfortably as of yore. For, as a human being, he still had certain expectations, exclusive of his larger social obligations. Certain of the latter, such as marriage and children, he hadn't yet taken up, though still of the intention to, as soon as certain things measurably faded. For, he still expected to itch, to weep, hopefully to love, and regretfully to die. Dark evenings, when he despaired of humans, or wild, sweet ones, when the Ramapo breeze blew as if water had truly followed it, were merely (he grew to reassure himself) like those first times after the war, when he had first had to admit to himself that though young, trim, not even thirty, he had grown too heavy, too old and un-nimble—for the parachute.

And he still meant to marry, as soon as—like any shell-shocked man – he got better used to certain tricks of shadow, noise and language which made him nervy, certain hopes of them which kept him continually waiting, even on the dullest social evenings, to see what came round a corner, a door. Though there was one common remark, one polite bit, which he would never get used to whether it came from a grizzled matron or curly damsel, or old codger – from anyone else in the world, instead of out. Faintly, someday he still expected to hear it at his side, in a voice he knew.

For it might have been anybody's voice, sitting by the tape recorder, busy at its legends – but it hadn't been. He'd been amazingly moved when that voice had addressed him as a person, and rather overwhelmed – for the fallible moment – when it had hoped to count him as a friend. And very much surprised when (though he hadn't actually heard it give it) a command had come, after all these shenanigans, to open the doors. But the voice's last comment fitted so well with all he knew of it. And so, deep in his heart of hearts he hadn't been at all surprised to hear it say – after that precociously heavy sigh for all that they both were still in for: "Well then – mind if I sit in your chair?"

The Envoy

AND so — I was betrayed. Not that I hadn't half expected it. No adventure of the soul is without betrayal; it is part of the stickiness which holds the soul in space. The small ones I had practiced on my own part, the mild lies I had scattered everywhere — birdseed for those left at home, chicken feed for those on ahead, and a little fruitening gardenseed for myself — would never have been enough. It took a betrayal in the highest, and by others, to make me admit that my adventure was of the soul as well as of the body. Though I meant to be human, not martyr. And though perhaps not as pioneer as I had fancied — and forced at present still to work at it — that hope is still high. All during the hours of my oration, I could hear privately — and with what astonishment, delight and giddy laughter! — my own gradual advances in that direction, but tone, or even the double consciousness, is not enough. When I heard, outside the doors I had in a way helped to seal, that long, thrilling whistle-cry from home, I had a moment's falter — my allegiance went to them, and when they entered, all my pride. At the moment of perfection, when all down the aisles a One leaning with a one made such a cloister of couples as must each have a flame-glass window to itself in the legend — my allegiance was, I truly believe, to the world of worlds that shall come, among worlds. And when

I saw the band of my colleagues, never, to be sure, of that close order here called "friends," but nevertheless a band; when I saw them turn tail — ah, what a dollop of bitterness it takes to be human! When I saw the doors open, as no doubt everywhere there were opening what had taken so much secret labor to seal — I was already human enough to be surprised. And when they vanished through them, leaving me behind, the patsy, to take the rap, to be the fall guy — oh I knew all your names for those of you who are too heavy with innocence to fly with the angels — then my allegiance went over forever, to you. Where, with the exercise of an occasional ingenuity, it has remained.

They do not trust you; there it is, in a nutshell likely never to be anything but a nutshell. They never have. Often and often it was argued me, even among my own cohorts, that we would do no better than the Christians had at bringing you to true ellipsis, whereas my part and theirs — to earn a permanent place here — would be the easiest of falls. "Let *them* emigrate," they said, "but of course not as they are; let them be refugees to the *nth*." How they had laughed to hear I had a name! "Always *naming*, they are!" a chorus of us said. "Always predicting new particles, too!" And "Oh marvelous!" sang the chorus on another groove. "Oh *smashing!* Let them come as particles or not at all."

It was only their bit of fun, I had thought at the time. I thought they already understood, as I had, that if it was We who had the distance, it was you who had the perspective, and that names of all sorts were only your vain effort to tick off the one little particle, not a pi-meson, not even an Omega minus, which made you human. And now I should never be able to tell them; or now perhaps, having seen you and leaned toward it, they were understandably frightened to smell what I already knew — that this one particle, which would never be named, came from the Beyond. It takes all kinds — your own sages are always hinting it.

And so I watched them, my kind, running, and I watched yours, and considered where I was. Only minutes back, at the very point when all our maneuvers had seemed at perfection, I had called for a mouth, in a carnal loss of control that was jolly unrefined; I could have my own guilts and humiliations too therefore, if betrayal were not presently enough. Or could save these for later. I watched Jack running, after having heard from me as much as I could spare and then a little over — and was this human of *me?* How many times, in the years to come, I should have to ask that! And in the grace of providence, or effort, or in the doom of both — be able to. I shouldn't expect to haunt him, Jack, unless I was very lonely — a word whose meaning I had learned by watching him. He had had all that he could bear, and if I could bear more, it must be because I wasn't human yet.

After him, the little secretary came peeping out from wherever in the wings she'd disappeared to, and tiptoed, wide-eyed and scared, to within a few paces of me, where she set down the tape recorder, then knelt so thoughtfully — but just out of reach — to start it going. Then she too ran. At the door, she blew me a kiss. At the door — though I had my back turned by now and didn't see him — I wouldn't have been surprised to see that at the door, he looked back. But I was confused now, and too tired to consider whether chivalry kept me at my post, or chargin — or tired muscles. Humanity never comes evenly. I would sit a bit. And there might be no more answer than this to much of human conduct. Some of us run; some stay.

Then I turned, from the depths of his chair. "*Shadows!*" I called after him. He was gone. But I sat in wonder. This is our last scream, before the crater. Here, it was my first.

And so, my long soliloquy was finished. But this had been

the formal one, hero that I had been; now I had one for myself. Everybody here is a hero at least for a day — the day on which he is born; and then forever, in the long night, all are heroes there. I looked out upon you until you were gone, all of you soon to lie, with your shields, in your slumber. But before then, in the between of those two poles, you are ordinary people, of the commonest betrayals, and with your own heroisms to make. I meant to be ordinary, and I had a few thoughts for myself on this, as even the unheroic do.

Now, meditating back there in the cottage in that summer lamasery of one member, as the violet passage of the hours was succeeded by the white, I had learned to watch all the equinoxes of the day. This is very important, though I do not mean to sound wise. And I do not know whether wisdom comes of it. But, when after my long sojourn, I was carried out of there, it was mysteries I was giddy with. I had never lived with mystery before. Your rooms were chock-full of them. So it was mysteries, not conclusions, that I presented myself with now.

They know their own queerness, I thought — meaning *you.* They understand that, by the one thin particle, they are born into the beyond. I shall become one of them, as — slowly into their vortex — so do I. And in this adventure, perhaps the appendages of the body, which I have all this time been so fixed on, need not antedate those of the soul. By nature, I am a virtuoso of images; by these I will plod on, but this time in their same danger — that my shadows, unlike my body, will not last my time. But consider that this too must have a bearing on what — to one in want of it — is of all their possessions, the sum. For consider not their death, but the manner of it. Everybody who dies here is a person. *Everybody who has ever died here, has been a person.* Repeat it, repeat it — for they have a repetition, they have a beat here also, and this is what they mean here when they say "the people." Everybody who dies here is a person. And nobody has ever known how it comes about.

The tape flapped, somewhere along in my reveries, and after a while, the machine ran down. That stops the recording! I thought, meaning forever, though of course I was wrong. But it did bring practical considerations once more to mind. And my mind was — somehow to go underground, yet remain among you. At first, my thought was to stay there in the neighborhood, where I knew the basements, and indeed there I did stay, until enough of the old pallor and intangibility overcame me, making me fit again to travel. Then, finding that I could travel safely in almost any weather except snow — when memory brought tints which were unsafe — I left the Ramapo, at least for many voyages to come. I had no wish to haunt the people there, who as it was — though they might no longer believe in what they had seen — would never again know for sure what object here might not have its images, or whether every object in their universe might not be a Trojan horse. Besides, there were not people enough, in just a valley and a mountain range, for my purposes. And what were, were too refined.

Think of me then, as in many public places — under the George Washington Bridge perhaps, by dawnlight, counting the first cars. Or listening to the radio that whines on happily in Filipino, in a whisky-box squatter town. Or watching all the diseases of Asia, and the buboes of gladness too. I often look in mirrors. I watch the babies always, for hints. Think of me wherever protoplasm really carbuncles, or shrinks or swells, or even dies. And as in private places also, for sometimes I am a beast in chambers, groaning moonward, like yourselves. One day, on that day when the hands and the feet, and the sex and even the full face finally come upon me — then at that point, I shall no doubt remember the shadows of my old home as celestial ones. And *at that point* — I shall be human. Humanity never comes evenly. Until then, I am an envoy, which has so many meanings and all of them rightful — an ambassador and a deputy, a dedication, a poem. Until then, think of me as where the people are — as you think of yourselves.

And say a blessing for all those in a state of between.

One night, after many wanderings which do not cease, I found myself on a small footpath, a meander, which if I wished, I could count as a place where I had been born, though I have many such places now. I was used now to there being no line of demarcation between the happening and the brooding; wherever there is difference, such a two must meld. I could see, to the south, a view. The views of your planet are from all sides, really, but for simplicity's sake let us say that it was only from the south. I saw what I now knew. I saw the great wallows of light between cities and their parks, between the park and the field and the desert, and on all, cherished as if within a wild sea, the closeness of the starved.

And I said to myself the old lesson for messiahs, that I now say to you. What is humane? The small distance. What is wild? The mortal weight. Wherever there is difference, there — is morality. Where there is brute death, there love flits, the shy observer. I had my feelings now, those mysterious pains which held them to living. And I said a blessing for all those who live in mystery. The wilderness was all before me — and I was glad that I had come.